The Statement

Other books by Jan Drabek:

Whatever Happened to Wenceslas? (1975)
Report on the Death of Rosenkavalier (1977)
The Lister Legacy (1980)

Nonfiction

Blackboard Odyssey (1973)

Children's

Melvin the Weather Moose (1976)

The Statement

A NOVEL BY
Jan Drabek

MUSSON BOOK COMPANY
A division of General Publishing Co. Limited
Toronto, Canada

Published in 1982 by
Musson Book Company,
30 Lesmill Road,
Toronto, Canada
M3B 2T6

Canadian Cataloguing in Publication Data

Drabek, Jan, 1935-
   The statement

ISBN 0-7737-0055-2

I. Title.

PS8557.R32S72   C813'.54   C81-094728-5
PR9199.3.D73S72

Printed and bound in Canada

It is quite easy, when one considers the three major forms of social change — elections, reform, and revolution — to give undue attention to the last one, the most spectacular of the three. Humans are naturally attracted to circuses and a full-fledged revolution is nothing short of the greatest show on earth. But there are many political thinkers who have doubts as to whether there are any deeper meanings attached here. Thomas H. Green writes, for example, that "among the animal species only man is willing to die for an idea. It is the source of both his nobility and folly. How much nobility and how much folly is for subsequent ideologies to judge."

I would go even further. I would say that the violent upheaval, an armed conflict such as a revolt, rebellion, civil war — call it what you will — for all its enormous emotional impact is, in the final analysis, only a simple statement. A non-verbal, nevertheless a clear and highly articulate statement of fact about how a particular society wishes to govern itself.

From the introduction to
Chronicles of Political Systems
by Dr. George Titus

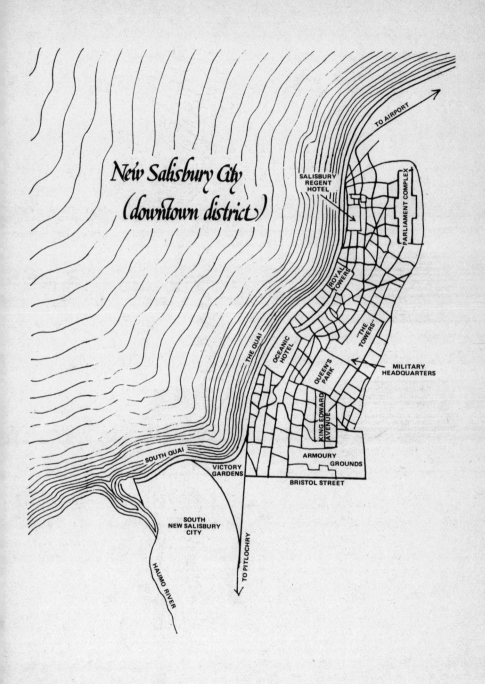

Part One

PREPARATIONS

Chapter 1

It was I who discovered George Titus, and it was I again who put him on his throne.

I have made that statement before. And it has also been countered before that I am immodest, that I lack the proper degree of humility — especially for a Jew.

I plead guilty on both counts; I am a Jew and I am immodest. In fact, I come from a long line of immodest Jews, people who have preposterously adopted the hyphenated name of Bech-Landau in the manner of the respected British families, people who have survived and prospered in Central Europe during the last century and the first part of this one — precisely because of the fact they have thrown all their burdensome modesty away.

During my relatively short lifespan I have been a successful businessman, a politician, and a revolutionary leader. Not one of those occupations carries modesty as a prerequisite for success. No wonder then that I take the credit for the making of George Titus and that I so steadfastly maintain that without me he would still be an ineffective professor of political science in Vancouver, Canada, groping his way through dusty library stacks, secure behind a thick belt of woods called the University Endowment Lands.

George was never meant to be a scholar — his whole early life had been that of a doer, not a philosopher. What's more, he had always been exceptionally successful as a doer. Of course, the successes came only after the traumatic straightening of his strangely twisted ways as he was about to enter puberty. And for this straightening out, again I must take full credit.

The remarkable incident occurred at the Herriott School for Boys, certainly the best private school on the islands of New Salisbury, if not in all of Oceania. At the time, we in New Salisbury were no longer a British Dominion but a sovereign country within the British Commonwealth of Nations, of which Norman Ruttledge Titus, George's father, was the first prime minister.

I, on the other hand, was the Head Boy at Herriott.

One would have to really know Herriott with its neo-Gothic red-brick buildings, its green lawns and gowned masters, to fully understand how incongruous it was to have a Hebrew head boy. In fact, up to this day I am the only Jew who has ever attended Herriott.

If George's academic performance at Herriott was barely average, his social one was an absolute disaster. He spoke, in what strongly resembled a high-pitched factory siren, often and on every conceivable subject. What only a year or two before had been an almost pathologically introverted youth had become a loud boor who wandered through the halls with his bodyguard in tow, dispensing unsolicited advice and cocky commentaries that never failed to alienate.

To lapse into my expressive mother tongue — a schnook.

And on that late sunny afternoon, as he was walking toward his waiting limousine after rugby practice (he was also a notably dispensable member of the Herriott team), I stepped into his path. His bodyguard discreetly kept his distance while I put my arm around George's shoulders, steering him to a bench underneath a clump of Pohutukawas in reddish bloom.

There, speaking softly and in a voice full of warmth and compassion, I asked him why it was that he insisted on being such an awful bloody bore of an ass. He looked up at me, his big blue eyes wide in wordless surprise. (George had expressive eyes even then. Along with his wavy brown locks, they still constitute one of his greatest political assets.)

In the words of a later generation it was all hanging out at that moment, and George had just heard a totally unexpected condemnation of his ways which, in his circumstances, he didn't think possible. Absolutely stunned, he rose and staggered a bit away from the protection of the giant trees. He took a few steps, then stopped and turned around to make sure that I was really there, that it all hadn't been a bad, bad dream. Slowly he joined his bodyguard and rounded the corner with him, until the very last moment eyeing me in mute astonishment.

The very next morning he called to invite me to spend a weekend at the prime minister's residence at Pitlochry. It was, not to coin a phrase, the start of a beautiful friendship.

Not that I wasn't apprehensive. As I've already said, I belong to that certain race. Even in New Salisbury, where my father had quite honestly and somewhat ingeniously made his wartime millions, and where before World War II the Jews were practically an unknown entity, we still weren't exactly welcomed with open arms. But we also weren't being gassed or otherwise pogromed; neither were we condemned as Christ killers, nor praised as composers of the *Wedding March*. Despite the ambivalent attitudes towards us, we were observed with vivid interest, which made some of us more nervous types apprehensive. But given certain excesses for which we tend to become known, no wonder we were being observed.

On Friday night I arrived at Pitlochry with its soft-stepping butlers and curtsying maids. At first I was regarded as something of an exotic curiosity — a bit like an African black brought over from the last safari or a pig-tailed Chinaman with a plate-like hat who added color to the master's household. Not to mention exotic cuisine: I claim credit for having introduced the Titus family to breakfasts of bagels and lox and lunch of Central European potato pancakes.

But all that came later. In 1948, when I was sixteen and first set foot inside the prime minister's residence, I was received (quite properly in the receiving room) by Mary Titus, George's diminutive but slightly imperious and somewhat doting mother. She looked me over, checked my manners, and once satisfied that my presence in the mansion would not constitute an embarrassment for either of us, she welcomed me. Then she proceeded to lavish attention on me to a degree I had not known during the five years since my own mother had passed away.

George's father was something else again. True, he had not worn a high collar since the demise of Neville Chamberlain, but some of the accompanying stiffness remained. The mother country had first been ravaged by the war and then Americanized. Not being quite certain which fate was worse, he was determined to maintain New Salisbury as a bastion of Anglo-Saxon stability. To him the Pacific was the perfect place for his stronghold, what with the reasonable people of New Zealand only a few hundred miles to the west and Australia (but here he saw certain worrisome cracks in the facade) not much farther.

Norman Ruttledge Titus was a towering man both in stature and vision. He was also immensely practical. It was argued that for a leader of the Liberals he was overly conservative. Perhaps. His conservatism however had not been the result of some overly emotional attachment to things archaic. It was rather due to the simple conviction that in the past more things had worked than hadn't, and that those that had should therefore be readily employed in the future. But while the elder Titus may have been noticeably conservative socially, he was less so politically and an absolute radical economically. His tenure as Chief of New Salisbury's Resources Mobilization Office during the war attests to that. At a time when other countries turned a blind eye, he sent the HMNSS *Aphrodite* to Dubrovnik just before the start of the war to collect highly skilled refugees who had been huddling there for months. My father was among a group of engineers brought over from Yugoslavia with their families to play an important part in New Salisbury's war effort.

Despite having to assess the European situation through Neville Chamberlain's blinkered eyes, Titus was indeed accurate, probably because he concentrated much more intently on the Japanese threat to the Pacific. And there he was dead right in his estimates. Preparing diligently for a naval war, he waged it successfully and emerged from it with New Salisbury ready not only for independence but for his leadership as well. This tower of success in a striped dark suit and homburg would ask politely each evening that I spent at Pitlochry what George and I had been doing, if we found what we had been doing amusing, and if we learned anything from it. Only moderately enlightened by our answers, he would then formally excuse himself and go about his business.

During the early years of my friendship with George there were times, I must confess, when our activities were not *that* amusing. He was still a puny kid who regarded girls as embarrassing obstacles rather than exciting challenges. He was, after all, almost three years my junior and I missed my regular friends — the hairy, ribald story-telling hulks who were more my age and with whom I was used to cavorting about town.

But then there was the sparkling ambience of Pitlochry, the never-ending wash of the surf on the beach, and the constant stream of guests — ambassadors, ministers, and generals who could spin fascinating tales at the dinner table, and on occasion crack outrageous jokes afterwards. Then there was Mary Titus, who eventually regarded me as her second son. She seemed immensely grateful for my friendship with her George who, quite understandably, did not have all that many friends.

George submerged himself into puberty, became taller, mightier and considerably wiser until there wasn't that much difference between us anymore. By then I had left Herriott, taking a vacation from the academic world, and only occasionally putting in a day or two at my father's office at the Allied Shipyards. I was ostensibly acquiring a rudimentary knowledge of the family business, but much more important was experience I was getting elsewhere. While George was completing his last two years at Herriott (as a much improved student, and now registering moderate social successes), I had travelled throughout the Pacific as far as China in the East and the U.S. on the opposite side. I also fell in and out of love in a rather maddening cadence, but in this respect the truly great years didn't start until 1952 when George and I registered at the University of New Salisbury, aiming for degrees in philosophy and claiming our regular table at the Cafe Europa on the N.S. City Quai. That was in the afternoons; in the evenings we prowled through the small student clubs with their lilting Italian music — partying and dancing our way through higher learning while sharing a three-room apartment south of Queen's Park.

We were both outspoken but basically in agreement about politics, although George — at least during those early years — had always been a bit more left-leaning. To prevent depletion in party ranks it was important to George's father's Liberals that a youth organization be started and kept alive. So we travelled throughout the Lower and Main Islands, bringing together the young Liberals; George started to exhibit a fine feeling for strategy and organization. He silenced the critics from the radical left with vivid descriptions of Marxist horrors as they were spreading during the fifties across Europe and Asia. From the right there wasn't too much criticism; its association with fascism still hung like a millstone around its neck.

But there were still the religious zealots, the anarchists, and assorted pockets of malcontents to deal with. Most dangerous, however, was a group which was not discontented at all, and which we privately called "the idiot class." They were the uninformed, the lethargic and the lazy that could see no further than next week's paycheck.

So we beat the bushes to get them out. To hear the word and to take a stand. At this George was particularly adept; he could challenge, excite and, when necessary, even irritate.

All right, you would like to say, then it was really George coming into his own, discovering his own potential as the son of a revered but slowly ageing prime minister, as the man in 1956 voted by the readers of an Australian magazine "the most popular young person in the Pacific." He was the one who had really discovered the advantages of being related to power.

Except that there was this in-between period, when the discovery was painfully taking place.

Chapter 2

Shortly after New Year's 1958, with our university degrees finally in our hands — George shot up to cum laude during his last two undergraduate years — we booked passage on a slow freighter to Europe. It stopped at every godforsaken port in Asia and the Middle East until we were so thoroughly sick of earthen jugs, cotton print dresses, and Arab leatherware that we refused to leave the ship. Finally we were through the Suez Canal and into the Mediterranean. In Genoa we disembarked, and caught a fast train to Cortina d'Ampezzo where we skied and partied incessantly for almost five weeks — a record even for us. Then we slowly started making our way across the Alps in a rented Volkswagen, passing through the blooming Swiss and French springtime until we reached the Channel. It had been a valuable experience for both of us, but especially for George. For the first time he had not only left his English-speaking world, but had been also introduced to the sources of our culture. Still, gazing at the white cliffs, we felt enormously relieved to be able to slip back into the Queen's Own.

In New Salisbury, meanwhile, the Liberals had lost a confidence vote and gracefully retired into the Opposition to reorganize. Expecting to be out of office only temporarily, Titus, and his wife, hurried off on a holiday. We met them in London, then motored on to Oxford — Norman Titus's alma mater.

And there something happened. The awe on George's face was remarkable as we meandered through the hallowed halls dating back to the thirteenth century. He leafed through decrepit, leatherbound manuscripts, listened to his father's fielding of philosophical questions about his country's condition, and an enormous change began to take place in his thinking.

He returned to London to say goodbye to his parents, then abruptly cancelled a summer trip to Greece we had planned. In the end I went alone — confused, and bored. Sometimes downright miserable. When I returned to England he had already set up shop at Oxford, preparing for the fall semester. I was not yet altogether clear on what had happened to him.

I hesitated, then crossed the Channel once more to tour the chateaux of the Loire.

That trip, however, was cut short. I returned to England for the last time because time had run out. If there was to be a summer election in New Salisbury as the elder Titus predicted, and if George and I were to run for parliament as we had agreed, then we could wait no longer.

"It's a lark, Maurice," George explained. "Nothing else — this whole yearning for a seat in the parliament. It's just something we haven't done till now so we want to do it — to be able to say it was lots of fun. But the larks have to end somewhere and for me it's right here at Oxford. I want to find out what came before us and what's likely to come after. This is the place to do it."

I hurried back to New Salisbury aboard a rickety Comet, got the nomination and filed my papers in the riding of West New Salisbury City. In the fall of 1959 I was elected to parliament. I became a desk-beating, foot-thumping and, when occasion demanded, foul-whistling Liberal Party backbencher. Titus was returned to office with a slim majority, but he was rested, rejuvenated and relatively dynamic.

Three years later, with several ridings slated for by-elections, I flew back to England to try and persuade George that the Liberals needed him and that the nomination at Garrick was his for the asking. Actually it wasn't all *that* altruistic: the party had had several defections and the idea of having one sure winner in the prime minister's son strongly appealed to everyone in it. A successful outcome of my mission would have gotten me a junior cabinet position, although the prime minister had not promised it. He had not urged me to go to England — not N. R. Titus. He was too proud, too unbending for that. But by then I knew him well enough to know that he very much wanted me to go.

From the moment George welcomed me at Heathrow with a young lady alongside him to whom he was engaged, I knew he would not go. Kathy, the daughter of a minor Ford of England executive, enjoyed being seen with the son of a Commonwealth prime minister who was about to defend his PhD dissertation, then move on as a lecturer in Canada at the University of British Columbia — an obscure institution away from most academic centers. UBC's remoteness suited him well — he was already heavily into the first volume of his

Chronicles of Political Systems. Actually, his dissertation on the role of the individual in ancient Egypt was an integral part of it.

He looked different too, having forsaken his impeccably tailored suits and slacks for checkered shirts, soft shoes, and loose jackets with leather elbow patches. Instead of a cigarette a meerschaum pipe projected from his mouth, and while driving his Vauxhall from the airport he donned a corduroy cap to protect his thinning scalp from the wind.

He also spoke differently. He said little and what he did say he qualified in tautological banalities. One of the few times he showed genuine interest was when I spoke about his mother, now terminally ill and in a N.S. City home; but, on every other subject, any emotionalism had largely evaporated.

For a man of twenty-eight years he was unendurably tolerant. This, from George Titus! It was as if he had been training hard to suppress all anger and now was eager to show the fruits of his Gandhian self-denial. He wanted to know about the N.S. Parliament and its ways when I knew very well that he thought it a silly game compared to what he was doing — a fleeting pastime for people who had neither the inclination, ability, nor the stamina to dig deeper into the issues. According to him parliaments were staffed by people who either did not know any better or were notoriously opportunistic.

He didn't say so in so many words. As an academic he expressed himself much less concisely. But my administrative assistant had been duly collecting all of George's learned articles and there could be no doubt that in spite of all the conditional voices, in spite of the meticulous softening and diffusing of his statements, when one made his way through the footnotes and what was above them, there was nothing so evident as the haughty disdain.

It would be hard to say exactly why. I suspect that at Oxford that afternoon with the dons rushing to greet his father he sensed that in politics he could be nothing but a follower of a great leader. So he rebelled, chose an entirely different route, and since then had spent much of his time in justifying his rebellion not only to himself but to the whole world.

The by-elections didn't take; the Liberals became a minority government and Norman Ruttledge Titus, thoroughly unaccustomed to the undignified haggling sometimes with grossly inferior individuals, began to show every one of his seventy years. But then yielding to pressure, he once more led the Liberals into the election campaign. This time they won a fairly comfortable majority.

Only a week after the successful campaign, Titus collapsed on the marble steps in front of the New Salisbury Parliament. I have seen pictures taken at the scene by a *Times* photographer which never appeared anywhere because the editor thought them too morbid. But they should have. Even in death there was an undeniable dignity about him as he lay there with his attaché case nearby. It was the kind of dignity we so sadly miss in our public figures nowadays.

George returned to New Salisbury for the funeral. He was impressive as he walked behind the casket leaving the Christchurch Cathedral, praying at the cemetery and reading a statement to the press which indicated he would not be coming home to live. His wife Kathy made a pleasant impression too, saying very nice things about the islands before flying off.

Three months later Harold Simpson, the late Titus's foreign minister, lost the temporary leadership of the party at a conference in Wampaha, and the faction-ridden Liberals chose the dull Charles Stirborn as their compromise prime minister. A staunch rightist, he had been Norman Titus's assistant during the war, in the process becoming an enthusiastic admirer of the man but not so much of his party. At Titus's bidding he reluctantly chose to run for parliament on the Liberal ticket.

Possibly because he was too acutely aware of his weaknesses, Charles Stirborn was not an outspoken man. An excellent administrator, he was at his best with tasks which required hard work and precision, but he was totally devoid either of imagination or of the ability to quickly improvise. Most significantly, he lacked vision, something that had been behind all the accomplishments of the Norman Titus government.

Stirborn came to power in the mid-sixties when the world was daily becoming a more intricate place, when in the West men's expectations had become unreasonably great and the conflict in Southeast Asia was about to produce a savage maelstrom that would markedly enlarge the Marxist domain. He knew precious little about such things. All he knew was that the state's books had to be balanced and alien ideologies kept at arm's length.

He had never travelled farther than Australia. Essentially a dedicated conservative, he was at the head of a Liberal government at a time when radical socialism had become an enticing ideology.

Exiting from the great hall of the Oceanic Hotel after the conclusion of the leadership conference, I couldn't imagine a worse choice for the Liberals to have made.

Chapter 3

Charles Stirborn then proceeded to compound his problems by appointing me his minister of immigration. The post was nothing spectacular, I was not exactly his favorite. But I was the youngest Liberal in the house and, as such, certainly an asset to the minority cabinet as a minor minister.

I lasted exactly two months. At the end of that time, I called a press conference to announce a new, comprehensive immigration law for the islands; the next morning I was called on the carpet to the prime minister's office. Without so much as lifting his head from the papers in front of him, he wanted to know what the hell I thought I was doing. In spite of it being a question, it was the most definite statement I had ever heard him make.

Without waiting for an answer, he explained that I had been empowered *to commence a study of the desirability* of a new immigration policy — a far cry from bringing in a comprehensive immigration law. And it all took place at a cabinet meeting where decisions made, he reminded me, were highly confidential.

I then asked if he wanted me to retract the statement. He was absolutely horrified at the thought.

"No, no. That would only whet the appetite of the press. What we have to do is lead them away from the issue — make some other announcements and policy moves. Bring up other problems," advised Stirborn, the great master of smoke-screening that he was. But he certainly wanted no more fire from the Immigration Ministry.

"I see. And the new comprehensive immigration policy?"

He looked at me the way one looks at a child one suddenly realizes is severely retarded.

"Well, it certainly cannot be a priority this year. Or the next."

I saw my role of a drone more clearly now. And I didn't want to be the youngest minister in N.S.'s history anymore. More than that, I didn't want to be associated with Stirborn's government from which, I strongly suspected, would someday begin the despondent slide into dictatorship. Once again I repaired to the back benches. Of course, I also didn't want to be the spark that would trigger its downfall. Sometimes I voted reluctantly with the Libs, but more often I simply abstained.

I was really at a loss of what to do. Labour had elected its new leader, one Kevin Moorehead who was thirty-six, wore his hair down to his neck, and was champing at the bit to introduce the country to the welfare state along with several other nifty left-wing innovations. Nothing for me there.

The Conservatives, on the other hand, were staid, dusty types that had never commanded more than twelve per cent of the popular vote. They seemed to see salvation mainly in the retention of the Union Jack and by keeping the national emblem — the dumpling-like cone of the Kauri tree — off the New Salisbury flag.

There was one exception among the Conservatives though — a former assistant New Salisbury police chief with a mind so sharp that it crackled, who had been elected by his South New Salisbury City riding with the largest majority ever recorded in the country.

Though he still half-heartedly followed the Conservative caucus decisions, he also had a unique program of his own. It included heavy doses of nationalist fervor along with vague shades of racism, religious respectability, economic protectionism and, for labor, job guarantees. His name was Lucius C. Liefenbarger and he sure had something for everyone.

By 1968 even Stirborn must have realized that he had reached the end of his rope. He had then been in power for almost four years without having once won an election as a party leader. In Vietnam it was the year of the Tet Offensive — an event of particular interest to the country because a New Salisbury brigade had been serving there for two years. When the critics became too vocal, Stirborn characteristically solved the problem by failing to replace personnel lost through casualties, retirements, and reassignments. Then, for good measure, he started to skimp on the brigade's equipment and armaments, thus managing to alienate the hawks as well.

Medical care was mediocre, educational policies were uninspiring, and taxes and prices soaring as Stirborn reluctantly led the country into elections triggered by the Vietnam issue.

To everyone's surprise I retained my seat in the next parliament, where the Liberals weren't even the official Opposition anymore. Aside from the Independents it was fifty-three per cent Labour, twenty-four per cent Conservative, and twenty per cent Liberal.

Labourite Moorhead trimmed his beard, railroaded through the Kauri cone flag bill and proceeded to print money at a breathless rate. Anti-poverty schemes, racial equality blueprints, grandiose pension plans and health insurance programs — they all now proliferated and rapidly managed to drain the country's resources. Worthless money was then printed at an extra fast clip, but at least some of it was saved: the boys were back from Vietnam two weeks after the elections.

The first real challenge came from Lucius Liefenbarger just after his arm had been grazed by a bullet from an assassin. There were no clues and the former assistant police chief announced that since the left-wing political appointments had rendered the police force impotent, he was hereby establishing his own force. The initial number was 100 men, but with auxiliaries its strength was much closer to five times that number. Plagued by a rift between the radicals and moderates, the inexperienced socialist Moorhead failed to respond properly. He merely spoke and condemned — in effect leaving all executive action to a thoroughly indifferent God.

I guess that is the real reason why I view socialist-internationalists with much suspicion. Not because they sincerely try to help the poor working stiff — that could be nothing but commendable — but because in a crisis they are so consistently ineffective. The German and French socialists failed in both wars to stand up to militarism and/or defeatism. In Eastern Europe they failed to stand up to the Communists, and in New Salisbury their naivety had practically handed the country to Liefenbarger.

In the midst of all the excitement George arrived for his mother's funeral, and stayed for a Christmas visit. From the welcome he got it was clear that the Titus name was still quite a drawing card. That didn't escape Moorehead's attention, who quickly organized a mammoth barbecue at Victory Gardens where hordes of shirt-sleeved working-class freeloaders made George visibly uneasy. An ugly monument to Norman Ruttledge Titus was unveiled that George's twins — a boy and a girl — fawned over. Spread across the front page of the *New Salisbury Times* the next day was a picture of Kevin

Moorehead, beaming at Titus in the midst of an animated discussion, both looking relaxed and good-natured with beer mugs in their hands.

I wasn't there, being a part of a parliamentary delegation to my native Eastern Europe, an experience I didn't want to miss. But George and I met a week later, when he was already ensconced at a mountain lodge in Lower Isle's Cheviot Hills. Once more he doggedly refused to become involved in a discussion of New Salisbury's politics, claiming that he was really an outsider, a foreigner with no interest or right to meddle. His wife Kathy smiled prettily, then insisted on hearing all the long-forgotten details of my one-time romance with New Salisbury's own Diana Mulgrave. It was really ancient history: Diana now reigned in Hollywood, endeared to the Academy, with her third husband and the previous year's Oscar as Best Actress.

When George and his suntanned family flew off to Vancouver, I again returned, brooding, into the back benches, watching the depressing scene's final act unfold before me. With the economy sliding, Kevin Moorehead moved leftward, clamping all sorts of crippling controls on business, finding all sorts of ingenious ways of killing the golden goose, not the least of which was the compulsory presence of inept workers' representatives on directorial boards of large companies. In various parts of the country, clandestine workers' action committees were being formed and supplied with arms while the police continued to look the other way. (Credit should be given where it's due: Moorehead most probably initially opposed such moves, but soon he was receiving and becoming more and more dependent on aid from the Russians. The Russians, it is rumored, tend to favor radicals with arms.)

The Americans, on the other hand, were not about to hand eastern Oceania to the Soviets. They bet on Liefenbarger and the money poured in for his well-organized National Unity Movement as the only viable alternative. It was particularly strong in New Salisbury City and even along the industrialized north coast where clashes between the workers' militia and the National Unity Movement's troops were becoming more frequent.

Twenty people lost their lives in such clashes during the 1972 elections. The Conservatives and Liberals together got only twenty per cent of the vote. The rest was split within half a percentage point between the Labourites and their left-wing associates on the one hand, and Liefenbarger's NUM on the other. With promises and veiled threats of civil war, Liefenbarger in the end got the tacit support of the Conservatives and Liberals. Further help came when five ultra-left-wing radicals refused to sit in a parliament dominated by National Unity.

One by one the workers' militia units were now being disarmed. The NUM's organization was strengthened and Russian involvement in New Salisbury's politics exposed daily in newspaper articles and television reports.

Having finally lost my seat in the latest elections, I now sat uneasily in the press gallery, reporting the dismantling of the country's democratic framework, knowing full well that the newspapers' time had to come soon if the Lief was to be successful in his bid for total power.

The year 1973 couldn't have been more suitable for the final push. New Salisburians who had practically no oil and very little coal were beginning to panic. And in the midst of all the hand-wringing, the Lief announced a tough new policy, whose cornerstone was to be a government-imposed industrial peace. Labour promptly fell into the trap. Moorehead called for demonstrations against the proposal, forgetting that his radical wing still controlled a few armed workers' groups. Referring to the recent bloody skirmishes, Liefenbarger called them "a national crusade." Then he declared a national emergency, silenced the media, and centralized his grip on power through the demotion of provincial governments. Finally he suspended New Salisbury Parliament itself.

He also had no trouble finding Labourites who were willing to change color instantly and serve in his National Unity Government as ministers. It gave the whole terrible charade a bit of an aura of legitimacy. But the real power now lay with his advisors — mostly handpicked cronies from his police days — and, of course, with himself.

The jails started to fill. People also disappeared — sometimes were found dead, and sometimes not at all — and the rest of the country couldn't have cared less. New Salisbury had bet on Lucius C. Liefenbarger and it was expected that a few hotheads had to roll. Moorehead and most of the Labour leadership were among the first to enter the newly established camps on the Partrawa Plain and I thought it typical of their general helplessness that they were still around to be so easily bagged. Then it was poor old Stirborn's turn. The same day that I heard about his arrest I paid a sizeable sum to a fishing-boat captain to take me to Wellington.

My father sent word there that the following morning Liefenbarger's police had come to the house for me.

Chapter 4

Initially the New Salisbury Freedom Committee received substantial if somewhat indirect help from el Presidente Augusto Pinochet Ugarte of Chile, because he came to power about the same time that Lucius Liefenbarger did. Although the two of them had never met, they proceeded with equal speed and equally hard fists against all dissenters. It therefore soon became accepted journalistic practice for New Salisbury and Chile to be mentioned in the same breath whenever the press chose to speak out about the world's injustices.

Which was often. At least, as I said, initially. As a result I, the ranking Liefenbarger dissenter abroad, never stopped lecturing, giving interviews, exhorting and prophesying. From the committee's headquarters in Honolulu I sent out monthly newsletters based on information brought to Hawaii by messengers aboard the three weekly flights from New Salisbury City. The Americans, surprisingly, weren't too disturbed about having on their soil a revolutionary movement directed against a regime which they had helped to establish and now fully supported. It took me a few months to figure out why: the committee served as a reminder to the Lief that an excessively and, for the U.S., embarrassingly bad performance would swiftly bring on the next act. Mine.

Then there were the Algerians who, the Americans felt, needed a bit of competition. Billed as the New Salisbury Liberation Front, the quartet of John Leahy, Victor Channing and two other Marxist former youth leaders had first gotten together in Cuba. But Havana had a certain undesirable aura; it made the Marxists thoroughly suspect in the eyes of most Westerners. So they moved on to more remote Algeria where they were being trained and groomed by the Russians for an eventual revolution in New Salisbury.

Things would have continued smoothly for all three of us — for the Americans, for me, and the Algerians — had not Pinochet and the Lief proven to be fairly fast learners. The excesses of their regimes soon were toned down and only carefully edited news left the country. Pinochet and Liefenbarger then went on the offensive by granting selective amnesties and employing statistics which proved a substantially improved economic performance over the preceding regime. They also kept executions and atrocities within the ranks. The result was a markedly reduced interest on the part of the press, universities, and clubs that in the past tended to lionize Hawaii-based New Salisbury's former minister of immigration.

Then my father suffered a second stroke and died a few days later. The ass of my cousin took over Allied Shipyards. The first thing he did was to freeze all foreign accounts that dad had conveniently left open for me. The second was to publicly throw in his lot with Lucius C. Liefenbarger. I was broke, and the New Salisbury Freedom Committee faced at best an uncertain future. My secretary was replaced with a $200 answering service: the weekly newsletter became a monthly. The future was bleak. Reluctantly I started looking for a job.

That was when George flew into Paradise and checked in at the Princess Kaiulani. Late August was definitely out of season for Hawaii, but George would have been a surprise any time of the year. He was alone, in the cool of the bar volunteering only a bit of stark factual information. So we talked about redundancies and inanities, both feeling highly uncomfortable especially after all those times we had enjoyed raging against all the redundancies and inanities around us.

And then came the confession. In small drops at first, about how there had been disagreements and family arguments. Then a steady stream of disaffection, and finally a dam-busting torrent of confusion about goals — his, his wife's, the twins', and those of his native country.

By midnight it was clear that George had reached a middle-age crisis and that he had tried to solve it by increasing the production pace on his *Chronicles of Political Systems*. That may have temporarily pushed back gnawing doubts about himself and the direction he was heading in, but it also further reduced the time spent with his family to beyond the critical point, he realized later, as he failed to heed repeated warnings in the form of increased disdain in his daughter's eyes, and indifference in his son's. First there were minor eruptions. The final, big one came early in the spring and in the pouting mood that followed he had no trouble convincing himself that ingratitude ruled the world. He packed his bags and rented an apartment on the university grounds, determined to teach his family a lesson.

In the end it was a lesson he had neatly taught himself.

Without the sprawling house on University Boulevard which he had thought to be such a hindrance, there was nowhere to escape. Certainly the bare studio flat in which he slept was no substitute. Once more he stepped up his pace, but he experienced moments when his mind started to balk, when he could no longer register things on the printed page in front of him, where much of his alertness disappeared and he had to do constant battle with ennui. And it grew worse. Some nights he couldn't sleep for the pressure at the back of his skull; there came the sensation of vertigo and mild attacks of claustrophobia — both in his university carrel and at home.

He was forced to change his thinking, to look around and communicate with people, whether it was at the laundromat, at the supermarket checkout counter, or during those walks along the beach at Spanish Banks that he found so therapeutic. Reluctantly he arrived at the conclusion that he had been wrong, that he needed the family at least as much as the family needed him.

And then came the ultimate jolt: When he called his wife it became obvious that she no longer needed him, that no one at the house needed him, that they had found life much more tranquil without him. What was worse, his wife had found a lover. There was no place for him to return to, the bridges had been burned.

From the other side.

He had no idea where he belonged and, remembering that I was in Hawaii, he came to find familiarity again.

"How did you know where I was? I mean I don't have you on the mailing list and — "

"But you have the UBC Library on it, don't you?"

"I suppose. Why didn't you keep in touch?"

George smiled enigmatically. "You wouldn't understand. At the department it's *de rigeur* to keep aloof. If you act as a campus guide for visiting PLO members, or if you accept an invitation to be an observer at the South African elections, you quickly acquire a political label. Aside from inviting a hostile response from your opposites, you are also looked down upon by the dyed-in-the-wool theoreticians that rule most universities. And for some inexplicable reason what the effete scholars thought of me used to be terribly important."

"Hence no *New Salisbury Newsletter* delivered to your address?"

"Hence no newsletter. But I did manage to contribute $300 via Toronto last year."

My eyes widened. "So the C. R. Thames Company was you. No wonder I couldn't find it in any phone book."

George grinned for the first time that evening. I smiled back a bit idiotically because I still had no clear idea what role he expected me to play — Father Confessor or the much more active Ignatius Loyola?

He went on, asking about the Partrawa Plain camps, the maroon-shirted National Unity Corps, and about Lucius Liefenbarger. He listened, nodded, and asked for further details until it was obvious that here was more than just a curious interest. Much, much more.

"I would like to join you and your group," he said finally.

"You mean you would lead us?"

"No, I just want to be part of it."

"Titus as a footsoldier is no great contribution, believe me. But the importance of a Titus at the head of a movement you simply can't imagine, George."

"I can't lead a revolution, Maurice. Don't be ridiculous. I've never even fired a gun."

"Have you ever seen a picture of Lenin with a submachine gun? But how many times have you seen him with his mouth opened, exhorting the crowds? In an hour or two we'll teach you how to shoot a gun and then we'll concentrate all our efforts on making damn sure that you're nowhere near when guns are fired. Don't you understand George? You're much too valuable."

He grumbled something that made it clear he was not yet convinced. Then he asked, "Can we do the whole thing with regional help? I mean with Australia and New Zealand?"

"You've been in your carrel too long. Revolutions nowadays are conducted either by the Americans or the Russians. Sometimes the Chinese test the water, but only in Asia and only when the Americans are neutral. We have to go to Washington on this."

"Garbeau?"

"Garbeau," I nodded, delighted that he remembered.

Chapter 5

The elegant Kenneth Garbeau owed us at least the early part of his career at the State Department. We had provided the all-important initial push. When Garbeau arrived at the American embassy in N.S. City during the fifties, Titus was prime minister. We met Garbeau at some dull party which the American proceeded to liven up with his imitations of Groucho Marx and Marilyn Monroe. He also managed a passable Jawaharal Nehru and Churchill. With such talents he soon became an indispensable member of our group of young, fairly prominent New Salisburians to which the appalled radical left loved to refer as *jeunesse dorée*. Garbeau thus gained entry into circles he could have never managed without us. For a young Foreign Service officer on his first assignment, this was a feather in a cap that was clearly visible all the way to Washington's Foggy Bottom.

Now he was a deputy assistant secretary with a suite in a posh San Francisco hotel, rented because an annual international trade conference was held there although it didn't particularly interest him.

He had aged in a standard American way — flannel suits showed a bit more stoutness around his waist; sideburns were meticulously trimmed; he sported greying and also thinning hair; he expressed himself more slowly, and frequently with more emphasis on delivery than meaning.

After some weak introductory humor and coffee I fired my question. Garbeau leaned back in one of the loveseats, rubbed his hands together and began: "I'm sorry, Maurice, it can't be done like that. To come up with a policy the U.S. would have to know what sort of an armed uprising you're talking about — a few fanatics disrupting traffic through the Cheviots with hunting pieces or a genuine grass-roots movement? And on both islands or just on the Lower Isle? What are its chances of success, how capable are its leaders? And then what exactly is its political orientation? Which major powers support whom and what is likely to be the future ideological orientation of the revolutionary regime?"

He looked at me, then at George, then smiled to soften the whole thing. "The U.S. has had bad experiences with revolutions, you know. We should have kept Batista in power at least temporarily, and left Castro starving in the Sierra Maestra. And in the meantime we should have cultivated the moderates. And we should have been satisfied with Sihanouk."

"Could it have been done?" George asked.

"Christ, I don't know." Garbeau scratched his chin. "But it sure as hell would have been worth a try. It's something I wish we were trying in Africa these days. But — "

"There is no moderate movement in New Salisbury," I reminded him.

"I thought you were one," said Garbeau.

"We're not in New Salisbury and Liefenbarger is no amateur. We've looked at the thing from every conceivable angle. An armed revolt is the *only* way to get rid of him."

Garbeau studied us silently for a moment. Finally he came out with, "That's what our people say. But that's right now, at present. It could all change."

"Well?" I asked after a decent pause.

Garbeau took a sip of coffee, evidently without any great desire for it. But it gave him time to think.

"Look, Maurice, I have to go back to what I started with. How can we be sure that in the end the whole thing will not provide the Russians with a sorely needed satellite in the South Pacific and us with a Marxist threat to both New Zealand and Australia? O.K., so Liefenbarger is an embarrassing tyrant now with considerable blood on his hands. But who could replace him — the Gulag people? Your names could be nicely used until you were no longer needed, then you would be replaced with a hammer and sickle. For Christ's sake, it wouldn't be the first time — whatever happened to all those highly-touted democratic elements in the Viet Cong?"

"With American support we could get rid of Liefenbarger and keep the Russians out as well."

"You have a bloated view of what we can do nowadays. Maybe in a two-bit banana republic somewhere, but your proposition is particularly difficult. We're talking about New Salisbury, a country with no illiteracy, practically no poverty and a strong tradition of social consciousness."

I changed to a different tact. "In Algeria there is an outfit called the New Salisbury Liberation Front. I think they're about ready to transfer their operations to New Salisbury."

"I know."

"And you want them to land first?"

"No, we certainly don't. We also know that they won't be beaten with monthly newsletters."

A mysterious smile flew across Kenneth's face. He got up and walked to the dresser. He took a piece of paper from his attaché case on top of it, then handed it to me.

"At this address you can get anything from a sawed-off shotgun to an anti-tank missile. You might want to pay them a visit. They're in Los Angeles, can deliver anywhere in the world. A very kind uncle has arranged for a certain amount of credit to be extended to you there."

He paused a moment, thoroughly enjoying our astonished faces. "It's part of a brand new policy of ours, highly unofficial as yet. Code name is Put Up Or Shut Up."

Chapter 6

Diana Mulgrave lived on a crescent in Beverly Hills that became a fairytale in the early evening with thousands of city lights below. A black servant ushered us into a foyer that displayed a small marble fountain full of tropical fish, then into a sunken living room dominated by a wall of glass. Seated on a white leather couch, we faced a massive stone fireplace while silently viewing the many and varied excesses of the Hollywood school of interiors surrounding us.

The first time I saw Diana Mulgrave she was still a struggling young actress, known only to the most dedicated of N.S. City theatre habitués. She had just begun receiving invitations to the Saturday afternoon affairs at Pitlochry, where painters mingled with poets and journalists with potters, then stayed on for a buffet supper, usually followed by some cultural presentation.

From these gatherings evolved the Saturdayers — the group which came to Pitlochry each week, whether the prime minister was in town or not. I remember Douglas MacArthur coming to Pitlochry just before Christmas 1950 to personally thank New Salisbury for its help in the Korean War. During dinner on the mansion's balcony with the surf and the glittering lights of N.S. City in the background he rose, a champagne glass in his hand. Within months he would be ignominiously relieved of his command and the war would start winding down, but then he was still the invincible seventy-one-year-old warrior with the brilliant Inchon landings just added to his credits. The words of his proposed toast had since become part of the large, leatherbound guest book, where he had written them down at the request of George's father: "At magic moments like this we tend to think that there can be no defeats or even disappointments in our efforts. There can be; there are. I should like to propose a toast not to our victories and certainly not to our defeats, but to our ability to learn from them."

Later the general delivered a stiff, sabre-rattling address about U.S. goals in the Pacific. In the end there was appropriate if not enthusiastic applause, and then the gathering broke into clusters. Diana, in breezy chiffon, politely listened for a few minutes to an excessively pedantic description of present-day Nippon, provided by one of the general's more wooden aides. Then, unexpectedly, she chirped in with a totally innocent expression: "Tell me, general, don't you find that lately there has been entirely too much emphasis on solving the world's ills through the use of military force?"

There ensued a somewhat stunned silence, eventually broken by the venerable warrior who reluctantly explained that when one is dealing with an ideology based almost entirely on violence, there really isn't that much of a choice. Then he promptly excused himself.

Her charming audacity propelled her into a full membership of the Saturdayers and into my arms, although not for long.

Now she emerged at the top of a staircase, the perfect set for dramatic entrances just above the living room. It was clear that she had the ageing process entirely under control: through a series of holding actions she had channelled it in the proper direction rather than doing battle with it. There were wrinkles, true, but she was actually thinner and I would say even more attractive than when I last saw her in New Salisbury. Nostalgia momentarily engulfed me, but then regrets over lost youth were overpowered by our need for her voice.

"Maurice and George!" she sang out on the last step, her arms outstretched. "How nice of you not to have forgotten me. Sit down, sit down. What can I get you?"

We finally settled on Scotch which Diana produced from a mahogany liquor cabinet beneath a Grandma Moses original. Then we spoke about her career.

It didn't seem to have slowed down. She had recently toured the country in a production of *A Streetcar Named Desire* and she was hosting a public affairs program on human rights. Her next film was to be based on the life story of the wife of Salvador Allende Gossens but first the money had to be found.

"Please don't think, though, that I have forgotten all about home," she hurried to explain. "How could one possibly forget about it when it's being destroyed by a fascist monster like Liefenbarger? Of course, he couldn't do it alone. He wouldn't last a day if it weren't for the Americans — the CIA, the fucking Pentagon, the whole damn industrial establishment. I thought I knew, but of course I had no idea of the scope of the whole thing. None at all. But two weeks ago Vic Channing was here — do you know him? Well, I had a few people over — Shirley McLaine, Jane Fonda with her hubby, Robert Vaughn and so on. You know, those that would be interested and who have shown some interest in the human condition. Well, Vic Channing certainly opened our eyes. The Partrawa camps, the torture chambers, the whole bloody maroon shirt business. And it's all financed from this country. Right from here. He couldn't stay in power otherwise. Not for a day — the people would trample him to death!"

At just about the same moment George and I realized that she had no idea of the existence of our New Salisbury Freedom Committee and that she would not join our ranks. The Algerians had gotten to her first.

"Vic Channing has a complete record of all the transactions between Liefenbarger and the Pentagon," she continued. "There is a man in the Towers in N.S. City who works with them."

"With whom?"

"With the Liberation Front. There are just a few of them in North Africa right now and they need money — lots of money — but we'll get it for them. They are dedicated people. You can't imagine just how dedicated; you'd simply have to hear Vic Channing."

"I've heard Channing," I said to George later in the cab on the way to the airport. "He used to be an assistant to Mel Hardwick. You remember Hardwick, don't you? The only man who voted against the Korean war credits in the entire New Salisbury Parliament. Grudgingly he would now and then allow people to refer to him as a Marxist, but never as a Communist."

"What happened to him?"

"He must have been crazy. Absolutely off his rocker. As soon as Liefenbarger dissolved parliament, Channing and the others were on their way to Australia. But Hardwick stayed. His trail ends at Partrawa about two years ago. But Channing, from what I've just heard, knows where to be and what to say at exactly the right time."

Chapter 7

It has become fashionable to blame the Renfrew Peninsula disaster on Garth Boyce's betrayal. It's quite in tune with the present-day tendencies toward simplification and search for scapegoats. Also toward just plain telling of lies.

The truth is we had originally planned to come ashore not on the Renfrew Peninsula at all, but on the Lower Isle — at the remote, largely deserted Precarious Sound. There Boyce would not have been able to inform anybody of our landing and we would have disappeared into the high mountains within hours; as well, our contacts among local residents would have been much more extensive. However, George chose the Renfrew Peninsula on Main Island over Precarious on the Lower Isle.

We had been planning the Precarious landing for weeks when George first heard about it after his arrival at Honolulu. He confessed that he found it decidedly undramatic: "It isn't the way for a Titus to reenter New Salisbury," I recall him saying. So in between training sessions with a U.S. Marine Corps sergeant, George and I bent over a map of Main Island, studying roads and military installations near the Renfrew Peninsula.

From all sorts of clues Boyce probably figured out that we would land somewhere on the north shore of Main Island and he quite likely had been able to send word to the Lief. Liefenbarger knew that there wouldn't be more than a handful of us and that George Titus and Maurice Bech-Landau would be in the group, so he did little about it. He didn't strengthen shore patrols and he did not provide for air reconnaissance of the coast. As a matter of fact, in some communities, police presence was actually reduced. The idea was to get us all safely ashore, to lull us into a false sense of security, then pounce.

Garth Boyce had been planted among us in a way that was nothing short of brilliant. He came to us a month after the murder of Charles Simpson, the former foreign minister. Simpson, because of his international contacts, was the last of the prominent democratic politicians not held in Partrawa camps. Living alone in Weymouth, he was watched by National Unity Corps agents, but not closely enough. Simpson's friends managed to smuggle in an Italian reporter who interviewed him for six hours. The interview, along with a harsh eye-witness description of Liefenbarger's New Salisbury, appeared in the world's press.

According to the diaries kept by Liefenbarger's executive secretary Frank Copithorne, it was at that point that the Administrator decided that Simpson must go. He was disposed of during a storm when a falling branch supposedly struck him on the head.

But no one doubted that he had been murdered. There was enough consternation at the United Nations for the General Assembly to appoint a special commission which was to go to New Salisbury and investigate the entire affair. Initially the Lief had been vehemently opposed to the idea, but when he found out that the commission would consist of the third-grade dropout Ita Nzambwe of Zambia, a thoroughly corrupt crony of James Mancham from the Seychelles named Royton, and an anonymous Hungarian party man, he changed his mind. The Magyar, it turned out, felt thoroughly uncomfortable in the group, returning to New York in disgust a day after the committee arrived. Meanwhile the Lief lavishly wined and dined the other two and, for a fleeting moment, showed them the body of Simpson with the bullet holes carefully camouflaged. After that the outcome was never in doubt. The committee published a report which was in reality a paean to Lucius C. Liefenbarger's statesmanship.

Garth Boyce had been owner of the tavern in front of which Simpson had been killed after partaking of his nightly brandy. Because of this, Boyce claimed, he had to go into hiding. Eventually we managed to smuggle him out of the country to New Zealand and then to Honolulu. There he gave several moving addresses describing Simpson's last hours and the harshness of the Lief's murderous regime. A former army sergeant, Boyce soon became part of our group. None of us had any reason to suspect him.

How could we not accept him? It was simply inconceivable that the Lief could have been so secure as to recruit him while Boyce still ran the tavern, then order him to go into hiding and to make strong anti-government statements in order to become a trusted member of the Committee for a Free New Salisbury. But those were the halcyon days of the Liefenbarger regime and the Administrator felt strong enough to weather all of Boyce's staged attacks. With reason because, as I've already said, the Lief *was* strong. In the beginning we all tended to underestimate his abilities, and overestimate George Titus's.

It wasn't hard to do. While bobbing up and down in the sun aboard two rusty Samoan fishing boats, we became convinced that we were thoroughly in command of the situation. Although there were only five of us so far, it would take at the most a few hours after we landed to rally entire communities to our side through underground groups we knew about.

The whole thing had acquired a movie scenario unreality. From the first day that we drove through the gate of Schofield Barracks on Oahu, I couldn't rid myself of the suspicion that soon I would see Burt Lancaster firing a heavy machine gun from his hip at the attacking Japanese. The conspiracy sessions at my garden apartment near Waikiki conducted to the heavy beat of disco tunes from a nightclub across the way were a bit fantastic too. Then there was the Hercules with our supplies in it, warming up on the breezy runway to eternity, while the incredulous Garbeau was listening to George explaining all about the new landing site on Main Island.

"Do you agree with this?" Garbeau turned to me.

"No, but it's not my show. I am not in charge."

He studied my face for a brief moment before turning back to George. "Are you sure you want to do it this way?"

And when George nodded, he said, "It's against what our people advise."

But that seemed a bit pushy and George was instantly up on his hind legs. "Your people have been wrong."

"It's also against what Che Guevara says — and our people have been right much more often than they have been wrong, except that you haven't heard about it. O.K. Just tell the boat captains at Neiafu."

The dialogue was straight out of a Bogart movie. When we set down at the island of Vava'u the scenery changed, but the mood remained. Two British-built trucks took arms and our supplies to the dock at Neiafu, where we loaded up the crates aboard the tuna boats with the backdrop of a moon-dappled lagoon and surrounding hills of gently swaying palms.

At close quarters aboard the *Pita,* we got to know each other pretty well. The fourth one in our group was Mel Adams, a marvelously inventive man Friday who had been with me close to ten years — as a campaign manager and an administrative manager, as an advisor, and a very dear friend.

The fifth member was a woman, Meg Winters. She had been a graduate anthropology student when Liefenbarger came to power. One of a small group who saw clearly what had happened and what was about to happen, she helped to organize the February '74 demonstration at Victory Park. It was so well disguised as a rugby rally that it caught the National Unity Corps completely by surprise.

But the reprisals were furious. It was the first operation directed by the newly appointed NUC Chief Eddie Mayfield, a ruthless crony of Lucius Liefenbarger from his police days.

With swiftness and uncommon penchant for efficiency that later became proverbial, Mayfield closed the university and proceeded to divide its student body into three parts: those who were to be arrested, those who would be suspended and those — mostly in the professional faculties — who could continue their studies. When, in about a month, the university reopened, Meg's name figured prominently in the first group. But she was in hiding, looking for a way out of the country.

She was also convinced that it had been the university that had failed her more than anything or anyone else. That place of such hope-giving enlightenment, where she had felt brightly alive, figured prominently in Liefenbarger's own special brand of *Gleichschaltung* — that Nazi method of bringing everything and everyone in line with government policy — that had been carried out so fast and with so little resistance that it made a joke of all the moralistic, liberal pronouncements taught in its classrooms. She didn't blame her fellow students too much. After all, the puerile, stilted defenses of man's rights during the afternoon seminars, the awkwardly written editorials in the student newspaper, and the haughty ideals regurgitated during bull sessions in the dormitory — they had all been inspired by the profs. With very few exceptions the faculty of UNS pledged allegiance to the Liefenbarger regime ensuring tenure for its supporters.

George Titus was a university prof parachuted into the leadership of our group not because we thought he had exceptional abilities but because of his exceptional name. Meg greatly resented his tailored slacks and Florsheim loafers, and his detachment from the Committee's efforts until his own, personal crisis made it into a convenient escape route.

"You wanna know something Maurice?" she once confided in me on the way back from a tough day of training at Schofield Barracks, "He's a lousy leader, but the only one we got. It really hurts to think we might die on some desolate rock of the old homeland just because our boy here is a slow learner."

Even though Meg took time out to knock out the new planks at every opportunity, George really did try to mend fences. The third day out of Neiafu we sailed into a storm. The *Pita* slid down the sides of giant waves, leaning precariously to one side, its screw frequently out of water. We were terrified. The captain — an overweight, smiling Samoan who couldn't speak a word of English but who insisted his name was Jack Smith — guided the boat with a sure hand through the churning sea.

During one such slide, George got down from his bunk and went out on the tiny deck just outside our cabin. There, leaning over the stern of the boat, was Meg. Her clothes were soaked and her hands clutched the railing as she retched over the side, pained by the effort as well as by the indignity. Moving along the railing, George approached her.

"Meg, this is no good, by yourself here…"

"Get away from me, damn it! This isn't any of your business!"

He stood there beside her for a moment, amazed and baffled by her powerful vehemence, even after the toll her nausea must have taken. She turned away from him, her body succumbing to even more terrible spasms. She tried to vomit again but nothing came up. Then, exhausted by the exertion, she slid down the railing, and finally setted on the wooden deck beside it — a spent bundle of human misery. She didn't look at him again; her head fell on her chest and her eyes closed heavily.

Chapter 8

We arrived at a spot on the north shore of the Renfrew Peninsula shortly before dawn on a warm November Sunday. Quickly disembarking, we then watched the *Pita* and the *Sesa* disappear from sight. They would be waiting offshore for forty-eight hours, until we had established contact and decided on a place to unload the guns and supplies with which the *Sesa* was laden.

What we saw at Renfrew reminded me of those knowledgeable Western journalists who arrive in totalitarian countries, somberly reporting about the calmness of the populace, sometimes only hours before the outbreak of a major revolt. Except for a few obnoxious posters and banners strung across streets exhorting people to show a greater degree of unity behind the stellar Administrator, we were in the middle of a typical holiday resort. People here cared mainly about the available ice-cream flavors, and the water temperatures and weather forecasts almost to the total exclusion of everything else.

Each one of us carried a revolver in his bag, but it made us feel more incongruous than safe. Divided into two groups we walked the streets of Renfrew, thrilled to be back home, although at the same time quite apprehensive because the mood here was nothing like we had expected it to be.

I don't recall just why it was Garth Boyce who had been assigned to make the phone call; it was probably simply because he had volunteered. It suited his purposes admirably. While I waited outside he dialled the number, then mumbled something into the phone, listened, mumbled something again, then hung up. When he opened the door of the booth he asked for another coin, explaining that he had dialled a wrong number.

Granted that had the booth door been left open, he would not have been able to alert the police, but we were just outside a noisy milkbar with a blaring jukebox. For me to have insisted on the telephone booth's door to remain open would have been asinine.

Later in the afternoon we were picked up by the Mc-
Elroy's blue truck and taken to their farm near Te Lame.
Ellen and Grant McElroy were an engaging couple in their
twenties, excited by their lifestyle, but greatly disturbed over
the direction in which the country was heading. Ellen served
us a sumptuous dinner and, because only one bedroom of the
house had been finished, we agreed to sleep in the haystack
outside; perhaps at that moment we were still romantics and
the idea of a starry sky above us seemed most appealing.
Mel had discovered that he and the McElroys had some
mutual friends, and he and Garth stayed behind in the farmhouse to talk.

A word about Captain Trevor Greytrix in charge of security
in the Renfrew District that night — a man whose towering
ambition was only matched by his gross incompetence.
Thank God for him. Very early during Liefenbarger's rise to
power he had grown to realize that his place was among the
meaty thugs of the National Unity Corps. That was while it
was still the Lief's private army; after he assumed total power
Greytrix was rushed through the academy, commissioned,
and within two years promoted to captain. It should be noted
that even the ruthless NUC had its more rational side —
Greytrix was consciously kept out of command. At Renfrew
he had been the executive officer to the district commander
of the NUC. But it was a long holiday weekend — the first
one of the warm season — and the commander was out of
town. So was, it would seem, every senior NUC officer at the
capital.

After the Renfrew incident, there naturally came a drastic
shake-up of the entire Liefenbarger security structure, but the
moment that Greytrix was informed through Boyce's
phone call of our landing, there were still many communica-
tion gaps.

Greytrix assumed that it was up to him to lead the counterattack. It was up to him to save the country from the
arrogant Bolsheviks. He didn't call for the crack security
troops stationed at N.S. City partially because he was convinced that time was of essence and partially because command would have likely slipped from his hands. Instead, he
requisitioned two howitzers along with fifty reservists from
the nearby Fort Kerry. The insurgents' choice of an isolated
farmhouse, Greytrix felt, had been a magnificent stroke of
luck. The rural setting placed practically no limits on what he

considered to be a masterful assault plan. Through it he planned to exhibit, he felt, his not inconsequential martial prowess. In fact his plan did not differ too much from all mediaeval battle plans. Like a blow with a sledgehammer, it was a show of force without much sophistication or concern for consequences.

The second shell constituted a direct hit on the farmhouse. Within seconds came the next one, also a direct hit, which set the butane tank ablaze, sending the sides of the frame house high into the air. By that time our haystack was on fire in several places and the three of us were scampering away in the direction of the river. Typical of Greytrix's martial prowess was the fact that he had had the vicinity of the farmhouse surrounded — except that his men were positioned *on the other side* of the Sewena River which flowed through the McElroy property.

For no discernible reason we had been neatly divided into those who would live and those who would die instantly. Among the latter were Garth Boyce, Mel Adams and the McElroys — their six-month-old son as well.

I really don't recall how I reached the river. By the time I fell through the bushes into it, I saw two dark spots in the distance, immediately assuming that they were part of our group. The surrounding countryside was bathed in the eerie glow from the fires started by Greytrix's howitzers. There were shouts and sporadic firing of submachine guns, the crackle of flames and the crash of collapsing structures — a veritable hell of heat, chaos, and terror. Keeping my face in the water as much as possible, unharmed I floated away from Greytrix's perimeter, away from the burning farm with its five corpses and my very first encounter with fiery, violent death.

And I don't know what I was more at that moment — scared or angry. But whatever it was, it was far less noticeable than that which was happening to George as we reached the mouth of the Sewena at daylight. He had been hit by an assortment of significant realizations all at once, somehow having to come to terms with the fact that the Renfrew Peninsula had been a bad decision, that he should have posted guards around the farm and that his failure to do so had probably cost five lives. Also that we may have been betrayed and that, quite unlike the storylines of movies, we were hungry, cold, hopelessly bogged down, and probably surrounded. It didn't look like a happy ending at all.

At least one of our problems was being solved, though. As

the sun kept climbing it also dried our clothes and rid us of those trembling spasms that had been plaguing us all, especially George. Only Meg was still armed. Only she had remembered to bring her bag through the melee, although her gun by now was probably useless.

All three of us still expected either to be killed or captured. When by 10 A.M. we were still at large, and had not noticed any increase in activity either on the road or on the river, a slight hope rose in us that there was a chance we might make it back to the beach. As the day advanced, we started to suspect that something had inexplicably gone our way after the disaster. But we still had no idea what it was.

It was the legacy left behind by Captain Greytrix. By then, of course, he had long been relieved of command by an NUC lieutenant colonel named Crossley who, as soon as he uncovered the reasons for the fiasco, placed Greytrix under arrest. It was late in the morning when, the area having been thoroughly checked and the charred bodies identified, it was established that other members of the group were probably at large.

Not even Colonel Crossley and his staff, however, had seriously considered the possibility of the insurgents escaping toward the sea. It had been naturally assumed that we would take to the hills. Roadblocks were therefore set up on all routes leading to the interior. Meanwhile we skirted the shore and, mixing with the holiday crowds, proceeded towards the rendezvous beach on which we had landed less than forty-eight hours ago.

The inept Greytrix, to whom we owed our lives, was eventually court-martialled. He was then demoted to a corporal and transferred to the regular army. He died a little over a year later of wounds suffered while fighting with the N.S. Guards in Wahira.

Chapter 9

Totally spent by the effort of the last few hours, the three of us lay on the canvas covered afterdeck of the *Pita*, parched by the sun and with the depressing lead-colored sea around us. Through it the tuna boats noisily chugged their way north, toward Neiafu in the Tonga group. There, or perhaps when we returned to Hawaii, we would have to make some sort of a decision. There really weren't too many alternatives; we would probably break up, all of us going separate ways, all the while tormented by thoughts that leaving behind the bodies of four adults and one infant could somehow have been avoided. Captain Jack Smith and his crew unobtrusively went about their business while we quietly ate our rice and sausages and drank beer from the captain's refrigerator. Most of the time, though, we just stared at the eternal sea.

On the second day and already out of danger of interception by the N.S. Coast Guard, Meg came out of her cabin, seating herself on the mat beside me. "Where are we going?" she asked.

"Neiafu. Where we came from."

"Why?"

I turned over in her direction. "Christ Meg, we have to rethink the whole thing."

"Oh . . . Is that what the Americans ordered? More thoughts?"

George spoke. "Nobody ordered anything. Try to understand that we've just lost two men — practically half of our force. The whole Renfrew coast is full of police now. What would you have us do?"

Meg totally ignored George, speaking only to me. "We still have all our supplies, don't we? I mean the *Sesa* over there — "

"Yes, we still have all our supplies," I said tiredly.

"Well, let's go somewhere else. Down the coast somewhere."

"To have more young farmers and their children killed by the NUC?" George asked softly, but not at all sarcastically. It was rather a challenge for her to meet. I found it hard not to

admire George's control. Meg was still refusing to acknowledge his presence, as she had ever since we had reboarded the
Pita. And he, in place of an angry retort, seemed to respect her
right to hate him.

"How about the Precarious plan?" she asked.

And at that moment I started to realize that the revolution
was by no means over for us. There would not be much time to
talk and reassess our chances. Returning to Hawaii would
mean accepting defeat not from the Lief or Greytrix but from
ourselves. John Leahy and the Algerians would come, not us.
Taking time to regroup would also mean giving time to Lief to
gloat over his victory. We were only a few hundred miles from
the target. Our presence in the area was unsuspected — the
tuna boats had not been discovered and we were fully in the
possession of the all-important element of surprise. We still
held the precious initiative.

I watched George and read his mind unashamedly as he sat
up, staring at the sea. He put on his sandals and got to his feet.

"Let's go and see the captain," he said.

Three days later we entered Precarious Inlet. Within moments
the sea calmed down, the wind barred from entering by the
five-hundred-meter high ridges that shot up almost vertically
from the water. At the head of the inlet was the village.

Precarious *was* Branko Justac. His sons lived in houses
scattered throughout the tiny fishing community, at the foot of
rocks so high that the sun only reached them at midday. There
was another son, Peter, who had gone to study architecture at
N.S. City and had been arrested there during the 1974 anti-
Liefenbarger student demonstrations. Twice Branko had
journeyed to Partrawa to find out what had happened to him
and twice had come back without success. The second time,
when an arrogant young NUC lieutenant ordered him out of
his office, Branko let go with an oath. As a result, he returned
to Precarious cut and bruised.

There were perhaps some in the village who would have
preferred to stay aloof from politics, to go about tomcod
fishing, leaving destiny to New Salisbury City. But the Justacs
had founded the village, the Justacs had been running
its affairs for thirty years now, and the Justacs chose its
political and moral stance.

This time both the *Sesa* and *Pita* came to shore together.
Halfway through the inlet we were met by young Tom Justac,

whose boat we followed to a low-lying island filled with bushes and stunted trees at the mouth of a stream. Here we unloaded our supplies.

Branko Justac welcomed us in his house full of rough, wooden furniture with heart-shaped carvings. A bearlike figure, he had fought with the partisans in his native Yugoslavia, but thoroughly grew to despise the Tito regime which replaced the Nazis. Making his way to Italy, he emigrated to New Salisbury after the war, along with a sizeable group of his countrymen who refused to recognize Communist Yugoslavia as a political entity, calling themselves — somewhat to the delight of the canine joke devotees — the Dalmatians.

Branko's clumsy appearance and infrequent words were sometimes mistaken for the demeanor of a slow-witted man. I knew him from Liberal Party conventions where he had figured prominently among the ethnic delegates. Those of us who had seen him in action in the middle of a confrontation took care not to arouse him. When challenged, his slight speech impediment vanished, and his eyes became alive and ablaze. Every one of his gestures suggested power one should definitely have on his side.

We dined on mushroom soup, home-made bread and shrimp casserole, washing it all down with New Zealand wine. It was a welcome relief from the monotonous fare aboard the tuna boat. And when cigars were lit afterwards, Branko spread a survey map of the Precarious area before us, noting that the nonofficial possession of such maps was now illegal. He pointed to a spot only some six kilometers from the village, but separated from it by so many contour lines that in places they merged into a black mass. It was over a thousand meters above sea level.

The Seismo Camp consisted of no more than a lean-to which had been abandoned by a team of seismologists a year before. It was about two kilometers west of the Precarious Trail — the only connection between the inlet and the rest of the Lower Isle. To reach Devon, the first town of any size on the inland plain, required a fast-paced four-day hike.

George overruled my suggestion that we wait until morning before starting up. Meg responded with a smirk on her face, doubtlessly seeing in his insistence that we begin the ascent now only a pathetic attempt to show signs of great leadership. We were joined by Sid Capadouca, a locksmith from Garrick who had fought against Liefenbarger's domination of the unions until he was forced into hiding. For a year now he had been living in Precarious under an assumed name, going out on boats and repairing them, all the time waiting for some opportunity to openly do battle with the Lief's forces.

Led by Dragan Justac, Branko's oldest son, each one with a voluminous rucksack on his back, we started up the steep trail shortly after 3 A.M. Two hours later, government helicopters landed at Precarious and a team of fifteen NUC men searched the houses. It was at best a peremptory search. They were looking for people who were not resident at Precarious, but by that time the four of us were miles away. They only searched the houses — the arms and supply cache on the island remained undisturbed. As the helicopters again rose into the air, the troops still knew nothing about our landing at Precarious. The general search of all New Salisbury coastal settlements had been ordered because of our encounter on the Renfrew Peninsula.

Chapter 10

All sorts of mysteries would have been solved had Lucius C. Liefenbarger's diaries been found. There is no doubt that he kept them — fairly regularly and meticulously. But he also saw ahead. He must have known when he came to power that a totalitarian system in New Salisbury was at best a chancy thing. He saw around him a world that was disorganized, confused, afraid — a world that would at least temporarily help to keep his regime in power.

Still, there is no evidence that he actually destroyed his diaries. Perhaps they are with a friend who will publish them in a decade or two, maybe in fifty years. It's, of course, also possible that they are being properly aged by some entrepreneur until their value rises right along with the curiosity of the historians and professional nostalgists.

But Frank Copithorne's diaries *have* survived. They had been plucked from the sea practically page by page, dried, preserved, and made available to those with a legitimate need to study them.

They are fascinating reading; as time went by and the pressures on the Lief intensified, Liefenbarger became almost totally dependent on his secretary. Copithorne kept and severed contacts, organized administrative procedures, and constantly gauged the country's mood. Copithorne was, in effect, the Lief's Bormann, but with a far less mysterious past. He came from an upper-middle-class background, studied law, and was a latent homosexual. He detested violence but got over that hurdle by carefully remaining ignorant of the way that the regime he served had been built.

Also unlike Bormann, Copithorne was tall, dark, capable and thoroughly attuned to the nuances of power. In his youth he had flirted with Marxism but he was soon out of the phase, moving on, quite naturally, into fanatical egocentrism. What Mozart had been to music Copithorne became to opportunism. He easily elbowed his way into the Lief's favor, past the limited early devotees of National Unity, who in the end had to content themselves with no more than regional vice-chairmanships.

He was welcomed with open arms. The Lief badly needed to be identified with the upper bourgeoisie, to be advised about its ways, and counselled on how to deal with its idiosyncracies. He very much wanted to become its darling without, of course, losing the confidence of the masses.

Because of the ever-dependable Copithorne, the Lief had been able to concentrate on broad, long-range policies that he carved, refined and smoothed — frequently with exquisite care. Thus, the day-to-day affairs he was able to leave to the ubiquitous, sometimes sly, sometimes threatening, but always thoroughly charming Frank Copithorne. Frank attracted or repelled on the Lief's behalf; he set up appointment schedules and got the recording machines started once the audience began. It seems neither Copithorne nor the Administrator bothered to edit the tapes.

Copithorne's Diaries
Tuesday, November 22nd

At ten o'clock the Administrator received Bishop Kewley at Pitlochry and the weather was pleasant enough to sit out on the patio. The A once more outlined the state's need for continued support of the church, thanking Kewley for last week's Anglican Synod's statement against terrorism.

The conversation then turned to more general subjects, the mood becoming less official. In that spirit toward the end of the meeting the A suggested it would be useful if the Anglicans condemned Titus's terrorists and the Algerian Communists by name. The bishop somewhat evasively replied that the Synod indeed considered both groups to be thoroughly reprehensible, but that it felt it should not involve itself to such an extent because it might then lose some of its spiritual authority and be regarded as sycophantic hangers-on. This would not be of advantage either to the A or to the Anglican Synod. I didn't feel that the A was fully convinced, but he did not press the point any further.

On our way to the city I suggested to the A that perhaps now was the time for stronger overtures to be made to the Catholics and to the fast-growing fundamentalist sects in order to twist the Anglican Synod's arm and make it condemn both the Algerians and Titus. He disagreed, saying that the Anglicans, as the official church, had the legitimacy and respect needed by the government. Of course, we should take care not to alienate the fundamentalists and Catholics, but never at the risk of losing the Anglicans. The fundamentalists mostly represent the lower class which can be reached more effectively — as had been amply demonstrated during the 1973 takeover — by fear on the one hand and by promises of economic advantages on the other. And there was still latent suspicion of the Catholics by many New Salisburians — the Catholics, after all, bore allegiance to a foreign, non-English-speaking power. In the light of that explanation I had to agree.

Over lunch at the Oceanic Hotel the A listened to a detailed report on the Renfrew Peninsula landing, delivered by (National Unity Chief Edward) Mayfield. Also present were (Foreign Affairs Minister Matthew R.) Diebel; (Economy Minister Bernard) Metcalf; and (Chief of Staff, General Richard B.) Ormsby. Afterwards the discussion broke into embarrassing squabbles between Ormsby and Mayfield over the failure to capture the entire Titus gang, even after the group had been infiltrated by one of our people. There is no doubt in my mind that Mayfield is primarily responsible. At times he gives the distinct impression of lacking the necessary educational background, experience — the *Weltansicht,* really — to handle the increasingly demanding duties of the security chief. But, of course, he also possesses undeniable zeal and ruthlessness, and he lacks Ormsby's haughty stuffiness. Above all, he harbors unquestionable loyalty to the A. After a while the A toned down the discussion and asked that a thorough military analysis be made of the affair so that mistakes wouldn't be repeated.

No doubt that must be our priority. It takes a man of the A's calibre to see that emotional arguments over the Renfrew affair lead to nowhere. At the end of the meeting we were not necessarily convinced that the problem of the terrorists had been solved, but felt that under the A's leadership effective action would be taken.

The most interesting meeting of the day came at 4 P.M. in the Royal Towers. Along with Metcalf came John C. Clark of the National Association of Farmers and Industrialists, and Derek Wheeler from Pacific Petroleum. There is no doubt whatsoever now that there is oil at the Thames River Delta in Renere Bay. It is a major field with between 750 million and a billion-barrel potential. I was excited over the find and proceeded to ask questions which, I suspect, the A found as a good

way to get all the pertinent information. Because our needs
here in N.S. are relatively small, there is no doubt that the
export of crude oil will prove to be extremely beneficial to our
economy. After the economic repercussions of the find had
been explained, the A pointed out that the newly discovered oil
can be certainly counted on to increase the importance of New
Salisbury in the eyes of the superpowers and that we can expect
to be under increased pressure from them in the future.

Metcalf said that he was fairly certain the full details of the
oil find had been kept secret. The A stressed that for the present
an all-out effort must be made to keep it that way.

We heard the news at Seismo Camp a day after the meeting
took place. The coded message came in as a lengthy dispatch
about weather conditions in the Antarctic, containing a series
of temperature, humidity, and barometric pressure readings,
and gave us all the background we needed on Lief's oil deal-
ings: Shortly after he came to power the Lief commissioned a
study of New Salisbury's future energy requirements and
supplies. When it had been completed two years later, the
prospects were so dismal that he promptly suppressed the
whole thing. But it was too late — the business types in the
Association of Farmers and Industrialists had already sniffed it
out and they managed to press the government into financing
forty-nine per cent of a crash oil exploration program. Being
fanatical free enterprisers, that was about as much as they
would allow the government to become involved. Half of the
rest was put up by the association through intricate arrangements with N.S. banks, the other half was offered to the Pacific
Petroleum Corporation, the only company with majority of its
stock in the hands of New Salisburians. The PPC smacked its
lips at the prospect, but because it was a local company, it was
naturally impecunious. The PPC therefore approached Shell
and Shell provided a loan, anonymously channelled through
Switzerland. Because this was also start of the greatest excesses
of the National Unity Corps, which had violently aroused the
usually non-violent Amnesty International chapters throughout the world, an overt move would have been bad for the
already shaky corporate image of Shell.

But Shell's participation in the scheme did not escape the
attention of other large oil companies. As soon as there was
even a hint of oil under the Thames Delta, Exxon's spies heard
about it. And Exxon, in turn, was under surveillance by the

U.S. Central Intelligence Agency. In Washington they must have known about the find long before Liefenbarger had any inkling of it.

The original intention in the U.S. was to file it away for future reference, except that Garbeau, being one of those directly involved with New Salisbury across whose desk the secret memo from the CIA passed, argued that we at the Seismo Camp should be informed. After all, Titus and his group were part of the U.S. initiative in the area.

Washington reluctantly agreed.

Chapter 11

The calmness of those first few days at Camp Seismo was never experienced again. It enabled us to settle in the mountains and to haul supplies up from the island in the sound. That had to be done on our backs at night over the narrow path which seemed to take us straight up. Every bone in our unaccustomed bodies ached, and the red welts from the shoulder straps and the broken blisters became well neigh insufferable.

But soon we could see the first results of our efforts — the two small repaired cabins and the lean-to. We made radio contact with the Americans at Christchurch, and scouting parties went out to look for campsites. It all required great physical exertion, but there was the consolation of the marvelously tranquil forest around us, the camaraderie, and the realization that all of us were working toward the same goal. We were tired but happy. We were beginning to feel that there was now at least a possibility it might all go our way.

Not that we weren't aware of the pitfalls. A functioning Resistance network started throughout the islands. To assure absolute secrecy, its regional leaders had not been told about our plans to land. We were now planning to activate it, but we also wanted to make damn sure that we were permanently ensconced in the country before we made any announcement about our return.

We harbored no illusions about the network being already infiltrated by the Algerian group and we suspected that the Communists now knew about the oil field. We were in the middle of a race, and the winner would be he who first established a credible presence on the islands. New Salisbury, with the only sizeable oil fields in Oceania, had become an energy plum. There was now no doubt that the Russians would be coming. And soon.

The greatest excitement came from an unexpected direction — from the crazies — the unholy alliance of Trotskyites, Maoists and anarchists, malcontents of all shades who had been pushed together by the NUC's ruthless methods. There had never been more than twenty, and of those, eight were now dying on the Partrawa Plain, the rest being picked off one by one in skirmishes noted for their lack of purpose, meaning or objective. The so-called People's Council had alienated the local population as well as the government. Their mindless raids were also deeply resented by people within the Resistance network because they invariably disrupted more serious efforts.

The People's Council existed not to overthrow the government or to provide an outlet for the oppressed populace, but primarily as a therapeutic device for its demented members. In a tightly knit group that was constantly pursued by governmental hounds there seemed to be at least an implied precept however: suffering was a cleansing process, death was a fulfillment. To their febrile minds it had all become that simple.

In the process the crazies became expert men of the woods. For weeks they could subsist on what they found in the wilderness. Unfortunately they also tended to become increasingly animalistic. While spending a night at Renette just days before our landing at Precarious, the People's Council, now reduced to five members, had been ambushed by the NUC. Only two escaped into the Cheviot Hills — Louis Guernsey and Rod Litvin. The rest were either killed or put into a local prison to be taken to the capital for questioning the next day. Litvin didn't even have time to put on his shoes when they started running. The two of them huddled in the hills through the chilly night, not coming up with any better idea than to storm the NUC headquarters at Renette in order to free their comrades. At dawn they struck, their guns blazing, and they got as far as the front hall before realizing the futility of it all. By that time Litvin had lost a lot of blood through a wound in his shoulder. Guernsey had to literally carry him back into the hills.

Even there they were still in trouble. They crossed and recrossed streams to make the pursuing hounds lose their scent. The pursuers quite naturally assumed that they would be heading back toward Marsbury, along the only road that connected Renette with the interior. It was the pursuers' insistence on expecting what was logical from this highly illogical pair which saved this tiny remnant of the People's Council.

Not from the elements though. Without food and with scant clothing they staggered through the mountains for two miserably cold and wet days until Litvin could go no further. He died on the morning of the third day. That evening Guernsey staggered into Camp Seismo. At first he was ready to fight with us for its possession but, when he realized that he was welcome, that there was food and warmth, he changed his mind. He ate a bowl of soup with bread, reluctantly told his story, then slept for thirty hours.

His sudden appearance electrified the camp, reminding us that we were not a construction team but the vanguard of a guerrilla movement. It had shattered the tranquility of the mountains, jolting us into a new sense of awareness.

Meg was affected more than anyone else. True, now and then she would address George, but only to exchange the most essential information. The night of Guernsey's arrival we were sitting around a small campfire. Meg turned to George and asked, "What now, chief?"

"What do you mean?"

"I mean that I've earned my brownie points now. I can make a cup of tea in teeming rain, fire a Colt .45 and find my way along the ridge above Precarious Inlet. What next?"

"Patience. We have to establish our presence here so that — "

"Oh Bullshit! Bullshit, bullshit, bullshit! You are just establishing your cushy presence, so that the great Titus name will again be on every pair of lips far and wide — delightfully, marvelously, gloriously!"

At that point I intervened.

"Look, Meg, we're preparing a revolution. It probably won't be tomorrow or even next month. But we're here so that we'll know these mountains inside out."

Meg pointed to the cabin where Guernsey was sleeping. "*He*'s not sitting around and holding study sessions. He's doing something."

"We don't want to — " George started calmly but I, now just as aroused as Meg, interrupted him.

"What the hell is he doing besides committing suicide? We've gone through that phase already, remember? This is not some straw man down there waiting to be toppled by moral force and schoolboy zeal. It's a goddamn ruthless fascist dictator with his own maroon-shirted SS troops, a man who has held effective power in New Salisbury for the past five years. A cunning, powerful bastard. He is capable of going through these mountains with a fine-tooth comb the minute he believes that George is here. To him, hunting Guernsey is like shooting clay pigeons for sport but Titus would be like a big game safari."

She said nothing more. We sat around, staring into the flames, and I realized that I was getting slightly tired of George's battles. I disagreed with Meg, but so did George and it would be nice if now and then he raised his voice to defend himself.

Next morning Meg left on a five-day trip, scouting for future camps.

The same day, Copithorne's diaries tell us, the Lief met with Diebel and some other economic advisers. The idea of raising prices on a wide range of foodstuffs tightly controlled by the government had been advocated for months by the three major retail food-store chains. Up till then the Lief had skillfully avoided making a decision on the proposal. But this was the week during which the Lief was preoccupied by the preparation of the contingency plan for another landing, when he was uncertain as to where our group and the Algerians actually were, and when the People's Council's attack on the Renette headquarters sent a bit of a shock through government circles. The Lief needed a viable economy. He needed allies in the industry so he approved some price increases, although they were nowhere near as great as the food chains would have liked them. An interesting footnote to the approval is that Copithorne notes that Copithorne himself strongly opposed the move. In his diaries he referred to the attitude of the industry to be that of "greedy vultures."

Small demonstrations in the working sections of Garrick and Sidwell were quickly suppressed. News about them, however, caught the attention of Leahy and Channing and the rest of the Algerians in the middle of the Pacific, steaming toward the Lower Isle aboard the Czech freighter *Vitezny Unor*. To them they were a godsend — they had been presented with just the kind of a diversionary tactic needed for a safe landing. The freighter pulled into Suva, ostensibly for repairs but really to let off one of the group so he could catch a flight to New Salisbury under an assumed name. This all happened during the time we were still out of touch with the Resistance network, so their man had no trouble organizing demonstrations in various parts of the capital. The Lief's agents reported some sort of activity being planned, but its date and place had been kept effectively under wraps. The advantage for the protest organizers lay in the fact that the protest really had nothing to do with food prices. Its purpose was to divert the NUC's attention from the landing of the Algerian group. The safety of the demonstrators was not an important factor: most of them were not Marxists and therefore expendable. Then there was also the sacred doctrine of the end justifying the means.

During the night of December 10th, a Saturday, minor riots flared up in various parts of the capital, mostly in working-class sections of South and East N.S. City. The police, soon strengthened by NUC units, responded swiftly and brutally. For all practical purposes it was over by midnight, leaving ten people dead, scores injured, and countless arrested. Several blocks of storefronts had been destroyed, the streets littered with debris, and the air was pungent with a mixture of smoke and tear gas.

But by then the Algerians had safely landed, coming ashore near Hawar on the south coast of the Lower Isle, to establish a camp in the southern Cheviots near Lake Ormatoro. They seemed better organized than we, although that may have been a mixed blessing in the long run. They had ensconced them-selves some 700 meters up in the mountains but were still accessible. Leading up to their camp was a rough logging road that could be negotiated by an all-terrain vehicle. From the *Vitezny Unor* they brought ashore three prefabricated huts and enough supplies and ammunition for at least six months. There was no problem getting the trucks through the town of Hawar which had been taken by the Marxists' local suppor-ters. But a New Salisbury Coast Guard patrol boat spotted the *Vitezny Unor* offshore and it waited for authorization from New Salisbury City to board it.

Such authorization never came. With riots raging through the capital there was little interest in an obvious smuggling operation off the Lower Isle. It was fortunate that the crew of the N.S. patrol boat had not been authorized to board the *Vitezny Unor*. Concealed guns aboard the Czech freighter would have torn the Coast Guard vessel into shreds.

So there were two groups now. The eleven from Algeria in their spiffy prefabricated housing on Lake Ormatoro, openly controlling the small coastal town of Hawar, and us, perched high above Precarious Inlet in two drafty cabins, without a road to the sea, somewhat divided and enjoying at best a benign neglect from the village below. We had a weekly radio contact with the Americans at Christchurch, but as yet no supply route. The Communists were in constant touch with the *Vitezny Unor* which cruised the international waters just off the Lower Isle, providing a direct link with the Algerians' advisors, supplies and ammunition — all available on a moment's notice.

Examining our merits, it was clear on whom the smart money would go.

Chapter 12

Before Lucius C. Liefenbarger came to untrammelled power, one N.S. City columnist commented that the only public relations conquest he had missed so far was narrating *Peter and the Wolf* with the N.S. Symphony. He visited workers' cafeterias, retirement homes, football matches and university commencement exercises. He spoke whenever it was convenient and to whomever listened. He appeared on the cover of the Pacific edition of *Time* magazine as the personification of the theme of New Nationalism and was the keynote speaker at the twentieth annual conference of the highly influential Oceania Trade Association. He was a smiling, easy-going, highly accessible public figure who had an immense appeal primarily through his reasonable, accommodating image.

But charisma there wasn't — there never had been. Any mystic appeal was entirely missing from his personality. In its place, as best he could, he substituted a "guy like you" approach, that carried with it the possibility of appearing perilously fallible in times of stress.

This attitude changed almost overnight once his absolute power had been established. Often Copithorne mentions in his diaries occasions when he counselled and even pleaded with the Lief to return to his old ways, to reestablish his rapport with the masses that would ensure their unequivocal support. In vain though.

It seems that even the astute Copithorne failed to grasp the obvious truth: the quiet, brooding and remote Liefenbarger was the real one and the baby-kissing, quipping, folksy uncle was an aberration. It was a character the Lief had created against all his natural instincts: he saw quite clearly that without it he had no chance of coming to power. From an entirely different political angle it was the end justifying the means once again. It was the immensely enticing lure of unlimited power turning up the corners of his mouth when seriousness was so much more natural; making him talkative and neighborly when silence and detachment were more characteristic.

On Sunday, December 11th, the day after the Algerians' landing and the New Salisbury City riots, Copithorne wrote that, "It all simply cried out for a calming television appearance by *A.*" But he refused. Instead, Copithorne read a statement to the press which stated that the capital, after a night of vandalism and rioting, was once more under control, with all the instigators taken into custody. Nothing was said about the Communists at Hawar and, since there were no questions allowed, the subject never came up. (It could have been raised only by a foreign journalist, of course; the local ones knew better.)

Afterwards Copithorne hurried to the Lief's offices in the Parliament Building where an emergency meeting of the cabinet, and military and security chiefs, was about to begin. Both Ormsby and Mayfield delivered situational reports, Ormsby concentrating on the problems of the military, Mayfield on those of security. It would seem that these aspects were inseparable, but not to these two. To Copithorne's great consternation they broke into invectives, accusing each other of gross incompetence. Mayfield's attack intimated vague hints of treason on Ormsby's part, while Ormsby obliquely suggested that Mayfield was not up to his task because of his limited intelligence.

At that point the Lief, who up till then had said nothing, broke in and silenced the two men. Calmly, without referring specifically to anyone or anything previously said, he thanked them for their reports and also for the work they had done toward the preparation of the contingency plan, designed to counter attempts at insurgency on the islands. He then dropped a bombshell, telling them about the existence of a document called the Extraordinary State Act, designed to cope with threats to the government. It would be promulgated that afternoon.

There came something of a hiatus while the news was being digested. Eventually — of all people — the diminutive, prissy Foreign Affairs Minister Diebel decided to speak up. Diebel had always constituted something of a joke when it came to internal matters, where his judgment was almost invariably dead wrong. His forte was the outside world and even then not in any particularly sophisticated way. He merely possessed the uncanny ability of remembering the views of leading world diplomats and the exact wording of treaties, reports and position papers. As a result he was an extremely useful living resource library. Based on Diebel's faultless recollections the Lief, with copious advice from Copithorne, often made instant foreign policy decisions.

From the transcript of the meeting:

Diebel: "If I may express an opinion, sir, there seems to be very little likelihood that the group from Algeria and the George Titus terrorists would ever join together, since Titus is a confused liberal and the Algerians are hard-line Marxists. Their goals are really much too diverse for such a union!"

(At this point the tape is full of nervous coughing along with sounds of paper and chair shuffling. One senses a distinct feeling of embarrassment from it.)

Liefenbarger: "Their goal, Mr. Diebel, is to topple you and me and everyone else in this room from our positions. Granted, in the process they are quite likely to try and outmaneuver each other. Make no mistake about their ultimate goal, though. And it is this goal of theirs of taking power from us that so effectively unifies them.

"I would like all here to know that I consider our performance during these last few days to have been thoroughly inadequate. The fact that we know nothing about the present whereabouts of Titus and Bech-Landau and that our information about the strength and numbers of the Leahy-Algerian group is totally unreliable makes us quite vulnerable. These people are not Maoist maniacs operating out of inaccessible hills, but the nucleus of potentially well-organized movements. You have heard about the military and security aspects of the Extraordinary State Act. Others will be added soon. Mr. Metcalf: For tomorrow afternoon I would like to have a general plan for the mobilization of the economy, stopping just short of war status. We may have to temporarily convert some civilian facilities into military ones. We should consider such things as the use of commercial harbors as refuelling bases for patrol boats, the conversion of fishing vessels for patrol duty, and the utilization of railways, lorry transports, aircraft, etc. Please get together with General Mayfield and General Ormsby on this. Let them tell you their needs and then do your damnedest to satisfy them. Mr. Diebel: I would like official and unofficial reactions to these last few days from our embassies in London, Washington, Peking, Moscow, Paris, Tokyo, Canberra and Wellington. Also a proposal outline on how to deal with the reactions. There will be two other parts to the

Extraordinary State Act. They will deal with the mobilization of the media — Frank Copithorne is working on that — and the succession of power. That is already completed and in Frank's possession, to be released in the event of my death or total incapacitation."

One can't help seeing Copithorne as the Lief was saying this, characteristically leaning against the wall to the Lief's right and grinning like a Cheshire cat. From Copithorne's diaries we know that it was Copithorne who had written the succession document and who had also put together most of the wording of the Extraordinary State Act. Upon the Lief's death it was to be Copithorne who would determine the successor. It should be also noted that the succession document has never been found.

The Extraordinary State Act was a device with which to combat the Algerian group (the Lief still was not aware that we too had landed), and to prevent the repetition of the events of the last few days. It was also a cleverly thought out weapon with which the economic unrest within the country could be effectively quelled. From here on any discontent would be understood as unpatriotic slander against a government honestly trying to deal with a serious emergency. There was a name for the crime such discontent now constituted and the Lief, through the Act, was serving notice that it would be dealt with accordingly.

It was the last time that the full cabinet and the defense and security establishment met together. Mayfield accompanied the Lief and Copithorne part of the way back to Pitlochry. Copithorne describes the pensive, philosophical Liefenbarger who spoke up in the car: "You know, Eddie, Solzhenitsyn once said that all which is distant, which doesn't threaten that it will reach your house today, seems to have a generally bearable dimension. I've never forgotten that, because it's true. So true."

"Don't worry Lucius," Mayfield tried to reassure him, "we'll push them right back into the sea. We'll — "

"And I'm going to make damn sure," the Lief continued as if nothing had been said, "that it's us who'll be putting the Reds up against the wall and not the other way around. We have to stay awake on this."

"What is really needed is a general tightening up," Mayfield suggested eagerly. "There have been too many stories about what has gone wrong and nowhere near enough about all the things that have gone right."

It wasn't the first time that Mayfield had argued for a tighter police state. The Lief must have known his song by heart now. To Mayfield increased efficiency came with increased terror. Like the fanatical Moslem who believes that greater morality comes from cutting off people's hands, Mayfield's world was entirely a two-dimensional one — without any gradation or nuances. If the loss of an eye was to be repaid by another eye, an unfavorable newspaper report should be repaid by a firing squad. Up till now the Lief had eagerly resisted Mayfield's pressure, in many instances, but the proclamation of the Extraordinary State Act signalled a significant shift toward Mayfield's way of thinking.

Chapter 13

It took a week for the madman Guernsey to fully recover. In the meantime we had successfully camouflaged the camp from the prying eyes of the government planes which now flew regularly over the area, searching perhaps for the Maoists, perhaps for the extent of the Algerians' influence. From Precarious the Justacs reported no unusual activity; there was some aerial surveillance but no sign of greater vigilance either on the ground or the sea, probably because there were several hundred kilometers between Hawar and Precarious.

Ten days before Christmas an American Navy plane, supposedly gathering weather information, strayed into New Salisbury air space. It then dropped fresh vegetables, mail, and other supplies to us. The amounts were token only, but the exercise was really a practice run.

Guernsey's presence constituted something of an irritant. Around the fireplace (because of the aerial reconnaissance we had stopped having open fires) he never tired of explaining that, according to Chairman Mao, the first phase of a successful insurgency consists of agitation and of informational efforts, which eventually leads to the second, guerrilla phase, with hit-and-run raids and control of some territory to be used as a base camp. Then comes the final push in which the existing government is toppled. Guernsey claimed that by establishing a base camp we were already in the second phase, and that George was a typical stinking liberal hypocrite, afraid to take the all-important and irretrievable step of opening up hostilities.

In a calm tone and complex, qualified sentences suitable to an academic symposium, George patiently pointed out that we were not dealing with rural China, that down in the valley there were no starving, superstitious peasants but affluent farmers, loosely scattered throughout the countryside, living in ultramodern ranch houses with heated swimming pools. To most the revolution had constituted a big bother. How then could the thoughts of a nineteenth-century German, and an egotistical Chinese cult personality who had never been to a

Western country, be taken as the gospel in twentieth-century, fully industrialized, prosperous New Salisbury?

"Coming out shooting would be close to placing our heads on the chopping block," George concluded.

"You should've thought of that before you decided to get into this bloody business," smirked Guernsey. George started to say something, but I interrupted.

"We have. We have thought about it very carefully. That's why we're still intact — with our communications and supply lines established. And with a population down at Precarious which we have managed not to thoroughly alienate. What about your group? Both Mao and Guevara considered keeping peasants on a friendly footing to be the basis of revolutionary success. Guevara died because he didn't practice what he preached."

But Guernsey spoke the way he fought. The main thing was to deliver a blow — verbal or otherwise; he was totally uninterested in our response to it.

When we returned from yet another terrain-familiarization hike, Dragan Justac was seated in the headquarters hut of Camp Seismo waiting for us. He had been to Muldoon to see his fiancée. On his way back he passed through Hawar. According to him, the town was firmly in control of the Algerians, although there were no visible signs of it. The local police were still in charge but they were now supervised by Leahy's men. Traffic between Hawar and Muldoon had not been disrupted, but each truck, boat or freightcar that arrived in or left the rebel enclave had its contents carefully checked. It was crazy, as if both Liefenbarger and the Algerians had signed some sort of a truce.

"At Hawar people have really accepted the Algerians. In Muldoon they talk about nothing else. They think in a few days Leahy will extend his control there too. The National Unity types are pretty nervous," reported Dragan.

"Are there lots of uniforms at Muldoon?" I asked.

"I didn't see a single one."

"What about the local papers — have they written anything about Leahy?" I pressed further.

"Nothing. And there was nothing about it in the *New Salisbury Times* either while I was in Muldoon. Not a word about any rebels."

"We should come out too, and pretty quickly," advised

Meg. "Claim Precarious and all the other towns along the coast."

"Aaah, but you forget that you're not primarily a fighting force," smirked Guernsey. "You're a talking one. Your ultimate weapon is your jaws."

George still remained silent.

"They've said nothing on the radio at N.S. City about Leahy," reported Sid Capadouca. "I've been listening to the news broadcasts."

"Then what are we waiting for?" asked the impatient Meg. "It's pretty clear that Liefenbarger *can't do anything* about Leahy. He is weak. No wonder, after all those demonstrations. Right now he's probably licking his wounded paws, so let's not give them any time to heal."

"Two hundred people have been arrested because of the riots and twenty-five have been sentenced to death. Our organization in the lowlands has been decimated. N.S. City has been quiet for days now. Leahy and the Algerians have provided a smoke screen for their landing, but that's all. N.S. City and the rest of the country are still very firmly in Liefenbarger's hands, make no mistake about it," said George grimly.

"Then why doesn't he simply clean out Leahy and the Algerians," she asked defiantly. "Why is he waiting?"

"I don't know."

Meg left after a moment and went to her cabin.

When she came back with her rucksack she said goodbye to Dragan, finally turning toward me. "We've disagreed on this already in Hawaii, Maurice. A superstar billing is no guarantee of talent, is it?"

She then stepped out into the darkness, totally ignoring George. Sometime during the night, Guernsey disappeared as well.

A week before Christmas Sid Capadouca ran out of the radio shack and dragged George back with him. Disguised as a novice ham radio operator's fumbling, a prearranged signal had been diligently sent daily to the Americans at Christchurch. But this time came a reply disguised as a weather report for McMurdo Sound. When decoded, Christchurch was telling us about a regiment of crack New Salisbury Guards being readied at St. Enoch, that practically the entire New Salisbury fleet had taken to sea and was heading toward the south coast of the Lower Isle, and that two squadrons of fighters had been transferred to a field near Muldoon. I immediately started down to Precarious in an attempt to somehow warn the Algerian group. But I doubted that it could be done on time.

On December 19th some forty tanks and troop carriers moved into position around Muldoon as part of a plan conceived jointly by Ormsby and Mayfield after they were ordered to come up with one by the Lief. At sunrise the force moved into Muldoon's streets. Ten tanks remained there in reserve, a visible reminder that the city had been placed under martial law. The rest of the assault force continued on its way toward Hawar.

Then two companies of paratroopers descended in the vicinity of Richardson Pass, the gateway to the southern Cheviots. An hour later the tanks and troop carriers rumbled through the pass on their way to Hawar. The N.S. Navy's light cruiser *Balaclava* started its barrage of Hawar at precisely 7 A.M. The fighters then arrived and air attacks continued for over an hour, ending only with the arrival of the tanks. Two hours later there was little left of the town. Its dazed, blood-spattered inhabitants wandered aimlessly about, one by one being picked up and taken away for questioning in an official truck of the National Unity Corps.

By 10 A.M. Hawar was deserted. The operation had been a model of planning and efficiency. Tanks and troop carriers were refuelled from supplies brought ashore by ships. The paratroopers returned to Muldoon where they boarded planes for another drop in the area, some five kilometers from the rebel camp at Lake Ormatoro.

The Algerian group saw the paratroopers land on the opposite side of the lake; moments later fighter planes were overhead, spraying the rebel camp with machine-gun fire; others followed dropping small incendiary bombs. Several dinghies with paratroopers were approaching the camp and at that point the rebels scattered. Those who hesitated and did not immediately head into the deepest wilderness were either killed or rounded up, in most cases badly wounded.

On Mayfield's orders each phase of the operation had been carefully filmed. The idea was to emphasize the total control the government had over the country. On film survivors freely admitted that they were Communists and that their goal had been the overthrow of the legitimate government. The intent of the footage was to place the Liefenbarger regime squarely in the Western camp as heroic defenders against onslaughts of international Marxism.

But the effort missed the mark. In spite of the stirring, martial music on the soundtrack and the smiling, excited faces of the soldiers, the film produced widespread revulsion. I guess it had not been fully grasped by the triumphant Eddie Mayfield that the tradition of a stirring documentary on the swath of destruction cut by tanks and gunfire dated back to World War II — to Dr. Goebbels's newsreels.

Chapter 14

In spite of the effectiveness of the Hawar operations, Liefenbarger's priority remained the security of Main Island. On this score he started giving Mayfield and the NUC almost a free hand. Through the increased role of the security forces, effective command over all N.S. armed forces was being placed more and more into the hands of this half-educated former policeman with a racist record. The Polynesians, according to him, were people unable to cope with the twentieth century because their attitudes had not yet fully moved out of the Stone Age. Instilling fear was the only method of dealing with them.

The result — seething discontent in the multiracial N.S. Army — should have been brought to the Lief's attention. But Ormsby, the aloof, Sandhurst-educated chief of staff, was too much of a stuffed shirt and he had too much disdain for the Lief's humble beginnings to protest directly and effectively.

Eventually Mayfield decided to try and extend his power to the Lower Isle as well, but here things were a bit different. The week before Christmas, Mayfield flew off to St. Enoch to confer with Governor Allan McAlpine. The two men met for the first time and instantly developed an intense dislike for each other which soon matured into undisguised hatred. But even before they met, Mayfield had already urged Frank Copithorne to try and influence the Lief's thinking in the direction of getting rid of the governor and placing the Lower Isle under direct NUC rule. Copithorne, however, remained strictly neutral on the matter.

Liefenbarger had always been a bit uneasy when it came to dealing with the Lower Isle's affairs, recognizing that people there were different, living at a slower and probably more satisfying pace, marching, as it were, to a different drummer. Less interested in such things as efficiency, order and the proper scheme of things, people there found Main Island's preoccupation with them to be a ready target for their sharp brand of humor.

Ever since his days as a member of parliament and later as the elected governor of the Lower Isle, McAlpine had always been a popular figure there. Because of his following, which the Lief definitely wanted to keep on his side, McAlpine was the only regional administrator who remained in his position even after the promulgation of the Centralization Act in 1975. In a way the Lief even trusted McAlpine, but only to the extent that he was able to trust anyone.

McAlpine was neither a democrat nor a totalitarian. Both of those concepts to him constituted merely a foundation on which personal power could be built. When he graduated from secondary school, his family had expected him to take part in the farming of the fertile soil in the fields south of St. Enoch, but he first surprised and then angered them by announcing he would soon be leaving for Australia.

At the end of that first year of law study in Sydney he married a homely, silly girl of twenty — the same age as he — who was pregnant. Her embarrassed, nouveau riche, beer-brewing family was shocked and also frightened to death of a scandal just as they were beginning to make their first inroads into the upper crusts. They hurriedly assented not only to the marriage but also to a healthy stipend which would enable young Allan McAlpine to finish his studies in more than just relative comfort.

In 1960 he was admitted to the bar. Two weeks later his divorce became final and the millionaire brewers were laughed out of court when they asked for alimony from a pennyless law student.

Back in New Salisbury, he established an effective political base by practising law on the outskirts of St. Enoch, and charted a course for himself which led through county clerkships to administrative assistantship and into the echelons of cabinet ministry. Eventually came his own election to parliament, and finally his rise to the governor's position.

The appearance of the Liefenbarger phenomenon on the political scene somewhat altered McAlpine's schedule for his own arrival at the top. On the other hand there was consolation in that he, as the only major elected official on the island, had managed to successfully maneuver through the prime minister's treacherous dictatorial waters.

So far, anyway.

It was McAlpine's first trip to Main Island in three years. Of course he spoke with the Administrator on the phone several times each week, but he was convinced that the main reason for his survival had been his aloofness from the affairs of the capital. But this time there was no escape. He had been summoned and had to go.

Christmas was only two days away. At the terminal McAlpine was met by a young Guards officer with gold braid on his left shoulder, indicative of the Administrator's personal staff. The young man started off on the wrong foot by congratulating McAlpine on his part in the capture of the Lake Ormatoro rebels. Having seen the documentary on his television set the night before, the governor knew where the young officer had gotten his information.

"No small part in the success of the operation," explained the narrator, "had been played by the timely and accurate information about conditions in the area provided by Governor McAlpine and his staff."

It was basically true. McAlpine had known where the rebels were and he had divulged it to the Administrator. Now he regretted it because one hundred and fifty civilians had been killed or wounded as a result. Hawar had ceased to exist and most of its inhabitants had been flown to Bristol Street prison in N.S. City. The governor did not at all like being publicly identified with such carnage.

Inside the Mercedes the officer rambled on about the proposed magnificent architectural transformation of the city; McAlpine thought about the upcoming interview. He sensed that there were changes in the offing for the Lower Isle and he was not a great admirer of changes. That is why he had participated in the rounding up of the rebels at all. Whatever else they may have been, the rebels were primarily a threat to his own lust for power which, to a large extent, depended on as many factors as possible remaining constant.

At Pitlochry he was led to a receiving room on the main floor where coffee and some *petit fours* had been laid out on a coffee table with Christmas decorations. He began chatting with Copithorne when the Lief entered, wearing a sports coat with a small green disc in his lapel identifying the bearer of the Supreme Order of Merit of New Salisbury. He took a seat across the coffee table from McAlpine while Copithorne moved discreetly into the background.

After a polite inquiry about the health of some mutual acquaintances, Lucius Liefenbarger paused for a moment. Then he abruptly opened up a new subject, firing the opening salvo largely for its shock value.

Lief: "My chief of security advises me to fire you immediately, governor."

McA: "May I ask why?"

Lief: "He feels that the chain of command, the whole administration of the Lower Isle would be streamlined. What do you think?"

McA: "I don't think so."

Lief: "Why?"

McA: "I don't think he understands the atmosphere down there."

Lief: "In what way doesn't he understand it?"

McA: "We are a strange breed. We do things differently. Maybe a bit too slowly for some tastes, but there is much more time for reflection, more emphasis on the way we do them. Most of the people there support you. They are in favor of law and order, of the policies of the National Unity Movement. But if the island was administered directly from New Salisbury City, there would certainly be much less enthusiasm. It would feel a lot like a foreign occupation."

Lief: "I haven't asked Mayfield to be here because I wanted to talk with you first. You do know that he doesn't particularly like you?"

McA: "I've had my suspicions."

Lief: "I see."

McA: "The Lower Isle is a sensitive place right now, sir. Big administrative changes would certainly not contribute toward stability there."

Lief: "You may be right."

McA: "The Hawar and Lake Ormatoro affairs have shown how well we are able to work together against the Communists."

Lief: "Yes, in a way. On the other hand it came as a surprise that the terrorists were able to operate unchallenged in the Hawar area for weeks. Many of the people at Hawar seemed to be actually working with them. I guess they must have been a part of that very small minority that doesn't support the policies of the National Unity Movement. Am I correct?"

McA: "There are malcontents in every society, sir. And the Communists traditionally know best how to effectively exploit them. For the rest — well, the Communists know how to use fear too."

Lief: "There are some people who seem to feel that not all the terrorists have been rounded up. They talk about other terrorist hideouts on the Lower Isle. There is suspicion that there may have been more Communists at Lake Ormatoro than have been found. What do you think?"

McA: "I think that they have either died at Hawar or of exposure somewhere in the wilderness. It's only a matter of time before the bodies will be found."

Lief: "When the Titus group landed at Renfrew, they were found out within hours."

McA: "But not destroyed, sir. Do you have any idea where George Titus might be right now?"

Lief: "General Mayfield assures me that he is definitely not on the islands. Perhaps Pago Pago. We don't know."

McA: "There is one more thing, sir."

Lief: "Yes?"

McA: "You have mentioned the need for a quicker response to possible terrorist landings. I fully agree, but let's be practical about it. The quickest way we can respond is to have troops at my disposal. Not too many would be needed if they were highly mobile. There should be paratroopers among them who could be dispatched to a rebel landing site within minutes."

Lief: "We already have NUC detachments at St. Enoch, and where else Frank?"

Copithorne: "At Renette and Castlereagh, sir."

McA: "But the NUC detachments have no real counter-insurgency ability, sir. They're even vulnerable themselves, as we have seen at Renette. What's needed is a well-trained, highly mobile group with a short chain of command."

Lief: "What do you think Frank?"

Cop: "There is the third battalion — some people in it have had experience with anti-terrorist operations at the McElroy farm. Lots of them are Lower Isle boys. They would be suitable."

Lief: (After a pause.) "I'll look into it, governor."

I have quoted most of the exchange here because I consider the meeting to have been one of the most important that Liefenbarger ever held. McAlpine had been called into N.S. City at best to be relieved of his post, at worst to be taken into custody. The very fact that he arrived and walked into the Lief's office without any evident trepidation must have greatly impressed the Administrator. Copithorne notes in his diaries that when McAlpine, "this very short and chubby but also incredibly calm man" arrived, he too was forced to sit up and take notice. "The man had definite presence," he continues, although he also admits to wondering if McAlpine was not simply too conceited and ignorant to sense the danger. This notion, however, was dispelled as soon as McAlpine spoke.

It was an important triumph for McAlpine. Aboard the plane back to St. Enoch and the relative safety of the Lower Isle, he had every reason to be pleased with his performance.

Chapter 15

The Extraordinary State Act had pushed us onto the defensive. With increased government air and sea patrols, Camp Seismo was no longer safe. On Christmas Day we began moving into two new camps which were being built some ten kilometers to the northeast — away from the sea and nestled among far less accessible mountains.

More people started trickling into the hills, but this was a mixed blessing. Resistance people throughout the islands had learned to channel people who were escaping from the NUC's clutches to the Justacs at Precarious. It was possible that there were agents among the new arrivals and it was certain that by now the Lief had at least a general idea as to who and where we were.

Shortly before New Year's, Dragan Justac brought up a two-day-old copy of the *New Salisbury Times* with the headline:

25 ARSONISTS, LOOTERS AND MURDERERS EXECUTED

It referred to the demonstrators arrested during the night of Leahy's and the Algerians' landing. We were stunned. It was a ruthless, cold-blooded declaration of war and most of us had serious doubts about being able to wage it successfully.

There was also a letter from Garbeau, short and coded. He congratulated us on establishing a camp and once more asked us for a detailed report on our organization and activities. As he had done with the previous requests, this time too George chose to ignore the plea. This way, even if the mail was intercepted, the Lief would only know that we definitely exist. Nothing more. The interception of a letter with even a carefully coded report on our whereabouts and activities would have dangerously bared us before the NUC.

On the third of January, the last night we spent at Camp Seismo, we were awakened by a noise outside the tent. When I opened my eyes, Sid already stood next to the entrance, his carbine in his hands. Just as I reached for my revolver I heard Branko Justac's highly accented, somewhat coarse voice yell: "Anybody home? I brought you new recruits — different beliefs but nice guys all the same."

The grinning Branko stood in front of the tent with a dismayed sentry nearby. A bit to the right stood John Leahy and Vic Channing. The third man I guessed to be Gino Baracolli. I had never seen him before.

Leahy had grown a beard and the disaster at Hawar coupled with the long trek through the mountains had hollowed his cheeks. There was no elegance left in the usually dapper Channing. During the escape he had suffered a dislocated shoulder and his arm was now resting in a sling made of a dirty rag.

Baracolli was a thick-faced, stocky man with an expression on his face that seemed to be continually challenging someone or something. The tight lips and piercing eyes strongly suggested brutality which his substantial build seemed to back up. But he said nothing. Leahy was doing all the talking.

They stood awkwardly in the chilly morning air, until Sid Capadouca finally broke the impasse. He stepped forward and asked them to come inside, offering to cook some breakfast in the lean-to, the only permanent structure not yet dismantled. We all adjourned there.

I studied George's reactions to it all, once again gauging his leadership abilities. He must have realized that he was at a distinct disadvantage: Leahy had had a chance to prepare for all this. He explained how they had headed for Precarious at first because they had heard about Dragan Justac asking about them at Muldoon and they assumed that through him they would find a way to get out. But they immediately changed their minds about leaving when they heard that we were in the mountains.

"Does that mean that the NUC knows about Dragan?" George asked with distinct coolness. "Because they seemed to have known about everything else that happened at Hawar."

The implied criticism didn't escape Leahy. He looked up sharply, then remembered where he was. He forced his face to relax. "I don't think so," he replied softly.

"Not too much of a chance," said Branko. "Dragan spoke with Milan Plavesic who could be trusted. And Milan is dead. Died during the assault."

Later, when the Algerians were catching up on their sleep, I chose to play a bit of Iago. "How come they are still alive when everyone else who was at Ormatoro is either dead or in jail?" I asked George.

"I don't know about Lake Ormatoro, but we certainly are in no position to start being too selective so far as extra hands are concerned."

"But they are Communists, aren't they?"

"Yes, I know."

"And they'll turn on us the first chance they get, won't they?"

"We'll just have to make sure that they don't get any chances, that's all," he replied in the exasperating professorial tone of his, starting to walk away at the same time.

At dinner Leahy broke the long silence. "I would like to thank you," he said hesitantly, turning to George.

"For what?"

"For the way you welcomed us."

"Just like we have welcomed everyone else."

Leahy nodded, considering it all for a moment. "Even though we aren't exactly after the same thing?"

George looked up, surprised. "But we are. We *are* after the same thing."

"My men and I want a *socialist* New Salisbury."

"So do we."

Leahy looked at him questioningly and George put down his fork. "We just have different definitions for socialism," George explained. "We're for the type where everyone that needs caring for will be taken care of and where no one has to pay for it with his individuality. But all that's less important right now than giving everyone down there a chance to say what they want. That's why we are up here — isn't it why you are up here too?"

Leahy ignored the question. "You don't really expect a country that has just gone through a bloody revolution to hold elections which would mean anything, do you?"

"I hope there'll be a minimum of bloodletting from now on, and I would expect a revolutionary authority to remain in power until the country was stable enough for elections."

Leahy grabbed his forehead, now completely losing the mild-mannered image he had tried to project a moment ago. "Man, are you a dreamer!"

"In Ghana or Afghanistan I might be, but not in New Salisbury. We happen to have quarter of a century of democratic traditions here."

Now Leahy erupted: "Of bourgeois, capitalist democracy! With all the ugly exploitation and with a reactionary parliament to stamp it legal!"

"But without political prisoners, hangings or barbed wire fences. And with legally guaranteed rights."

"Rights? Oh Christ, it must have all looked so beautiful from that Olympus of yours. With the workers quickly legislated back to work whenever there was a major strike and the police on the alert to smooth over the rough edges. And no political prisoners? Every Poly thrown into the drunk tank on Saturday night is a political prisoner because it was your democracy that drove him to drink. The desperate, unemployed man who finally resorts to armed robbery — isn't he a political prisoner? Who took away his self-respect and made him pick up the gun? Not I, nor any of my comrades!"

George took out his white pipe, loaded it to the brim with tobacco, then slowly, meticulously, lit it up. The whole maneuver had been designed not only to give him time to think, but also to defuse the argument.

"I don't know about the causes," he said finally, "because I have not yet found a key to the history of this world. When I look around for that brand of socialism you seem to regard so highly, the only thing I come up with is a vast, regimented anthill called China, or a mediaeval fortress called the U.S.S.R., neither of which seems to me as a particularly enticing example to emulate."

"We shouldn't emulate anyone. We should learn from their mistakes."

"Is that why you are financed and ordered about from Moscow?" I jumped in.

"We got some help from the Soviet Union — yes. Don't you get money from the Americans?"

"Ah yes, the Americans with the odious CIA, FBI, and their stranglehold on the world. They have dared to win the last world tussle and yet the way they scrape and bow before the yen and the Deutschmark it doesn't look to me like they're ordering the Japanese and the Germans about. On the other hand the Czechs and the Cubans are good boys, they — "

"We're not talking about the Czechs and the Cubans for Christ's sake!"

"Oh, but we have to talk about them. How else are we to know what might happen if we don't look closely at what *has* happened?"

Leahy paused. He was clearly anxious now to find some road toward reconciliation, not because dialectics went against his grain but because under the circumstances at least a temporary truce was more expedient.

"Look," he said with his voice an octave lower, "we're not in this to create another China or Cuba. We all have an opportunity here to put together something new, that hasn't been tried before — a nation with real equality where the freedom you talk about would have a real meaning even for the lowest guy on the economic totem pole; where medical care and housing will be adequate, and where everyone will get a crack at the best possible education. We have plenty of oil now, so we'll also have energy. And we're an island far away from any foreign influence, but only if we want to be. It's right down there, all of it, along with a two-bit fascist dictatorship that is beginning to crumble. And with such a tremendous opportunity are we going to quarrel and fight like dogs among ourselves?"

I didn't believe it. Not that stuff about a two-bit fascist dictatorship that was beginning to crumble. There were no signs of it; none whatever.

Chapter 16

In a world where rich, arrogant, strong men have traditionally been accorded greater honors than even the greatest prophets of righteousness, New Salisbury's oil discovery added substantially to the Lief's international stature. Internally, the proclamation of the Extraordinary State Act served notice that the hand which had been holding the country tightened its grip. Meg was in the lowlands, organizing the Resistance network, but on Main Island the Resistance, shattered by the needless exertion on the night of the Algerian group's landing, was in total disarray.

We were now certain that the NUC knew about us in the mountains. Air patrols flew low over the ridges almost daily, hoping that someone would take a shot at them or that they would spot a telling wisp of smoke. January went by and half of February before we were securely ensconced in several remote camps, constantly expecting to be attacked by an NUC assault force. Toward that end we trained practically day and night. Our number had grown to about forty and, because of our increasing familiarity with the terrain, we judged our actual strength to be at least twice that number in relation to an attacking force. Against a massive, well-conducted assault we could hold out a week, perhaps two. At the end though, there would be no organized revolutionary force left in the mountains.

But the attack never came. The Lief wasn't really so sure he could depend on the loyalty of his troops. A near mutiny took place among pilots who had participated in the Hawar-Lake Ormatoro operation when they later saw the carnage through Mayfield's cameras. Followed by the installation of NUC advisors at each military unit — according to yet another provision of the Extraordinary State Act — the loud discontent at one field near Muldoon was quelled only through the personal appearance of Governor McAlpine who had to promise that never again would the pilots be asked to fly missions against civilian targets. It would have been unthinkable for the Lief to launch a military operation on Lower Isle without air support, but of course we did not know it then.

There was also the Precarious problem to be considered. Any assault against us would have to be through the village. The bloody memories of the Hawar operation were still too vivid in the minds of the military that would have to take part in the assault and in the minds of the civilian population of the island that would have to support it.

The truth was that, at the end of five years in power, Liefenbarger was far from crumbling, although there was still no more than a tacit acceptance of his rule. The gentle nuances of this situation were particularly difficult to grasp for the over-zealous and excess-prone Mayfield. Mayfield favored spectacular operations for which the Lief would have required mystic qualities of leadership that he clearly didn't possess. Unlike Hitler, who through his electrifying presence, spiffy uniforms, martial music and racist pseudo-science at least initially commanded the hearts of Germans, and unlike Stalin who had been blessed with a strong ideology, and a backward country to cement his rule, the Lief had nothing but the petrol shortage and economic panic of 1973 to fall back on. He was at best the lesser of several evils. The deterring alternatives consisted not so much of other systems of government as of the radical upheaval itself. A massive military operation in the Cheviots would have served notice that the Lief regime had failed to prevent such an upheaval. It would also force the New Salisburians to choose sides which, of course, was the last thing the Lief wanted.

Then there was the oncoming winter. There was a good chance that it would obliterate all traces of the Cheviot rebels without the slightest effort or risk to the Lief regime.

All of this was not so clear in the Cheviots, where we were plagued with more than just a mild case of paranoia though toward the end of February it became more obvious that we should be spending more time and effort in figuring out how to ward off at least the major discomforts of the oncoming season. Occasionally an American plane from Christchurch would drop the barest necessities to us, but otherwise there was no real contact with the outside world. There were vague American promises of a boat cruising off the Lower Isle which would provide more frequent and two-sided contact via a helicopter, but we weren't supplied with a timetable. The fishing boats from Precarious were now confronted by N.S. Coast Guard cutters the moment they left the inlet. They were usually boarded and searched, and their crews harassed in the process. Because we wanted no repetition of Hawar, it had been decided that no communications should be routed through the village.

The constant military drills combined with our feverish pace of construction made me work harder than I had ever worked in my life. When I could no longer stand on my feet I would crawl among the blankets on a cot in the corner of my cabin at Camp Beta which was stocked with supplies piled to the ceiling. Then I would instantly fall into a deep, dreamless sleep.

On Friday, February 24th, I was in the midst of just such a deep sleep. Two hours earlier I had staggered into camp from a conference at Camp Alpha at which the only interesting item had been George's third and final rejection of Leahy's Fort Wellington plan. The fort was reportedly defended by only about fifty government men and Leahy wanted to take it, hold it for a day or two, then retreat into the mountains. The rebel flag would thus be shown, supplies and ammunition acquired, the Lief's knuckles rapped — all in one fell swoop.

The trouble was that Fort Wellington had too many characteristics of a baited line. It was conveniently near the foothills of the Cheviots and it had been reactivated only a month before. Our assault and subsequent retreat into the mountains would have given the Lief far too much information about us — our numbers, equipment, tactical know-how and probably even the shortest route to our camps.

By refusing to authorize the raid George invited all sorts of critical innuendos. It was also obvious that Leahy was grandstanding — demonstrating his leadership qualities and building his more-ready-to-fight-than-thou image. But George was also something of a blessed peacemaker. In order to make his final refusal less bitter, he allowed Leahy and his Marxist friends to establish a new camp — Camp Gamma — in the western Cheviots from which they would at least be able to periodically observe the happenings at Fort Wellington. I thought the arrangement not particularly wise, but I was also much too tired to object effectively.

So I slept deeply, not hearing the door to the cabin slowly opening, not hearing the soft footsteps that neared my cot or a coat being unzipped. The thing I finally heard was the sound of my name being whispered close to my ear. It was unmistakably Meg's voice.

I sat up, staring into the darkness, when her face brushed against mine. Then her hand held my chin and I was being kissed, passionately. With one hand I searched for her through the darkness; I touched the curve of her waist — she was soft, warm, and eager — and gently pulled her down to lay beside me. It was all accomplished without the slightest thought given to consequences, precedents, implications. Certainly not decorum. All such things had been shed in the mountains where the satisfaction of the moment played a major and an all-dominant part, where sex in the arms of familiar warmth was of such paramount importance.

We made love in the darkness — noisily, passionately and hungrily, with all the bizarre accompanying smells of our inadequately washed clothing, of oiled canvas and hemlock crates, and the sound of the mountain beeches rustling in the wind and birds beginning to awaken in their branches. Then we slept and made love again, but this time the sun had begun to rise magnificently over the surrounding mountains, over the camp, lighting up a cloudless sky and sending down the first hint of a promised warmth. Meg lay in my arms, now fully visible as well as tactile, staring at the rough-hewn ceiling above.

"I've been wrong Maurice. God, have I been wrong!" she rolled onto her side and out of my arms.

I immediately assumed she was talking about defeat and started to reassure her about our vitality in the mountains. She rolled back, held my face in her hands, saying, "No, I mean I was wrong about George. Dead wrong. Did you know that last week the NUC ordered all corduroy caps and meerschaum pipes off the shelves of the stores? Not that there had been any left anyway."

"Because of George?"

She nodded. "Because of George."

"How do they know what he wears and smokes?"

"Remember that picture from Honolulu? It's all over the place. I went down there with the crazy idea of making *you* into the revolutionary leader with maybe myself catching a bit of the glory too. But he is it. You were right: the Titus name has absolutely miraculous qualities. You could be the greatest leader since Napoleon but he has the name. And *he* can do no wrong."

"Fine. What are we going to do now?"

"I don't know...I'm not too good at being apologetic."

"What about down there? Are there more people willing to risk their necks?"

"A few," she said. "How about up here?"

"Some people want to come out right now. Mobilize whatever friends we have down there and take St. Enoch."

"What? Which people?"

"The Marxists. At least they'd like to make a showing."

"That would be crazy. Totally mad."

"But you've just said — "

"There are a few heroes and lots of sympathy down there. We're just slowly starting to get organized but those that really want to fight are already up here. The only people down there who are really organized are the NUC. They'd crush us, roll right over us. There isn't anything they'd like to see better than us coming down to slug it out. They have air support, artillery and all of Main Island to use for reinforcements. It'd be idiotic."

She was indignant now, much more of a soldier than a lover.

"We have the winter to face up here," I tested her some more.

"So let's get ready for it. Let's survive it. Sure it won't be a picnic, but maybe that's what we need — a little Valley Forge. If next November when the snow is gone we're still here we've won. But we can't take shortcuts."

We lay silently on my cot for a few moments.

"Where have you been, Meg?" I asked.

"In Kilmaron, Castlereagh, but mostly in St. Enoch."

"Have you heard about the executions?"

She nodded. Then she sat up, and abruptly changed the subject. "I almost forgot: I brought a newspaperman up with me. A guy named Asmatar Surgit Sahota. A hack par excellence, but he could be very helpful if used properly to further build up the Titus mystique."

"Where is he?"

"Camp Alpha. He was too beat to go any further, and I wanted to talk to you first anyway. He's from England. Well, from Fiji actually. I met him in Muldoon. He's been itching to get up here."

I climbed over her to get off the cot. "Well, then we should have some breakfast and get over there. And you'd better start thinking about the wording of your apology to George."

She grinned at me from the depth of our blanket lair.

I fixed breakfast on the Coleman stove and over bacon and dried eggs explained about the Americans, about the supply drops and their promise of a boat permanently stationed off the coast which would fly its helicopter back and forth between the mountains and its deck. "They've been helpful. Really helpful."

Meg stopped eating and stared at me. "Maybe not as helpful as you think."

"What does that mean?"

She reached into her bag and came up with a tattered brown envelope. She rummaged through its contents until she finally pulled out a newspaper clipping. "Here."

It was the upper part of a front page from the *New Salisbury Times,* about three days old. ARMS PACT WITH THE U.S. SIGNED, blared the headline. The story listed the armaments the Americans had promised to deliver to Liefenbarger "for the increased needs of New Salisbury's national defense." Included were two squadrons of jets, several troop transport planes, armored vehicles, destroyers and patrol ships.

"There must be something to this. The Lief wouldn't just — " I started to say.

"That's right. There is."

"Well, what the hell do the Americans think — have they gone crazy?"

Meg smiled. "Like foxes. They're keeping everyone on the ball and competing. That's the good ol' American way, isn't it? They're making sure that whoever wins they'll be right there at the finish line, offering congratulations and presenting a bill for services rendered."

"They're fighting against themselves. That puts American equipment on both sides."

"Yeah, but that way the odds are much better than the Americans on one side and the Russians on the other, aren't they?"

A feeling of helplessness came over me. It must have shown because Meg came around the table, sat down beside me and put her arm around me. "Come on, it isn't the end of the world, Maurice, not by a long shot. I think I have a pretty good explanation. Look, the Americans always like to insure themselves. It was they who invented double indemnity."

"So long as they're happy who are we to complain, right?"

"Well, not exactly. Because I don't think that the Lief is *that* happy. At least he shouldn't be. I don't think he's likely to miss the fine print in the agreement. Not him."

"And that is?"

"The date the deliveries are to start is January 1st."

"Next year?"

"Next year," she nodded. "And that only means that by that date they're required to *send* the first shipment. Probably from New York. Via the Panama Canal and with long stops in San Francisco, Honolulu ... maybe even Pago Pago. It gives them something like an extra two months to divert the shipment if something happened that would make it in their interests *not* to deliver in New Salisbury."

"But why go to all the trouble of outfitting us and then promising the Lief jet fighters?"

"Because that's all they have done — *promised* him something. They'll deliver only if we don't perform."

I was still confused. "Then why start doubting us now? I mean after we have already established ourselves?"

"It might have something to do with the Gamma problem. With the Communists at Camp Gamma."

"They knew there would be Communists among us. It only stands to reason."

"All in one camp?"

"George thought that — "

Meg waved her hand. "I know what George thought. But the Americans are obviously hedging about the way George is handling Leahy. A revolutionary movement isn't some Canadian university department full of drawing-room Marxists, you know."

"I know," I said.

"We have to get to him on this. We really do."

"It won't be so easy. Anyway, is this why the Americans will equip the Lief to swallow us?"

"No, Maurice. They *threaten* to equip him. By next summer it should be pretty clear just who is in charge up here. And if it isn't George the Lief gets his jet fighters."

Chapter 17

On March 12th Liefenbarger held one of his inner cabinet meetings in which he delighted so much. He listened to Bernard Metcalf's report on the economic repercussions of the Extraordinary State Act, which were considerable. He listened attentively but lost his cool when Foreign Minister Diebel suggested that the "Act was strong medicine indeed" which would "affect, mostly detrimentally, practically everyone in the country," that perhaps parliament should be recalled "to put its official seal of approval on it."

"I have a better idea," the Lief commented acidly, "let's have the National Unity Corps and a few tanks put their seal of approval on it instead."

But he must have immediately regretted saying it; that was not his style at all. Few things could have more aroused his ire than the idea of recalling parliament, which had not been in session for over four years and many of whose members were either in exile or on the Partrawa Plain. Two had even been executed for treason. The constant squabbling and electioneering, the jealousies, maneuverings and half-hearted compromises that had characterized the last few parliaments had provided the Lief with some of his most potent ammunition in his bid for power. "The weaklings and the windbags," as he frequently characterized its members, had been one of the most visible targets of his National Unity Movement.

The Lief then abruptly dismissed his cabinet, retired to his adjacent apartment and, according to Copithorne's diaries, wondered aloud if Diebel should not be replaced by a younger man. Not one of them, however, could count on the contacts that Diebel had so assiduously cultivated throughout his decades with the Ministry. Diebel would have to stay.

Copithorne then read to the Lief a milquetoast petition signed by ten fairly prominent New Salisbury poets, writers, professors and artists. It did not criticize the regime but suggested a liaison with the academic and creative communities so that "problems particularly of the working people" could be examined "in an atmosphere of complete mutual trust with a common view toward further improvement of lifestyle in our country."

It was a document that betrayed fear and at the same time asked for a crumb or two from the Administrator's table. According to Copithorne the Lief quickly discerned an opportunity to recruit the intellectuals on his side with the appointment of some sort of a largely dormant consultative committee, with the handing out of titles and functions, with a dignified reception at which the profs would get a chance to wear their colorful academic gowns and he his dress uniform. In a mood that was now much improved, he wistfully asked why it was that in the entire recorded history the working people had never been aroused by injustices committed upon intellectuals. It was always the other way around.

At 11 A.M. the Lief received Clifford T. Lattimore, Jr., the U.S. ambassador to New Salisbury. It wasn't the first time that the Lief had talked with Lattimore since his accreditation some two months earlier. But they had never spoken alone. Lattimore had, of course, been present during all the negotiations preceding the armaments agreement, but the mechanics of it were handled by an experienced team sent over from Washington.

Lattimore was a career diplomat of the drier type, careful not to initiate anything on his own without specific authorization from Washington. Perhaps because of his previous service in Greece under the colonels and in Portugal under Salazar — both of whom were removed in relatively bloodless coups — he tended to underestimate the Lief and his organization. In his memoranda to Washington, Lattimore envisaged some sort of a bloodless coup in New Salisbury during which everyone — including Eddie Mayfield and his goons — acted as Victorian gentlemen, followed by the rule of a military and authoritarian but well-meaning government in the short period of transition to a truly parliamentary system. A readily noticeable weakness of such a theory was the total lack of personalities qualified to lead such a group. Would it be the aloof, unpopular and highly unimaginative Ormsby or the mousy Diebel? Possibly a candidate for the post would have been the quiet, introspective and perhaps a bit too mysterious Air Marshal Pentland-Garaudy, head of the N.S. Air Force. But the air force didn't provide a sufficient power base for a coup. It was all Lattimore's own idea of how New Salisbury's affairs of state should be handled.

Lattimore, the efficient administrator and a decent enough chap, was not exactly the best choice for a U.S envoy in New Salisbury, certainly not after the oil discovery and after our landings in the Cheviots. There is also evidence that the crafty Lief was well aware of his weaknesses and a substantial part of his policy toward the U.S. was built upon the assumption that Lattimore would remain in New Salisbury.

Copithorne welcomed the ambassador in the anteroom, brought him in to meet the Lief, then discreetly withdrew. After the formal greetings and assumptions of seats, the ambassador opened with, "You are certainly fortunate to be the head of state of such a beautiful country — especially on a day like this."

It was a seemingly innocuous statement, but a bit of an uncomfortable pause followed. Liefenbarger was not the head of a state; that was Henry Hathaway, once one of Norman Ruttledge Titus's closest friends. As Governor General, Hathaway was the legal link to the Crown, although now a senile, white-clad, impotent and pathetic figure in a wheelchair, he suited the Lief's purposes exquisitely.

Conversation turned to the defense agreement. Lattimore explained that U.S. congressional approval of the arrangement was assured although, of course, some left-wing elements were still busily trying to undermine the confidence between the two countries. The Lief must have certainly been aware that not only the left wing but the isolationist right one, and the liberal faction, opposed providing the New Salisbury government with arms. But he said nothing, allowing Lattimore to conclude his overly optimistic summary.

"Are you happy with the agreement, sir? I know that we are," Lattimore commented and at that point the pleasant part of the conversation came to an end. The Lief brought out his big guns.

Lief: "As happy as a small nation could be, Mr. Lattimore. I'm trying to deal with a Communist insurrection supplied by mysterious ships, sometimes of Australian registry. Twice a week such ships send out helicopters which furnish the rebel terrorists with everything from toothbrushes to howitzer shells, and I am forced to wait until next January to deal with them effectively. Is it really any wonder that I am not exactly deliriously happy?"

Latt: "It takes a few months to assemble the supplies, sir. Also, the president must consult with Congress."

Lief: "It is curious that such arguments are not there whenever the state of Israel needs military supplies."

Latt: "Mr. Prime — Mr. Liefenbarger, Israel is strategically placed in a highly volatile area. New Salisbury — "

Lief: "Is in one too. Of course, our propaganda machine is running less smoothly, but then we're not Jewish. Perhaps you could tell me more about your country's policies."

Latt: "I shall do my best, sir."

Lief: "Please help me with this one: Are we still fighting the Communists?"

Latt: "Of course we are. The only thing that has changed, perhaps, is that the struggle has become part of a much larger picture — on behalf of human rights and consequently against all forms of totalitarianism." (Lattimore was a true liberal. He would not have sanctioned any bloodletting to depose the Lief because deep inside he still quite sincerely believed that the Administrator could be toppled through the use of great oratory.)

"You see, it is difficult to come marching out against Communism and find oneself right in step with a Boer from South Africa who believes that only the Communists oppose his ideas on apartheid."

Lief: "The world is becoming more and more complicated, isn't it?"

Latt: "Considerably so, sir."

Lief: "You know of a gentleman named Leahy, don't you?"

Latt: "Yes, sir."

Lief: "You know that he is a rabid Communist who has been trained by the Russians?"

Latt: "Yes, sir."

Lief: "And you know that he is in the Chevior Hills right now?"

Latt: "Yes, we know it, sir."

Lief: "Mr. Ambassador, your country must be aware by now that in the Cheviot Hills there is an organized insurrection against this country's legitimate government. Am I correct in assuming that?"

Latt: "We know that there are insurgents there. Yes sir."

Lief: "And you are also aware that such an insurgency requires supplies — tons of supplies?" (Lattimore must have merely nodded.) "What about the strategic value of this country? Does the U.S. recognize it to be the same as Australia's or New Zealand's?"

Latt: "I don't think that there can be any doubt about that."

Lief: "Why can't there be?"

Latt: "Pardon me, sir? I — "

Lief: "Why can't there be any doubt about it?"

Latt: "Well, there are treaties that — "

Lief: "I don't believe that the treaties guarantee anything. You and I both know that they are riddled with escape clauses. There was nothing in the way of your country abrogating its treaty with Taiwan once Chairman Mao was dead and there were new winds blowing from Peking. I should like to have your commitment to New Salisbury reasserted by you, its official envoy, here, right now."

Latt: "Sir, my country is the biggest maritime power in the world. Surely you don't think we would stand idly by while our enemies established themselves in the South Pacific?"

Lief: "It has done precisely that when Castro established himself ninety miles off the coast of Florida. And Cuba has been a festering ulcer ever since."

Latt: "There are considerable differences."

Lief: "There certainly are. For one thing I'm no Batista. Please tell your president that there is no chance at all that I will run away. None at all. I intend to fight."

(There is another pause on the tape at this point during which the Lief must have indicated the interview was over.)

Latt: "I appreciate your making your position clear, sir."

(There follow some footsteps indicating that Lattimore was on his way to the door, probably feeling quite uncomfortable under the Lief's blazing eyes and unequivocal declaration of determined intent.)

Lief: "You should be told, Mr. Lattimore, that this entire conversation has been recorded; I think that your country is making a big mistake with the Australian boat and I want to be on record as having warned you."

Lattimore then icily bid his farewells and left. Most of the conversation has been transcribed here because I consider it as crucial. The Rubicon had been crossed, the die cast and the gauntlet flung. The Lief had officially announced that he knew about the Americans' risky game and that he was not about to roll over and play dead.

Lattimore must have arrived back at the embassy a worried man. From the information I have I gather that he was also quite angry with the State Department generally (and with Garbeau specifically) for having decided to play the double game in New Salisbury, thereby forcing the Lief into a corner. The ingeniousness of U.S. policy toward New Salisbury was now up against the Lief's overbearing belief in his messianism. It was also quite likely against Leahy's mixture of nineteenth-century Marxism and his own fanatical ruthlessness. Unlike the efficient, stainless-steel variety of U.S. policy, both the Lief and Leahy were thoroughly irrational. They were impulsive and therefore highly volatile. Added to the unknown was George Titus, who could prove to be no leader at all and who could very well disappear from the chessboard with the arrival of winter.

If Titus was not up to the job, then the arms deliveries to Lief would have to start much earlier. His demise and a Marxist takeover would not only constitute a serious strategic loss but also a diplomatic and prestigious debacle of incredible proportions. Lattimore must have realized that Lucius C. Liefenbarger was neither one of the crude, slow thinking Greek colonels, nor the ridiculously monocled Spinoza.

He was something else entirely.

Chapter 18

Romance, chivalry and adventure aren't dead; they live in the wilderness of the Cheviot Hills on the Lower Isle in New Salisbury. So began the first in a series of articles about us by Asmatar Surgit Sahota which was picked up by several publications, mostly in New Zealand and Australia.

There, among the giant ferns and clusters of pigeonwood trees, beats a heart as outraged as that of Thomas Payne, operates a mind as profound as Thomas Jefferson's and evinces a talent as practical as that of Benjamin Franklin. All of these qualities are embodied in the name of George Titus. He is the leader of a revolt against the dictatorship of Lucius C. Liefenbarger, the strong man who has been mercilessly holding New Salisbury in subjugation for five years now.

A few weeks before Christmas there had been an attempted rebel landing on Main Island's Renfrew Peninsula. Led by Titus, the son of New Salisbury's first prime minister, it had been repulsed by government forces with several of the rebels killed in the skirmish. But Titus himself survived to lead a much larger movement in the Cheviot Hills on the Lower Isle, far from New Salisbury's capital. The "hills" by the way, are a misnomer: some are towering peaks more than 3,000 meters high.

There is considerable sympathy throughout New Salisbury for the revolutionary movement. A schoolgirl living on New Salisbury City's fashionable West Side told me that, right next to John Travolta and Burt Reynolds, "I have a picture of George Titus on the wall of my room — and it wasn't so easy to get."

Why would today's teenager place a picture of a middle-aged academic alongside her favorite movie stars? "Because he's real. There's no playacting about him. And he fights for what he thinks is right. It's great to have someone like him in this plastic, computerized world. It really is."

A young lawyer from New Salisbury's Main Island city of Nelson told me that he is trying to work up enough courage to go and join George Titus in the mountains: "There really isn't that much to do down here. There's not much law left."

A *farmer's wife* on the Partrawa Plain, in the area where Lucius Liefenbarger's dreaded prison camps are located, says that the rebel movement is much overdue because she no longer wants to "live next door to Buchenwald or Mauthausen."

But there is still much support for the Liefenbarger regime. Devotees of the status quo like it, those who believe that no matter how bad things are they could still be worse. His virulent anti-Communism is also a strong attraction that Liefenbarger holds for many people.

"It's good that we're finally planning to go after the Communists," says a young army lieutenant stationed near Muldoon, a port on the Lower Isle near which one group of rebels not associated with Titus battled with the government recently and lost, "because so far they've been going after us — in Czechoslovakia, Rhodesia, Angola. You name the place and they're there. Even here in New Salisbury they've been making their grab for power but things are bound to change now."

Some leaders in New Salisbury may not be overly enthusiastic about Liefenbarger's heavy-handed running of the country's economy, but they are also highly suspicious of what might come after him under a government headed by a university professor from Canada.

"A violent overthrow of government seldom benefits a country," opined an electronics company vice-president in New Salisbury City, "because the scars left behind — the loss of life, destruction of property and the dislocation of both energy and talent — take much too long to heal. Sometimes more than a lifetime. Look at the Russians, they're still today trying to find their way out of a revolution that took place more than sixty years ago. A revolution is no solution. It is really a way that any civilized country admits a defeat."

"Is it — an admission of defeat, I mean," I asked the trim-looking George Titus over some coffee at the Revolutionary Army's headquarters deep in the Cheviot Hills.

"It's certainly not the best way to change a government," he replied thoughtfully. "But sometimes it's the only way available. The first thing I've learned here in the mountains is not to get overly optimistic, dogmatic or even theoretical about revolutions. Each one is different. Many a university savant has run into tremendous trouble trying to find a common thread between them without becoming overly tautological."

George Titus uses much smaller words when speaking to his followers; there is misunderstanding in the Cheviots on what it *is that he stands for. At present a committee of his camp commanders is working on a draft of a document which would effectively summarize the goals of the revolution for anyone who would care to look at it.*

Such concepts as "democratic procedures," "universally accepted principles of human rights," and "the rule of law" make frequent appearances in the document, right alongside "tolerance of opposing ideas" and "the spirit of compromise." These phrases may explain to George Titus's followers what it is they are being asked to die for, but they also raise some questions: Does each of them really have only one accepted meaning? Isn't it possible that each member of the Revolutionary Army will interpret them according to his or her personal ideology?

Titus allows for this possibility. "It could be. But to provide any further definitions, to write out a complete nomenclature for what the future government of New Salisbury should look like, is to indulge in exactly the kind of thing we're fighting against. How and who will govern must be decided by the people themselves."

The democratic leadership vacuum which had existed in New Salisbury during the 1970s, during Lucius Liefenbarger's takeover, has been filled. Almost without an exception everyone I have met in the Cheviot Hills has nothing but the highest regard for George Titus and his leadership abilities.

How many revolutionaries are there in the Cheviot Hills? Probably only George Titus and those around him know for certain. They, however, are not about to divulge the number and thereby aid Liefenbarger's efforts to dislodge them. There seem to be countless camouflaged camps into which the narrow trails widen every ten miles or so. They are supplied by air by a consortium of powers whose identity no one is ready to disclose.

"You could say that they are a group of concerned nations. Concerned lest the ruthless dictatorship which today rules New Salisbury be replaced by another one. And such concern is a very good thing," says Maurice Bech-Landau, one of Titus's lieutenants. "And quite unprecedented in this day."

(Tomorrow: Life Among the Revolutionaries.)

Chapter 19

Aside from clearly establishing Sahota as a pompous ass of the first order, several things became clear with the publication of his articles. Our period of even semiclandestine presence in the mountains was over. From now on we would be subjected to scrutiny right alongside the Lief, and we were now a part of the international scene and the terminus of an official escape route for all discontented New Salisburians with all the heavy accompanying responsibilities.

Most important of all, though, Sahota had single-handedly crowned George Titus as the king and placed him on his throne.

To this day I am convinced that Sahota initially worked for Liefenbarger. For various reasons I suspect that Meg was discovered by the authorities while organizing the Resistance at St. Enoch. But she was not picked up. Instead, Sahota was introduced into the picture by the NUC to be taken back into the mountains by her and provide a much needed, firsthand report for Mayfield.

Something happened to Sahota while in the Cheviots, though. He became convinced that the future was ours. He then quietly crept out of our midst and out of New Salisbury altogether, knowing full well that his association with Mayfield was eventually bound to come out and that in such volatile times he could easily lose his head on account of it.

A few days later Meg Winters moved to Camp Alpha to be nearer to the center of power. The apology and reconciliation had been much easier than expected and she was quickly accepted into George's inner circle. Her knowledge of the situation in the lowlands was found to be extremely valuable.

In April, though, came the rains. At first they were just intermittent, occasional showers that settled the dust in those areas where camp construction had destroyed the natural ground cover. The rain renewed the greenery, but only temporarily. Soon came the night frosts which turned the grass yellow. The bothersome insects were now gone, but after the first frosty night we were out in force, busily caulking the chinks between the logs of our cabins.

Morale dropped. It was now clear that we were locked in the mountains for the winter, and there was no hope of a triumphant march into St. Enoch — a hope which most of us harbored secretly in the back of our minds. We were now face to face with the reality that this was no longer a summer camp but a tough endurance test that not everyone would pass.

Then came the invitation from Ken Garbeau. He was cruising aboard a U.S. Navy supply ship just off New Salisbury's territorial waters and wanted to meet with George. I fully expected that George would want to take Meg along, but I was asked to go instead. Meg would stay and tend the shop while we were gone.

The trouble was that George was sick. He had been nursing a cold for days and it wasn't quite clear yet if it would progress into a case of pneumonia. To make things worse, rain had been falling all morning on the day of our departure, followed in the afternoon by gusts of howling, freezing wind. The landing area was at least a brisk two-hour walk away and we set out after lunch with heavy odds against us that in this weather the helicopter would arrive. Too dark to start back to camp, we would have to spend the night outside. I was definitely against going, but we didn't really have much choice. Garbeau would not be cruising the New Salisbury coast forever and there were some pretty important issues to be resolved.

And we were lucky. At four o'clock there came a partial clearing and shortly afterwards the helicopter appeared. Without a word we were pulled aboard into our seats. When we looked out the window there was below us only thick, seemingly impenetrable cloud.

When we left the coastal range behind we were out in the clear again, but by then darkness had settled. The sea below looked grey and sinister. The Sikorski was flying low in order to avoid Liefenbarger's radar and I added to my growing depression by reflecting on how easy it would be for a patrol boat to shoot us out of the sky.

I looked at George. Never a relaxed flier even under the best of conditions, this sort of travel produced perspiration on his furled brow. Garbeau would have a lot of questions to ask and it was imperative that his answers made sense.

The helicopter banked slightly to the left and through the window we saw the vague outline of a ship — the Australian *Constant* we had heard so much about. When the Sikorski had touched down — the landing pad was camouflaged by an ingenious combination of crates and canvas which could be easily rolled away — several dark figures appeared and connected a fuel hose to the machine. From the cockpit emerged Russ Nichols, whom we already knew, to supervise the operation. He told us to go into the wardroom for a cup of coffee.

George had a bit of problem getting up. His forehead had become moist again and he was dabbing it with his handkerchief as we stepped out of the machine.

"This way sir," directed one of the figures that had been waiting there.

The wardroom was immediately below and we were both glad that it was deserted. The dark figure that had escorted us there turned out to be a boy who couldn't have been older than eighteen. He poured coffee for us, mixed it with cream and sugar, then quietly disappeared when the job was done.

We sat down, George looking increasingly feverish. Outside the porthole the ocean seemed less sinister toward the horizon as it reflected the dying rays of the sun. George let his head drop, enjoying the aroma of the rising steam from the coffee mug around which hands were tightly clasped. I was worried. The whole atmosphere was not exactly conducive to miraculous recoveries.

Then another man entered, taking off his white hat. He closed the door but remained standing beside it. "Good evening," he said.

"Evening," I answered, and George's head came slowly back up.

"I'm the first officer of this tub. The name's Garfield."

"Pleased to meet you," George replied with some effort. "I'm George Ti — "

"Yes, I know who you are," Garfield interrupted, coming closer to our table. He had deep-set eyes and wiry blond hair. I noticed his enormous hands as he raised one in a greeting.

"If you don't mind, I'll have a cup of coffee with you."

He pulled up a chair. "I wanted to meet you," Garfield started explaining. "You see, I'm from New Salisbury — "

"Oh? From where?"

"Main Island. Ayman, but you probably haven't heard of it. It's a small town near Garrick."

"I've heard of it," George said. "That's where Firestone has a plant."

"Yes sir. My father worked there for thirty years. He is now retired. I live in Australia, at Surface Paradise. Married an

Australian. I guess I couldn't go back anyway. Not while I'm attached to the *Constant.*"

"No, I guess you couldn't," said George mechanically. He must have felt terrible at that moment, but he had also sensed that Garfield came in for something more than just a chat and he was curious to find out what it was.

Garfield stared into his cup for a few minutes, then suddenly looked up. "Do you think it's worth it, sir? I mean with all the killing and misery?"

"Wha — What? The revolution? Yes, I'm afraid I do. Otherwise I would be either a bloody fool or a hypocrite, wouldn't I?" He sensed that he had probably come on too strong, but the way he felt he simply couldn't cope with too many gradations.

"No, I'm sure that you yourself know why you are in it, sir. What I meant was that whatever your own reason, is it good enough for everyone else? Do several hundred dedicated men really have the right to plunge a nation into tragedy?"

It was obvious that he didn't think so, and that he had been thinking about it for quite some time. I suspected that whatever it was which made him think that way resulted from a close loss. Obviously, George did too.

"Was it someone in your family?" he asked.

"My brother," said Garfield quickly. "Actually my half brother; my dad remarried after my mother died. He was studying philosophy — that was a new one in our family. He used to say he wanted to study something that couldn't possibly by any stretch of the imagination be considered a useful skill. That he would be able to collect unemployment and do what he wanted with his life."

His attempt at humor was forced and it fooled no one, least of all himself. Garfield paused. In his mind he seemed to see his brother before him.

"He was picked up with the rest. I found out about it on Christmas Day. They carried signs and marched out into the streets to join the riots. Comrade Leahy was landing at Hawar and needed a distraction." There was a bitterly sarcastic tone to his last sentence. Garfield stared into the shadows ahead and his knuckles turned white as his grip tightened on the coffee mug.

"What they had done with them during the last two weeks before the trial I wouldn't want to know. But once the verdict was in they took all twenty of them and put them into a special cell with nothing but a concrete floor and a trough along the side. They stripped them, then injected them with something that produced diarrhea and vomiting. Do you know why? Because they didn't want messy hangings — sometimes those who are being executed, especially when they are young — lose control."

The ship creaked unpleasantly in the silence that followed. George obviously wanted to lie down and sleep. Sleep for days. Leahy's slaughtered sacrificial lambs, along with the destruction of the whole underground organization in N.S. City — what could one really say about it?

"That was the Marxist group. We — " George started to explain.

"They're with you now, aren't they?" Garfield quietly interrupted him.

"Yes."

"Then it isn't that easy. I mean whoever lives by the sword automatically gets the ball rolling. He is equally to bl — "

"Now wait a minute. It wasn't the revolution that killed your brother. It was the mud that came up to the surface along with Lucius Liefenbarger. People whom he put in charge of the police and courts," I shouted.

"Liefenbarger is in a vise. He has to defend himself, doesn't he? I mean, I don't agree with the guy in the slightest, but I do understand that." Garfield spoke with increased conviction. My head was spinning with the warped logic, misplaced emphasis, and meandering causation. Then he was finished and I was about to argue, but George spoke up.

"We are the ones in a vise, Mr. Garfield," he said quietly. "We are the ones holed up in the mountains, blocked off on one side by the ocean, on the other by a well-equipped fascist army. The winter's coming and we are not at all sure we'll be around to see the spring."

His forehead dripped sweat, his cheeks were flushed. In spite of it, he tried his darnedest to appear statesman-like in dealing with Garfield. Here in the wardroom with a dry ceiling and white tablecloths he seemed to be succeeding, but how many in New Salisbury thought the way Garfield did?

"It was your decision," Garfield reminded him softly.

"That's right, it was. Now think about the people in Partrawa prisons who are waiting for us. Who was it really that started the snowball of violence rolling?"

Garfield's thoughts seemed already far away. "My dad tried

to see him the night before but they refused...his own son...
What's happening to the country?"

Garfield had voiced his doubts, told his story, and that
seemed to be all he needed. They sat alongside each other —
George and he — neither having anything more to say. All that
Garfield wanted was his brother back. I looked out the porthole at the dark sea again, at the cold drizzle and the uncertainty ahead. I shuddered.

Suddenly I wanted my own past back too.

Chapter 20

When we arrived aboard the USS *Richard Thompson,* George was only half conscious. He was brought out of the Sikorski straight to sick bay, where a doctor injected antibiotics and bedded him down to rest under the watchful eye of the sick bay orderly. Exhausted, I too collapsed on a bunk in my cabin after a few words with Garbeau, explaining that we both could do with some rest. About 4 A.M. I woke and eventually found my way back to the sick bay. George was asleep and the orderly was devouring a pocketbook.

"He woke up a few minutes ago," the orderly reported. "Wanted a glass of orange juice and a Milky Way."

"A what?"

"A candy bar — a Milky Way. He must be improving," he grinned.

"Where is the doctor? Has he been back to look at him?"

"The doctor? Back in New Zealand, sir. He said he'd be back in a day or two."

I went back to my cabin, lay down and fell asleep to the hum of the engine. At ten I woke up again. I shaved and showered, then made my way back through the maze of the ship to the upper deck. It was by far the most modern vessel I had ever seen. Beneath the weather-beaten exterior, it was spotlessly clean, with carpeted passageways and indirect lighting. When I emerged on the upper deck there was a futuristic, aerodynamically designed superstructure. The Sikorski which had brought us aboard and then probably taken the doctor to New Zealand was now secured on a pad below. Off the starboard side a destroyer serving as an escort bobbed up and down on the bronze sea.

Garbeau was in the captain's wardroom, along with our pilot Russ Nichols and another man in civilian clothes. The captain was not present. All three rose as I entered and Garbeau advanced toward me with his hand extended. But it was a different Garbeau from the one in the States. He seemed more respectful. After all, this time he was welcoming an active guerrilla, not just a dreamer.

"Welcome back among the living. Now we won't have to be assuring them back in the Cheviots every hour on the hour that you're O.K. You can tell them yourself." Garbeau then casually introduced me to Clifford Lattimore, the U.S. ambassador to New Salisbury. I promptly erupted and scared the hell out of him. "I certainly have a bone to pick with you. About those F-16s you're selling to —"

But Garbeau quickly intervened. "Whoa, Maurice. Sit down first. Cliff here had nothing to do with that. It was the man before him. And in any case, it isn't the ambassador who decides about U.S. foreign policy."

He directed me to a vacant seat and I felt like a complete ass. "Would you like some coffee?"

"I would really like some breakfast. I'm hungry."

The steward produced a plate laden with eggs and sausages. Garbeau informed me that George seemed on the mend, that after I ate we would go down to the sick bay to have our talk there.

"Not that I'm hurrying," Garbeau continued, "because a sea cruise like this sure is great for one's shattered nerves."

I felt like I was being closely scrutinized by Lattimore from the moment I had entered the wardroom. He must have found it strange to meet a representative of the major threat to the government to which he was accredited. Unusual, anyway.

"So you've decided to spend the winter in the mountains," Garbeau started by getting right to the point. "Can you make it?"

"We'll know early in November," I answered, perhaps a bit too flippantly.

"What about supplies? We've got all sorts of winter clothing, skis, snowshoes and things that we'll get to you before May. Before the snow really starts falling. What you'll need even more, I guess, is morale. Do you think you have enough to see you through?"

"I think so."

"That's what Russ here thinks too. You didn't know that he was really our agent, did you?"

"Geez, that would be hard to miss. Anybody who keeps asking over and over if you've ever stood on skis must be either a U.S. Olympic team scout or something like an agent."

That took care of the obligatory humor. I had finished my breakfast and we rose to go down to the sick bay to talk with George. We found him sitting up, looking pale, but much better than the night before. He too had just finished breakfast and was now munching on another Milky Way. There were introductions, comments about his health and then we all settled in a circle around his bunk.

Garbeau took in his breath and considered various ways of jumping into it. "The main thing to remember is that the U.S. is primarily interested in the stability and maintenance of status quo in the Pacific," he began. "And anywhere else in the world for that matter."

"I'm afraid that's your problem," George commented softly.

"What is — the status quo? That's been the policy of all major powers throughout history. It's nothing new. You — of all people George — should know that."

"I do know it. And I am also well aware of the results. Henry Kissinger once wrote with considerable wisdom that whenever the maintenance of status quo has been mankind's main preoccupation, the international system depended on the tender mercies of its most ruthless member. Reluctantly, I'd even allow that something like the status quo should be defended — if something like it existed on the islands. But how can you possibly talk about a status quo with the Extraordinary State Act and the wartime economy on the one side and several hundred revolutionaries in the Cheviots busily planning Liefenbarger's downfall on the other?"

"I meant the international status quo. The South Pacific is firmly within our sphere of interest. We wouldn't want to have that changed."

"So what you really mean is that we'll be spending the winter in the Cheviots as part of the holy quest for an international status quo, is that correct?" I butted in.

Garbeau turned to me. "Look, Maurice, we've known each other too long for me to start sugar coating it for you: yes, that's basically it. The U.S. wouldn't be in this at all were it not for the Russian effort via the Algerian group."

"Aren't there any other — *moral* issues?"

Lattimore turned to Garbeau. "Could I answer that?"

"All right."

"Well, I just wanted to say that we know about the National Unity Corps' tactics at the Bristol Street Armory and on the Partrawa Plain. Do we need a revolution to correct them though? We've had some pretty bad results with revolutions in this century. Just like — I'd be the first one to admit — we've had some bad results with our attempts to keep things as they are. The status quo usually costs fewer lives though."

Garbeau smiled as he suggested changing the subject. "Would you be terribly upset, gentlemen, if we called a halt to this rather haughty moral and philosophical discussion? I would like to talk about something much more specific."

"What?"

"Camp Gamma — Force Gamma."

"What about it?"

"It's led by what remains of the Algerian group, right?"

"That's right."

"Do you think it's wise to concentrate them all in one place like that?"

George shrugged his shoulders, then decided to return the shot along the same lines. "Would it be wiser to scatter them through the Cheviots?"

"We don't know. We'd kinda like you to convince us. I mean I live in Washington and Lattimore here lives in a marble palace in the middle of New Salisbury City. You, on the other hand, live in a rebel camp in the Cheviot Hills."

George thought for a moment. "Leahy requested his own unit. Not to give it to him would have meant the start of another conflict. We just aren't strong enough yet to play Tito to Leahy's Chetniks."

"That's not too accurate," Garbeau corrected him. "Leahy is ideologically closer to Tito, you to Mihailovich. And we all know what happened to Mihailovich: Tito had him hanged."

"Shot," George corrected him. "It happened because the Western allies decided to support Tito against the Chetniks. So it's really all up to you once again, isn't it?" Sarcasm was slowly beginning to seep through. He was tired and probably still had a slight fever.

"Why do you think the Algerian group can be trusted — because they say so?" asked Lattimore, as if relieving Garbeau on the attack.

"I don't know," George shrugged his shoulders. "They really haven't given us a reason for not trusting them. And we have to trust someone."

We were all silent for the next few moments, the Americans evaluating what had been said so far as things must have seemed quite different from Washington or from the marble palace in New Salisbury City, I thought.

Then Garbeau spoke up again. "Well, that's something for

you to decide. Our main interest in this thing is to keep you in charge of the Revolutionary Army. Not to be replaced either by John Leahy or Gino Baracolli. You say that you have to trust someone and you're probably right. On the other hand the Algerian group really wouldn't have landed on the Lower Isle with all the hullabaloo just to become a part of George Titus's Revolutionary Army, would they?"

"Probably not," George allowed. "So what should we do?"

"I don't think there's much you can do. Not now. Except to be highly suspicious of every move they make."

"What happens if we're not — if Leahy takes over?" I asked.

"Is there a chance of that?" Garbeau shot back.

"I don't know. I hope not," I said.

"I'm not sure of anything anymore. Except that there are close to two hundred of us holed up in the Cheviots. But I'm not sure if there should be that many because I feel responsible for them," George said.

Another pause followed. It was Garbeau who finally spoke up. "Look, the way we see it the immediate danger to you lies not in Lucius Liefenbarger: it is a) the winter, and b) Leahy and the Algerians. And not necessarily in that order either, because we sure can help with the weather. We also feel that there is better than a fifty-fifty chance that enough of you will make it through the winter to constitute a strong enough foundation on which to build in the spring."

"Fine. Now what happens if we manage to keep up morale, but not John Leahy out of the headquarters cabin?" I asked.

Garbeau scratched his head. "Then we'll put our money on Liefenbarger," he said reluctantly.

"In spite of the Partrawa camps, National Unity Corps, torture chambers and everything?"

Garbeau nodded. "Liefenbarger we can control."

I was carrying the conversation now, George listening intently. "You haven't so far."

"We haven't really tried to. And don't forget he's under tremendous pressure right now, from your rebels. Would it really be so logical to expect him to perform like a wide-eyed liberal when his ass is on fire?"

"If you bet on Liefenbarger, how far will you go to support him?" asked George. Garbeau paused. The answer would really summarize everything that has been said.

"All the way," he said finally.

"Troops? The works?"

Garbeau reflected on it for a moment but in the end he must have decided we really were entitled to the information. "Yes," he allowed uneasily.

"American?"

"No. This is a regional affair: Anzac."

"Oh, sort of like the Warsaw Pact and the Brezhnev Doctrine, right?"

Garbeau didn't seem a bit offended by the comparison. "I suppose. Except that without Russia the Warsaw Pact is nothing. The Australians and New Zealanders on the other hand can take New Salisbury away from Leahy quite easily."

"Does Liefenbarger know just how safe he is?" asked George.

"Of course not. But we wanted *you* to know. You are our first choice. Liefenbarger is second — not Leahy."

George thought for a moment, then managed to conjure up an uneasy smile. "Fair enough," he said. "About as fair as one is apt to get in this business, I suppose."

George was tired. Garbeau, Lattimore and Nichols rose to leave. Kenneth Garbeau suggested that we get together again that evening and George tentatively agreed. When I started to leave too, he asked that I stay behind.

"What do you think?" he asked tiredly when they were gone.

"I think... I think that after this if either of us succumbs to that dangerous and alien doctrine of idealism he should be shot for treason. That's what I think."

George just nodded. He slumped down in his bed and closed his eyes. In the afternoon George slept again. Garbeau and I talked inconsequentially for a while; I also played cards with Russ Nichols. Then I walked out on deck, buttoning my parka against the brisk wind. I gazed toward the west, where I thought I could see what must have been the first lights of the dimly outlined Chatham Islands. Beyond them was New Zealand. In that direction lay tranquility. Having experienced warm baths and clean sheets again, I had to admit that shipboard life had its advantages. The other way lay the uncertainty of winter in the mountains. Coupled with the American penchant for testing us, the prospects there were far from enticing. Revolutions, when one got closer to them, looked nowhere near as glorious as that picture of the Bastille being stormed I remembered from my history book at Herriott.

Probably because I had been born so far inland, the sea held a double fascination for me. Gone was the mild claustrophobia induced by the mountains, the fears engendered by the myriad of hiding places in the forest, and the living, threatening darkness at night. The bow of the *Richard Thompson* cut effortlessly through the sea and the steady progress of the ship was accompanied by the incessant but reassuring rumble from below. The fatigue abated. My mind, uncluttered by the daily duties of the mountains, lay as if dormant. The feelings had taken over. There was warmth, contentment, and a total lack of anxiety. It was all so bloody marvellous.

In the evening we watched an idiotic American horror movie on the closed circuit television, had a few drinks, then welcomed the doctor flown in by Russ Nichols. George seemed improved. The doctor patted him on the shoulder, shut his bag with a flourish, and was on his way again. George asked for another night of sleep and we scheduled a meeting for the following morning to discuss details of the supply plans. Before turning in I came out on the deck again. The Chatham Islands' lights were clearly visible now and the mild swell had abated. The *Richard Thompson* was making its way ahead without the slightest roll. It would be ideal for sleeping.

Without so much as a peremptory knock, Ken Garbeau walked into my cabin at 6 A.M. and sat down on the bunk across from mine. He was dressed in a bathrobe. "Some of your men have gone down into the valley south of Marsbury. Have you ordered it?"

I rubbed my eyes and shook my head simultaneously. "Was it Fort Wellington?"

"Fort Wellington," Garbeau nodded. "What is it all about?"

On the way to the sick bay I told him. "Leahy's Force Gamma. Liefenbarger keeps a skeleton garrison at Wellington — probably as bait in hope we would try and pounce on them. Leahy always wanted to. The trouble is that the new Anti-Insurgency Unit can be flown to Fort Wellington within minutes. Do you know how many men are involved?"

Garbeau shook his head. "We intercepted a message which must have been for the Unit at St. Enoch."

George listened carefully, then swung his legs out of bed. "We have to go back, Maurice. This thing can break us."

"If you're willing to wait an hour we'll be close enough to

the coast for the helicopter to take you straight to the Cheviots. You won't have to refuel aboard the *Constant*."

During the hour we agreed on supply routes and methods. George had a talk with Lattimore, who was waiting for a boat which would take him to the Chatham Islands. From there he would fly to New Zealand and back to N.S. City.

When we were standing out on deck with our rucksacks, another message arrived. The rebel force was less than thirty men strong and there was fighting inside the fort. Government reinforcements from St. Enoch were on their way. There was no doubt now that the rebels were Force Gamma and that Liefenbarger and McAlpine had them exactly where they wanted them.

As the Sikorski's blades started to whirl, we shook hands with Garbeau. Just then the sick bay orderly emerged from a passageway, with one hand holding his hat against the wind, the other clutching a small package. He grinned as he saw George and fought his way toward him against the gusty wind.

"Here," he said when he reached him, handing him the package. "This should keep you in good health."

George took off the lid and looked down at what he was holding. It was a box of Milky Ways.

According to Copithorne's diaries, it was he who woke Lucius Liefenbarger with the news at Pitlochry. The Lief quickly put on the uniform of a general in the New Salisbury Guards and ordered his car. He was clearly excited but also quite capable of not showing it. While the Lief was shaving in the limousine on his way to town, Copithorne, over the car phone, received the news that Fort Wellington's defenders had successfully evacuated the place through a tunnel passage, and also that McAlpine's Anti-Insurgency Unit was already in the air. Local gendarmerie had blocked off all the roads to the mountains that could be used for escape.

The Lief didn't head for the military headquarters in the Towers, but for the Armory on Bristol Street — the notorious headquarters of Eddie Mayfield's National Unity Corps. That was certainly significant. From there the Lief called McAlpine, congratulated him on quickly getting the Anti-Insurgency Unit into the air, and asked him about the mood on the Lower Isle. McAlpine told him that things couldn't be quieter and that all the people stood unequivocally behind the Lief.

The Lief couldn't have been overly convinced by this rather

transparent piece of flattery. After all, it wasn't as if McAlpine had already been out early that morning, conducting a public opinion poll. But as a statement of personal loyalty on the governor's part, it must have been welcomed and appreciated.

There are two roads leading back into the mountains from Fort Wellington, one along the Thebe River and the other along the Stewart River Valley. It was into those valleys that the anti-insurgency troops were dropped. Once in position, the shelling of the fort began and local gendarmerie moved against the fort. At about 3 P.M. the phone rang at the Armory and Major Felstad, commander of the Anti-Insurgency Regiment, reported personally that Fort Wellington had been retaken.

Now the Lief was almost dancing with joy. "How many casualties?" he asked.

"Five men wounded on our side — none seriously — and eight dead on theirs, so far, sir."

"Have you got any prisoners?"

"Two sir. But one of them is not likely to live."

"Where are the rest?"

"Dispersed through the countryside. We'll get them tomorrow when we make our sweep."

"Were there thirty of them?"

"It's been scaled down, sir. More like twenty."

"Well, keep me posted. And congratulate the governor for me."

The Lief hung up the phone, thought for a moment, but was interrupted by Mayfield, who opened an ostentatious cabinet in the corner of his office and extracted a bottle of Scotch. He filled a glass for everyone present and proposed a toast to victory; the Lief, who almost never touched anything stronger than a glass of Chablis, downed it along with everyone else. It was an elated Administrator who stayed a bit longer, shaking hands and chatting amicably with the NUC officer-types around (there was no regular army, navy, or air force officer in the room), then ambled over to Copithorne, grabbing him amicably and uncharacteristically around his shoulders, saying, "Let's go back to Pitlochry, Frank. It's been quite a day."

Again he shook hands with everyone, his face now a picture of total contentment. In the door he turned around and still beaming, observed, "Yes, sir, quite a day."

Chapter 21

In the helicopter, I had an opportunity to study George's face: it reflected all the strain. If his world had not yet totally collapsed, it had at least developed a dangerous tilt. Fort Wellington couldn't be compared to the Renfrew Peninsula fiasco: at that time his world — the revolution — had not yet truly existed, his expectations still an unknown quantity. And the problem at Renfrew had been created by the Lief's forces, not by an insubordinate group.

I suspect that for George the word "conflict" until now had meant that a dusty prof had boldly challenged his thesis on political change at some obscure colloquium. After a spirited afternoon session the faculty would adjourn to the cocktail lounge of the club to discuss inadequate National Research Council grants.

An unpredictable and *ipso facto* unfair opposition meant that during a question period following his "Marxism in Today's World" lecture some radical refused to wait his turn in line behind the microphones at the Alma Mater Society Auditorium.

About forty minutes after taking off from the USS *Richard Thompson,* the dark grey coast of the Lower Isle appeared before us, but we were not about to approach it right away. The Sikorski came nearer and followed its contours for a few minutes before Russ Nichols appeared beside George's seat. "We can't get you home," he yelled into his ear. "Look, it's completely fogged in."

George followed the direction of Nichols's forefinger, studying the outline of the coast. "How about down below?"

"Down to about a hundred feet, I'd say."

"Well, let's go under it," George shouted.

"But I still can't get you into the mountains."

"Doesn't matter. Drop us off at Precarious."

Russ thought about it for a moment. There were other perils — there might be patrol boats in the inlet and he would have to fly at almost sea level.

Suddenly I was afraid. Thoughts of turning around and

returning to the *Constant* or the USS *Richard Thompson*
figured prominently in my thinking in spite of my best efforts
to the contrary. I wanted to speak out, but George beat me to
it. "Look, Russ, if I don't get there soon we might lose the
whole thing."

Nichols stared at him, then turned around wordlessly to get
back to the controls. The helicopter banked sharply to the left,
then entered the inlet. At its mouth and even a bit beyond, all
went well. The sea was calm, and Russ maneuvered the
helicopter between the sheer mountain slopes that rose out of
the sea. On the left, thin strings of cascading water showed that
at the top it was raining hard, maybe even snowing. We
banked to the left, with the sandy island in a cove just ahead of
us. This was where the *Pita* and *Seta* had dropped us off a few
months before.

And then I felt them, several slight vibrations out of sync
with the engine. Russ pulled up the helicopter's nose. We were
flying straight into a wall of dark rock, but at the very last
moment Russ abruptly changed course, this time parallel to
the island. The patrol boat was in sight now, and we were close
enough to see men scampering about its deck, two of them
behind a machine gun. Only beyond the next bend did Russ
reduce speed and George pointed to the window, punctured by
two bullets, beside his seat. By then we were hovering near the
Precarious dock, now deserted, without a boat tied to it.

"This is as far as we go," Russ yelled. George started to undo
his harness, then picked up his rucksack from the helicopter's
floor. A thought flashed through my mind how fortunate
George and I were not having to go back out through the inlet.

The copilot then took over the controls. Russ Nichols came
into the cabin and helped us into the breezy vicinity of the
Sikorski, now seated on the dock. George jumped out, then
squeezed Russ Nichols's hand through the opening.

"Are you sure you can make it back?" he asked.

"We'll make it."

"You've got guns?"

Nichols shook his head. "Not allowed to use them from the
chopper. Not even if they shoot first. Our orders are to ditch it
in the sea somewhere if forced to do that, then claim we are
mercenaries if captured. They're worried about an incident."

For more there wasn't time. George scampered from the
diameter of the whirling blades, turning around just in time to
see the Sikorski lift off and start rising toward the clouds. They

were going to fly blind to avoid the patrol boat and we wished them luck.

Although Precarious looked completely deserted, we didn't take any chances. Carefully skirting the village, we headed right to the trail we had travelled so many times before. Within moments sweat rolled down our backs.

The sun broke through the clouds, our shadows appearing in a clearing among the trees; they lengthened, then disappeared completely. We were hoping that the sun might have helped Russ and his copilot, but then realized that by then they must have either cleared the inlet or were now at the bottom of it. Dusk came, then increasing darkness.

Slowly we made our way up the muddy trail, George's aching muscles not yet having fully recovered from the illness and inactivity. We set what seemed to be a comfortable pace, and soon became something like automatic walking machines. We were alone in the stillness of the wilderness, also in a sort of vacuum. In a limbo between the Revolutionary Army, its American sponsors, and Liefenbarger's defenses.

We seemed to be standing apart from it all, not having any idea what was happening and what already might have happened on the other side of the ridge. But the prospect of the eight-hour climb seemed to be a palliative for George's anxiety. Others would have to make decisions in his absence.

We now began to discuss things in earnest. What was coming? If successful, our precious revolution could unleash forces that had created men of such disparate ideologies as Kerensky, Danton and Robespierre. Kerensky had spent most of his life in exile, Danton exhorted himself to show no weakness as he marched to the guillotine, and Robespierre could say nothing at all because his jaw had been shot off.

And the result was either Lenin or Napoleon — hundreds of thousands dead.

According to Meg, the lowlands were seething with discontent over which George towered as the leader to a better tomorrow. There was no blueprint, just George Titus. There had been a vague, professorial and probably unduly idealistic emphasis on something called democratic procedure, but no revolution could really be democratic because it consisted of acts of force and violence — exactly the opposite of what is considered to be democratic. Yet, until then we had carried on the business with the camp commanders as if they were all members of some sort of a parliament. We had argued, cajoled, compromised and persuaded; and there had even been the odd time when George rescinded an order because he felt it had not been supported by the majority.

We listened to the rhythm of our boots being sucked and then released by the mire of the Precarious Trail. George suddenly complained that he would be even more alone now — without his university-induced preconceptions, having to override his quite natural desire to be liked, and, when necessary, dropping all standards of fairness. He felt that there were blood and enormous suffering ahead and that it was all part and parcel of that great beast to which he had chained himself. It all could be in vain unless we made it clear to ourselves what we stood for, unless we could come up with some goals.

"And we can't come up with those goals through discussions among reasonable men because the definition of what's reasonable has undergone a great change here in the mountains. For God's sake, we're trying to kill and destroy and reasonableness carries with it the great danger that it could be mistaken for weakness," he said at one point.

We sat down on two tree stumps to rest. George reached into his bag and produced a couple of Milky Ways. The candy bar seemed to restore at least part of our strength and in a few minutes we were ready to move on again.

George then continued with what was increasingly becoming his monologue. We had been pushed into a corner, he said. The emergency, the dire threat facing us, has been brought home not only via Leahy's flagrant disregard of his orders, but also by Kenneth Garbeau's cold-as-steel spelling out of the U.S. policy toward New Salisbury. And emergencies and dire threats cannot be solved by tribal council meetings.

No revolutionary democracy was possible. That had always been the gobbledygook of the Marxists which meant nothing but the unbridled reign of those in power. There could be no revolution in a democracy, just like there could be no such thing as a revolutionary justice. There had been no Glorious Revolution for those who had been maimed and who died in it. It was important to be honest — not because of the revolution but because of one's self. Under the stress that was coming George had to be absolutely sure of what he was doing. Mainly to retain his sanity.

Two hours away from the top of the ridge George announced he had to sleep. His knees were weak and he was starting to get dizzy. We found a relatively dry spot under a felled tree trunk resting against a tall Rimu. As we laid out our bags, we frightened a covey of Kakas whose flight and raucous ka-aa disturbed the slumbering forest around us. The drizzle had stopped. Against the shadowy sky sailed torn clouds and George was back in his youth, remembering aloud one of our hiking trips in these very same mountains, when we trudged our way through the rain all day. Smelling of wet wool, we put up our pup tent and, unable to start a fire, were forced to eat our food uncooked.

The damp sleeping bags were not at all conducive to sleep and, while lying there inside them, we promised ourselves that never again would we spend a night like this. We fell asleep and woke up several times until, in the middle of the night, we crawled out of the tent to relieve our tortured bladders and found ourselves in a different and much more hopeful world — one with a moonlit sky and a breeze portending great change. Soon the morning sun would appear and quickly dry out the soggy hills. And, between the time that it stilled our shivers and later when it produced hot, perspiring foreheads, painful sores from rucksack straps, and parched lips and dusty trails, the sun would be regarded as our best friend.

Recalling that hopeful note of many years ago — I would say at least twenty-five — we fell asleep. When we woke up again, our bodies half-paralyzed by the hardness of the ground, the clouds above us were brighter. By the time we had finished massaging our hands and feet it was dawn. Again we were thankful to the anonymous orderly for another Milky Way. While chewing on them, warmth was slowly returning to our hands and feet and we wondered if Russ had made it back, if he had managed to avoid the patrol boat and the steep slopes of the inlet — if George's insistence on going through to Precarious had not caused Russ Nichols's death.

In a few moments we were on our way again. The sun grew warmer and the spasms of self-serving nostalgia were gone. Then, as we reached the top of the ridge, from a place we knew we could be easily recognized, we shouted across a small ravine to the still, hidden camp. In ten minutes we stood face to face with a two-man patrol, enthusiastically shaking hands with them.

Chapter 22

Force Gamma had been decimated. Within hours of the raid more than half of its members were dead. A skeleton rebel crew had been sent from Camp Alpha to the now empty Camp Gamma to take whatever supplies there were and to burn the rest. It was likely that Liefenbarger had prisoners and more than likely that he could make them talk. To make plans for such an eventuality, George called a special meeting of all camp commanders for the morning after our return.

"There is something else that happened while you were gone that you should know about," said Meg over lunch at the headquarters cabin. Earlier, George had summarized the discussions aboard the *Richard Thompson*. "I don't know how to begin. It's so far-fetched that it almost doesn't make sense. It has to do with McAlpine."

"What about him?"

"There is this new arrival, picked up from a patrol from Camp Chi. His name is Lawrence Saunders. We've kept him here at headquarters because he's pretty special."

"Why?"

"Well, for one thing, he's McAlpine's nephew. His mother is our beloved governor's sister."

"How does he strike you?"

"Young Lawrence? Fine. Just fine. I think he's the genuine article."

"Well, keep a close watch on him," George said.

"Oh, but that isn't all," Meg smiled mysteriously. "It's what he brought with him."

"What did he bring? What are you talking about?"

"He says that dear old uncle Allan is not exactly an enthusiastic Liefenbarger fan. Lawrence Saunders thinks that with a bit of persuasion he could be made to switch sides."

George put down a loaded fork. It literally took his breath away. What was the maxim from his *Chronicles*? "No revolution ever succeeded without the government in power dividing, weakening and finally destroying itself."

He was a tall, finely sculpted youth who at first gave the

impression of being too handsome to be capable of serious thought. Because of it I found myself immediately viewing him with distrust. But Lawrence spoke shyly, softly, and modestly. In answer to the question of what made him come to the mountains, he described his final form class at a fashionable St. Enoch Grammar School. He said it had literally been broken up. Several of his friends had been picked up by the National Unity Corps. Some returned after being warned and threatened, one didn't return at all.

Their parents spoke about nothing of consequence any more and some relatives occasionally disappeared on the Partrawa Plain. For Lawrence himself the extent of his country's degradation was reached when his favorite teacher — a white-haired venerable gentleman who taught history and was only a year away from retirement — suddenly disappeared for a few days. When he returned his face was bruised and his eyes were dulled. Gone was the color, humor, the vitality and wit which had been the hallmark of his lessons. He now read from carefully prepared notes, clearly discouraging any questions. His face at times betrayed numbing fear of someone in the class who had informed on him.

"We've heard about things like that happening in Nazi Germany or Russia, but New Salisbury?" asked Lawrence of no one in particular. "Six of us couldn't stand it any more so we decided to come up here."

Only one of them arrived in the Cheviots though. The least likely to. The rest had fallen by the wayside for a variety of reasons which all boiled down to the fact that when they were faced with the deadly reality of joining a revolution, they couldn't surmount the awesome implications of it. One by one they came up with ingenious excuses, one even persuading himself that the existence of a revolutionary movement in the Cheviots was a myth.

George Titus listened to Lawrence Saunders as if spellbound. The youth told of his uncle who lived in a mansion only a few blocks away from his own home, and about his father who was one of Allan McAlpine's administrative assistants. At noisy dinner parties at the Saunders' residence, McAlpine would arrive from some official reception, complain about the lack of availability of imported cognac, and then launch into a ridicule of Lucius Liefenbarger which was so unabashed that Lawrence's easily frightened mother would begin to reprove him.

Lawrence was careful not to imply that his uncle had ever suggested or even hinted that he might favor the rebels. But he was convinced that this was because he knew so little about them, because he probably suspected that their goal was merely to replace one dictatorship with another.

"To tell you the truth, sir, I'm still not so sure about it myself. We've talked a lot about that part of it with my friends."

The lad's frankness was disarming and George was visibly moved, more than I could remember ever seeing him. Here was a self-avowed realist, a romantic who had made his way to the mountains not because he thought he was not earning enough or because his Fijian vacations had been unduly restricted, but because he felt that the stringency of Liefenbarger's Extraordinary State Act had limited his freedom and robbed his history teacher of his dignity. Lawrence came to the mountains in spite of the fact he had justifiable doubts about us. He came because the land around him was no longer the New Salisbury of his youthful dreams.

There was still doubt in some of our minds as to Lawrence's sincerity, but it also became clear to me that there was really only one possible use for young Lawrence Saunders.

"Outside of the other five, who else knows that you were thinking of coming up here — to the Cheviots?" I asked him.

"My friends...they all know."

That was good, even better than I expected. I said so.

George asked why.

"Because he can go back and tell them that he couldn't find us." I turned to Lawrence: "But make it sound convincing — as if you really changed your mind about being a rebel when you saw the big, snow-capped mountains."

"But why? I want to stay up here. I want to fight."

"Because you are much more valuable at St. Enoch. We can't win this thing without the help of your uncle or someone like him, no matter how many guns and stout-hearted men we have up here. It can't be done. But with you down there we at least have access to the governor. You're more important to us than one hundred gun-toting revolutionaries."

He didn't like it. It was all too quick. For weeks, maybe months, he must have been preparing himself for his decision to come up to the Cheviots. "You want me to organize my friends down there? We could have St. Enoch in our hands even before you got there."

But even here we had to disappoint him. Meg stepped in. "No Lawrence. You must stay clear completely of our people at St. Enoch. Don't take part in any demonstration or Resistance activity. You'll be our contact in the governor's mansion. Our only real hope at the moment."

"Should I talk to him? Tell him who's up here, what's happening?"

"Not right away," said George, now also taken with the idea. "And don't change the way you act too much. If you used to tell jokes about Liefenbarger, keep telling them. But don't get yourself involved in anything so that you end up in jail. That's the last place we need you."

"When do you want me to go back?"

"Right now. Tonight. Tell your family you've spent a couple of nights thinking it over in the foothills. But make sure that you have your story straight. Where you spent each night and what you did. Then go back to school and wait. Wait for us to get in touch."

Lawrence got up. He gathered his things and started toward the door. That's when George got up to shake his hand. "You could very well be the key man, Lawrence. Because of you the Liefenbarger era could come to an end on the Lower Isle."

He thought about it for a moment, then looked at George, a broad grin slowly spreading across his face. He was convinced. "I didn't know being a key man in a revolution could be so boring," he said just before disappearing in the darkness.

Not one of us said a word until I got up, added a couple of pieces of wood to the fire, and stopped before returning to my chair. Finally I shook my head a couple of times in sheer disbelief, and commented, "Goddamn it George, you're turning out to be a helluva leader. Better than expected."

The planes came soon after it got light. There were three of them and they knew exactly where they were going. One after another they passed over the headquarters camp to get the lay of the land, then climbed back into the clouds. That gave us time on the ground to scamper.

Few things were still standing when they had gone. Half of a stone chimney remained, sticking out of the rubble that moments ago had been the headquarters cabin in which George had been sleeping. The radio shack and the dormitory on the other side of the clearing weren't there anymore either. The twisted wreckage of what had been the radio antenna rested on top of the shack's roof. The roof had remained largely intact, now prone on the ground.

Slowly we emerged from the safety of the forest. From the opposite side came Sid Capadouca with a pronounced limp. He had twisted his ankle as he hurriedly left the radio shack where he had been sleeping. We then realized that we had been almost incredibly lucky: in spite of the almost total destruction there had been no casualties.

"Luck, hell," Meg muttered, surveying the damage. "We have friends in the New Salisbury Air Force. I'd say there were at least three minutes between the time they first passed over and when the attack actually started. That's not the way to take advantage of the element of surprise. That's the way to give the people enough time to get the hell out. And at the same time they were still following orders — they just needed time to line it all up."

By noon we had salvaged all that was salvageable and set fire to the rest. Leaving three enormous bonfires behind, we set out toward Camp Delta. It was the nearest camp, but still at least a four-hour brisk walk away.

"Was it that guy Saunders?" asked Sid Capadouca, limping alongside George and me, trying to take some of the weight off his ankle by supporting himself on our shoulders.

George didn't answer, but I did. "Couldn't have been. He only left here late last night, so he couldn't have reached Precarious until this morning. A strike like this takes a bit of preparation. I'd say at least twelve hours."

"So who told them exactly where we were?"

I shrugged my shoulders. "Could've been almost anybody. We've had plenty of people go down into the valley."

"But wouldn't it be too much of a coincidence that they bombed us on the day that Saunders got back?" insisted Sid.

"Coincidence, sure. And two days ago they also got some of the Gamma Force Communists. I'd say that is a lot more suspicious coincidence," said Meg.

Of course. All of us had forgotten.

Sid Capadouca skewed up his face in pain. "Geez, I sure as hell wouldn't wanna fall into their hands alive. They can get anything they want out of you."

"That's if there actually had been any torture," mused Meg. The meaning of what she was saying escaped Sid who was concentrating on his painful ankle. But George must have understood: what better way was there to get rid of uncomfortable leadership than to have the enemy do the job for you? Stalin waited for the Germans to kill off Polish democrats before ordering the Red Army to liberate Warsaw.

I saw George shudder; then he flatly refused to believe it.

Chapter 23

Major John P. Dingwall of the Royal New Salisbury Air Force levelled his grey Skyraider, then once again found the outline of the boat on the horizon. He went into a shallow dive in its direction. At two hundred meters he was still descending and directly opposite, across the ship's bow, he saw another fighter in a dive. At thirty meters he jettisoned his load. The plane, lighter by two torpedoes, sprang upward. As he completed a half turn he levelled off, looking over his right shoulder at the billowing cloud of pungent grey smoke.

With relief he counted the three dots in the sky behind him. Everyone was safe. Then the smoke had cleared enough to see that most of the eight torpedoes must have hit. There was nothing but a patch of debris spinning in what seemed like a violent whirlpool.

In the east, Major Dingwall already saw the laboring, clumsy Catalina putting down into the calm water, leaving behind a trail of white foam. It was all taking place so beautifully on cue, thought Major Dingwall, as if in some carefully prepared documentary on air power.

The Catalina stopped not too far from where the boat had been. Four men quickly inflated an enormous rubber raft, then started making their way toward the debris, scooping up the larger pieces. When they finished their job, they loaded the debris inside the Catalina and deflated the raft. One of the men looked up and waved to the circling planes, which replied by dipping their wings.

The Catalina then maneuvered into the wind for takeoff while the Skyraiders assembled in formation above it, heading east, toward the coast.

Anatoly Blavatsky's appearance on the colorful canvas of New Salisbury's revolution is fairly ephemeral. He was an asthmatic, unimaginative, perfect Party Man. Also the wrong man at the wrong time in the wrong place when it came to minding the Soviet embassy in N.S. City. Late April was the time of highly flexible big-power policies in relation to the Lief, a time when almost anything seemed negotiable. The Lief was flexing his muscles and it was important that it be correctly assessed just how justified he was in doing that. Blavatsky was singularly unequipped for the job.

On April 24th his large frame was inserted in a chair at the Royal Towers building where Liefenbarger had taken over a floor under the cover of the National Resources Bureau. Blavatksy had been summoned there for an urgent conference with the Administrator. The Russian, of course, had no idea what it was all about. That brought on a mild asthma attack which he tried to relieve by periodically inhaling a decongestant. Copithorne found the sweating, obese Russian humorous, the presence of his political watchdog Chubar preposterous. Shortly after 10 A.M., he ushered them both into Liefenbarger's presence.

Liefenbarger had taken to wearing his uniform now, usually with its collar open to avoid any suggestions of pompousness which he found so distasteful in Ormsby. According to Copithorne, the Lief "projected an image of strength, of almost God-like invincibility." While that observation may be debatable and attributable largely to Copithorne's adulation of the Lief at that time, there was no doubt that the Lief emanated strength. The Russians in their ill-fitting suits — the sweating Blavatsky and the cowering Chubar — were certainly on the defensive.

But their defenses were further weakened when Liefenbarger unceremoniously threw Chubar out, sardonically remarking that this was not meant to be a social chat. Blavatsky and Copithorne had conversed in English before this; the argument that Chubar was needed as an interpreter was negligible.

Without witnesses Blavatsky must have felt deplorably naked even in front of what he considered to be nothing but a two-bit fascist dictator. They had never met before. The Soviets had recalled their ambassador in protest over the Lake Ormatoro slaughter and the First Secretary Blavatsky had been serving as a chargé d'affaires. Quite likely he must have been convinced that this new job would consist only of keeping the fifty-strong contingent at the Soviet embassy in line.

Blavatsky seemed uneasy because as yet he had no idea what his country's policy toward the Lief would be — it had not been decided on. Some fairly vicious attacks on the Lief had appeared in the Soviet press, but similar views had also appeared in *The New York Times*. To compound what constitutes for any Russian such dreadful uncertainty, the Americans were supplying the rebels in the mountains and at the same time promising to arm the New Salisbury government.

Were it not for the oil in the Thames River Delta, Soviet attitudes would have been fairly easy to predict. The Lief was a fascist reactionary; one of those petty, posturing dictators whose carcasses filled history's garbage pails to the brim. On the other hand, if Liefenbarger was judged by Moscow as able to survive the rebels, the oil would remain his and some sort of an accommodation would then be necessary.

After Chubar's departure the Lief asked Blavatsky to sit down. There was no introduction, just a stunning accusation from the Administrator which must have sent Blavatsky reeling:

Lief: "We are disturbed, shocked and greatly annoyed by your country's arrogance. We find the fact that you would not hesitate to engage in waging a naval battle in our territorial waters to be utterly deplorable."

Blav: "I do not understand — "

Lief: "Your country's cruiser, the *Admiral Timshi... Admiral Timoshenko,* has been cruising off the western coast of the Lower Isle for days now. Until yesterday we didn't know why. Now we do know."

Blav: "I do not understand. I am not usually informed about my country's ships — where they are, what they are doing."

Lief: "Do you deny that your country's cruiser this morning sunk an Australian fishing ship called the *Constant* because the *Constant* was in reality an electronics detection ship keeping track of the Marxist rebels in the Cheviot Hills?"

Blav: "Of course. It is nonsense. Why not have the Australians themselves protested?"

Lief: "Because the Australians have no proof. We do."

Blav: "I do not see how — "

Lief: "Mr. Blavatsky, this is not some American courtroom drama. Everything here points the blame to your country's cruiser, the *Admiral Timoshenko.* Twenty-five men are dead."

(At this point Blavatsky must have had at least a vague idea of what it was all about. Had the *Constant* been sunk in New Salisbury's waters, Liefenbarger would have been expected to protest. He was doing it now.)

Blav: "My country's government categorically denies sinking any vessel in or out of New Salisbury's territorial waters. Is that all?"

(Now the Russian was really aroused. Unilaterally terminating an audience cannot be considered as anything but a gross insult to a head of government. Quite probably it was meant to be just that.)

Lief: "We will be protesting officially in writing. I think you will appreciate the fact we consider this flagrant breach of international law and common decency to be extremely serious."

Blav: "It *is* a very serious matter — for those who have fired on the *Constant*, Mr. Liefenbarger."

On the same morning another character in New Salisbury's revolutionary drama made her first appearance. Ann Schorez, the chic first secretary of the U.S. embassy, had been at her job for several months. Only after Lattimore's return from the USS *Richard Thompson* did the U.S. ambassador fully realize just how complicated the whole situation had become and he sought help.

The natural choice was Ann — the ambitious, thirty-five-year-old native of Lynchburg, Virginia; a graduate of the prestigious Sweetbriar College. She had already served at the embassies in Tokyo and Moscow, collected accolades and promotions, and eventually became convinced that she was destined not only for an important ambassadorial post, but later for something even among the policy makers in Washington. The fluid situation in New Salisbury was a godsend for directing attention to herself.

As she sat alongside Lattimore in a waiting room inside the Parliamentary Building in her tailored suit, her shapely legs supporting an attaché case, she anxiously glanced at the clock which indicated they had been waiting for almost an hour.

The Lief had staged the charade beautifully, exhorting the wheezing Blavatsky in the stark surroundings of the Royal Towers for sinking the *Constant* and at the same time keeping Lattimore and Ann Schorez incommunicado in the much more opulent milieu of the Parliamentary Building. While the business-oriented, aluminum-trimmed air of the Royal Towers promised no mercy, the Persian-carpeted mahogany-panelled ambience of the Parliament Building suggested an amiability and warmth. Shortly after ten-thirty the news about the disappearance of the *Constant* reached the U.S. embassy in N.S. City. It is unlikely that it was immediately clear just what had happened; nevertheless, it was imperative for the ambassador to be informed-of it. A messenger arrived at the Parliament Building, but he was no match for Copithorne's interceptors who quickly directed him into another wing. There he cooled his heels, waiting for Lattimore and Ann Schorez who, quite unaware of his presence, were waiting for the audience across the courtyard.

When Liefenbarger did arrive at the Parliament Building shortly before eleven, he had already skillfully transposed himself from Mr. Hyde to a very urbane and charming Dr. Jekyll. Profuse apologies for his tardiness were offered, but without any clear explanation of it. Copithorne, the great connoisseur of the chameleon's art, must have been thrilled by his master's performance.

Quite unlike the very clear tape of the Blavatsky audience, the recording of the Lattimore-Schorez-Liefenbarger conversation is frequently unintelligible. There is no doubt that the entire interview had been conducted in highly informal manner. In the middle of all the introductory mirth, the Lief complimented Ann Schorez on her looks, even engaged in some light flirting. At times Lattimore must have felt a bit superfluous, particularly due to his fairly straight-laced nature.

The Lief apologized once again, this time for summoning the ambassador over on such short notice. Lattimore replied graciously that he was honored to be there and that he hoped every moment of their discussions would prove immensely profitable to both their nations.

"Yes, we would like to keep each other informed — as allies, of course," the Lief emphasized the last word especially.

Copithorne poured coffee from the famous heavy silver service and the conversation lagged for a few moments as a result. Refreshments then taken care of, the Lief started.

"Well, now, Mr. Lattimore, I understand you have been out of the country a few days."

Lattimore must have gulped a bit. It was like being caught with one's hand smack in the middle of the cookie jar.

"Yes, I was in New Zealand. In Wellington. We had a sort of a regional ambassadorial conference of people in this area."

"Ah yes, but Mr. Coulter, your ambassador from Canberra, wasn't there — was he?"

And Lattimore had no choice but to admit aloud that Coulter hadn't, and that the so-called regional conference actually included only himself and the New Zealand man. The Lief possibly knew much more except that he was far too clever a man to let him know just how much more. The Lief then explained that the New Salisbury government had been entrusted with the responsibility of providing for the safety of all diplomats on the islands, and that in the future he would appreciate being apprised of Lattimore's whereabouts at all times so that proper security measures could be taken.

And then, suddenly, the slightly ominous Liefenbarger was transformed again into a kindly uncle who enjoyed caring for his children. There followed some comments about the quality of the cake they were eating. The Lief asked jovially if American diplomats were instructed in cooking and quite in the spirit of the joviality Ann replied that this was expected to have been part of their general education before entering the foreign service. The Lief then offered her a job and a promotion to New Salisbury's chief cook. Ann graciously declined the honor, instead extending an invitation to New Salisbury's Administrator to come to dinner at the embassy, promising that she would prepare some typically southern dishes. The Lief smilingly accepted and changed the subject once again, this time to the *Constant*.

Lattimore, promptly and quite logically under the circumstances, pleaded ignorance about the name and the Lief apologized for not explaining properly. He said it was a fishing boat registered in Australia that for some time now had been cruising off the Lower Isle's western coast with an unusual amount of electronic gear aboard. New Salisbury's intelligence service thought it was also capable of landing helicopters.

"I'm sorry sir, but I still don't understand. If it's Australian —" Ann Schorez started.

"Well, yes, it is Australian. But in the opinion of our intelligence people it is also engaged in tracing the movements of the Marxist terrorists in the Cheviot Hills. As a fishing boat it is, of course, perfectly within its rights to operate in our waters. We have a reciprocal agreement with Australia on that. And we also certainly understand the Australians' concern over international terrorists who are camped in our mountains. It should be of great concern to everyone in the Pacific region, shouldn't it? That suicidal raid on Fort Wellington just a few days ago should cure us once and for all of all our tendencies toward complacency."

Some inconsequential variations on the same theme followed and then Lief offered further explanations: "No, we're certainly not opposed to the Australian initiative. On the contrary, it serves to strengthen our own resolve. But unless there is a clearer understanding between the Australians and ourselves, there is the grave danger that mistakes will be made. Mistakes that could cost lives. A few days ago one of our patrol boats in the Precarious Inlet fired at a helicopter which was apparently lost and had violated our airspace. Fortunately the gun crew was stopped by an alert officer before any damage was done. Thank God ... but the incident only underlies the necessity for some formal understanding between us. After all, the Precarious Inlet is really one of the important gateways to the mountains."

"We understand your concern sir," said Lattimore, "but how could the United States possibly — "

"Yes... that, of course, is the crux of the whole problem. Let me explain. We feel that contacting the Australians directly might give them the impression we are somehow trying to chastise them, that we are demanding that they give account of themselves and of their presence in our waters. That is, of course, far from our intentions. We are simply worried that a supposedly unarmed fishing vessel in our territorial waters, which is clearly monitoring the movements of the terrorists, is also quite likely to provoke the terrorists' sponsors — the Soviets. The South Pacific, as you know, is full of Soviet warships..."

Lattimore and Ann Schorez couldn't have had much of an inkling just where he was heading. The messenger from the embassy could have cleared a few things up for them, but he was still seated in the waiting room across the courtyard, wondering why it was all taking so long. When Lattimore reluctantly agreed that the U.S. would act as an intermediary between New Salisbury on the subject of the *Constant,* he of course had no idea that at that moment the *Constant* was already resting at the bottom of the ocean, not far from the International Date Line, with twenty-five bodies inside its hull.

Nor did the U.S. ambassador know yet that in the cunning eyes of the Lief he had performed superbly. There is no doubt in my mind that the Lief had carefully rehearsed his performance that morning, down to some of the key lines he had delivered to Blavatsky and Lattimore. His performance, of course, had not constituted an ironclad alibi. Not by a long shot. On the other hand, it came about as close to such a thing as one is apt to get in international politics.

Chapter 24

Based on the information brought by Meg, George decided it was time to project an even stronger image for the masses. This was accomplished through the use of a fawning photographer who accompanied him everywhere, capturing such scenes as George Supervising the Construction of a Cabin, George Monitoring the News of the World on the Shortwave Radio Set, George in Rapt Conversation with Camp Leaders, George Having His Breakfast and George Bedding Down.

The idea was to whip up revolutionary enthusiasm in the lowlands, but there was also great need for such a campaign in the Cheviots, now sprinkled with the first snow and hardened by first frosts. Some of our people started drifting back into the lowlands. It wasn't anything catastrophic yet, but our group was down to about a hundred and seventy. Two camps had to be abandoned — the Nu and the Delta — because they became too inaccessible in wintertime. Only a trickle of supplies had arrived since the sinking of the *Constant*. The perennially cloudy skies dictated high-level drops that were not nearly as accurate as the low-level ones.

There had been a near mutiny at the badly led Camp Psi over some food rations, and George wisely closed that one down too, dispersing its people among other camps. Snow started to fall more frequently and by the beginning of May the general mood in the mountains was perilously close to sheer despondency.

It was not at all helped by the sudden arrival in our midst of a group of Fort Wellington survivors led by John Leahy — Baracolli, Vic Channing and John Tolway.

"We have no idea where the others are — probably dead," Leahy tiredly answered George's first question. He told how the four of them after the assault had reached a friend's house in Devon, how they then realized that their escape route to the mountains had been cut off, and how they had been frequently forced to change their hiding places as the searches intensified. Then, inexplicably, the searches stopped. It was as if the National Unity Corps had either given up or come to the conclusion that the entire Force Gamma had perished in the wilderness. The four men slowly made their way to the mountains.

They went in to eat and I grabbed George by the arm, leading him up the path above the camp where he had often walked together. "How now brown cow?" I asked. "What're we going to do about this plant?"

"About what?"

"The boys from Algeria. The ones that seem to survive everywhere and everything — they'd probably manage to strike a deal with the SS guards while undressing for the gas chambers. The naughty boys who disobey your orders because they are bushwa orders and contrary to the dogmas of the class struggle...what will you do about them?"

George sighed. "How do you know that they're planted?"

"How the hell have they survived without being captured and how have they managed to make their way up here? Remember Lenin and the sealed car in 1917?"

"That's a very poor historical analogy."

"Oh, is it? Then what about the levelling of the headquarters camp?"

"We have no proof that it was connected with them."

"George: if we keep waiting for definite proof it will be in the form of a noose around our necks. That's the god-awful truth."

"And if we start acting on suspicions and hunches we might as well bury ourselves. We're trying to keep this movement united — we already know how to splinter it."

George met with them, but he did it alone. In the end they too were dispersed. There was some grumbling that they were guilty of gross insubordination and of acting against specific orders, and opinions were voiced that they should be tried in some way. But here George was right: he really had only two options. One was to banish them, and the other was to accept them without any recriminations. A court-martial of some sort would have certainly split us right down the middle. It would have been an exercise in inflaming emotions, not in judicial procedure. The simple fact is that to this day no one knows for sure if the four of them had been sent by the NUM. No proof exists either favoring or discounting the theory.

But there is still no doubt in my own mind as to the existence of this misalliance.

That same night one of those increasingly rare moments

occurred when George wanted to talk with someone who would not be hanging on his each and every word. That night George had succumbed to nostalgia mixed with considerable loneliness. He needed to talk with friends and he was also painfully aware that there weren't that many of them around. There never had been. So I was resurrected for cards. So was Meg, who now lived in the headquarters tent, her bunk separated from George's by only a flimsy partition.

We played rummy for about an hour, drank hot herb tea and talked about nothing memorable. Then, when we had stopped playing, George told us that Leahy had apologized for Fort Wellington, that he explained at the time he had sincerely believed it was time to show the revolutionary flag. Leahy now saw clearly he had been wrong and also that because of his mistake fifteen men had died. But Leahy had also explained that they had expected to die because they realized that this was a revolution, not some academic debating society.

"I've heard it all before, of course," George said. "I've read the same message over and over again in the *Collected Works,* put out on cheap paper by the Moscow State Publishing House. In those pamphlets with a badly reproduced, tasteless picture of Lenin on the front."

And then something totally unexpected happened. Something that — at least for me — for the first time bared another side of George Titus.

He started to tell us about England, about the graduate students at Oxford who would never pass up a good dinner, and for whom he had always managed to wrangle invitations to receptions whenever someone noteworthy visited and George was trotted out because he was a Titus. And at Oxford they occasionally met East Europeans who came there to study, to gain experience, to be able to go back home and boast that they had been abroad. In their square-cut, dark grey suits, they struggled with the language, with currency, with prosperity. Officially — and also unofficially whenever more than one of them was present — they recited dull, endless statistics and casual opinions which sounded suspiciously like printed slogans. The Western academics around them were, however, most forgiving. Theirs was, after all, a new system — as yet without sophistication and tradition.

At a reception for an East European commercial mission, the graduate students had dined and wined with the Bulgarians, who were overnourished and — almost to a man — unilingual. The Slavs stuck together in an unnatural cluster, entertaining themselves in a horseshoe-shaped arrangement of armchairs near the buffet.

But there was also another man — a heavily drinking official of some exporting agency who had come with the delegation but whose mother tongue had been English and who was consequently fully bilingual. He began to circulate, crossing the parqueted floor toward George's group of university-connected people. For a while the wandering Bulgarian listened to some bawdy jokes on the fringes of the group and then, during a lull, grasped his opportunity: "Well, that may all be well and good, my dear fellows," said he in a lilting, decidedly upper-class accent, "but of course the biggest joke is on you, isn't it?"

Unfazed by the hostile glances, he took a sip of his champagne, then introduced himself by some thoroughly unpronounceable name, and finally informed the graduate students that his countrymen had come to see how best to bring about the demise of this dying colonial power. Naturally, the demise was expected to come as predicted, but that also the Eastern bloc was becoming somewhat impatient with such ruddy slow progress toward that end.

"Of course, there *is* a smattering of commercial people among them, but most of them are spies. Well, that's perhaps putting it unduly harshly for the tender ears of the British liberals, but let us say that they are keen students of the various, mostly secret aspects of your national life."

Not one of those around George believed him. Or rather, the whole idea seemed so preposterous by their standards that they quickly decided to ignore it. Instead, they quizzed the bilingual official about the system under which his country operated.

"Make no mistake about it," the Bulgarian in turn totally ignored their generally puerile questions, "Marxism, Communism, Socialism — whatever euphemism you want to use for that type of police state with unlimited powers — is a dead end. It's a brick wall built in the middle of the street to put a stop to all those wanting to travel after their dreams or even toward finding a logical reason for one's existence. But there's one thing the Communists are good at, and that's painting. They have painted such beautiful pictures over those bloody bricks that as long as you stay far enough away you won't notice any wall at all. But from close by it's ugly — so very, very ugly."

George then explained how the Bulgarian's haunted imagery stuck in his mind and how in all this time he was unable to shake it. How it drove him to visiting Russia and Eastern Europe over and over again, hiring interpreters so he could speak with people on the street, fascinated by their tenacious hold on ignorance. He tried to see what it was that made so many people meekly and sometimes even proudly submit to a system that had been so much built on lies and subterfuge.

George finished. We sat in the dimly lit cabin, now silent.

"And how about it — have you figured it out?" Meg finally asked.

George shook his head. "No. When I left Europe it seemed even more confusing, because mere force can't be the answer, at least not in the long run. But I was already working on the *Chronicles* and you can only do so many things — "

It was about a half hour's walk back to my camp that night. On the way I thought about George's Bulgarian story and started to realize that George had thereby lost the excuse that so many North American academics regularly but largely unknowingly claimed in regard to practical Communism: the excuse of total ignorance.

Chapter 25

Things got even worse as the bleakness of winter settled on the mountains with its awful aura of permanence. Because there hadn't been much snow we kept in touch between camps fairly well, but there was precious little contact with the outside. Communications with the Americans at Christchurch were now limited to a few seconds of identifying signals each morning.

More of our people started making their way down into the lowlands; a few, we suspected, had tried to reach Precarious, but the village was now occupied by an NUC detachment. To elude patrols in its vicinity, one had carefully circle it, then start another arduous journey across the ridge south of the village. An easier route down was eastward, toward the now deserted and gutted Camp Gamma and from there down to the plain south of Marsbury. But even there the NUC had increased its patrols. No one knew exactly what was happening to those who were captured, but it was safe to assume that their end was neither quick nor painless.

In the middle of May we completed the count: there were now five active camps with greatly reduced contingents. Barely one hundred rebels remained in the mountains and winter had not yet struck in full force.

The very next day, however, something happened that raised our morale enormously. The regular morning transmission from Christchurch included a weather forecast, supposedly for Cape Adare which, when deciphered, advised us to be at the southern shore of Lake Mawusituki at noon the following day. The lake was some fifteen kilometers away. We followed a trail that took us three-fourths of the way and finished the journey along a streambed which fed into the lake.

Ten of us were on our way long before sunrise. The trail hadn't been used since the summer and progress was slow. We wondered just why we had been summoned. Obviously the Americans wanted to establish contact again. But how? Perhaps a small plane would try to land on the frozen lake. Maybe a few of them would try to land together, or three or four Sikorski S-61s would try and bring in supplies without actually landing. There could also be parachutes.

Lake Mawusituki had a thin blanket of snow over the ice. I judged it to be five to seven kilometers long before it turned out to be almost ten. The south shore was generally rocky and bleak except for some patches of thick bush. In the north the lake washed against a sheer wall of forbidding rock rising into a craggy mountain range. The mountains were slightly lower on the lake's two other sides, but any approach with a fixed-wing plane would have to be made from the south.

Seconds before noon two jet fighters made a pass over the area, swooping high and settling into a holding pattern of figure-eights; only the vapor showed that they were there. No American bases were within their range — they must have been Navy planes from an aircraft carrier and this realization had a heartening significance for us. The days when the Americans were under orders not to defend themselves even when fired on were obviously now over. After the sinking of the *Constant* such sensitivity to international niceties must have completely disappeared.

Shortly after the appearance of the jets, the whole area started to reverberate with deep, hollow sounds of laboring engines. What eventually emerged, seemingly vaulting over the low hills in the south, was an enormous Lockheed Hercules with its black nose immediately dropping much lower once it had cleared the hills, wafting over us near the clumps of bushes, its flaps down and steadily losing altitude so that when it reached the lake it was only meters above its frozen surface.

Knowing that in the next moment its enormous weight must crack the ice, I wanted to shout to the pilot to pull up, pull up for God's sake. But just then I realized that the Americans were no fools. One by one the striped parachutes fluttered in the plane's immense airwash, like a magician's trick pulling out of its fat belly pallet after pallet with supplies that settled on the lake's surface with a sharp, crackling sound, heard even above the roar of the engines.

Halfway down the lake, now speckled with giant bales, the plane banked to the left, managing to complete its full 180 degrees of turn long before it reached the mountain. Then it was gone, its impressive show now over. But for a while we crouched in the bushes, still awed by the gorgeous efficacy of it all.

Then someone started to clap, then another and still

another. Until all of us there, our beaming faces turned to the sky, were shouting and jumping up and down in noisy delight which crassly disturbed the placid wilderness around us.

Just as we reached the first bale, it became clear that the impressive show was not yet over. The Hercules appeared again, this time much higher and still climbing toward the sun which emerged from behind the high, scattered clouds. Out of its rear door fluttered another parachute — this time with a figure dangling at the end of it. The plane then made its way back toward the ocean, its escorts once more painting long stripes across the sky.

Not far from the bushy southern shore the figure landed and rolled gamely with the parachute before he skillfully got up to collapse it. Then he folded it neatly into a bundle, waiting for us who were on our way toward him to reach him. But, standing in front of us, was a stout woman of about fifty, dressed in U.S. Army fatigues. On her head there was a fur hat with its flaps tied underneath her chin, in shape and style somewhat resembling that favored by Quebec's *habitants*. She also wore a touch of lipstick and her fleshy face broke into a smile that strongly suggested a sense of humor as well as wisdom.

"Hi. Rose Kubatan from the *Washington Post*...I hope I'm not too late for the revolution?" She stripped off a colorful, hand-knitted mitten and extended a hand toward George. She flickered her eyelashes at him.

"A journalist?" the disappointed Branko Justac asked. "We were hoping for a heavy weapons expert."

But by the time he finished asking, Rose Kubatan already had her arm around George's shoulders, marching him in the direction of an as yet unknown destination, constantly explaining: "Nothing to worry about, all the stuff in these CARE packages has lots of instructions packed in with it. And I don't require much care — as you see I don't eat much and I've brought my own sandwiches anyway."

"You realize you can't leave here until spring now?" George finally got a word in edgewise.

"That's all right, they know where I am. It's a slow season for news anyway. It's summer back home. Washington is hell in June. Come to think of it it's not too nice in July and August either, and the rest of the year isn't much of an improvement. I'm really much better off here — much better off."

The black tarpaulin-covered giant bales contained fresh

food and vegetables, clothing, and some arms and ammunition. There were two snowmobiles, several canisters of gasoline, also radio equipment and snowshoes. But most welcome was the last bale, the one nearest to the center of the lake. It contained mail, piles of newspapers, magazines and books.

The immediate task was to get the stuff into the bushes and out of the prying eyes of government planes which flew regularly over the area. Our providers had foreseen our problem: the pallets on which the bales rested were actually sleighs. The snowmobiles regretfully had to be left behind because there wasn't yet enough snow on the ground for their use. But we divided some of the food and all of the mail among ourselves, filling our backpacks with it. As the sun started to set we were on our way back to camp.

The wind started to pick up. Even with the approaching darkness we could see heavy clouds crawling into the sky. The weather was changing and we hurried to be out of its reach.

We almost succeeded. The blizzard struck in full force about half an hour away from camp and we took almost three hours to cover the distance. Still, we were thankful that by then we were out of the open country, sheltered from the howling winds and pin-like snowflakes. At midnight we staggered back into camp, dead tired, answering in monosyllables the hundreds of questions with which we were immediately showered. Rose Kubatan took off her coat and watched all the excitement from a few feet away — in her mind she must have been filing her first story.

Chapter 26

By next morning the snowstorm had tapered off into intermittent flurries and George called a general meeting for that
evening. In the meantime we built a gigantic fire in the hearth
of the newly completed headquarters cabin. Then we made a
pot of tea, into which Rose Kubatan poured generous amounts
of rum from her silver filigreed flask.

She had already told George about her telephone conversation with his wife Kathy. His family was fine. Then she reported on her talk with Garbeau in Hawaii. Nothing new
there — the test was still in progress and he sincerely hoped
that we would pass it.

Rose also brought a letter for George from his dean at the
University of British Columbia which stated he was being
advised that the reasons for his absence had not been
adequately explained and that he was therefore suspended
according to some regulation which must have sounded awesome in Vancouver but was positively hilarious in the central
Cheviots. George remarked that he could almost hear the
horrified sighs of his concerned colleagues who must have
regarded his foresaking of tenure and of the accompanying
pension as the first sign of raving insanity.

In the evening the headquarters cabin filled to capacity. I
was surprised. Of course I had heard of Rose Kubatan, but I
hadn't expected that so many others had as well. But having
heard of her was probably not that important. Most of all she
was a new face — a foreign journalist who had dropped from
the sky by parachute because she considered such stunts to be
well worth the trouble. That was fascinating.

At the start of the meeting someone asked why she came.

"Jesus, I was wondering about the same thing, looking
down through that plane's asshole yesterday, with you milling
around down here like cockroaches and all that goddamn
wilderness everywhere. And now I know: If you're successful,
if you manage to topple Liefenbarger, you'll be the first rebels
since 1776 to bring in a democratic government. That
would be quite an event in this totalitarian world of ours and I

want to be right here when it happens. And please notice I say *when* it happens, not *if*... By the way, you *are* still in favor of democracy, aren't you Dr. Titus?"

George smiled and got right into the spirit of the thing. "Democracy forever: Yesterday, today and tomorrow!"

"Well, that's good, then the whole dreadful effort of mine has not been in vain. You see, I've become something of an expert on revolutions. I've covered Fidel in the Oriente province, marched with him into Havana, and counted the bodies produced by his firing squads. Then on to greater gory glories with the Khmer Rouge to Phnom Penh and with the Popular Movement to Luanda. And we shot hordes of imperialist lackey swine and anyone else who showed signs of getting in the way. We cut down all the Khmers who were not Rouge and all the errant Ovimbundus, Kimbundus and Bacongos. It sure was hard work keeping all these revolutions pure, but the boys stuck with it and today you have all these snow white, er, righteous regimes in Africa, Asia and in the Caribbean. Everywhere. Now that the dust has settled down though, the picture is not exactly the way lots of people imagined it would be. Particularly if those doing all the imagining are the dead ones and those living in jail or exile."

The fire crackled in the hearth and Rose Kubatan had obviously acquired an audience paying rapt attention. She pointed to George. "I saw the piece that ass Sahota wrote about you. And right then and there, reading about George Titus, Superstar, I began to suspect that you really were up to something big. But for reasons that Sahota couldn't possibly understand.

"So I went to Hannah Arendt to make sure. You guys — and gals — are on the threshold of something so big and profound that it blows one's mind. No, I mean it. The question of winning here is much more important than just the future of New Salisbury or even the South Pacific. If you manage to lick Liefenbarger, you'll have transformed the Jeffersonian democrats of this world from a whimpering, apologetic bunch of fatalists into a thundering herd of dynamoes. And that hasn't happened since the end of World War II."

"Who is this Hannah Arendt?" I asked.

"Was. She's dead. A philosopher," explained Rose. "Maybe more of a practical political thinker, actually. There was nothing airy fairy about her. She was a German Jew. Came to the U.S. in the 1940s, had lots to say about totalitarianism, the nature of evil, the human condition — things like that. But her most famous book — on revolution — wasn't exactly high on the hit parade with the university profs who taught political science."

"Is that right, George? Did you really ignore poor Hannah?" Meg asked.

"Not entirely. But Miss Kubatan has a point."

Rose paused to relight her cigarillo and in the process caught sight of George lighting his pipe. Her eyes lit up. "Aah, so there really is a meerschaum. I thought it was only something that the P.R. boys at the State Department thought up. Good for you. I take it you have the famous corduroy cap as well?"

"I do."

"Excellent, I must remember to downplay it all greatly. It has always been my policy to give the masses a lot of what they need and as little of what they want as possible. That way you make them whopping mad and thereby manage to hold their undivided attention."

It was more than enough to start a highly animated discussion. Rose Kubatan was a roaring success. I remember thinking, we must bring in more acts like her. George wasn't totally convinced, though. Rose was, I suspect, a bit too much of an emancipated woman for his taste and while he was able to deal with the younger version of the type — something like Meg, who was now his constant and very intimate companion — he found it all very confusing in a woman of Rose's age. She was, after all, in her early fifties.

Shortly before midnight we started to disperse. George dropped a greeting here, a remark there, until everyone had left, except for a small group consisting of the three Justacs, Sid Capadouca, Meg, George, Rose and me. Rose then lit another cigarillo and without the slightest preamble opened up a totally new subject.

"I take it Leahy is safe with you here, right?"

"He was here tonight. In the back row — nicely hidden," I said.

"Well, then keep him. Put some nice warm clothes on him, then put him into the cradle and rock him gently, making sure that he's nice and comfy. Because you're gonna need him."

"For what? He's a bas — " I started.

"Tut tut, becalm yourself, sir," smiled Rose. "Granted that he's a slippery eel, sometimes a barracuda. But unless you have a democratic spectrum you can't have a democracy. The trick is to keep the middle strong enough so that the left can't gnaw through it. It's a good idea to have an extreme right too, but you won't have it for a while after you march into N.S. City and string up Lucius Liefenbarger. Because he's pretty much it. And it'll take a little while after you do the stringing before all the other little Liefs dare to crawl out of their holes again. That's only natural."

George remained silent, but he followed the conversation with avid interest.

"You know about the Fort Wellington raid?" Meg asked. "Two-thirds of the Algerian group were killed in it."

"Not really. At least not according to the information that Lattimore keeps sending to Washington. The intelligence boys think that three, at the most four, of the Algerians have been killed. It's not clear just where the rest are — if they've escaped on their own, are hiding or if they're in Liefenbarger's jails. Maybe they've even been let loose so that the National Unity Corps could see whom they're talking to. What does Leahy say?"

"Nothing. He says he doesn't know what happened to the rest."

Rose Kubatan sighed. "As expected. But you must admit that without him this whole revolution business would get pretty tedious, wouldn't it? He represents the ye olde irritant. Without Iago, Othello would've been an awful bore of a Moor. Of course, the idea is not to let him get too close to you. Old King David said it rather nicely in the 55th Psalm:

> My companion stretched out his hand
>   against his friends,
>   he violated his covenant.
> His speech was smoother than butter,
>   yet war was in his heart;
>   his words were softer than oil
>   yet they were drawn swords.

"I've looked that up. Rather gives weight to my copy, don't you think? I believe the Bible will figure prominently in all my copy from now on."

"What does Garbeau really think? Does he think that we can handle Leahy?" I asked.

Rose thought about it, taking a couple of deep puffs on her cigarillo. "I don't think they would've risked the Hercules if he didn't. Of course, it isn't Garbeau who will ultimately decide. The supplies will have to start appearing on accounting sheets and at that point congressional committees will get involved. There are some business interests lightly lobbying against you already because they're doing business with Liefenbarger and he is complaining. And Garbeau, you should know, is part of a new program which is at best so far experimental. Usually operations like yours are handled by the CIA. Because of the CIA's fairly recent indisposition and because there are some other complications and embellishments involved, it's the State Department's show this time. But such a change of policy isn't inscribed in stone anywhere. It's just something they want to try out for a while and any day Garbeau may be replaced by some double-oh-seven type. That's something to keep in mind. And then there's the oil. Oil has a strange effect on people. It makes them jettison things. Moral principles go first."

"You're quite a cynic, aren't you?" George asked with a mild smile on his face. But Rose wasn't smiling when she answered. Like all doubters about human values who expressed their doubts via irony, she considered herself a supreme realist, not a cynic.

"All right, consider this: it was oil that smothered Biafra and effectively erased all public concern afterwards. It's oil that makes us treat mediaeval Saudi Arabia and the sheiks on the Peninsula as if they were our equals. Some people believe it's the lack of any coherent energy policy — that's really a very nice euphemism for yes we have no oil today. Oil has changed the once almighty dollar into an insignificant piece of paper. Do you think that oil couldn't stop a hundred men playing at Valley Forge in the New Salisbury mountains?"

"Look, we've heard about Hannah Arendt and Kenneth Garbeau," George tried to defuse the argument. "Now, what do *you* think about our chances?"

Rose stared thoughtfully at the fire crackling in the hearth. "All right, I'll tell you what I think," she finally said. "I don't think that any goddamn revolution is going to be won up here in the mountains. All that you have been doing so far is gathering the lore which will eventually make its way into primary readers and wide-screen movies. Which is pretty important but by no means indispensable, because we all know that whenever necessary, history can be made to look like anything you want. It can be kneaded like dough, I once heard some unusually inspired critic of Marxist thought propound.

Your dramatics up here are also important because they will fire the imagination of a few wide-eyed romantics down there. I wouldn't count on them too much, though, because if that's all it takes, they can easily be fired in any other direction. And, of course, the Cheviots are a handy staging area from which you can come marching down in full battle gear, with dust on your tunics and a gleam in your eye. Great stuff — full of macho glory and blood and guts — the steel jaws and dignified determination. Righteous and fully justifiable wrath.

"But only if you're actually marching down. *Fighting* your way down would be considerably more messy. To prevent the need for fighting you need an extensive organization down there — at St. Enoch, Muldoon and in Castlereagh. You've got lots of sympathy down there, and you, George Titus, have a lot of personal appeal coupled with the admiration for your father and his times. But an organization you haven't got. At least not yet. There is no coordination. None. Before I came up here I spent a couple of weeks on both islands. And that's what I saw."

It took a few moments to sink in. Then Meg spoke up.

"She's right. We're hoping for some sort of a miracle in the spring. There won't be any. We've got to start organizing, George. They've got to be ready down there. Just surviving up here isn't enough anymore."

We all went to sleep on it. Rose was heady stuff. Also a bit disturbing. But I liked her from the start. Her antics and the uncanny amount of information she carried in her head were fascinating. I suspect, though, that to George she constituted something else: an avid fan of the game who was, nevertheless, comfortably seated in a special box in the audience. Theoretically, she was under his command. But only theoretically and definitely temporarily.

In the morning when I was ready to start back to my own camp, I stopped off at the headquarters cabin to say goodbye to George. But Meg was there also, saying goodbye because she was going back into the lowlands to start organizing. George was naturally not too enthusiastic but he was hard pressed to come up with an alternative.

"But they know you down there. They'll — " I started to say.

"Big deal, so I'll dye my hair and make myself look like a man. That's no problem. It's not as if the Lief had the greatest sleuths in the world manning the NUC outposts, is it?"

George's manner plainly showed that he was afraid for her. Terrified. But I couldn't think of a thing more to say. There was no doubt that she was by far the most logical one to be going.

Early in June, Paul Felstad's A-I Unit was officially designated as the First Royal Anti-Insurgency Regiment and Felstad himself was promoted to a full colonel. The occasion was marked by an impressive full dress parade with the presentation of the new regimental colors and an inspection of the Unit at St. Enoch by the Administrator himself. In tow were Eddie Mayfield, General Ormsby, and practically everyone in N.S. City who carried any military or political clout.

More significant, however, were the exchanges that took place afterwards aboard the Boeing 727 that flew over the Cheviots, piloted part of the time by Copithorne, with McAlpine and Felstad pointing out the areas probably infested by the rebels. Ormsby felt obliged to comment that the whole exercise was superfluous because the rebels wouldn't be there in the spring anyway.

The Administrator then somewhat tiredly explained to those seated around him that he hoped the rebels would not pick up and go too early, because they would then disperse into the cities and become difficult to track down. Much more advantageous would be a situation in which the half-frozen, demoralized rebels could be found in their mountain lairs in the spring and then liquidated once and for all.

Ormsby uneasily replied that he understood what the Lief meant, but Liefenbarger must have doubted it. Ormsby was a Sandhurst man who had seen only very limited action in Korea as a young subaltern. Since then he had acquired a paunch and a penchant for electronic gadgets but little else. He was thoroughly incapable of deductive reasoning. It may have been this simplistic approach that had once so endeared him to his officers and troops.

Later, when everyone else had sat down again, Mayfield managed to maneuver himself into a seat across the aisle from the Lief. Next to the Administrator sat Copithorne who pretended to be dozing off but who was in fact listening very attentively to the conversation. Later he recorded it verbatim in his diaries:

May: "Look, Lucius, I've been thinking. We've been trying to run the National Unity Corps from two places — from

Main Island and from the Lower Isle as well. And it just can't be done."

Lief: "Why not?"

May: "Well, because that way we can't respond immediately. We just have to be right there when we're called."

Lief: "Haven't we been? I thought the Fort Wellington operation was quite a success."

May: "That's only one instance. O.K. But suppose the terrorists strike at three places at the same time. Suppose an effective response requires a hell of a lot more coordination."

Lief: "Then we'll still require expert assessment from the Lower Isle. Eddie, these people down here know their island. For God's sake, let them be more helpful."

May: "McAlpine is no soldier. He knows nothing about the military — "

Lief: "McAlpine's tremendously popular. He's trusted by the people on the Lower Isle. He's also a very capable regional administrator and he has always been loyal to the ideas of National Unity."

May: "Fine. Then let him run the administration. The *civilian* administration. What he has now is his own private army."

Lief: "No, no. The Anti-Insurgency Regiment is very much a part of the national armed forces. It's made up of men of the Lower Isle and who have strong emotional ties with the island. It's a potent force. We certainly don't want to tamper with that."

May: "And they can turn on you. Overnight."

Lief: "Even faster than that, Eddie. The idea is not to give them a reason to. We can't hold the Lower Isle by force. Unless we make the people down there feel like they're part of the whole effort, we've lost them for good. And having pride in their own island is very important to them. Very important. That's why we are building up the Anti-Insurgency Unit to regimental strength, promoting Felstad to a full colonel and providing all sorts of incentives: hazardous duty pay, insignia — to show that they're really appreciated."

May: "Then at least do this. Name the Unit the Lucius C. Liefenbarger Regiment and appoint a liaison officer who would come from the National Unity Corps. Will you at least do that?"

Lief: "No. We can't do that, Eddie. I'm not starting a personality cult. Any appointment of an outsider would suggest that we don't trust them, and we do. Eddie: Do you know what your problem is? It's that you are able to think only in terms of the National Unity Corps and military strength. Running a country, even in time of an emergency, is not just shuffling divisions. If it were, all the countries in the world would be run by generals. And damn few of them are."

Copithorne notes that aboard the Boeing the Lief again spoke with him about Ann Schorez. He had met her for the second time at the British High Commissioner's reception on Victoria Day and in the plane he was wondering aloud if he should accept the invitation to the Bonn embassy to celebrate the German Unity Day. And, more importantly, if Ann Schorez was likely to be there.

Later Copithorne landed the Boeing smoothly at St. Enoch Airport and, while bodyguards anxiously scanned the surroundings, the plane was refuelled. The Lief said goodbye to those who were getting off here — to Governor McAlpine, Colonel Felstad and a couple of others. Then the Liefenbarger party got back aboard and the plane taxied to the runway for the takeoff and the journey back to the capital.

While in the limousine on their way back to St. Enoch, the governor told Felstad that the Lief wouldn't hear of changing his directive that all captured rebels should immediately be handed over to the NUC. Felstad became agitated: "Did you mention what it would do to the morale? I mean if they know that the prisoners will be tortured then — "

"Paul, he's aware of all that. I have — "

Horrified, they stared mutely ahead of them where an invisible knife had cut the lead policeman in half. His severed head flew in one direction while his motorcycle skidded and in the next moment lost its decapitated body.

When we heard about the wire strung across the road, it was clear to us in the Cheviots that the insane Guernsey had struck again. It was certainly his brand of revolution.

Chapter 27

The arrival of Rose Kubatan had a decidedly beneficial influence on our situation in the Cheviots. Close on its heels came the inauguration of a regular flight from Christchurch, dropping bales on Mawusituki Lake every week. A new spirit began to fuel the camps. There was now adequate winter equipment for the almost incessant training maneuvers and six new snowmobiles provided a breakthrough in transportation. Eventually we even built a cabin near Mawusituki Lake. It was manned by a three-member patrol so that each arrival of the American Hercules had an immediate, on-the-spot response.

Of course, we realized that the Lief must have had by now at least a general idea where we were, but that only increased our optimism — because he was doing nothing about it.

Rose took advantage of the now frequently foul weather to pump George on all sorts of things. I was present at one such session where the subject was the future — just how exactly George saw the coming New Salisbury. The one without Liefenbarger. Rose asked the questions and also took down the answers verbatim in shorthand.

"In the end what you're really offering is the replacement of Lucius C. Liefenbarger with a George Titus, accompanied with some largely amorphous thing called democracy. The last time *that* system had been tried in New Salisbury it all ended up with Partrawa camps, the National Unity Movement and crude police tactics. How'll it be different this time?"

"Elections. Periodically we hold free elections and in between we have something called the rule of law."

You had to hand it to him — the answer was simple and to the point. Sahota would have probably used it as his lead, but not Rose. She looked up from her pad with a message.

"Mmm...Do you know what it's like holding elections in a revolutionary atmosphere? I saw it in Vietnam. It was a farce. One of the most difficult points for us English-speaking people to grasp is that *we* are the aberration and that the dictatorships and police states are much more the normal thing in the world. *Real* elections are the most fragile of all the democratic paraphernalia. They have to have peace and stability and strong traditions and, most of all, people who want to play fair. If you hold your elections too damn soon you'll get too much fawning from your claque along with an embarrassingly big majority because liberated people tend to deify their liberators. And, if you wait, there'll be a growing temptation not to hold elections at all because as the euphoria evaporates so does the claque's enthusiasm for you. Then there's of course the safest way — eat the cake and have it too: rig the elections."

George thought it over. "What exactly do you want from me, Rose?" he asked after a while. "What's the next question?"

"Well, I'd kinda like to see a blueprint. I guess I'm a print-oriented person as the P.R. boys say. In my business you sort of have to be."

George took a noisy bite on a biscuit, washing it down with a swallow from a cup of steaming coffee he was holding in his other hand. That gave him plenty of time to arrange the answer in his head. Not to think of it, because obviously he had already done that.

"I want a written constitution. And in that constitution I want things like a unicameral parliament, without proportional representation, an elected governor general, an independent and appointed judiciary, a bill of rights, sharply limited police powers and an army under civilian control. I want a strong social program that will guarantee freedom from want but which will not discourage individual initiative. I want equality for females and Polys — socially, economically, culturally. But most of all I want emphasis placed on the little guy. Because somehow between big government, big business and big unions he has been lost. I want to find him and put him on his pedestal where he belongs. I want to say to all those around him that from now on everything they do — and I mean *everything* — must be done primarily for the benefit of that little guy *above* them." He paused, as if suddenly reawakening to where and who he was.

"Or the little gal?"

"Sorry. Sure. The little gal as well."

During the pause we refilled our cups, then settled down again.

"I know where it'll be the toughest," George continued. "We can run Liefenbarger out of the country and we can get rid of the whole NUC thing and muzzle the army again. But it's not the physical institutions. It's our thinking."

"Meaning?"

"Meaning labor strife, for example. We've learned to accept it. Some of us even make sounds as if this was the integral part of our democratic system, all those strikes and lockouts. Something like unalienable rights. But no matter how you look at it, it's all basically a form of blackmail. The very type of thing we consider bad in any other field. It doesn't make sense."

"I had no idea you were such a right winger, Dr. Titus. I mean for a university prof — "

"Don't tell me that you've fallen in the trap too. He doesn't like strikes so he must be right-wing reactionary. That's nonsense pushed by those who consider industrial conflict their bread and butter. And I consider big business to be part of that group too. They actually budget for strikes and lockouts now and consider them as a pretty useful weapon. There isn't any right and left involved any more. That's outdated. What you have now are the big guys — the unions, corporations, the government. Then the little ones — the working stiffs, the small business operator and the pensioner — in the end he is the independent, thinking, creative kind of a guy who must be the backbone of any truly progressive society. It was the threat of a general strike that brought the Lief to power — and you ask how do we propose to keep out all the future Liefenbargers. That's easy: By understanding where they come from." George suddenly paused for greater effect.

"O.K., I apologize," said Rose after a while, putting her pen down. "I have been asking to see a blueprint and you have the house practically built."

"And there's more. Much more. Ninety-five per cent of the households have a TV set but we haven't made any real use of them yet. Referendums, samples of public opinion, elections, recalls, initiatives — it's all there just for the taking. All of those things that can make us participators in public affairs rather than — as your Hannah Arendt says — someone who is only represented. The Polys should have the power to initiate things dealing with their race so that they won't have to live under white paternalism — "

Rose smiled. "Jesus, you'd better take over pretty soon, otherwise there won't be enough time in your life for it all."

"It sounds pretty utopian, doesn't it?"

"I don't think Jefferson sounded that much different."

"And we have a lot going for us. We'll be coming to power without being tied to any regime before us. On the other hand there have been almost thirty years of democracy on these islands. We can bring in things no Western leader could even dream of. Later on we can keep them or throw them away according to how they work out. But the point is that we'll have a clear runway to take off on."

"Power *is* exhilarating, isn't it? Even when one just thinks about it. That's where it's so different from liquor. On the other hand it's very much like sex."

That was no less profound a statement and we all ruminated on it for a moment. Not for long though.

"I make jokes and sometimes tend to be cynical for a wide variety of reasons," Rose began. "When I'm awed, for example. And that's what's happening now."

"Awed by what? Our plans for the future?" I asked.

But Rose was her old self again. She had recovered. "Not really. Awed by my own uncanny ability to spot the right kind of a story worth spending the next three months on."

Chapter 28

One of the first persons who Meg saw in St. Enoch was Lawrence Saunders. She told him to contact his uncle to say that he was in contact with the rebels. Then he was to report to her McAlpine's reaction.

It should be kept in mind that this was the period of Governor McAlpine's greatest triumphs. He not only remained fairly secure in his office, but got his own Anti-Insurgency Regiment. He enjoyed as much of Liefenbarger's trust as the Administrator could give. The terrorist action that killed the policeman on the way back from the airport served only to increase his own popularity on the Lower Isle. General dissatisfaction with the provisions of Lief's Extraordinary State Act and the consequent belt tightening had not been transferred to the governor because McAlpine was most careful with his public statements. He constantly stressed the need for stability, loyalty to the government, and for reasonable accommodation, but seldom was there any mention of Lucius Liefenbarger by name and almost never of the National Unity Movement or Corps. Sometimes it seemed as if the whole Lower Isle was something of an onlooker so far as the regime in N.S. City was concerned. All the horrors of Partrawa Plain and of the Bristol Street Armory were the results of orders issued from the capital and, since all three institutions were on Main Island, they really had little to do with St. Enoch. That was unmistakably McAlpine's message.

The governor had always liked his nephew. Much more than he cared for his lazy, sycophantic father who agreed with anything or anybody so long as he could keep his prestigious government job, acquired through the governor and for which he was badly suited. Lawrence's father's basic philosophy was really that of McAlpine himself, except that he lacked the brains and sophistication with which the governor so effectively camouflaged it.

Lawrence Saunders, on the other hand, was an ardent idealist, determined to see all injustice in the world eradicated — preferably while he was still in his teens. It was important, though, not to patronize him. McAlpine had once tried that route and in return got an itemized list of all the wrongs his office had perpetrated during the past three years. The list was perceptive and so astoundingly comprehensive that the governor found the whole exercise quite disquieting.

After that, he countered Lawrence's arguments point by point, sometimes evoking as his defense the need for the avoidance of greater evil, sometimes plain expediency, but most of the time misunderstood motives. It was never dull. Lawrence may have been inexperienced in that he often saw his country in absolute rather than relative terms, without relevant comparison or without adequate historical depth, but he also produced some of the most original thinking the governor had ever heard.

That's why McAlpine was delighted to meet with his nephew for lunch at the Winter Garden at St. Enoch. He was a bit puzzled, though, when Lawrence asked that the partition between their table and the rest of the restuarant be closed. The governor commented that in spite of Lawrence's assurances to the contrary, his face showed that everything was not fine. He asked what was bothering him.

Things were unbearable at school, replied Lawrence. Everyone was watching everyone else and he did not like it one bit. McAlpine reminded him that the Extraordinary State Act had been declared and that there was a good reason for it. Lawrence smirked that the primary reason was for the act to keep one man in power.

Even that didn't unduly surprise the governor. He allowed that they held different opinions on the Administrator's role, and that this was probably due to the difference in their ages. Then Lawrence told him that he had been in the mountains. McAlpine tried to ease the growing tension by jokingly asking him if he saw any Communists there, but soon saw that this was definitely the wrong kind of humor for the occasion. Lawrence angrily informed him that he had met with Meg Winters and George Titus and that he was up there because he wanted to join them. And no, in answer to his question, he had not seen any Communists there.

McAlpine was flabbergasted by the revelation, although he managed to hide it fairly well. Instead he began to lecture: "All the rebels are Communists nowadays, Lawrence. It can't be done otherwise. Sure they hide it the best way they can, but the moment they're in power the masks come off. The supposedly once democratic Viet Cong was quickly abolished once the Reds got into Saigon. And who do you think is running all those black liberation movements? Do you really think that Angola with half the Cuban army within its borders is evolving into some sort of glorious parliamentary democracy?"

"This isn't tribal Africa," Lawrence hissed back.

McAlpine was startled by his vehemence. Lawrence spoke about the American support for the rebels, about the absence of any prominent Communists in leadership. He spoke about Liefenbarger's sinking of the *Constant* and then asked if his uncle thought that the Americans would support the Administrator's regime after that.

"So with twenty revolutionaries Titus is going to take over the country, right?" smirked McAlpine.

"Twenty? No sir. Several hundred. Maybe a thousand by now. And there are thousands here in the cities, getting ready for the spring. Is that why Liefenbarger put the country on a wartime basis — because of twenty revolutionaries?"

McAlpine said he couldn't believe the numbers, but he was obviously on the defensive.

"I came to tell you that things are really happening in the Cheviots — it's later than you think. You'll have to take sides."

McAlpine's head shot up. "I've already taken sides. I'm on the side of an orderly, stable society. That's the side I'll always be on, Lawrence."

His food didn't seem to taste right after that. McAlpine left his dessert half finished, then put his napkin on the table. As he stood up, he spoke, "I'll treat the whole thing as if this conversation never took place. I'd like you to do the same. For the sake of your parents, Lawrence. Because believe me you're playing with fire. You really are."

But there was no doubt in Lawrence's mind that he had connected. The governor was visibly shaken.

On the same day that Lawrence managed to plant the first serious seeds of doubt into his uncle's mind, Ann Schorez managed to put a slight dent into Lucius Liefenbarger's armor a few hundred kilometers to the north. She had met the Administrator at a Fourth of July party in the American embassy. Frank Copithorne stood guard at the little salon, where they engaged in increasingly intense flirtation, keeping out such notorious irritants as Rohlicek, the Czech ambassador who unceasingly sought permission to establish an assembly plant for Jawa motorcylces at Garrick, and Pariseau, the Belgian envoy, who insisted on telling unfunny, bawdy jokes in abominable English.

The flirtation progressed nicely, until each one left separately to be reunited in half an hour aboard the Administrator's yacht *Trafalgar*, anchored in the bay. What went on after that can only be surmised, although it may safely be assumed that the only fireworks in the harbor that night were not those supplied by the U.S. government.

Actually, the U.S. government had supplied the other ones as well. The sleek Miss Schorez with her witty repartee was a perfectly obvious choice for her role of a temptress and it was also assumed that the Lief would see through it immediately. On the other hand, it was also assumed that he would be flattered by the attention of the Americans, or that he would treat such an obvious plot to get near him as a joke — that he would be amused by it. It was also possible that he would try to use Ann Schorez as a conduit for information he wanted the Americans to have. All of that would be acceptable because the Americans were convinced that eventually the Lief would become powerless and succumb to her charms. It was just a matter of time.

Of course, the Americans never allowed for the possibility that the situation could be reversed.

In a way Ann Schorez was an interesting equivalent of both Lucius Liefenbarger and Allan McAlpine. Like the two, she had been born into a lower middle-class environment with a burning ambition to climb into a position of power. But, while the two men had chosen politics, she had chosen diplomacy. Her climb, as a result, had been often circumvented by the customs of the rather conservative U.S. foreign service. Its regulations on seniority made her impatient and in the Liefenbarger assignment she saw a way of circumventing them. She didn't flinch from providing the Lief with the ultimate of her favors even at the risk of her activities acquiring a different, more unsavory shape. And in that the Lief, McAlpine, and she were absolute equals.

Her father had been a minor official in the Rockbridge County in Virginia and she was fully expected to acquire a minimal education, to marry a local beau, bear children and then quietly fade into oblivion. Instead, she was singled out in grade school as an exceptionally bright student, and in high school won the top scholarship award. That, in turn, lead to a scholarship at the prestigious Sweetbriar College in nearby Lynchburg, where she must have suffered countless indignities from the hands and minds of exceptionally rich girls who regarded the school as nothing more than a posh marital agency.

Ann didn't. She graduated at the top of her class during the mid-sixties, then proceeded to Columbia for her graduate degree.

But in New York she discovered that she really didn't want to be a scholar; she took the foreign service test, passed it with flying colors and within a year was at her first overseas posting in India. Her rise in the service was by no means phenomenal, but it was steady. There was no doubt that she was capable as well as knowledgeable, but there was also little doubt that she had discovered, albeit somewhat belatedly, the power of her svelte body and her charm. There had been several amorous involvements, but they had been neither memorable nor excessively erratic — they were precisely what would have been expected from a woman with Ann Schorez's qualities and position.

The Lief was a product of a union out of wedlock; he carried with him the stigma which affected his views on sex not uncommon to people with his predicament. He seemed to distrust the urge, because it had a tendency to slip out of the rigid control which he had learned to impose on everything else that he did. There is little evidence of any sexual activity on his part while in his teens and absolutely no indication of any homosexual tendencies, as some seemed to suggest because of his reliance and definite affection for the clearly gay Copithorne. It wouldn't make much sense: if he mistrusted normal sex because it could interfere with the rigid standards that he had set for himself, he would have been quite likely to mistrust homosexuals even more.

It's true that while on the N.S. City police force the Lief had allowed himself a bit more freedom, but even here they were fleeting affairs, predominantly physical, that had left little effect on him or his partners. As he rose on the political scene even these grew rarer. Possibly because there was less time for them, but also quite likely because the Lief knew that in conservative and basically puritan New Salisbury more than one politician's career had been ruined by jaded love — whether imaginary or real.

So, on the night of July fourth, under the dazzling fireworks, their affair had been consummated. Neither of them could have had any idea just how far-reaching the effects of their liaison would be.

Chapter 29

Corporal Richard Merridew of the Royal New Salisbury Air Force came to see Eddie Mayfield at his office in the Bristol Street Armory late in the evening on January 24th. A mechanic formerly stationed at the Dernvale Field outside St. Enoch on Lower Isle, he claimed that he overheard talk among the pilots stationed there which would indicate that, during the destruction of the terrorists' former headquarters camp, they had deliberately allowed the rebels to escape before destroying their empty buildings.

After the raid, an order had come from the Administrator that no further raids were to be conducted until further notice. But that was unimportant. Of utmost importance was that if the expected spring offensive against the terrorists took place, the pilots could not be relied upon for air support.

As Mayfield saw it, Merridew's testimony only added to his suspicion that McAlpine would bolt the Lief's ranks at the first opportunity; also, that Colonel Paul Felstad and other senior officers in charge of the First Royal Anti-Insurgency Regiment were McAlpine's cronies, spelled nothing but disaster.

The trouble was that Mayfield had nothing concrete with which to approach the Administrator. The Poly air force corporal-informer now sitting across his desk was a well-known troublemaker who had twice been demoted: once for threatening an officer, the other time for brawling at an enlisted men's club. He was everything that Mayfield detested among these people — the kind that strengthened the stereotype of the Polynesians as drunken, thick-headed louts.

In spite of it, Mayfield probably didn't doubt for a minute that what Merridew was saying was truthful. The pilots were an elite group which was fiercely determined to preserve its exclusiveness. There were instances of third generation fliers among them — men who mingled socially almost exclusively among themselves and who, although they didn't openly oppose him, welcomed Lucius Liefenbarger's rise to power with lukewarm enthusiasm at best. They remained loyal primarily to General Pentland-Garaudy, the quiet, thoughtful and largely mysterious officer who seldom spoke up at staff meetings but still headed an air force which ranked among the best in the Pacific.

There were disguised National Unity Corps agents at all airfields in New Salisbury, but none among the pilots. Their ranks remained closed to security penetration no matter what ploy was used.

"The trouble is," wrote Mayfield in a memorandum dated late in July, "that we are slowly beginning to fall for our own propaganda. There is much more in the Cheviots than a few wild Communists who in the spring will be making suicidal raids into the lowlands until they are gradually wiped out. There is every indication now that they have strong and important ties with subversive elements in the lowlands and that these ties will become apparent the moment we decide to mount an offensive against the Cheviots. If that offensive fails, very soon afterwards we can expect a counter-offensive led from the mountains."

Leahy's Camp Gamma rebels captured at Fort Wellington had all died. Not one of them had survived more than three months in the cellar at Bristol Street Armory. But on the day of Mayfield's talk with Corporal Merridew the last of them — a thirty-year-old teacher from Hamilton named Leslie Smith — was still alive. As I've said before, I am convinced that some of them gave information to the NUC without being tortured, but Leslie Smith was certainly not one of those.

Liefenbarger summoned the NUC duty officer at the Armory, a certain Captain Severn, and together they walked down the wide steps, built when space in downtown N.S. City was not at a premium. They passed through the darkened entrance hall where a sleepy private on duty snapped into attention, then down another, much narrower flight of steps into what was commonly referred to as Hades. At the entrance to the corridor a sergeant became rigid at the sight of Mayfield. He listened to his request, then promptly unbolted the heavy metal door behind him.

Now they were in a totally different environment. Here the stark corridors had been recently whitewashed and the stone floors were spotlessly clean. The lightbulbs in the ceiling at three-meter intervals were red. The effect was incredibly eerie. It was as if the very sound of one's speech and footsteps had been altered. The sergeant stopped at a cell with a large figure

54 on it. He inserted a key in the door with a heavy metallic click, then leaned against it with all his weight until it slowly started to open. The floor of the three-by-two-meter cell was covered by a wooden grill. Lying on it in the bright, harsh rays of the red bulb, beside a metal pail with a lid on it, curled up for warmth, was a man — fully naked and with his head shaven.

He responded only very slowly to the sight of the three figures in the doorway. Mayfield stepped forward into the cell, running his hand along the smooth tile wall as he did so. The man then slowly sat up, pulling his knees against his chin. He stared at Mayfield, taking in the gold stars on his collar, then moving on to his eyes but without being able to adequately focus his own.

Mayfield knelt on one knee beside him. "Which camp were you at in the Cheviots?" he asked.

The man stared at him without a word, his head unsteady on his shoulders.

"Listen, you scum," Mayfield picked up the man's chin with his forefinger and thumb, "we need to know which camp and you need a bowl of soup. It's time to trade."

There was no response. For a moment even the man's eyes closed. But then they opened again and with his lips barely moving, he said almost inaudibly, "I was not ... in ... Cheviots."

Mayfield disgustedly pushed him aside so that the body slumped back into a heap. Leslie Smith was by far the toughest of those captured, never admitting that he even knew Titus and Leahy, that he had ever been in the mountains. But he also couldn't adequately account for his whereabouts during the three months before his capture. The evidence was stacked up overwhelmingly against Smith and yet he refused to give in on even the relatively insignificant point of having been in the Cheviots. Smith was as completely aware as Mayfield and his inquisitors that a single crack in his story would provide an opening through which the crowbar could then be inserted. Smith wouldn't break. But he was also unable to retreat into insanity as did some of the others.

Leslie Smith would soon die on the damp wooden grill next to the slop bucket.

What surprised me personally when I later interviewed Captain Severn, was that Mayfield apparently wasn't aware of the Fort Wellington raid being a rebellious Communist caper. He had no idea about it being unauthorized.

Severn tells of Mayfield inviting him up to his office for a cup of coffee. He reports talking to a deeply worried Mayfield — worried about the Liefenbarger regime increasingly finding itself built on quicksand. He felt it could collapse with all of them being swallowed up by circumstances almost without a sound.

What frightened Mayfield the most, however, was that for the moment he could see nothing — absolutely nothing — that he could do to prevent it.

Chapter 30

In addition to the Hercules drop, early in August the Americans inaugurated a weekly helicopter run to the new headquarters camp. The first Sikorski that made its way in between the ridges was piloted by Russ Nichols. With the blades still rotating noisily, Russ jumped into the snow. He looked around briefly and as soon as he spotted George and me, he made a beeline for us. We knew that he had survived the Precarious Inlet adventure, but we weren't sure if he had not been aboard the *Constant* when it was sunk.

It was a joy to see him again, just like it was a joy to see five men in full U.S. winter fatigues, carrying submachine guns and bulging packsacks. They constituted a new kind of arrival — the New Salisburians who had made their way to New Zealand and had been trained and outfitted by the Americans. Nichols claimed several dozen of them were there now. He also wanted to know if we would be ready to go into the lowlands in the spring.

"Tell them back there that we're doing fine, just fine. Everything is going all right," replied George noncommittally.

Russ gazed into his face in vain effort to wean out the exact meaning. Then he squeezed George's shoulder, grinned, and without another word climbed into the helicopter. At that moment Rose Kubatan suddenly appeared beside it, shouting up to Nichols: "Do you have space to take me out of here? I'm Rose Kubatan."

"I know who you are," Russ shouted back. "Sure we do. Come on, hop aboard." He offered her his hand.

But Rose looked around indecisively until her eyes rested on George. Nichols leaned further out of the helicopter.

"No," she said finally, shaking her head. "I can't go, I'm really not ready yet. But here, take this with you." She reached into her canvas bag and came up with a large brown envelope. At that moment, George suddenly stepped forward and put his hand over hers.

"Sorry, Rose. I can't let that go yet. I have to see what you wrote."

I fully expected her to be angry. But Rose merely shrugged her shoulders, then put the envelope back inside the bag which she reluctantly handed to him.

Nichols grasped the situation, waved, then disappeared inside the Sikorski. The blades then started to whirl around more frantically and the machine lifted itself off, quickly gaining altitude as it neared the mountains.

"You really wanted to go, didn't you?" George asked as we walked back to camp.

"No," she said, stopping in her tracks. "Like I told the pilot, I'm not ready to go yet. But the thought of a Bloody Mary, a white blouse, or my cashmere coat and a posh Sydney restaurant got the better of me. Did you ever notice that when you're forced to wear decent clothes you can't wait to get into bluejeans and then, when you're forced into U.S. Army fatigues, you'd give your right arm to be able to put on the dog again?"

She stopped, looked us over from head to toe carefully. "No, I guess you wouldn't notice that," was her final verdict. "Only us good looking gals do."

One of the new arrivals brought a report from Meg. She had established contact with the Cheviots via the British embassy in N.S. City. Having met with Resistance groups in St. Enoch, Muldoon and Castlereagh, she reported widespread discontent throughout the Lower Isle. National Unity Corps agents were everywhere. There had already been several acts of sabotage, mostly in the coastal cities. Prices were rising sharply and productivity was dropping although official statistics did their best to mask the situation. Nothing could disguise the steady drop of the New Salisbury dollar on the world market, though.

Meg's conclusion was that the present wave of discontent was a highly potent force. She suggested a course of action to be followed in harnessing it:

1. Cells should be organized immediately in the three largest cities. Each cell would have a specific task to perform on the day that we came down from the Cheviots.

2. Agitation among the military and its subversion should be increased with the goal of rendering the armed forces useless for all practical purposes by the time we came down.

3. A basic, comprehensive time plan for our descent should be drawn up as soon as possible. It should include strategy for the revolutionary forces as well as their support by sympathetic groups and individuals throughout the islands. The plan

should be flexible enough so that the malfunctioning of any one part would not jeopardize the entire operation.

Part of Meg's report dealt with her meeting Lawrence Saunders and with his news concerning Governor Allan McAlpine. Lawrence reported that more than anything his uncle's response was that of shock and he concluded that three or four weeks should go by before he tried to contact him again. Meg agreed.

In the personal mail there was a letter from George's son David. He had seen the Sahota article plus several other press reports about the rebels and he was excited. There had been requests from local press and television for interviews with George's family, but it had been decided around the dinner table that they would not give any. Here, however, David added that although he had reluctantly gone along with the decision because of his mother's insistence, he wasn't sure that complete silence really was the best approach. He suspected that eventually it would cause fictional stories to be written about the revolution.

George was visibly touched by the boy's loyalty. He said that for the first time he noticed a desire in his son to be actively involved in what his father was doing. I remember thinking that it was the first time in a long while that George was doing something one could get excited about. Because of his letter, far more than his mother, David started to symbolize the lost family to his father.

The most exasperating piece of mail in the pouch was a copy of a report by an international humanitarian organization based in London called World Concerned. It documented over one hundred and fifty deaths in New Salisbury either by execution or mistreatment in prison. Its pages described the stark tile walls of the Bristol Street Armory basement, the hopelessness of the dusty and unbearably hot Partrawa camps in the summer, the shivering cold of its winters. It warned of the ever-growing power of the National Unity Corps, the rise in its ranks of people who in most other societies would have been considered the criminal element.

"In New Salisbury, as seems to be the case in most totalitarian countries both on the left and right, this element has become the mainstay of the country's politicized police force," read the report.

All that was perhaps wordy and on occasion betrayed a bit too strongly the influence of the academic, but there could be no doubt as to its good intentions. But then there was the last part: "The presence of revolutionary elements in the mountains of New Salisbury's Lower Isle's mountains has significantly increased some of the more paranoid tendencies of Lucius Liefenbarger's regime," the report concluded. "In more than sixty per cent of the documented cases of death in this report there had been a connection between the activity of the revolutionaries and those who have died at the hands of the National Unity Corps. It is, of course, beyond the scope and mandate of this report to express opinions on the merits of the revolutionary movement in New Salisbury. But it should nevertheless be noted that those who advocate warfare in place of persuasion and other non-violent means of altering the present situation in New Salisbury must fully take into account the human costs in life and physical suffering, the destruction of property, and the general social dislocation that the use of arms invariably entails. Also considered should be the precedents of other such conflicts which have taken place in this country. The establishment of a functioning democratic system following a violent revolution is a state of affairs that is practically unknown among them. The ballot box has invariably proven to be a much more effective means of altering the policies of the government."

"What ballot box?" George asked angrily as I slammed the report shut. I agreed. Where was there a ballot box available to New Salisburians? It was precisely because such a ballot box was lacking that we were freezing in the Cheviots and not occupying some well-heated professorial or journalistic offices, sharpening our powers of persuasion.

But I was also immediately wondering what George would have said about the World Concerned report had he been sitting in an easy chair at his Point Grey home, below the Polynesian tapa cloth decorations, answering questions from a *Vancouver Sun* reporter who had put a slow news day to good use by remembering that the son of New Salisbury's first prime minister was a respected professor at the local university.

He would have most probably wholly and tactfully agreed with the simple thesis that all violence was bad. Remembering the tranquil, almost soporific New Salisbury of his youth, he would have publicly expressed his abhorrence at an attempt by a group of Marxist-oriented revolutionaries (after all, what other kind could there possibly be?) to shatter those traditions which have framed the political life in his native country for the past thirty years. Perhaps he would have even quoted himself, adding that each act of political violence really constituted a serious failure in the civilized man's attempts to govern himself. Then he would have added other tautological statements wrapped in the cloak of prefabricated phrases and comfortable jargon. He would have also taken adequate care to intersperse them with educated witticisms, providing the whole thing with a dose of personalized vitality clearly pointing out that the learned author of it all should by no means be forgotten when views on other world problems were being solicited.

But that sort of opinion could only have been given without knowledge of the Renfrew Peninsula; Captain Greytrix's fires and bullets on the McElroy farm; the memory of the cold waters of the Sewena River on that dark night; the roaring planes over the old headquarters camp; and the steeply banking helicopter in the Precarious Inlet with the bullet holes in its side.

George pushed away the chair and walked toward the fire. "Do you know what's happening?" he asked after a while. "I'm beginning to have the growing suspicion that what we're doing up here is not half as important as what people *think* we're doing up here. Here you have people ready to give their lives, to practically lay themselves into a fire because they can no longer live with what's happening. And this incredible sacrifice of theirs is being cheapened by some comfortable pundit sitting in a cozy room in London, England, because he doesn't like violence. For God's sake, who likes violence? I can't stand pain but I'm well aware that without it children couldn't be born, nor would one recognize an inflamed appendix."

Suddenly he stopped talking. He gazed at me; I was standing before him, trying my best to be his friend. Little by little I had relinquished every last bit of leadership. George alone was now in charge; he had to make the decisions.

World Concerned and its reports on New Salisbury wasn't really that important. Much more important was Meg's assessment of the situation and her recommendations for action.

"We have to start making plans for the spring," said George after a while. "About where we are going and how we are going to get there."

My face instantly lit up. "Jesus," I almost yelled, "I thought you'd never get around to it."

It was midnight when the door to the headquarters cabin opened and Rose Kubatan walked in. She shook the snow from her coat, then came nearer, into the light. "Aah, still pondering the famous report, eh? The boys in the dormitory have been discussing it for hours. I don't think they'll be going to sleep at all tonight."

"That's good," George commented tiredly. "It should be talked about."

"What do you think?" Rose asked, taking off her mittens and sitting down.

George thought about if for a few minutes, then smiled. "I think we will have a revolution in spite of what World Concerned thinks about it," he finally said.

Chapter 31

Several chinks appeared in the Lief's armor the following week. But they were in the back, where he as yet couldn't see them too well. For example, McAlpine called in Colonel Felstad and two other high-ranking officers from the Anti-Insurgency Regiment for consultation. Instead of discussing the army's ongoing dispute with the NUC concerning jurisdiction over captured rebels, McAlpine told them that, according to his sources, the information they had been given about the rebels was incorrect — that their number was far greater and political make-up more varied than officially allowed by N.S. City. He pointed out to the officers that the Americans seemed now to favor Titus over Liefenbarger, but they were still not fully committed; that the whole thing could really go either way. Finally he said to them that he had information which indicated Leahy was no longer in command of any rebel troops and that the Fort Wellington suicide raid had quite likely been the Communists' last gasp.

All of this, or course, had been fed to him by his nephew, but McAlpine never revealed his source.

The three officers were stunned. Felstad recovered first, asking McAlpine what he thought they should do. Instead of answering, the governor asked him a question: "How much can you really rely on your officers — I mean captains and through to the top?"

"A lot I would say," Felstad said after some thought. "Yeah, I would say quite a lot."

"Would they obey you or Eddie Mayfield or Ormsby or whomever?"

"I don't know. Me, I suppose ... Jesus, you're not thinking of — "

"I'm not thinking anything yet. Just checking on what we have and what we don't have. That's all."

Felstad nodded and got up, the others following him. McAlpine walked them to the door.

"The main thing is not to get too excited and do something silly. I know it's a shock — I've gone through it myself. Go home, take a hot shower and get your wife to give you a back rub. I hear wives are pretty good at that sort of thing," he said, grinning, as he showed them out.

They smiled back uneasily, then filed out one by one. Felstad was the last to leave, but before closing the door behind him he stopped for a moment, studying McAlpine's face. "Jesus Christ," he repeated softly, "Jesus Christ."

Liefenbarger, in August, was going through the most important transition of his life.

During his days as a policeman he had learned well that the so-called public opinion or public pressure amounted to practically nothing when confronted with fear. What he had to guard against was the rise of another leader whose magnetism was strong enough to offset the fear. He prided himself on being fully aware of these principles that kept him in power. He often talked to Copithorne about them, claiming that he never fooled himself about having the charisma or the skill of a demagogue. He merely knew, probably instinctively, what made people act the way they did — not in the theoretical manner of a clinical psychologist, but on a much more practical level. He was thus able to quickly and accurately assess each politically important development on the islands. For this purpose he had instituted a chain of communications which assured that the required information reached him immediately so that he could react with equal speed. Up till now at least he had been in control. In total control.

Ann Schorez was the one unfamiliar note in it all. Still, the music she produced sounded increasingly heavenly to the Lief. First of all, she constituted a welcome diversion of his time which up till now had been spent entirely on matters of state. They had met only three times since their first night on the yacht. Twice they had been in Pitlochry and once they had gone for a drive to Garrick, where they lunched at a seaside restaurant on superb sole. But she must have been on his mind constantly and that meant that his finely tuned senses were no longer used exclusively for ruling the tense country. It's difficult to say when exactly Ann Schorez stopped regarding their liaison as an official assignment, but I am fairly convinced that there had never been any plan in Liefenbarger's mind to use her. She came to his life when he had a great need for someone like her — the general anxiety and his own ensuing loneliness of middle age simply cried out for such a diversion. But he paid for it.

For one thing, he totally misjudged the Russians. It can be

argued that he could never have gotten over his personal aversion to Communism with or without Ann Schorez, but I don't believe it. The Nixons of this world have proven quite conclusively that even the most avid Cold War warriors can become the ablest negotiators when they put their minds to it. With Ann on the scene so prominently, the Lief was simply unable to concentrate deeply enough to properly think of all the ramifications of the new situation. The Russians shouldn't have been so summarily dismissed. I am not suggesting that the Lief should have immediately concluded an allegiance with them, but I am convinced that had he not been so preoccupied by his affair his antennae would have clearly picked up the changing frequency of the Slavic vibrations. He was certainly in no position to indulge in as much grandstanding and muscle flexing as he did.

The first sure sign of the Russians' changing attitude came when they not only didn't drastically curtail their relations with New Salisbury after being accused of sinking the *Constant,* but decided to ignore the incident altogether. Then, in a personal letter to Liefenbarger (in which he referred to him as the *able* Administrator), Brezhnev stated that the Russians were "most anxious" to avoid past misunderstandings between their two governments and that a newly appointed Soviet ambassador would soon be arriving in New Salisbury. The asthmatic chargé d'affaires Blavatsky was being recalled because — as Brezhnev allowed — it may have been Blavatsky's behavior that had been the cause of the deterioration of "historically friendly relations" between their two countries. Also included in the letter was a hint that the Soviets were preparing a series of specific proposals for the improvement of relations between New Salisbury and the U.S.S.R.

Two weeks later the new ambassador, Alexandr Voinovich Velikovsky, duly called on the Lief to present him with his credentials along with a picture book on Siberia and a set of newly minted coins commemorating the upcoming Moscow Olympiad. The coins as a gift were quite ironic because the Russians had been strong supporters of a growing movement to ban authoritarian New Salisbury from participating in the games.

With the help of an interpreter, Velikovsky plunged into the customary platitudes about the beauty of New Salisbury's landscape and about the general goodness of the people. Eventually he changed the subject to that of the Siberians' surprising friendliness. In the end, however, Velikovsky smilingly had to admit that since Novosibirsk was his home town, he was slightly biased. They had a nicely forced laugh over it.

That was all. Velikovsky never even hinted at the existence of the new proposals let alone their contents. The Lief didn't ask, probably deducing that the Russians were quite likely gauging the level of his anxiety. The audience ended on this neutral note.

But much more may have been said than had been immediately noticed. The coins, for example, may have been meant to indicate that what the Russians had been saying should have been viewed quite separately from what they were doing. And Velikovsky's chatty visit may have been an attempt for the two of them to get to know each other better — to be on an informal basis before attempting to tackle important issues.

Perhaps. But immediately after Velikovsky's initial visit the Soviets, as far as the Lief was concerned, were still an unknown entity. Something like a gigantic wooden horse at the gates whose insides could contain a Bolshoi Ballet or a crack unit of the Red Army plus a number of KGB agents. It could go either way, the trouble was that the Lief was not bothering too much to read the signs.

But on August 23rd a unique opportunity presented itself for doing just that as the Lief prepared to receive Velikovsky for the second time at his Parliament Building office. Some excerpts from their taped conversation follow:

(After the initial greetings there is a lull in the proceedings. There follow some barely audible Russian whispers, followed by Velikovsky's translator's voice:)

Veli: "The presence of the other gentleman is disturbing. What must be discussed is of a highly confidential nature."

Lief: "Mr. Copithorne is my executive secretary...very well, Frank if you would — "

Veli: "The government of the Union of Soviet Socialist Republics is well aware that at present the relations between our two countries are at a somewhat low ebb. At the same time, it is also aware that your country is being invaded by imperialistic, reactionary forces which are recruited and supplied by the United States of America, with the full participation of ruthless generals in the Pentagon bent on militaristic adventures, by the international monopolies, and by the CIA. Under the circumstances it is the duty of all socialist countries to be concerned with the fate of New Salisbury. The U.S.S.R., being the acknowledged leader of such countries, is ready to offer aid in this brave endeavor. Specifically, this is what we propose:

"1. We shall make contact with all the truly Marxist revolutionary elements in the Cheviot Hills, and explain to them that the revolution is no longer a socialist one and urge them to withdraw from it.

"2. We shall increase our naval presence in the southern Pacific, even to the point of visiting New Salisbury's ports and cruising within New Salisbury's territorial waters — but, of course, only to the degree your government should deem it advisable.

"3. We shall supply your government with defense material and possibly with low interest credits so that the present emergency with which you are faced can be successfully overcome.

"4. We will undertake diplomatic initiative on your country's behalf, and express internationally your small country's predicament in the hands of ruthless imperialist invaders.

"5. The Union of Soviet Socialist Republics — preferably through the aid of one of the smaller allied socialist nations — will bring up the foreign invasion of your country before the Security Council of the United Nations Organization and request a thorough discussion of it as well as a clear condemnation of the imperialist policies of the United States of America and of its allies."

Lief: "Does your government propose to include all this in some sort of a formal, public agreement?"

Veli: "No, Mr. Administrator. We wouldn't think it wise."

Lief: "Yes, I see. You are right, because that could present difficulties. It could affect our agreement with the United States concerning defense weapons."

Veli: "Does your government seriously expect the United States of America to honor that agreement? The first shipment is not to be sent until six months from now."

Lief: "Mr. Ambassador, we expect all the agreements we enter into to be honored. Otherwise we would not bother entering into them."

Veli: "Mr. Administrator, perhaps I have not made it sufficiently clear that the Union of Soviet Socialist Republics is extending its hand of friendship to your country. It is willing to forget past misunderstandings and difficulties. That is why it has recalled its former envoy to your country and why I have been posted here. I assure you that I come without any prejudices or past encumbrances so far as New Salisbury is concerned."

(Liefenbarger must have merely nodded. There is a slight pause on the tape.)

Veli: "In view of this I am most anxious to reach some sort of an understanding between us."

Lief: "Why?"

(Another pause follows along with excited whispers between the ambassador and the interpreter in the background. In the end the ambassador begins to answer, but even in Russian it is obvious that he speaks more excitedly and in a higher-pitched voice.)

Veli: "Why we are offering help? Because we wish to be friends. We consider it a very good thing to have friends."

Lief: "Hmmm... Would you like some coffee? Or perhaps tea?"

(At this point there's a sound of the door opening and in hurried whispers a message is delivered to the Lief, most likely by Copithorne.)

Lief: "I am sorry Mr. Ambassador, but I must go. The governor general of New Salisbury has just died."

(After a brief period of stunned silence Velikovsky begins rattling off condolences like a giant locomotive gathering all available steam.)

Veli: "The Government of the Union of Soviet Socialist Republics wishes to express its deepest sympathies on the loss of this great statesman.... Will you consider my country's proposal, Mr. Administrator? The various points are, of course, all negotiable. That is all it is — a proposal. A basis on which to begin negotiations."

Lief: "You will be called, Mr. Ambassador."

Veli: "May I ask how long it would be before I am called?"

Lief: "Soon. You will be called soon."

Velikovsky must have been stunned by the cool reception his proposal got. He had arrived in New Salisbury under the impression that the Lief was preparing for a deadly battle. New Salisbury's streets bristled with uniforms. Its jails and detention camps were full of political prisoners while there wasn't a single true international friend in sight. And here came a major power, offering concrete help that could very well make the difference between victory and defeat. The Lief, however, acted as if he were bored by it all.

While Velikovsky doubtlessly fumed in the back of his limousine on the way home, the Lief was explaining to Copithorne that among the Soviet proposals number two was pivotal. The presence of the Soviet fleet in the south Pacific for the specific purpose of defending New Salisbury would practially obligate New Salisbury to provide them with port facilities. A naval base. Such a base would then establish Russian presence at the gateway to the Antarctica, at the same time placing them in a threatening position both in relation to Oceania and South America. There was also New Salisbury's supply of oil. The Russian base would be completely self-sufficient in fuel.

"The trouble is, the Russians still think that we can't put it all together," Liefenbarger said to Copithorne. "And this has always been their Achilles' heel. They have been boasting so long, they now believe that all other systems are crumbling. Stalin had so vastly underrated Hitler that the country was almost levelled as a result. Since then, through such miscalculations, they have had to take their missiles out of Cuba, lost their foothold in Egypt, and control of most Communist parties in western Europe.

"The difference between the Russians and the Americans," the Lief concluded, "is that while the Americans simply keep you in blissful ignorance, the Russians insist on telling big black lies."

Chapter 32

On the same day that Hathaway was given a state funeral and the Lief walked bare-headed behind his cortege, God had also officially died in New Salisbury. The process, of course, had been going on for quite some time, but it was on August 14th that it was complete in the notorious Bishop Kewley article published in the *Times*. It began with the now familiar "Extraordinary times require extraordinary measures" passage and ended by officially placing the entire Anglican organization on the islands under the goverment's control because of "our common struggle against atheistic materialism."

The plan for killing the church in New Salisbury had been Copithorne's. It consisted of several stages, of which the first was the total dispersal of all minor sects such as the Hari Krishnas, the Unitarians, and the devotees of Reverend Moon, along with the more fanatical fundamentalist sects. Some of their leaders protested and quickly disappeared on the Partrawa Plain, but most docilely accepted the new situation. In return the NUC tolerated an occasional prayer meeting in a private home if conducted discreetly and without any political overtones.

The Catholics and all non-Anglican Protestants were next. A papal nuncio flew over from Canberra to plead against governmental advisers being imposed on the Church. He was copiously photographed with various officials including the Administrator himself, but there were no other concrete results. Along with the Methodists, Presbyterians and the Baptists, the Church of Rome was slated to become the religious arm of the NUC. Before he departed, the nuncio called all New Salisbury's priests together to announce that in the future the Church would likely find itself under increased pressure, but that each one of them would have to face each turn of the screw individually. The Church would not officially condemn Lucius Liefenbarger. At least not yet. It believed that such a move would end all Catholic influence in present-day New Salisbury and that this would be highly undesirable. But such a move was not excluded in the future. Following his announcement, the venerable white-haired nuncio gathered his robes and boarded a jet which took him back to safety.

That left the Anglicans and their sizeable following of almost eighty per cent of the population. Their churches had traditionally served as community centres, providing facilities for every sort of cultural activity from square dances to Boy Scout meetings. But the Boy Scouts had become junior NUCs years ago and chances were that at least one couple in each square had been planted there by the government. What remained relatively intact, however, was the Anglicans' strictly religious function. Supported by a group of sophisticated liberals who considered Liefenbarger's crassly anti-Marxist orientation to be below their dignity, Bishop Kewley continued speaking out publicly for the separation of religious and secular affairs — characteristically long after all other organized religion except Anglican had ceased to exist on the islands.

But this sweetheart arrangement was suddenly terminated by the government's demand that the Synod accept an official dictum from the Ministry of Cultural Affairs with a de facto veto power. Even while negotiation on this point continued, the Reverend Bleeker from Sidwell was murdered, supposedly at the home of a well-known homosexual. It didn't help the Anglicans' cause much when Kewley repeated ad infinitum that there was a big difference between being a homosexual and being a spiritual adviser to the homosexuals. Few heard him because he had no platform but his own church. On the other hand the innuendos on television, radio and in the press placed Bleeker squarely in the middle of the homosexual scene.

Kewley still didn't seem to quite get the idea, so a Catholic priest named Father Fariseau and an Anglican minister named Stern were killed during a reported shoot-out with the NUC at Nelson. Both clergymen were accused of having organized a Resistance group. Again, there was just enough circumstantial evidence to make it plausible: they both had known Marxist leanings and both had spoken from their pulpits against NUC tactics.

Kewley then requested a meeting with the Lief, but got no further than Copithorne. There it was spelled out to him that the Lief was losing patience and that the next target would likely be the bishop himself. Whatever the method, it had been successful. Within a week the "extraordinary times" article appeared in the *Times*. It was thought that the Anglican Church no longer constituted a potential Fifth Column.

But only on the official level was this true, because soon after all this our ranks in the Cheviots started to swell with disenfranchised ministers and laymen. Among the former the most notable was the erudite Reverend Henry Motherwell.

Chapter 33

I still can see the damn thing in front of me as I write this — the egg-shaped death symbol that terrified me far more than the cool waters of the Sewena River or bullet holes in the side of Russ Nichols's helicopter. To this day I can pinpoint the exact spot where it happened. I also remember what kind of smell there was in the air and just how loud the voices were coming from the valley below.

We had been to Mawusituki Lake again and the day was crisp, although not as cold as they had been lately. At the last moment George had decided to stay behind at the headquarters so I was walking with Rose who was replete with original *bon mots,* intermingled with generally witty comments on the harshness of a revolutionary's life. The Hercules arrived on schedule, dropping tons of supplies on the frozen lake by the ground proximity method.

The Mawusituki camp now had its own ground control system housed in prefabricated huts. These were occupied by heavy machine-gun crews assigned the task of protecting the aircraft during its most vulnerable moments — when, heavy with its load and practically unmaneuverable because of low speed and the nearness of the mountains, it was approaching the lake. Two more such huts had been built on the western shore to protect the plane from possible ground attack as it made its turn and began climbing away from the lake. It seemed highly unlikely though that any government force could enter the Cheviots to mount such an ambitious attack without being immediately detected by us.

There really had been no great need for our coming, but the trip to the lake was a pleasant outing which provided a much needed opportunity to exercise our muscles. Accompanied by five men, we watched the plane drop its load, then picked up the mail and turned back almost immediately.

Rose was still musing about the international implications of the governor general's death when we came to the Slab — the most difficult part of the route, about two-thirds of the way back. The others, because of their snowmobiles and heavier packs, had gone around it through the valley below. But Rose and I, cutting about two kilometers off our route, were negotiating three hundred meters of the trail which in the shape of a narrow trough had been hewn into the barren side of the mountain.

Walking carefully, inching along, we were suddenly distracted by a metallic clang nearby. At first I thought one of us had dropped some piece of equipment. I looked down, studying the smooth face of the rock for some sort of a clue. In the next moment came Rose's terrified shriek. Directly in front of us, now comfortably nestled in the trough, rested an oval grenade with its pin pulled out. Its symmetrical, armored sections resembled some sort of a strange crustacean.

Frozen in terror I stared at the monstrous thing, unable to take my eyes off it, but Rose's terror drove her to quick action. Screaming *Jesus! Jesus!* she threw herself at me; we lost our footing, with a painful impact fell to the rock, and slid down the slope.

The deafening explosion was quickly followed by a pressure wave. But it had all happened too far above us, and we were showered with only dirt and pebbles. We were safe. Except for my bruised elbow and Rose's painfully dislocated shoulder, we were unscathed. I thought I heard several gunshots from the top, from somewhere among the tall Kaikawaka cedars, but it may have been the fire from our people in the valley below, aiming at the clump of trees over our heads. By then I too had my gun out of its holster, regretting that Rose had so steadfastly refused to carry a weapon. She regarded herself as a neutral observer — in my view a wholy obsolete designation she must have picked up from her readings about the Crimean War.

There was no movement among the trees. From below came voices of those who had taken the long route and who wanted to know if we were all right. Slowly we sat up, called reassurances into the valley, then again stared into the Kaikawakas. Rose was rubbing her shoulder.

"They must have thought we were someone important," Rose said.

"They must have thought I was George," I narrowed it down.

"Most would-be assassins forget that killing a leader is not like bumping off some hood. You're bound to get a wee bit nervous during a political assassination and it's natural that you'll try to compensate for it. Otherwise you are likely to screw things up by taking out the pin or throwing the grenade two seconds too soon." Rose eyed George closely. "Who do you think is after you?" she asked.

"Anyone from the 10,000-member strong National Unity Corps would be a safe bet," he replied.

"Oh? So you think everybody up here in the mountains is now crazy about you, eh?" she asked with a smirk.

I was on her side. George had announced he was going to Mawusituki only the night before, so there was ample time for the Algerians to organize an attempt. Then, when he changed his plans, it was too late to have changed theirs. Leahy, Baracolli and Channing had all been accounted for. Naturally. But the assassin or assassins would have been unknowns — people who would have been able to slip in and out of the woods without anyone outside the Party circles having been the wiser for it. I counselled an immediate investigation which George rejected out of hand.

"I'm not too clear about the Communists' motives — if they were Communists," he said. "They know well that Maurice and I work together, and that if I should die he would take over. So what would they gain by killing either of us?"

"Yes, that's fine ... now how about killing the two of you together?" asked Rose. "Originally the two of you were supposed to go to the lake and you always take the Slab rather than the valley route back. I may not be exactly the same height as you, George, and I have a far better figure, but I was wearing the same type of parka that you usually wear and my hood was up. In other words, one grenade would have forced a radical change in leadership — if dropped properly. With both Titus and Bech-Landau gone, there was bound to be a scramble. And we all know which group is traditionally organized to make best use of such a scramble, don't we?"

But George still wasn't buying it. Not because the arguments weren't convincing but because, without saying so, without perhaps even realizing it, he was already deeply imbibing from the cup of power and he was not about to throw out its entire heady contents just because there was a slightly sour taste.

Liefenbarger's policies and Meg's organizing in the lowlands had their effect. The Cheviot Hills were now filled with about 300 men and women. Divided into strike teams and aided by Resistance groups in the lowlands, we were beginning to constitute a formidable force. The newly hatched Plan of Descent involved a three-prong thrust at St. Enoch — pincer movements from the north and south and an eventual direct assault on the city across the plains. The northern pincer maneuver was the most worrisome. Here Liefenbarger may decide to reinforce Castlereagh with troops sent across the Wellsbury Strait. To prevent this possibility George had already asked the Americans if they would be willing to violate New Salisbury's territorial waters and send a fleet through the Strait on the Day of Descent, also assuming control of air space between the two islands.

The reply, delivered by Russ Nichols personally, was negative on both counts. But there was an alternate suggestion: the Americans offered to provide up to thirty planes that would be flown by our pilots from a U.S. Navy aircraft carrier, then land on newly-liberated territory on the Lower Isle. George was elated. Within hours twenty pilots who had up till then felt largely useless among us in the mountains were on their way to a training center in Florida.

The decisive factor, George confided in me one evening, had shifted. Our success was no longer dependent on Liefenbarger's mistakes. With the completion of the Plan of Descent we were already on the offensive. It was, George used his favorite imagery, as if a jumbo airliner had begun to roll, its engines roaring. It would eventually come to the end of the runway and either have to lift off or break into pieces. We were committed.

Chapter 34

There were only scattered clusters of people in the stands of the stadium, huddling against the crisp air and making little sound. It was early September and cold. Lawrence Saunders looked up at the last section on the right, where a figure huddled in a navy-blue dufflecoat and a woollen hat. The figure sat alone but there were two others nearby, some ten meters away. When Lawrence approached the figures rose, then sat down again as Lawrence took his place beside Meg Winters.

"He still wants to see you," Lawrence said to her.

"But why? There's no reason to. Everything can be taken care of through you. It's dangerous any other way."

Lawrence sighed. "I can't change his mind. He wants you to come to the farm tomorrow evening. It's about ten kilometers from — "

"I know where it is."

"He says to tell you that there'll be men from the Anti-Insurgency Regiment all around. But that you shouldn't worry about it, they can be trusted. You are to drive up and just walk in."

Meg watched the action on the field in front of her for a few moments. The game was slow and unexciting. It was a miserable evening to be playing soccer and the teams showed it.

"I can't do it," she said finally.

"Why not?"

"Because it's just too damn risky. It would be crazy to walk into a trap like that. And I would be the one risking things. Not him."

"Not necessarily."

She turned to him questioningly.

"Look, this whole thing is too important to let it go now. We need him. What if while you talked I spent the time with someone from your group — a hostage, kind of. After all, I *am* his favorite nephew."

Meg thought for a while, then looked at him, then smiled. "All right. Tell him it's a deal. I'll be there."

Meg arrived at the governor's farm exactly at eight, driving her Volkswagen. At the entrance she was met by Felstad in mufti. He ushered her inside, obviously fascinated by the sight of the determined, trim, female revolutionary who in a plain blouse and a skirt under her coat appeared fearless even inside this place which must have been more like a lion's den to her. In the background hovered the very able Major Stewart, Felstad's adjutant. He said nothing, but occasionally kept notes.

McAlpine came from the living room, his arm outstretched, but Meg pointedly ignored it. "If you don't mind governor, I'd rather wait with the handshakes."

McAlpine said nothing. They sat down together in the colonial-style living room, Meg refusing any refreshments and getting right to the point. "I understand you have some sort of an offer to make to us."

"Well, it isn't quite as precise as all that. I just thought it was the right time for exchanging views."

Meg expressed her impatience with his vagueness, where-upon the governor launched into an overview of the situation. He allowed that the number of revolutionaries in the hills was growing, but then cautioned that the Lief was strong and that he was only waiting for the proper time to pounce on the Resistance network — to simultaneously bomb, invade and otherwise disrupt the rebel camps in the Cheviots.

"They might not be able to destroy your entire organization but they will disrupt it enough to make it useless for the next few weeks. And that's all that Lucius Liefenbarger needs because — well, remember the arms agreement? In January the Americans have to start the shipments or come up with some sort of a story. The question is this: Would the Americans be ready to risk another winter with the rebels still in the mountains while Liefenbarger is busily negotiating with the Russians, or would they be more likely to abandon the rebels and shore up Lucius Liefenbarger instead? That is very definitely the key question, Miss Winters."

Meg's mind was racing. She needed more time to assess what McAlpine had just said.

"And Governor McAlpine — how does he fit into all this?" she finally asked.

"Frankly, I'm not quite sure," he produced a smile that was not reciprocated. "I do have a bit of following on the Lower Isle and a bit of loyalty among the men of the Anti-Insurgency Regiment. Above all, I'd hate to see this island drenched in blood, I really would. Except, I don't know exactly how to put all those things together. That's why I invited you here. Maybe you could help me."

He's not giving an inch, thought Meg. What he was saying was that this was a seller's market and that he was selling. It was an invitation to make this political whore an offer.

"Could the Anti-Insurgency Regiment be neutralized on the Day of Descent?" she asked.

McAlpine nodded his reply.

"Could we sabotage airstrips, port facilities and communications without police interference?"

McAlpine nodded again.

"What about St. Enoch? Could we get together and between ourselves and you make sure that there is no bloody street fighting?"

"I think we could."

Meg paused. "Well, what do you want in return?"

"Nothing that I don't already have. I want to remain governor of the Lower Isle and I want everything that goes along with it: the mansion, this farm, a guest house at Castlereagh. And, of course, immunity from prosecution for me and everyone who will be helping me to deliver this island into George Titus's hands. By the way, it is George Titus who is in charge, isn't it? Not John Leahy?"

"Not John Leahy."

During the ensuing pause Meg was thinking about what to say. She had to make a point; at the same time it had to be made in such a way as not to unduly alienate the governor. Because, she grudgingly admitted to herself, he *had* been helpful. Or, at least, he had been pretty good at making it appear so.

"Governor," she finally said, "neither George Titus nor I can promise any of that. If we could, nothing really would have changed except that George Titus and not Lucius Liefenbarger would be running the totalitarian system. We can promise you this much, though: as long as the country is being run by a military government, that government, under the leadership of

George Titus, will grant you immunity from prosecution. It will probably also want to retain your services in some sort of a consultative capacity, but I doubt that the position of governor as such will be retained. It just doesn't fit in with the concept of military efficiency. I will, however, let them know in the Cheviots what it is you want."

McAlpine seemed unconcerned. "Look, they really aren't demands, just requests. How long would you expect the Lower Isle to be under a military government?"

"That's hard to say. I think it will depend on what is happening on Main Island."

"I see. Then after I have handed this island over to you on a silver platter I'll be thrown to the military beast, then to the tender mercies of the so-called democratic electorate — which is, in reality, the mob."

McAlpine seemed to be joking, but only half so. Meg, on the other hand, was deadly serious.

"That's how you got elected in the first place. And you said yourself that you have a bit of a following here."

"You're right," the governor dismissed the problem. "That's not what's really bothering me. I think I am much more worried about the shape of post-revolutionary New Salisbury."

"Yes, the future is a hell of a thing. Tell me, governor, what about the present? Do you feel at all responsible for what's happening on the Partrawa Plain and for the murders in the capital?"

It caught him totally by surprise. He took a deep breath through his nostrils, his eyes ablaze. Like an aroused bull, Meg thought.

"No, I certainly don't," he said after a few moments to compose himself. "But I do feel fully responsible for the fact that on this island such things have been reduced to a minimum. We seem to respect only the condemned, who proudly open their shirts for the bullets. But the man who aims his gun slightly to the side of the condemned is generally overlooked. Probably because he isn't dramatic enough."

Meg said nothing. Each of us has to build his own defenses before his conscience, she thought. Then she got up.

"I think we now have a good idea what it is you want. Do you think you know what we want?"

He nodded. "When do you think you will have an answer?" he asked.

"A week at the most. We'll be in touch with Lawrence Saunders."

"Nice kid, Lawrence," commented McAlpine. "I hope nothing happens to him."

"We'll do our best."

"I'm sure you will."

This time the governor didn't even bother to offer his hand. Without a word Meg walked out of the door held open for her by Felstad. She got into her car and slowly wound her way toward the entrance to the farm.

"I was bluffing a lot," McAlpine said to no one in particular. Before Felstad had a chance to respond, he spoke again. "Listen Paul, if you wanted to make the Anti-Insurgency Regiment totally useless but at the same time you wanted to make it look like the men were being very cleverly deployed, how would you go about it?"

"I'd disperse them," Felstad replied without hesitation.

"But if you spread them out everyone would know right off what you were up to."

"If you went overboard with it, sure. But not if you just broke them up into three groups. You see, the Unit is designed for the offensive — for striking in full force at a particular spot, unexpectedly, fully utilizing the element of surprise to produce fear and chaos. Then the shock troops — paratroopers most likely — would withdraw and wait an hour or two for the rest of the regiment to catch up. Now, during the initial strike there is only a limited amount of ammunition, supplies and manpower available. All that would come with the second strike conducted by the men brought in by surface transportation along with armor and practically unlimited supplies. But all that at the moment is designed for a single target at a time. Say that the rebels had decided to take Marsbury. We would drop the first group of the A-I Regiment. They would surprise the hell out of the enemy, blast them, then quickly withdraw. Two or three hours later, when the trucks and the rest of the men will have arrived from St. Enoch, they'd hit again. But if the rebels decided to come down also at Muldoon and Devon we would be in trouble. We would have to face them in three places."

"That's it, then. We'll disperse them. We'll disperse them to Muldoon and Devon because that's where the rebels will be attacking as well, I'm sure."

"And feed the regiment to the wolves?"

McAlpine nodded. "And feed them to the wolves. Making sure that there'll be a chance for them to surrender. Nobody wants a massacre.

At the start of September (except for the fact that Rose and I had come close to being murdered and no one seemed to have been unduly concerned), the mood and pace in the Cheviots picked up. Such was not the case, however, with the government in New Salisbury City.

There was no greater than usual gloom down there either but there were — how does one put it delicately — *difficulties* on the horizon. For one thing the Lief was in a decidedly difficult position *vis à vis* the Crown. London was not about to approve the Lief's choice for a new governor general which was alternately rumored to be Copithorne (a move to strengthen the grip on the country), McAlpine (an elegant way to reduce his administrative power on the Lower Isle), and the puerile Foreign Affairs Minister Matthew Diebel (a move which would have brought into play Diebel's numerous international contacts, but at the same time returned the office of governor general into its previous state of debilitation). London quite likely would demand that before any appointment reforms first be made in New Salisbury — specifically through the curbing of the excesses of the Partrawa camps and the heavy-handedness of the NUC.

There were persistent rumors reaching the Lief regarding the increased activity of the U.S. in supplying us. Naturally the U.S. embassy denied it, but it did allow that occasionally surveillance flights had been made along the Lower Isle coast to make sure that the Soviets were not involved.

Then there were the leaflets which appeared mostly on the Lower Isle and which formally introduced George Titus as the leader of the Revolutionary Army that would soon take over the government in order to restore elective democracy to the islands. The language was a bit flowery for my taste, but in the end one had to admit the purpose was to inspire, to inflame if necessary. Not to reason. With pure logic there could be no revolution. Logic pointed in the direction of survival, while a revolution called for the gambling of one's life on the improvement of it.

On the whole, things were fairly quiet throughout the islands. When one carefully reads Copithorne's diaries from this period, one detects a certain note of apprehension over this quietude because Copithorne alone among Lief's collaborators correctly sensed that in face of the terror, economic shortages, the growing strength of the rebels and increased American supplies in the mountains, the tranquility was like the proverbial lull before the storm.

Chapter 35

Acting completely on his own, on October 5th Eddie Mayfield dispatched a force of ten NUC types to the Lower Isle. Their helicopter refuelled at Marsbury, then set down three kilometers north of D (Descent) Camp 3. The camp served as a gateway to the northern lowlands and the NUC had undoubtedly sent agents there disguised as rebels to scout the surroundings. The mission was faultlessly executed: the NUC knew exactly where everything was and what the situation was likely to be at three o'clock in the morning.

The destruction was total. Mayfield's men quietly killed the sentries, then entered the cabin, firing indiscriminately at the bunks around them until there was no more movement. Then the bodies and buildings were doused in gasoline and the whole camp set on fire. In all, sixteen rebels were killed.

There was no real strategic or tactical value to the slaughter. The NUC killers withdrew from the mountains immediately afterwards and flew back to Main Island. There was no subsequent attempt to exploit the success. Eddie Mayfield had mounted the operation to prove that the NUC was better equipped to fight the rebels than the regular army, and that operations such as this could be mounted from N.S. City. The NUC would make the McAlpine-Felstad Anti-Insurgency Regiment seem redundant, if not downright threatening, to the security of the Liefenbarger regime.

Of course, Mayfield had proven nothing of the sort. The whole thing was seen by Liefenbarger as no more than a superb bravura piece. He congratulated Mayfield on its success, then quickly ordered all such future operations to be cleared with him. Which meant, in effect, that there would be no such future operations. The raid had received some coverage in the press, but only on Main Island. And even there in the end Copithorne intervened with the Lief, pointing out that the bloody accounts of it were disturbing and unnecessary. The Lief agreed. The publicity stopped and the destruction of D Camp 3 faded into history.

Most of the men who had died there were new in the

mountains, having arrived from the lowlands only recently. But one of them we all knew — he was Branko Justac's younger son, Tom, who had been in command of the camp.

The raid was hardly mentioned at a meeting of the Lief's entire defense-security apparatus a few days later. It had been called because Mayfield's intelligence sources reported rebel concentrations near Marsbury, Muldoon and — what Mayfield considered most significant — fifteen kilometers south of Devon. The NUC chief summorized the development as "one hell of a threat."

General Ormsby who, according to Copithorne's notes, had up till then been staring absentmindedly out the window, asked why.

"Why?" retorted Mayfield, "with rebels less than a hundred kilometers from St. Enoch, I didn't think you'd have to ask that question, general."

And Ormsby, playing his high-born role with Mayfield which Copithorne seemed to enjoy watching so much, outlined in his impeccable upper-class accent the strength and equipment possessed by the First Royal Anti-Insurgency Regiment.

"Do the terrorists have Leopard tanks in the mountains with which they'll come hurtling down?" Ormsby asked. "Do they have howitzers, personnel carriers, and airplanes? Because if they don't, they will have great difficulty in reaching St. Enoch to say the least."

Mayfield then tried to point out to the Lief that according to his intelligence sources there is something called the Plan of Descent and that its first phase calls for the positioning of the terrorists in three places — at Marsbury, Muldoon and Devon.

Ormsby ignored Mayfield and turned to Admiral Lester, Chief of Naval Operations. "Do you have any reports of unusual activity around the Lower Isle?" he asked, and when he received a negative answer he turned to the Lief. "That would be the only way the rebels could get hold of firepower and equipment that would match ours. Via the sea. They cannot come down without transport and heavy weapons because they cannot move against us without them."

"Why do you think they're massing then?" asked the Lief.

"To test us. To see how long it will take us to react, to deploy the Anti-Insurgency Unit, how well organized and how strong it is. When they scurry back up into the mountains they will know much more about us if we overreact."

Mayfield argued that the idea of sending men into the lowlands just for a probe would be highly dangerous, that government forces could easily block their route back up into the mountains just as they had done after the Fort Wellington raid.

At that point Ormsby no longer bothered to hide his disdain for Mayfield. "That was a force of twenty men. Now we are talking in terms of hundreds, perhaps thousands."

"Then what the hell do you suggest we do?" Mayfield yelled at Ormsby who, however, again ignored him and addressed himself directly to the Lief.

"I suggest, sir, that we put all the Lower Isle police units on alert and stay calm. In a few days the rebels will return to the mountains, being none the wiser about our strategy. In the meantime we bring Governor McAlpine and Colonel Felstad up here and begin planning our spring offensive."

Unfortunately, this was the last major battle with Mayfield that Ormsby would win. But had we in the Cheviots been asked which battle we would want Ormsby to win the most, it would undoubtedly have been this one.

Chapter 36

Even in October there were still few outward signs on Main Island of the approaching struggle. But more and more uniforms appeared in the streets, the proliferating and lengthening lines in front of the badly supplied stores became more telling. So did the foreign protests against the ever more brazen tactics of the NUC.

There was also talk about the increased activity of the Resistance in the city but for the most part that's all it was — just talk. With the Day of Descent fast approaching, the Resistance cells on Main Island had been told to lay low, to be ready to hinder any attempted transfer of military reinforcements from Main Island to the Lower Isle, but otherwise to abstain from activity which would justify NUC reprisals and disturb the laboriously mended fabric of the Resistance network, torn during the landing of the Algerians. We would need the network intact once the Lower Isle belonged to us and it was being readied as a stepping stone for jumping northward.

The other side was having its problems and Copithorne was well aware of them. In his diaries he notes that the Lief was becoming unusually expansive, that Ann Schorez was on his mind almost constantly at the expense of adequate consideration being given to the steadily increasing problems with the economy. Ominous messages received from missions abroad indicated that world opinion was changing from just strong displeasure with NUC's activities to more precise calls for economic sanctions.

The Lief listened with only mild interest as Ormsby kept outlining the grandiose but somewhat less realistic plans for the assault on the Cheviots. He had had a spat with Ann, the following day heading south to inspect coastal installations. When he got back to the capital she had flown off on a Hawaiian vacation. Only with great difficulty did the Lief manage to keep his consternation from showing.

In his diaries Copithorne now began to question the Lief's constantly reiterated search for a single magic stroke that would all at once set everything right again. Still relatively mildly, but with growing conviction, he criticized the Lief for abandoning his previous attention to detail, then for an attempted one-step surgical intervention designed to exorcise the defects and restore the badly ailing patient to his spiritually healthy, pristine state.

Copithorne disliked the Lief's insistence on comparing himself alternately to Churchill and to Tokimune, the able thirteenth-century Hojo Regent who, along with the generous help of the divine wind Kamikazi, was able to repulse Kublai Khan's attempted invasion of Japan.

"Sometimes it seems as if the A is tired of the day-to-day rule, as if he distances himself from the increasingly serious problems that face us all and attempts to deal with them by using only his left hand. Of course, under the present circumstances this isn't nearly enough," Copithorne wrote.

But there was one masterly stroke which the Lief made late in October: he appointed the puerile but contact-rich Foreign Affairs Minister Matthew Diebel as Governor General Pro Tempore of New Salisbury. London immediately protested that such an appointment must be approved by the Crown, but in a message full of humility Liefenbarger pointed out that this was a new post of purely technical administrative significance, and that Diebel's temporary designation to it in no way precluded the appointment of an official governor general once the problems between the islands and the Crown were finally resolved. Theoretically at least, the matter remained in abeyance until the Commonwealth ministers met and the whole thing could be thoroughly thrashed out.

In the meantime, Diebel proceeded to reestablish his old contacts, which now, because of his supreme rank, were on a much higher level. In spite of official explanations Diebel, in the post of the Governor General Pro Tempore, provided New Salisbury with that fake air of legitimacy that in the tradition-ridden, thoroughly artificial world of diplomacy is ever so essential.

There is no doubt that it was Copithorne again who had counselled the move. It was also Copithorne who had organized a somewhat bizarre luncheon at the Oceanic Hotel, sponsored by the National Federation of Farmers and Industrialists. This was an uneasy alliance created by the Economics Minister Bernard Metcalf, who wanted to unite the two main pillars of private enterprise under a single, government-dominated banner. Having often experienced the effects of untrammelled free enterprise regime during his poverty-stricken youth in south New Salisbury City, the Lief hastened to dampen the federation's boisterous enthusiasm for a laissez-faire economy. The previous month, for example, he had raised the hourly minimum wage by twenty-five cents, which was considerably less than what the galloping inflation rate seemed to call for, but far more than the federation had expected. An interesting guest, lending dignity to the luncheon, was Bishop Kewley, the newly elected head of the New Salisbury Religious Unity Committee, who was skating some of the compulsory figures on the decidedly thin ice to the music provided by Lief's office. In return for a generous donation he was ready to bless all of the federation efforts — past, present and future.

Notably missing from the press table at the Oceanic Hotel on the 23rd of October were Robert Fenwick and Roderick Muser. Fenwick, a bit belatedly, had penned a scathing attack on the provisions of the Extraordinary State Act, then had it published not in the *Times* (for which he wrote a daily column but which also possessed one of the few literate NUC agents in existence who had the final say on what went into the paper), but in an underground newspaper called *To Battle*.

The latest editor of *To Battle* had been arrested the previous week. Within hours of being brought to Bristol Street, he divulged all the names of his contributors and Fenwick was now serving an indefinite term on the Partrawa Plain. As brave as Fenwick's attempt was, it came five years after the Lief came to power, during which he wrote his column obediently, safely and as a consequence, in an extremely dull manner.

It wasn't the moral indignation over what was happening to his country but anger over what was happening to his card-playing croney that caused the N.S. Radio commentator Roderick Muser to write an angry letter to the Lief about the fate of Robert Fenwick. He was promptly suspended from his job, awaiting the further disposition of his case at home. In the end the Lief would let him go with only a warning, but certainly not to return to radio.

Liefenbarger knew both Fenwick and Muser well because he used to be present at their card parties while still a policeman, occasions which would lead to arguing politics until dawn. Now he gazed at their places provocatively left vacant by their colleagues, adlibbing a few introductory remarks, then making observations on the conflict between the East and West.

Finally he brought the whole thing back home again, making an indirect, vague reference to us in the Cheviots: "There are those who find the present stability of our island country distasteful to their hot blood, those who write and publish fiery declarations about our supposed lack of freedoms, against our determined efforts to preserve a system that has brought us one of the most prosperous economies in the Pacific. They would like to change this system. They would like us to transform it into the Marx-Leninist model — the one that nowhere has yet been able to feed its own people adequately, whose representatives are forever begging on the various international money markets for their credits. It is the same system that is notorious for being thoroughly unable to provide enough housing for its people, that scrupulously measures the number of square meters of living space to be allotted to each of its citizens. It is worthy of note that those industrialized countries that have been forced to adopt the Marx-Leninist system are today among the beggars of the world.

"But why? Why would anyone propose such a system now that it has been discredited a thousand times over? The answer lies in the background of those who are in the forefront of advocating socialism. These are the professional rabble-rousers, radicals who have made violence, the creation of disorder and chaos the goal of their lives. Also the naive academics — university professors who cannot help seeing the world only from the ivory towers which they inhabit. They are fat, satisfied and comfortable in their unreal environment. Perhaps some of them even believe the lies they are spreading — although I don't think I would go as far as to call them sincere men. They are not all honorable men; they are men who don't know any better. Those men and women who know better are right here in front of me. They are the men who direct the farm and industrial production as well as commerce in our country — people who are in the know.

"Edmund Burke, that famous and enlightened eighteenth-century English thinker, hit the nail right on the head when he said: 'What is the use of discussing a man's abstract right to food and medicine? The question is upon the method of procuring and administering them. In that deliberation I shall always advise to call in the aid of the farmer and the physician, rather than the professor of metaphysics.' "

An enormous round of applause from the spiritually uplifted farmers and industrialists followed this particular passage. Since then I have noticed a certain renaissance of Burke's thoughts from the mouths of politicians throughout the world. I guess it is comforting for the late twentieth-century conservative to identify with this oracle, this one-time confidant of Dr. Johnson. Even more comforting must be the thought that, by using Burke, one is really fighting the academic fire with the very same element.

Like the Administrator, whose attention had been brought to the political philosopher's thoughts through the efforts of the seemingly omniscient Copithorne, they particularly like to use the paragraph with which the Lief concluded his October 23rd speech at the Oceania: "And again, we should turn to Burke for an exquisitely worded opinion of those whose advice on how to reform a society is so sterile that it calls only for carnage and suffering. This is what he says: 'These professors, finding their extreme principles not applicable, employ no resistance at all. It is with them a war or a revolution, or it is nothing. Plots, massacres, assassinations, seem to some people a trivial price for obtaining a revolution. There must be a great change of scene; there must be a grand spectacle to rouse the imagination, grown torpid with the lazy enjoyment of security and still unanimated repose of public prosperity.' "

After the speech, Copithorne informed the Lief that Ann Schorez was back, that she was sitting at the table reserved for diplomats and had asked to see him.

It had been a day of unusual triumphs, the Lief must have thought, as the chic Ann joined him in the back seat of the Rolls Royce, on their way to spend a night at the cabin in the wilderness beyond Lake Haumo.

Part Two

THE DESCENT

Chapter 37

It's time to reevaluate. Not the revolution itself , which at this point was puffing along quite nicely, but George Titus. Like comparing and contrasting the personality traits of Pierre Bezuchov before and after the Battle of Borodino; or, on a Comp. Lit. exam, like describing Pip before and after meeting Miss Havisham and Estella and being told of his Great Expectations.

The Day of Descent was certainly Borodino and Great Expectations combined, with Estella thrown in for good measure in the form of Meg.

But I am getting ahead of myself.

For three days prior to October 24th, the designated Day of Descent, we had been zigzagging through the Cheviot foothills with a group of about ten rebels, playing the old shell game with any government forces that may have been around. Where would we emerge — in the North, South, or in between? Obviously, the best place for the government forces to strike would have been where Titus was. We still worried about the Anti-Insurgency Regiment; its pacification by McAlpine was regarded as probable but by no means certain.

None of us really knew where George was. True, he was marching two paces in front of me on the narrow trail, but where he actually stood and where we all were as a result, that was a bit more difficult to discern. I already knew fairly well at that point what it was that made me tick. It certainly wasn't some aura of bravery enveloping me, a burning desire to do the right deed on a white steed. By this time I had discarded such self-decepting baggage. In Honolulu I had even found it difficult to fool myself that I could somehow monitor and coordinate a spontaneous uprising in New Salisbury, then return there triumphantly and after a proper period of jubilation resume my upper-middle-class lifestyle. No revolution would be possible unless I or someone else organized it. And the way it was being organized from Algeria didn't portend good things for my return to the ranks of the upper-middle-class. The choice was between doing the job myself or remaining in exile forever. I love New Salisbury with the nationalist fervor common to most of those who had not had the good fortune of being born there. The choice had been really made for me. I was in it on this soggy mountain trail because I still clung to my ridiculous dream of recreating somehow the pre-Liefenbarger New Salisbury, then building my nest in it. It may have been selfish, but it was also, I've always felt, crystal clear and perhaps even disarmingly honest.

Meg Winters's motor, on the other hand, was powered by something else. The Lief had interfered with her studies — i.e. her career. She hated him with a passion that grew by leaps and bounds, particularly after she had been forced into exile. She even started out by hating George and went down into the lowlands to show off his ineptitude and cowardice, also her own bravery. She came back to the Cheviots, consummated her desire that first night with me, then transferred whatever love there may have been to George. It wasn't that difficult. Meg was the passionate type and that's really why she was in it all — because revolutionary situations constitute something of a paradise for all passionate people.

Aah, but George Titus — he remained enigmatic. Mostly because he had become so adept at changing the fuel that powered him while hurtling down the road with his gas pedal floored. There were several factors to be considered in his case. Let's start with the fact that he never really had a friend. I was the closest that ever came to that definition, but our friendship changed in substance even faster than the phases of the moon, and there had even been long periods where there were no phases at all — when for all practical purposes we simply didn't know each other. At the end of one such period George flew to Honolulu, just as his marriage had fallen apart. Or, rather, just after he had realized that it was irreparable. We got him on the rebound. He was useful to the revolution and the revolution to him. Through us he had acquired a new wife and family; he was kept busy and occasionally frightened enough to be able to ignore the ravages of the male menopause which oppressed him, and he could dream about a coup which would dwarf anything he had ever done before.

The cold shower produced by Captain Greytrix on the Renfrew Peninsula probably put an end to what remained of George's romanticism. Lying listlessly on the deck of the tuna boat with plenty of time to think it over, he had not yet become a hard-line realist. But he also began to realize that in his own life there was nothing left to go back to. He had dabbled in enough history to see that even had he opted to return quietly into his library carrel in order to reach some sort of solution with his family and work, he would still rate at least a footnote in future histories of the islands. In that very important footnote he would be identified as the effete and somewhat cowardly son of a highly effective politician. He was committed, but as yet he didn't see too clearly what to. It took Meg and the landing at Precarious to spell it out for him.

But it still wasn't much more than inertia with the accompanying fear of loss of face that carried him on. Certainly in November — less than a year ago — he could not have seriously expected to be anywhere near to where he was now. And in the middle of May, when there were barely a hundred rebels remaining in the Cheviots, things seemed even darker in that narrow tunnel. There was no sign of any light at the end of it and no space for George to turn around in and crawl back.

The mood had changed drastically with the arrival of the first Hercules and Rose Kubatan — with guns and respect from the influential, intelligent press. A few days later came Russ Nichols, bringing the American-trained manpower in his helicopter — the third requirement for attaining the deliciously enticing power.

After that, we all should have realized that there was no stopping of George Titus's megalomania. Looking back, it is now easy to analyze; but just before the Day of Descent, with us sloshing through the damp underbrush, George still constituted — as I've already said — something of an enigma.

I also suspect that at that time I must have been the only one who found the time and opportunity to worry about it.

Toward evening of the second day we reached Cheviot's lower foothills, where the craggy peaks formed only a distant picturesque background. Here and there a patch of bush had been cleared to make way for grazing land and the occasional farm.

One such clearing with a red farmhouse nestled between two hills, which had chintz curtains in the windows, brought back a memory so vivid that I stopped in my tracks. I was dumb struck by its similarity to another farmhouse of long ago. Maybe twenty years ago now.

The place was Brempton, some hundred kilometers north of where I stood, where Mrs. Gladys Cooper's husband had once cleared the land only to find that he was too far away from the markets for effective truck farming. But he was close enough to a charming lake whose placid surface dominated the town of Brempton. So Trevor Cooper sold his herd, turned to land development and emerged not with a fortune but with the prospect of living the rest of his life in relative comfort. He died three years later aboard a destroyer torpedoed by the Japanese Imperial Navy off the Maryannas.

That had happened ten years before George and I looked down at the Cooper farmhouse for the first time at the edge of a clearing one particularly wet afternoon. We had been in the mountains for almost five days by then, three of them spent by retracing our steps to Marsbury. On the way to Renette we had been hit by a number of setbacks, including a steady, unrelenting rain which had swelled the gentle streams into raging currents, the ground becoming a sea of black mud in the process. Everything we wore and touched was wet, slimy, and wholly uncomfortable. To make things worse, soon after the rains started George had slipped, spraining his ankle and making us both instantly realize that the handicaps would prevent us from reaching Renette. We suspected it would be no piece of cake returning to Marsbury either.

So we started back. Twice during that first day George shook with what seemed like the first stages of hypothermia. First I threw his damp sleeping bag over him, then hugged him tightly to produce some of that warmth we both needed so sorely. George kept suggesting that he should stay behind, a strategy that would enable me to travel faster for help. I wouldn't hear of it. We had by then consumed all our supplies, in the end pouring the vile-tasting, powdered food into our mouths in an effort to produce extra energy. We were mostly silent. Talking, we had sensed, tapped our last resources of strength. With one of George's arms around my shoulders we moved on, gloomily contemplating another night in the wilderness.

Then we saw the light in the window of Mrs. Cooper's farmhouse — a scene from Hansel and Gretel. The immensely practical Gladys Cooper fell quickly into step, dividing her time between the kitchen, where she kept an eye on the steak and kidney pie in the oven, the bathroom, where she drew water for our hot baths, and the bedroom, where she had piled blankets upon the still trembling George, at the same time attending to his bulbous ankle with vinegar compresses.

She won hands down over all adversity. Later we sat in her overstuffed easy chairs in her doilied living room. It was then that Gladys Cooper, in her perforated brogues, khaki woollen skirt, and with a stylish scarf around her neck, heard that one of her guests was the son of the prime minister of New Salisbury.

She thought it over for a few moments, putting the time to good use by pouring us a cup of fresh tea. "I'm thankful to your father for making this a good country to live in. I must say I had some doubts about independence at first, but I don't any more. It is good. But independence or the Empire don't automatically mean that people will be decent. It helps, though, when there are decent people at the top. In the government, I mean. We have been lucky."

"Thank you. It's nice to hear about my own father. I'll tell him what you said," George replied.

Mrs. Cooper looked up from her knitting. "Yes, please do tell him. But make sure that you say 'decent', not just 'nice'. There is a difference, you know, although so many people don't seem to understand it. It's important to be decent even though sometimes it may mean forsaking being nice. But I am sure your father understands that very well."

The next day a neighbor drove us to Marsbury and the following night we were back home in N.S. City. The novelty of finding neither a witch nor a simple farm woman at the clearing but the lucid, homely and so immensely practical Mrs. Cooper couldn't be forgotten by either of us. We talked about her often, until the meaning of what she had said slowly started to emerge. To her, decency meant a permanent, deeply-thoughtful and deeply-caring state — a way of life with principles which supported one's humanism and without which life tended to become a desperate maze.

Occasionally we saw Gladys Cooper after that. Once we even invited her for a weekend at St. Enoch when George's father visited there and we introduced them to each other. But as had been the case with so many things when we were young, it had all been too rushed. Our friendship was eventually reduced to an exchange of Christmas cards and then, when George went to England, it was allowed to lapse completely. The memory remained, though. With time Mrs. Cooper in my mind became all that was synonymous with being truly human.

Someone nudged me as I stood there, gazing at the farmhouse. Reluctantly I started to move again, wondering if Gladys Cooper was still at Brempton inside that house with chintz curtains and if all would ever be well again with the world.

When I caught up with George who was walking a few meters ahead of me, to tell him about my deja vu experience, he merely grunted his reaction. Yes, he remembered Mrs. Cooper and her farmhouse, but from his tone it was obvious that she didn't seem to be that important at the moment.

Chapter 38

There is no doubt in my mind that by this time George Titus had already been seduced by power — that he lived and breathed it, that he wallowed in the thought of it, but that he was also incredibly successful in keeping all signs of this inside him. What I considered to be enigmatic about him was, in fact, nothing of the sort. By the time of the Descent, he had no problems in deciding what his ultimate goals were; he had no doubts about what he wanted, what he craved.

But he did have some problems in getting to his goals. Some fairly substantial ones.

On the night between the 23rd and 24th he couldn't sleep. While it was still fairly dark he got up in a highly nervous state, almost in a state of panic. He complained that he couldn't breathe. As I watched him from the other bunk while he stood in front of the tent, it seemed a tremendous effort each time to take in air, push it into his lungs, then exhale again. Sitting up had helped a bit, standing even more. I eventually followed suit, unzipped my bag and came out too.

The early glow indicated the sun was about to rise. A few paces to the right Sid Capadouca was furiously pumping pressure into a Coleman stove to boil some water for morning coffee. I recall that the distant Cheviots took on a sinister look, as if they resented our leaving — it was the kind of silly imagery we both indulged in that morning to keep our minds off the deadly realism with which we would soon be faced.

George was breathing easier now, but not much slower. Grabbing the upper part of my arm, he proceeded for a few minutes to pour out his doubts with astonishing candor. What right did he have to stand here, getting ready to command a revolution? To be a man who, in a few moments, would become responsible for countless deaths and maimings because of reasons which may yet turn out to be nothing but thoroughly naïve notions of right and wrong? In the end, how exactly would he differ from history's great mass murderers — from the Stalins, Hitlers and Maos? This freedom and liberty without which man has shown himself to be perfectly capable of surviving over and over again — whose concern was it really? Those dead-tired workers coming home from the graveyard shift at St. Enoch Steelworks — were they ready to die for it, did *they* consider it worthy of death? What sort of a mini-holocaust will it be that he — George Titus — will have unleashed by the end of this day? What right did he have — *what right?*

He kept shaking my arm for emphasis.

Then suddenly, he stopped. He walked off a few steps, pulled the lapels of his coat closer together and stared wordlessly into the rising sun.

I too felt cold. Tired of wet ferns, of the clammy air of early spring, of the patches of dirty, granular snow, of muddy boots, limbs bruised by sharp rocks, of the smell of wood fires full of burning sap and of icy waters from the glaciers.

This — the American army fatigues and boots that reached halfway up my calf — had been the only clothing I had worn for almost a year. I was tired of it, tired of the tasteless, dried food cooked in cast-iron cauldrons, tired of the last few days on the road, sometimes up to my knees in mud. I wanted no more of lengthy detours around raging streams and avalanche-prone valleys. We were twenty kilometers south of Devon, near a sleepy provincial town named Smithton populated by about 500 inhabitants. Below us, in what seemed to be only a stone's throw away, were the dying lights of Smithton, and waiting in its streets was a strategically positioned force of thirty rebels.

Like a man who had just vomited, George felt better, although he did not yet look it. Inside him the beckoning promise of sensuous power must have powerfully reasserted itself. There was now a beacon of light to follow again. He was no longer just groping.

He started to tremble, trying to hide it by covering one of his arms with the other, at the same time slowly approaching Sid, who was bent over the Coleman stove. Two paces away Sid spotted him. His face broke into a wide, good-natured grin that had an immediate and beneficial effect on us all.

"I was just going to wake you ... but I guess you weren't asleep anyway, were you?"

Not quite certain of the degree of control over his jaws, George just shook his head.

"Here. The water's ready. Let's make some coffee."

A few moments later George was warming his hands on a steaming mug. His shivers started to disappear.

"Any news from anyone?" he asked.

"Well, they signed in from Kilmaron and Justac did from Muldoon, but that's all. It really isn't light enough for anything yet," replied Sid. Then he took a sip on his own mug, adding as if an afterthought, "But we already have a casualty."

"Who?"

"A guy named Granby. Nick Granby. When we moved into Smithton last night they didn't figure the police would resist. But one of them started shooting from the hip."

"Is Granby hurt bad?"

Sid nodded. "One of the bullets went right through a lung."

"Is he in hospital?"

"No. They're waiting until light before moving him. That part of town is dangerous. They're afraid of snipers."

Nick Granby lay on a cot a couple of tents away. His eyes were closed when we came into the tent. He couldn't have been more than twenty. Next to him on a stool sat a nurse in ridiculously large fatigues, one from the group that had arrived in the Cheviots just a few weeks ago. She started to rise as George came in, but he motioned to her to stay seated. At the same time we realized that the gurgling, wheezing sounds emanating from the depth of the tent came from the wounded man with each laborious rise of his chest. Granby tiredly opened his eyes. I had a feeling that there was a trace of a smile on his deathly pale face, but I was probably all wrong.

"How is he?" whispered George.

The nurse then got up and gently led us out of the tent. "He has to be moved, sir — immediately. We haven't got a moment to spare." Her voice was full of urgency. "There's a hospital at Smithton."

"I know, but he can't be moved until the town is safe. That would help no one."

"But he'll die!" she shouted.

"Unless the town is safe, he can't be moved through it."

Her face twisted into a mixture of defiance and contempt. She seemed to be wanting to say more, even to shout her disagreement over the verdict, but suddenly she turned on her heel and disappeared inside the tent again.

"It shouldn't be long now," George said to no one in particular. He looked at me and again, only fleetingly, all over his face the same question appeared: *What right?*

Soon Sid's radio was crackling with reports about skirmishes at Muldoon and Devon. Half an hour later Smithton was secure. The boy was quickly moved to the hospital and temporary headquarters were established in the branch office of the Royal Bank of New Salisbury. It may have been an indication of the rising chaos or maybe of our own callousness that neither of us has checked into the fate of Nick Granby to this day.

At eight came the crucial message from St. Enoch: the First Royal Anti-Insurgency Regiment had taken to the air.

The fight was on. At Smithton, though, we couldn't do much more than wait and listen.

Chapter 39

At a remote retreat, high on a hill south of Lake Haumo, Lucius Liefenbarger spent the last night before the revolution with Ann Schorez. I knew it well — it had been built by my father; first as a hunting lodge, then expanded into a sort of a sylvan mansion to provide a luxurious centre for wheeling and dealing and contract signing. When Bech-Landau Enterprises were greatly reduced in size early in the 1960s, the place went to Air New Salisbury. Soon after the Lief's takeover, it was transferred to the Ministry of Foreign Affairs.

There was the main, sprawling complex with its jutting wings, built of logs and containing roomy bedrooms, all leading into a central hall with some twenty easy chairs, several skylights and an adjoining kitchen. A few hundred yards below all this was the small guardhouse, connected to the main complex by a wide driveway.

Copithorne and the military personnel that came up with the Lief and Ann Schorez stayed in the guardhouse. The soldiers, of course, immediately began patrolling the vicinity, discreetly staying away from the windows of the main lodge lest they spot the Administrator and his mistress in an uncompromising position. The whole expedition had been organized on the spur of the moment when the Lief and his lady friend had decided to make the outing but, considering the haste, it had not been badly organized; about twenty men guarded the main lodge and immediate telephone contact had been established with the town of Lake Haumo about thirty kilometers away. But this contact was soon severed by a man named MacPhearson who headed the local Resistance cell, and who had been listening to his shortwave receiver late into the night. Playing around with the dial he overheard some transmissions between us in the Cheviot foothills and the Americans offshore. From those he surmised that the Day of Descent had come.

He was also aware through his informers at the Lake Haumo NUC office that the Lief was at the lodge. Shortly after midnight he drove out with two of his friends and, at a sec-

luded spot, cut the telephone wires connecting the lodge with
the town of Lake Haumo. The amazing thing was that he had
received absolutely no instructions to do that; Macphearson
had done it entirely on his own authority thereby managing to
provide us with some essential minutes of governmental chaos.

When the lieutenant in charge of the detail at the mansion
tried to call in at 7 A.M., he realized that the line had been cut.
He then resorted to the radio in his jeep, which had been
turned off. Only then was he told about the fighting on the
Lower Isle. He immediately woke up Copithorne.

The usually dapper Copithorne, dressed only in a pair of
trousers and a shirt, stumbled across the roots in the driveway
in his slippers, hurrying to the main lodge. He hammered on
the door until the Administrator finally appeared, dressed in
his pajamas, for a moment listening to the disquieting news,
then interrupting his secretary in mid-sentence to say as soon
as he was dressed they were going to Lake Haumo.

There are some who claim that at that moment the Lief was
convinced beyond any doubt Ann Schorez had been planted in
his life, and her primary purpose was to have had him safely
away from the capital and incommunicado during the first few
hours of the Day of Descent, and that in a fit of anger he had
come close to killing her.

It is true that Ann was not in one of the jeeps that soon left
the lodge. She returned to the capital much later and quite
unobtrusively.

From Lake Haumo the Lief called Winthrop Reese who was
the duty officer at the Towers — the military headquarters in
N.S. City. "What's happening major?" he shouted into the
phone.

"The information is scattered, sir, but it looks like there are
three columns moving eastward from the Cheviots. One is in
the north — "

"Yes, I know. They're the rebels Ormsby thought were just
testing us. I want a plane or something to take me to N.S. City
from here."

"Yes sir. Except that —"

"Except what?"

"Well, there are reports from the Lower Isle about some
unfamiliar planes in the air. They aren't ours. Maybe you
shouldn't be in the air, sir."

"Oh to hell with that. Have you spoken to anyone in the south?"

"Yes sir. Governor McAlpine says that they're taking countermeasures."

"Good. Get in touch with him again and tell him he's authorized to do whatever he considers necessary until I call him from the capital."

"Yes sir."

"Now get me Eddie May — no, wait a minute, get me Ormsby instead."

Just before the helicopter bringing the Lief and Frank Copithorne into the capital landed, the Lief got hold of Ormsby on the radio. There was no attempt to code or scramble anything, the conversation went on the air and was recorded by the N.S. Army as it took place.

"We have to hit them at Devon," shouted the Lief. "That's where the A-I group is heading, right?"

"Just a small part of it, I'm afraid sir."

"Well, where is the rest? The reinforcements? Move up to Devon everything we have at St. Enoch. We have to hit them now!"

"The rest is not at St. Enoch, sir. Felstad and McAlpine have split the regiment into three parts. They claim you have given them a free hand on deployment, sir. The other two groups are north of Marsbury and south at Muldoon, but without supplies and support they'll be swallowed up like minnows."

"What about planes? Let's get at them from the air!"

"There's fighting on all Lower Isle air bases. At Dernvale, outside of St. Enoch, it broke out as soon as the A-I Regiment was in the air. Then there are all those unidentified planes around."

"Well, let's recall the other parts of the regiment — get it all together again."

"Where'll they land, sir? Where would be the staging area? It would be nothing but chaos."

For a few moments the Lief remained silent. "Well, what *can* be done?"

"There are some small units at Castlereagh and Renette but without any real equipment. They aren't fighting groups at all."

"How many men?"

"Two hundred. Three at the most."

"And they're probably full of rebel sympathizers."

"That is quite possible."

"Christ what a mess! What has gone wrong, Ormsby?"

"I would say that McAlpine and Felstad are working with the rebels, sir."

"What? Why?"

"Why I think so or why they are in with the rebels?"

"Both. *Both.*"

"Well, to disperse the Anti-Insurgency Unit is to destroy its hammer-like quality. Felstad knows that very well. That is the answer to your first question. The answer to the second one is either I don't know or that the rebels may have promised them something in return."

"All right," said Liefenbarger after a pause, "do we throw in the Castlereagh and Renette Units?"

"Not unless you want them destroyed, sir."

"Then what the hell *can* be done?"

"Cut our losses and run. Make sure that we have the situation well in hand up here, then wait for a snag to develop on the Lower Isle. The best we can hope for right now is to get some of our men back here on Main Island. That is, if the rebels are willing to negotiate."

Liefenbarger didn't respond to this. He handed the receiver back to the pilot and looked out the window. The helicopter was already starting to descend toward N.S. City.

Chapter 40

At the investigation of the Sumawa affair two months after it happened, one of the key witnesses was Corporal David Wingate, who served in the C Company, 2nd Battalion of the First Royal Anti-Insurgency Regiment. He was pushed in his wheelchair into the St. Enoch courtroom, where the inquiry took place. The left part of his body was paralyzed.

In the first part of his testimony he described his friendship with his cousin, Private Roger Wingate, with whom he had joined the army a year and half ago and with whom he took basic training at a camp near Nelson.

"Why did you volunteer for the Anti-Insurgency Unit?" the chairman of the inquiry committee then asked.

"Because we would be going back home to St. Enoch and because we wanted to be paratroopers; that was exactly what we wanted to do," Wingate replied.

"Could you tell us what happened on the morning of the 24th of October please, corporal?"

"Well, we had been confined to the base all evening, and the night before too, but nothing was happening. Like we were in the barracks, playing cards and reading or sleeping until right after reveille at six. And then we were told to get our gear together fast, real fast, and we mustered out in front of the barracks where they had trucks waiting to take us to the airfield, which wasn't very far, maybe a ten-minute ride. And there we got loaded up into planes real fast and we took off."

"Did you know where you were going?" asked one of the inquiry committee members.

"No. Well, at least not officially. We had a pretty good idea though, you know with all the talk that goes on. And then we were over a drop area so we hooked up and I think I was about the third one out. Rog was right behind me and there was no trouble at all, it was a piece of cake. No wind and it was sunny and the ground was nothing but pretty level pasture. So we got down and assembled by platoons and then we were told that we were near Sumawa and to move out, going east, and that our company was to assemble at the BP station on Memorial

Square. So we started out, but in about five minutes we heard these planes coming, so we got down on the ground, ready to fight it out, but I don't know with what. Each one of us only had a gun, that's all. But they weren't shooting at us, they just dropped those leaflets. Thousands of them. They were all around."

"Did you read what was on them?" the chairman asked.

"No sir, I didn't. I don't think anyone did much reading. There was lots of writing on them about who was wrong and who was right but I've never been much good in figuring that sort of thing. I mean I do what I'm told usually, I'm no hero. Besides, we had to get to Sumawa, those were our orders. We didn't have time to sit around and read."

"Tell me, corporal, did you ever discuss with your friends the possibility of having to kill your countrymen and did you think about that at all on that morning?" asked one member of the committee with a distinct edge to his voice.

"Not too often, sir. You see, the A-I Regiment wasn't exactly the right place for it. You were kept busy, training from morning till night because there was lots to learn and when you got a few hours off to go and drink some beer what you wanted to talk about was girls and football and things like that. Not politics."

"Whom did you think you were going to be fighting when you were on that plane and later on the ground?" persisted the committee member.

Corporal Wingate shrugged his shoulders. "I don't know. Communists I guess. Yeah, Communists. We knew there were Communists in the Cheviots and that it was our job to clean them out."

The committee chairman then told him to continue with his account.

"Well, we moved on toward Sumawa, where we got just before noon. It was getting hot, really hot. I remember saying to Rog that I was surprised how many people there were on the street there, I mean it was all sort of like a big show, like a circus or something came into town and everybody was gawking at us. So we straightened up and played the part of big-shot warriors, dragging ourselves into the Memorial Square and heading for the BP station. Our officer, Lieutenant Hammond, sent two patrols into the side streets to make sure we wouldn't be ambushed. And the square was starting to fill up. Rog and I were leaning against some empty oil drums, smoking a cig and there were four officers inside the petrol station office, calling up someone on the phone all the time and studying maps and things. We just started talking about moving closer, getting underneath the arch to be out of the sun when I was hit. I have no idea from where. I just lay there, and I was still conscious, I knew what was happening around me all the time except that I couldn't do anything about it because I couldn't move. I remember Rog leaning over me and asking what was the matter, but I couldn't talk so I just stared at him like some kind of an idiot. There was lots of screaming and blood around us and I guess that Rog felt that he couldn't do anything sitting there next to me, that he should go for some help. So he started to run but he only took a step or two before they caught him and he fell backward with his face toward me. And he kept trying to say something but all that he kept making was this gurgling sound, until finally he put all he had left into it and a whole mouthful of blood poured out before he was gone, but I knew what he was trying to say. I understood.

"He said momma — like a baby he would cry out. Just momma."

The chairman then adjourned the enquiry until the next day.

At about 10 A.M., Meg Winters walked into our headquarters at Smithton. She was wearing her favorite khakis, inordinately big boots and an open parka. Spotting George, she took off her hat and with her other hand she loosened her hair, then started running toward him, a canvas bag swinging from her shoulder.

Neither of them held back; they fell into each other's arms to the great delight of all those standing around, and they held on, buried deep in each other's heavy coat and obviously feeling warm, reassured. On occasion George had mentioned the possibility of her not coming back, trying to condition himself into accepting the bad news, I guess. But all that was now past, her presence here was much more than just a great comfort to him.

A few moments later they disappeared into one of the offices upstairs and the show was over.

Shortly after that word reached us that Branko Justac and his group had reached St. Enoch, and that he had set up revolutionary headquarters in the governor's office building; except for the sporadic and well-contained street fighting, the Lower Isle's capital was quiet.

It had not all gone as smoothly at other places. Castlereagh was encircled by the rebels, but within the circle ruled a ruthless National Unity Corps detachment. For hours now the commander of our Northern Force had been negotiating with them.

Sumawa was in the throes of a raging battle that had already destroyed parts of the town and in which participated rebel pilots launched in planes from the American aircraft carrier. Every government air base on the Lower Isle was now in our hands. For all practical purposes we had control of the skies above our island.

Most important, though, was the advance of the Main Rebel Force — the Middle Force in the Plan of Descent, which had easily taken the town of Devon during the early morning hours. With commandeered trucks, a convoy had immediately set out for St. Enoch. Some twenty kilometers out of Devon, though, the second battalion of the A-I Regiment had been dropped shortly after dawn. They now controlled the arterial road to St. Enoch; the battalion's officers were still unsure whether they should follow the oft-repeated orders of Governor McAlpine and Colonel Felstad to lay down their arms and allow our Middle Force to advance on the Lower Isle's capital. Finally a compromise was struck: the battalion's officers ordered their men to withdraw some hundred meters from the road, but they did not give up their arms. The frightened rebels then drove by. The road to St. Enoch was clear, but within sight of it waited the grimly determined remnants of the once-so-proud A-I Regiment.

Convinced that the presence of George Titus in St. Enoch was now essential so that he could appear on television and be heard on radio from there, we didn't wait for the negotiations over the right of way dispute on the Devon-St. Enoch road to end. Instead, we decided to get to St. Enoch via the southern route, where the A-I's Unit's Third Battalion had already laid down its arms. The Muldoon-St. Enoch road was now clear and with the Titus party I headed south from Smithton to connect with it near a place called Kingussie.

At his office in the Parliament Building in N.S. City, Lucius C. Liefenbarger grabbed the telephone, introduced himself, then brusquely ordered the operator to connect him with General Ormsby. Moments later Ormsby was on the line.

"How many men can you put together in an hour or two? I mean fighting men."

"Fifteen hundred, maybe two thousand. I don't — "

"Fine. Get them loaded up on trucks with all the ammunition they can carry and get them to the airport at N.S. City."

"But some of them are hours away — at Nelson, Partrawa, Wahira — places like that."

"What have you got within an hour of the capital?"

"About a thousand."

"All right. Get them to the airport."

"Are you thinking of flying them to the Lower Isle, sir?"

"Yes, I am."

"But they will be perfect targets for anyone familiar with the terrain there. Besides, we don't have the aircraft to — "

"Let me worry about that. Just get them there."

Liefenbarger cut off further conversation. Within moments he had Eddie Mayfield on the line.

"Eddie: Get all your men together and take control of the airport. I mean absolute control: nothing takes off and nothing lands."

"We've already done that."

"Good, now listen carefully. This is what you do next. I want you to commandeer all the available aircraft at the airport. I mean thirty seaters or more, pilots included."

"Even the foreign ones? Air New Zealand, Quantas, Canadian Pa — "

"*All* of them."

"They won't like it, Lucius, They'll — "

"Neither do I like fucking Commie rebels. Now get going. Get the crews together, make sure the planes are gassed up, ready to fly."

"All right."

Liefenbarger put the receiver down. Copithorne, who stood nearby, notes that for the first time since the news of the rebel assault broke, the Lief seemed on top of the situation. His decisions were no longer defensive. With the planes in the air filled with men he would hold the initiative. The rebels would then have to find the proper response to a move they wouldn't have thought in a thousand years that the Lief would dare to make.

Chapter 41

About five kilometers before Kingussie, the lead car of our convoy was met by two men who leaped out of a Volkswagen Rabbit which had come from the opposite direction. They waved their hands and yelled for us to stop; they explained that there was fighting at the Senelle River three kilometers down the road. The message delivered, they quickly piled back inside and disappeared around the nearest bend.

There wasn't much to do but wait. In the back seat of our car George promptly dozed off. The stressful last few hours had taken their toll. I sat down not too far from our car, periodically closing my eyes as well, but never really falling asleep.

George's sleep was uneasy. He woke up again in a little while, feeling uncomfortably hot inside the standing car. He then left it and came out to sit beside me. We were alone; Meg had gone on into St. Enoch with the Middle Force. Occasionally someone from one of the clusters nearby would steal a glance in our direction, but no one approached. We were out of the mountains and the attitudes inexplicably became more formal.

Eventually, though, one figure did approach. It was Henry Motherwell, the fiftyish Anglican minister who used to make his tireless rounds of the mountain camps and who loved nothing better than a lively discussion on the nature of morality. It was Bishop Kewley's acquiescence to Liefenbarger's meddling in religious matters that had brought Motherwell to the Cheviots. I got to know him fairly well and liked him, although I found myself vaguely disagreeing with Motherwell's approach to morality exclusively via the erudite, sophisticated mind.

"Excuse me, Mr. Titus. Please tell me if I am imposing, but I was wondering if I could talk with you, for a few minutes only."

George looked up. "That's fine. I think I'd rather enjoy talking to you right now."

Motherwell seated himself alongside us by the side of the road. "I must confess I didn't exactly come to offer spiritual comfort. More like to ask for it," he smiled sadly.

George looked at him questioningly, doubtlessly thinking that modern religionists can certainly be somewhat peculiar in their approaches. I did.

"I am fully aware that being a padre to the rebels carries much less responsibility than being their leader. Still, initially I was very, very reluctant to come up into the mountains. Not because there can be any doubt about the evil nature of the Liefenbarger regime, but because everyone — especially priests and ministers — should carefully search their conscience before participating in any sort of violence. Here I differ with my more liberal colleagues who naively tolerate violence in Africa and elsewhere on the very shaky grounds that it somehow might bring about improvement of the human condition. Violence very rarely does. Besides — it is very clearly in the domain that our Lord has allotted to Caesar, isn't it?"

George nodded and commented, "I suppose it then becomes a question of the lesser of evils."

But Motherwell wasn't buying that. "Not exactly," he said, staring into space and arranging the words. "Frankly, if I felt that this revolution was merely the lesser of two evils, I wouldn't be here. That wouldn't be sufficient. I could not knowingly participate in any evil — lesser or any other kind. Are you a believer, Mr. Titus? I don't think I have ever read anything about that aspect of you."

"Yes, I am. Not a particularly orthodox one, I'm afraid, nevertheless a believer."

"That's good. Now I feel much easier talking with you. You see, I am not particularly tolerant of atheists. They are like the domesticated cat, denying the fact that she has a master who feeds her and puts a roof over her head. One who has taken her out of jungle and made her what she is. The cat has an excuse for her lack of brains; man doesn't.

"I sincerely believe that God's will is being done here by the rebels," Motherwell changed the subject a bit. "I believe that democracy — which is, in reality, institutionalized liberty —is God's special gift to mankind. Oh, I know it sounds a trifle corny. But we are living in an age that is so blasé that practically anyone who has anything to say about liberty and democracy sounds pretty corny. Yet it can't be denied that wherever true democracy has taken root, man's potential has been realized in ways we haven't even dreamt of. Suffering has been reduced; man's right to worship his God has generally not been curtailed. But there is one, by far the most important aspect of a truly democratic system which makes it so eminently compatible with the spirit of Christianity: it is a homage to the infinite variety God has placed on this earth — variety in thought, action, in ways to serve him. And at the same time it doesn't rob a man of his dignity, of his place as the especially chosen being among all the living things on this earth."

Suddenly he stopped, now visibly relaxed. He smiled. "I guess that's part of my most effective sermon, although I will readily admit that I become carried away at times."

"I know the sermon," said George. "I especially like the part where the revolution I lead becomes part of God's design."

Motherwell studied his face to make sure he was not being mocked. He concluded that he wasn't. It simply wouldn't have been the proper time for it. "Well, all that is only an introduction to what I wish to say."

The minister took a deep breath and both George and me found a softer spot on the ground. "Mr. Titus, I read anything I could find on the subject of revolutions before I came to the Cheviots. And in practically everything that I read I found bloodshed, cruelty and death in such abundance that it made me shudder."

"The history of Christianity is full of them too," commented George.

"Without a doubt," Motherwell was quick to agree. "It is because Christianity is full of revolutions; small ones and big. In fact everything that is important in human history is usually full of blood and suffering."

George nodded.

"At the same time, though, I consider it a measure of the quality of leadership whenever slaughter and suffering is limited as much as possible. And I think on that score you have been an exemplary leader."

"Thank you. Unfortunately the day isn't over yet, padre."

"Yes, there will certainly be people dying."

Of course we all knew it, but there was something in the way that Motherwell said it that made it unusually vivid. We thought about the statement for a few moments, then the minister continued. "Look, I know there may be hundreds of people killed by tonight, I know it and I am trying to understand it and accept it and I am not quite certain if I will ever be able to. There will always be some revulsion within me, I know, whenever I will pass one of those memorial plaques to someone nineteen years old who died defending his country for freedom or whatnot. Likely he was killed when he became so afraid that he inadvertently started to run — away from his hiding place and straight into the line of fire. And I wonder how many of those people so temporarily immortalized on plaques, if given the chance to do it again — to die for their country and motherhood and other lofty ideals, I mean — would choose not to. But all that may be lowly, excessively human considerations when only death is the ultimate reality and all reality comes from God. We may question the highly dubious labels we put on it, but we can't question death itself — it is all part of the grand design.

"So what I am concerned with is the human aspect of it all. No, that isn't exactly right. What I am concerned with is our ugly, vengeful side — the killing that is not part of the battle per se, but that nevertheless seems to accompany all revolutions. I am concerned with Castro's breathless firing squads, Lenin's Kronstadt and Ekaterinograd, Robespierre's guillotine. The settling of tribal scores in Africa."

"I'm afraid, padre, that you can't have too much faith either in me or in the quality of my leadership," said George, and Motherwell hurried with explanations rather than with apologies.

"No, it isn't quite a matter of faith, Mr. Titus. I feel a bit divine, warning you not to betray your conscience before the sun sets, but that's precisely what I want you to do. You see, I think that a righteous, revolutionary slaughter takes place because the leaders are good, extraordinarily good, to their men. It happens because the leader comes to the conclusion that his men have earned it and so he caters to that which is basest in them, and in all of us. Sometimes he pretends he doesn't know what he is doing. He may choose not to know. But then he isn't a very good leader, is he? I'm afraid I'm beginning to ramble a bit — "

Surprised, we watched the usually well-composed minister with perspiration beading his forehead, speaking much more rapidly than was his custom, starting to leave his sentences incomplete, hanging in mid-space. He must have found his role of God's chosen instrument in heading off a disaster, a bloodbath of hatred, of villification and sorrow, quite difficult to play. After all, a few kilometers ahead men were killing each other for the right to cross a river.

"You see, there is so much hatred below all that civility I have come across in the mountains. There were sons of fathers up there who had died at Partrawa, brothers of those tortured by the NUC. So much humiliation and debasement. Tonight, when we reach St. Enoch, it is bound to come out in a fury most of us can't imagine. I am afraid sir, terribly afraid."

Now there were tears in his eyes. He was looking pleadingly at George, waiting fervently for a response that would reassure him, and relieve his tortured mind.

The padre had been successful in one thing and George was grateful to him for it. He spoke about them reaching St. Enoch, about being victorious, as if it all had somehow been preordained. It was something George had not quite yet fully accepted, what with the confusion of the incoming reports and scattered streetfighting. He was about to say something when he was stopped by the low passes of two planes that disappeared over the hills. It happened so fast that none of us had been able to take cover, but the planes must have been ours. They probably knew who was in the convoy and were merely checking to see that everyone was safe.

Their engine noise receded in the distance as George spoke. "I really can't promise you what you'd like me to promise, padre. No one can but God."

"But you will do your best? You will not unleash your men like a pack of wild dogs?"

George nodded. "I will. It's in my interest too, padre."

The dying sound of the airplane engines now mixed with the sound of an oncoming car. The Rabbit once again rounded the curve ahead of us and came to screeching stop alongside the lead car. Out jumped the two rebels, this time with ammunition belts across their chests. They looked around, spotted George, and quickly approached us.

"It's clear now, sir. Some National Unity Corps types at Kingussie wanted to defend the bridge. It was all wired with dynamite, but they weren't exactly demolition experts. The bridge is still there, but they aren't."

"How many were there?" asked George.

"Four."

"All dead?" asked Motherwell.

The rebel nodded. "There wasn't much we could do. They decided to take on the entire South Force. I don't know what they were thinking."

Then Sid Capadouca came running over from the communications truck. "The fighting's over at Sumawa," he shouted. "We hold the town."

"Have they surrendered?" someone asked.

"No. They just pulled out of the town. They might be on their way back to St. Enoch."

"With their guns?" asked George.

"Yeah, it looks that way."

"Oh, my God. That's just what we didn't want. How many are there?"

"Two hundred, maybe three. They don't know exactly because there have been some casualties."

Sid started back toward his truck while everyone else climbed into their vehicles. As George opened the door to our car he thought of Motherwell again and looked back. The minister was still seated on his rock, now slumped as if defeated by the killing at Kingussie and the suffering yet to come.

"Padre," he called to him, "come and ride with me. Maybe it will help us both."

The minister rose and studied him for a moment or two, as if trying to make sure that he meant it. Then he quickly started toward the car.

Chapter 42

At N.S. City Airport, trucks and armored vehicles were scattered across the runways, and bands of soldiers milled around the parked aircraft. The helicopter deposited the Lief near the terminal and a Guards officer with hand grenades suspended from the front of his tunic escorted him into the VIP lounge of Air New Salisbury.

A colonel was speaking on the telephone as Liefenbarger appeared in the door, but he quickly put the receiver down. "Glad you're here sir," he said approaching him.

The Lief sat down and listened to a quick report on the current situation on Lower Isle. Not much had changed. The rebels were still advancing on St. Enoch from the mountains in three streams, but the Lower Isle capital was probably in the hands of the Resistance.

"How many men do we have here at the airport?" the Lief asked.

"About two hundred so far."

"And planes?"

"More than a thousand seats ready to go, sir."

"Where's Mayfield?"

"At the Bristol Street Armory."

"And Ormsby?"

"General Ormsby is on his way here. He should be arriving any moment, sir."

"All right. Let's get the planes in the air. We'll tell the pilots where to put down once they're on the way."

"There is something you should know, sir."

"Oh, for God's sake, stop procrastinating. Of course we're taking a chance. That's what war is all about."

"We don't control a single airfield on Lower Isle, sir. Where will they land?"

"They'll establish control wherever they land. That's why they are being sent — to establish control. That's why they have guns."

"There is something else."

"I'm sure there is. Now get the planes loaded up and start taxiing. Then tell me about it."

The colonel departed and Copithorne retreated to the telephone. Liefenbarger literally fell into a nearby armchair. He gazed into a mirror which was mounted on a post in front of him, running his hand over the stubble on his chin, also straightening out his hair which hadn't been combed since early morning. Then Copithorne was back alongside, about to say something. But the Lief spoke first.

"Frank, get the airport cleared of nonessential civilians. I saw too many of them ogling around as I came in. This isn't a movie show."

Copithorne opened the door, summoned an officer standing nearby and passed on the order. At that moment the colonel came back.

"All right, now what?" Lief asked.

"The reason that General Mayfield isn't here, sir, is that there have been some disturbances reported on Main Island as well. He thought he could take care of it best from his own headquarters."

"Where are these disturbances?"

"In Nelson and Partrawa. The most serious one was in Wahira. There is still some fighting going on there."

For a while Liefenbarger said nothing. The news was quite unexpected. Suddenly he had been forced on the defensive again. He turned to Copithorne. "What's happening with radio and TV?"

"Television stations don't start broadcasting until the afternoon, sir, and radio is continuing with regular programming. Of course, anyone can tune in the Lower Isle stations."

"What's happening on the radio there?"

"They claim that all of Lower Isle is in rebel hands and that they are now waiting for George Titus to enter St. Enoch."

"What about McAlpine?"

Copithorne hesitated a moment with his answer. "He has already spoken. Declared himself in favor of the rebels."

They were interrupted by the arrival of General Ormsby and Admiral Lester.

"Our first concern now must be Wahira," started Ormsby. "From what we know the rebels still haven't got Castlereagh. But if they do get it, Wahira will then become the key to landing rebel supplies and men on Main Island."

"Can the Wahira airport take jets?"

"Yes sir, the runway's long enough."

"How many men would you need to make the city secure?"

"Two hundred at most."

"All right," Liefenbarger said wearily after a few moments. "Load the men into planes and get them to Wahira. Keep the rest on standby basis."

"Using only New Salisbury aircraft?" asked Copithorne but without the usual intonation for a question.

"Using only New Salisbury aircraft," the Lief agreed reluctantly.

"Don't you think, sir, that you should now consider making a statement over radio and television?"

"Looking like this?"

"I think it would be quite effective. There is no problem getting an electric shaver. Under the circumstances it is quite natural that you are not wearing a full dress uniform. In battle an open collar is just right."

"O.K. Let me think a moment about what to say. It won't be that easy."

Copithorne took a piece of paper from his breast pocket. "I've jotted down a few suggestions — "

An agreement was finally reached at Trafalgar School on the outskirts of Castlereagh at about four that afternoon. The town was now under rebel control and the disarmed, thirty-man-strong contingent of the National Unity Corps was loaded aboard a fishing boat to be taken across the Wellsbury Strait to Garrick. The rebel commander, Martin Seymayer, sighed with relief as he watched the boat pull away from the dock, glad that Castlereagh had not followed the example of Sumawa. He then climbed into his jeep and started toward St. Enoch.

Chapter 43

Two or three of the towns through which we passed showed signs of fighting: an overturned car or some debris on the road, and the pock-marked façade of a building, indicated that the NUC was not exactly giving up without a shot, although nowhere past Kingussie did anyone seriously interfere with our progress. Here and there a group of local people would stand by the road, watching the convoy as we passed, but they appeared too stunned to respond in any way.

Two jeeps now rode about three kilometers ahead of the convoy. Shortly after noon we stopped at a surprised village called Marston, about thirty kilometers from St. Enoch, and proceeded to buy out the entire supply of meat pies from a grubby little store by the roadside. Its toothless owner didn't seem to have the slightest idea of who we were and why we were there.

Seated on a curb across from the store, George, Motherwell and I ate our hot pies, finishing them off with coffee and stale doughnuts. George then lit his pipe and stretched out on a patch of grass nearby. It was warm for this time of year and the meadow buzzed with insects. A summer vacation scene, I thought. Certainly not a revolutionary one.

The reverend started to leave.

"No, don't go," said George, his head propped up by his arms, his legs crossed in a relaxed pose.

"I thought you might want to take a nap."

George smiled. "Not this close to St. Enoch. I'm not *that* relaxed, padre." Motherwell sat down nearby but his thoughts seemed to be elsewhere.

A helicopter, with its NUC markings crudely painted over, arrived and hovered over us for a few minutes, then settled down in a nearby playing field. Sid Capadouca hurried toward it. George followed him with his eyes, but he didn't get up.

"Things aren't too bad, are they padre?" asked George.

"No, not so far," Motherwell said, snapped back to the reality of the revolution.

"And I don't think they'll get much worse. We have the main targets now."

Motherwell thought about it for a moment. "The trouble is, that the worst slaughter usually takes place at the most unimportant and therefore unexpected places. At Guernica, Lidice and Katyn — and at Sumawa."

Sid Capadouca approached, holding situation reports from all over the island. "The helicopter's going back to St. Enoch, sir. They'd be glad to take you," he said to George, who thought it over for a moment, then looked at the papers in his hand.

"No, I'd like to have time to study these first," he said. "But Maurice should go." I got up and started on my way to the helicopter when Motherwell spoke up.

"I'd like to go too, sir. I may be able to do some good there."

George nodded in agreement. "O.K., Reverend. It's probably not such a bad idea." Then someone gave the signal for the convoy to move on and at the same time our helicopter rose noisily above the crowns of the surrounding trees.

We flew low enough above the outskirts of St. Enoch for us to realize that there things had not always gone so smoothly. A shopping district of the suburban town of Northfield was in shambles, its buildings damaged by shrapnel and machine-gun fire. None of the store windows was intact. To prevent looting, the area was being patrolled by men dressed in green fatigues of the Revolutionary Army.

As we were passing a city park I saw traces of blood on the sidewalks.

McAlpine argued gently that a trip to Sumawa had not been part of the agreement, that fighting there had already died down anyway, and that all that remained to be done was the forming of a tight circle around the remnants of the A-I Regiment, until the men saw the light and laid down their arms.

"And what if they don't?" I fired at him. More than just specifically the governor, I simply didn't care for his type.

"Then you hit them. There is nothing else you can do in such a case. They're fanatics."

"Bullshit," I exclaimed, sizing up the governor through my narrowed eyes. "They're good soldiers, that's what they are. Following the orders of their superiors whom they still trust. I don't know why, but they still do. And because they do they'll not take any guff from us. That's understandable. What's not understandable is that you don't give a damn about them. Now get your ass to Sumawa and tell your men that the fighting's over, that they're still alive and that we want them to stay that way."

I was leaning across McAlpine's desk; in one corner of his office stood the silent Felstad, intently watching the proceedings. My tone must have been far from what either the colonel or the governor expected, but McAlpine still remained calm; he argued well and without too much emotion.

"Mr. Bech-Landau, they've just been attacked. A substantial number of them have been killed and wounded by your rebels. They will not listen to me or anyone else from this side."

"They'll listen all right. If you walk among them, unarmed. And if you tell them that the whole thing has been an accident which will soon be thoroughly investigated."

McAlpine's eyes now betrayed alarm at the distinct prospect of a trip to Sumawa. But he was still fully in control of his voice. "You have radicalized and even crazed these men by firing in their midst and now you want me to walk among them as if nothing had happened. Don't you think it's a bit unfair?"

"McAlpine," my voice now had a definitely vicious tone as I spoke through my clenched teeth, "this is not some cricket field where you can get your rocks off by the scrupulous observation of the rule of the wickets! This is a goddamn revolution and until George Titus gets here I am running it and everything else on this island. Now there are two or maybe even three hundred men there near Sumawa and if they decide to march on this city there'll be slaughter like nothing we've seen so far. And in the end it still won't change a bloody thing because we have far more men and guns and ammunition. But what we don't have enough of is good men to start up a new country with. We can never have enough of those. Now, I think that to ask me if I would exchange one peacock-like turncoat governor for several hundred good men is to ask me an extremely unfair question. Wouldn't you agree?"

No one said anything. I had taken the discussion out of the realm of politics and wheeling and dealing and onto a level where McAlpine was reluctant to follow. But the governor's years in politics had taught him that there were moments when the best defense equalled no defense at all.

"I'll go — I'm the commanding officer," said Felstad. "I should have been with them from the start."

"Mmm, but that still isn't good enough, colonel," I said. "The regiment's really the governor's baby. They got their colors from him and he was constantly hanging around during training. They provided his honor guard and he'll have to do the disbanding."

McAlpine remained silent. I slowly got up and walked around the desk to face him.

"All right, McAlpine," I said. "I'll give you a clearer choice: either you go or I'll kill you." I reached inside the holster and took out my massive automatic. Before pointing it at his head I moved the safety catch on it.

A few minutes later the helicopter with McAlpine and Felstad rose from the park adjoining the governor's building. There was one more empty seat and Motherwell in the last moment managed to get it. From the window of McAlpine's office I watched it disappear in a northwesterly direction. I wished them well.

Chapter 44

Considering the circumstances, it was not a bad speech the Lief gave from the VIP lounge at the airport, stressing the need for calmness and cooperation with the NUC. I watched it on TV at St. Enoch and grudgingly had to admit that Copithorne's writing and the Lief's delivery were both exemplary. The conclusion was almost poignant because the head of the regime, who had used it so effectively, spoke about fear: "As I have said, one of the most potent weapons in any insurgency is fear. Fear of the unknown. But it can only be used if people allow it to be used against them. If we all cooperate to the fullest with our armed forces and with the National Unity Corps, then there is very little that our enemies can do to us. I am supremely confident that in the end such a powerful demonstration of this nation's will to resist imported violence and lawlessness will not only carry us triumphantly over the present crisis, but it will also serve to deter any future attempts to disrupt our lives by force and coercion. Let us work closely together so we can quickly defeat this present danger and thereby show the world that New Salisbury and the foreign-imposed evil of Communism are two wholly incompatible things.

"Thank you. May God bless us with victory in these trying moments."

According to Copithorne, the next few hours constituted the darkest despair for the Lief. If we are to believe the diaries (and especially at times like these when Copithorne's star was obviously on the rise, one would be well advised to approach them with extreme caution), then Liefenbarger even expressed thoughts about possible peaceful accommodation which bordered on outright capitulation and flight. Copithorne claims that under the circumstances this was understandable, but he pointed out to the Administrator that they had come too far for surrender or accommodation. That if the Lief's role in New Salisbury ended in anything but total victory or death, it would automatically become a trivial, even a comic one. Copithorne claims that this made the greatest impression on Lucius Liefenbarger's will to resist.

Liefenbarger and Copithorne watched another plane taking off to transport more men to Nelson where they were needed to bolster the government's strength. Two had already departed for Wahira where now, late in the afternoon, all was quiet. But there could be no thought of transporting any troops to Lower Isle. Castlereagh had fallen into rebel hands and the skies above it were controlled by rebel pilots.

What had happened? According to Copithorne, the Lief admitted that he had miscalculated when the rebels would come down. He thought it would have been late spring before paths and roads would have dried up. By then he would have completed the building of his Anti-Insurgency Regiment; credibly started flirting with the Soviet offer; and, most importantly, Mayfield would have begun his planned offensive against all known Resistance cells on the islands.

Copithorne notes though that none of this could have been achieved without McAlpine's complete loyalty. Mayfield, with his simple, almost paranoic distrust, had been right. He had, however, not been able to put his suspicions into words that would sound like anything but envy of the governor.

The diaries then claim that the Lief at this point admitted having once thought of sending someone like Copithorne to Lower Isle — a cool, able, mini-administrator with a proper grasp of the situation. But he discarded the idea when he realized just how valuable Copithorne was to him in N.S. City.

The Lief's thoughts then turned to the future. Diplomatic relations with the Americans would have to be severed, although it would have been handy to keep them at their embassy in N.S. City in order to be able to play cat and mouse with them a bit longer. New Salisbury would likely be divided between north and south like Korea, and as Vietnam used to be. If the Americans played their cards right (and judging from their past performance this was doubtful, Copithorne noted in his diaries), they would retain control of the south. The Russians would then be pushed into some sort of an agreement with the Lief to the north. He would have to think about all that much more clearly, but not now. Now he was too tired to think clearly.

Then a driver entered the lounge, announcing that the Lief's car was ready. It was after 5 P.M. and the Lief looked a hundred years old. He started toward the door, then turned to Copithorne once more. "What happened to Ann Schorez, Frank?" he asked suddenly.

"The NUC people say they took her back to the embassy, sir."

The Lief took in the information without much emotion. "Good. We're going to Pitlochry, Frank. I need to think."

The convoy pulled up in front the governor's building shortly after five. The area was thick with green caps of the rebels who kept back the small crowd that had gathered there soon after the small arms fire died down, some of them now and then still a bit anxiously scanning the windows in the vicinity. Meg and I greeted George as soon as he got out of the car, but with all the noise we found it hard to talk. A small cluster of photographers, and radio and television reporters began to crowd around us. I had no idea where they appeared from.

"Would you like to say a few words, George?" one of them yelled through the din. The unaccustomed familiarity of the tone stopped George in his tracks.

"No gentlemen, you will be invited inside in a few minutes where you will be given a statement."

I noticed Rose Kubatan standing a bit apart from the rest. I fought my way toward her while George disappeared inside the building.

"Don't glorify the whole thing, Rose. Play it without all the romantic-heroic overtones, eh?" I asked, adding, "He's gonna have enough to cope with without you people polishing up his halo."

"Have you ever heard this old cynic glorify anything?" she grinned back.

"What about the Sumawa business?" George was asking Meg when I caught up with them on the steps inside.

"Nothing yet."

"We've got to settle it soon," George said decisively as Meg and I nodded. At the entrance to the governor's office George shook a few hands, then we all went inside.

"Have you had anything to eat?" asked Meg. "I could get — " she began but was interrupted.

"No, that's fine. How does everything look?"

"There's still some sporadic shooting but I think we're holding. Just like we're holding everywhere else," I said. "Except, of course, the Sumawa thing."

"How did it start, Maurice? What triggered it off?"

I shrugged my shoulders. George dropped into a leather sofa

in the office with Meg beside him. The three of us were alone.

"Who knows? Who knows how these things get started — somebody got trigger-happy."

"On their side or ours?"

"We aren't sure yet. Probably ours."

"Where was Leahy?"

"I've checked that already. He was in the south. At Muldoon with Branko Justac."

"The Maoists?"

"Maybe. I've got a man checking, but it looks like Guernsey has been operating on Main Island for the past few weeks."

George was up again, pacing back and forth across the office. "We have to settle this thing. We just have to."

"Yeah," I agreed.

"Do you think there will be a counteroffensive by Liefenbarger?" he asked after a few moments.

"No, we can start rebuilding here. I don't think he has the means to hit us."

George finally found his chair again and fell into it. "God, I'm tired," he said.

"I know what you mean. I just got rid of my ball. You're carrying it now," I said.

George nodded. "I hope I won't have to do it alone, that you'll be around. Both you and Meg."

Sid Capadouca knocked and entered. "The TV people are set up now. Are you ready to make a statement?"

"Have you got anything prepared?" I asked

"Yes — God knows I've had enough time to think about it. Where are they set up?" George asked, getting up.

"In the auditorium. I'll take you."

"Are you coming? To help me ward off stage fright?" he asked in my direction.

"No," I said, "I think I'd better go to Sumawa."

Chapter 45

From the air I could see troops of the Anti-Insurgency Battalion huddled around fires and, just across the river, rebels warming themselves at their own behind a stand of willow trees. Having touched down at Sumawa, Felstad briefed me on the situation, saying that they had been in touch with the A-I officer in charge, Captain Williams, and that he sounded reasonable but was convinced Felstad was a prisoner and therefore not in command.

"What they want is a safe return to St. Enoch. They aren't prepared to discuss anything else," Felstad explained.

"With weapons?" I asked.

"Definitely with weapons."

I looked around. On a nearby rock sat McAlpine and Reverend Motherwell. McAlpine had a challenging expression on his face as if he wanted to know what I would do now. But he said nothing. He knew better.

"Isn't there a major with them? A Major Inkster?" I asked.

"No, the captain is in charge. They've had a lot of casualties," Felstad explained.

I looked across the river to the battalion's side and tried to think of something that would end the stand-off without anyone dying. What I finally came up with was dignity. It was dignity that the A-I men wanted so much and it was dignity that all of us overlooked when we planned the whole thing. The A-I soldier had left St. Enoch that morning, convinced that his day had come, that he was finally off to fight the Communists and that by the end of it he would be either victorious or dead. Instead, he now found himself in limbo in a field near Sumawa with dozens dying or dead. It was a situation he couldn't possibly understand and from which he saw the only escape in his blazing gun.

The rebel officer approached me. "Captain Williams wants to know who came in the helicopter," he said.

"Are you in radio contact with him?" I asked.

"Yes sir."

"And you told him?"

"Yes sir."

"Let me speak to him."

I went to the communications truck with Motherwell and Felstad following closely behind. Only McAlpine remained seated on the rock, as if this was not his ball game at all. The officer handed me the receiver. I identified myself and asked to speak with their commanding officer. A faint response indicated there was someone on the other end who had gone to fetch him. A few moments later a man identified himself as Captain Williams.

"This is Maurice Bech-Landau. Could you tell me what happened to Major Inkster?"

"Dead. So are Major Broderick and Captain Gavrilla. They were all at the service station in Sumawa when it blew up."

It had been a matter-of-fact statement that admitted the gravity of the situation but without a hint of hysteria. I couldn't help admiring the officer's control.

"I'm sorry. Look, I don't know yet what caused the ambush at Sumawa, but I assure you that it will be investigated."

"Yes."

There followed a few moments of silence while I was trying to figure out the best approach. "We don't want any more killing. None of us."

"No."

"We revolutionaries are not Communists. And we will not necessarily be the new government. That will be decided by us — the people — through democratic elections."

"Yes."

"We haven't had that chance under Prime Minister Liefenbarger. We haven't had it for quite a few years, but all that will change now."

"Yes."

His constant agreeing was beginning to irritate me. I decided to go straight to the point. "I would like you to lay down your arms, captain. We'll arrange to have you all returned to your barracks."

He was quiet for a few moments. Finally he asked hesitantly: "Is Colonel Felstad a prisoner?"

"No, he is not. He is a free agent, allowed to go wherever he wants to."

"Even to come here?"

"Yes."

"And Governor McAlpine as well?"

"Yes. He is here with me."

"Will all of you come here? Unarmed, to talk?"

I hesitated a moment. "Yes," I finally agreed.

"About a kilometer from the road there is a farmhouse near the stream. Do you know where it is?"

I asked the rebel officer, who said he knew. "Yes, we know where it is," I said.

"We'll send a boat there to take you across."

McAlpine was visibly unenthusiastic but he failed to come up with a sound reason as to why we shouldn't go. My gun was still casting its long, educational shadow over him. He trailed behind us slowly, his head bowed.

"May I come too? If there are wounded men — " Motherwell trailed off.

"Sure," I said, "come along, padre. You'll be needed."

The punt was already waiting, with a tall soldier in it, holding a long pole. In the rapidly increasing darkness he reminded me of the mythical Charon and my fervent hope was that on the other side we would not be met by the mad dog Cerberus. As soon as the four of us climbed aboard, the oarsman pushed the boat away from the grassy bank.

There was little current. We floated lazily down the middle of the stream, slowly edging toward the other side with the soldier guiding the craft with his pole. It was cool on the water and we buttoned our coats to the top, huddling in our seats, lost in our thoughts.

It was Motherwell who first noticed the slight movement in the bushes directly ahead of us. He turned his head toward the spot just as the barrel appeared. He started to rise and opened his mouth to cry out, but three shots rang out in rapid succession and Motherwell slumped forward. He lay staring blankly into the darkening sky, across his seat with one hand trailing in the water behind the punt.

The oarsman sprayed the bushes with his gun, while McAlpine looked too stunned to do anything, even to crouch down. In the next moment the soldier-oarsman put the weight of his entire body against the pole and, by the end of his third stroke, we had reached the opposite bank.

I staggered out while the boat was still being pulled up. A group of soldiers which had been watching the progress of the boat on the A-I side was now in full pursuit of the assassin, while an officer who must have been Captain Williams helped us gently move the wounded.

Motherwell wasn't dead; his eyes attempted to focus on the captain's collar insignia. The officer leaned closer to better hear what the reverend was saying.

"I hope you can settle this thing," he whispered with great difficulty, his mouth twisting into an awkward, painful smile. "Because it's...it's...awfully important."

I looked around me, sitting there on the muddy ground in the moist darkness. I saw someone else carried up the bank and slowly I recognized the body of Colonel Paul Felstad, the first and the only commanding officer that there would ever be of the First Royal Anti-Insurgency Regiment of New Salisbury.

Chapter 46

At the governor's office in St. Enoch, the guard at the end of the hall seemed uneasy when I asked him about George's whereabouts. He pointed behind him, to the end of the hall, where an office had been hastily converted into his living quarters. George might have been asleep, but the guard told me that just five minutes ago he had delivered some cold beer and sandwiches to the room. I knocked and, because I was anxious to report on Sumawa, walked right it.

I was immediately sorry. At the far end of the room, lit only by the glow of a desk lamp, was a convertible sofa. Its bed was fully extended and on it lay George and Meg. I mumbled something in a way of apology and got ready to walk out again as quickly as I could. But George, not the slightest bit put out by the intrusion, called me over. I figured he must have considered the whole scene to be part of the usual revolutionary activity.

It was obvious that he knew nothing about what had come before, nothing about Meg and me. Looking at her I realized I was the only one who was truly embarrassed by it. To Meg, I should have realized now, sex was not much more than a biological function and since one didn't hide while eating there was no need to hide while copulating. George's feelings toward her were, I suspected, considerably stronger. But it was also part of the victor's spoils. In a revolutionary situation precedents are suspended. The leader decides on matters of morality and the leader in this case thought it good.

Slowly, I started to tell what had happened in Sumawa; they listened intently and, when I was finished, there was a moment of silence.

"So Colonel Felstad is dead?" George finally asked.

I nodded.

"And McAlpine?"

"Not a scratch on him. That's the god-awful injustice of it all."

"And Motherwell — the reverend?"

"Not much of a chance he'll pull through according to the doctor at Sumawa."

I saw a flicker of concern in George's eyes. His talk with the reverend that morning must have left an impact; the irony of their subject was too apparent.

"Who did the shooting?"

"Two privates in the A-I Regiment who felt that McAlpine and Felstad should be made to pay for the shooting at Sumawa. We've got them, but it'll be hard to do anything with them. We should have been more careful — expected it."

George nodded, thinking for a moment before speaking again. "Well, we've won. Why is it that I don't feel like jumping up and down?"

Meg answered. "Because deep inside you thought — we all thought — that it wouldn't cost anything at all. We thought if we were well organized we could walk in here with only one or two recalcitrant NUC types on the floor. Now we know that it all doesn't work quite that way."

George nodded. "Is there fighting anywhere else?"

"No, everything's quiet."

"So now we'll have to start convincing everyone else on this island that we should have a rip-roaring democracy," George said, and I couldn't help feeling that his tone was a bit too light.

"Well, I don't think it'll be particularly easy," mused Meg. "We never got more than seventy-five per cent of the people out to vote. That's one in four who stayed home. And I would say that out of those who voted about ten per cent did it intelligently — they knew what the hell they were doing. The rest were always ready to put someone in office because he smiled nicely and reminded them of Uncle Willie in Nelson. And the seriousness with which people regard politics doesn't at all increase with age. The older a man gets the more prone he is to vote for the guy who promises to keep his world the way it is. Only the silly kids are ready to die chasing visions. The McAlpines among us always run alongside it for a while to take a pretty good look at the bandwagon before jumping on it. Then, of course, they are the ones who play the loudest. Give me the Lawrence Saunderses anytime. You can keep the McAlpines."

"The job isn't finished yet. It won't be until Liefenbarger is gone," I said.

"That's right, and someone has to organize Main Isle the way we did it here," said Meg. George's head shot up, his face betraying alarm.

"We can't wait. The momentum's started rolling and we have to roll right along with it," she said.

"I know, Meg, but you don't mean — "George started.

It was exactly what she meant. He would again be writhing in fear for her safety with each bit of news about a fresh Mayfield atrocity, each time that her name was mentioned in the *Times*.

"There are others now, Meg. There is no need for martyrdom," he said feebly.

"Do you think I want to be a martyr? How could I — of all people — have a death wish?"

"Then what *do* you want? What is this compulsion of yours?" George was afraid for her and mad at her all at the same time. I felt even more uncomfortable than when I came in.

"It's no compulsion. I got into this knowing damn well what I was doing. I am the one that's best qualified to get the network on Main Island going. I have the experience and it will save a hell of a lot lives. Others might do a good job too, putting it all together, but we just haven't got the time to train them. I'm the best bet on this, there is no getting around it."

I left, sensing where the whole thing was leading. George had already crossed into the big GEORGE LAND, where all revolutions had been designed to serve him. Meg, on the other hand, was still the same, incredibly self-disciplined and what the Germans call *konsequent* — she had that stick-to-itiveness and devotion to the revolution at the exclusion of any other personal interest. She loved ideas, not people.

I remember her once saying to me that most people realized damn well that knowing right from wrong was the very basis of our being human. Without such knowledge all that was left were simian reflexes. Most of us didn't like paying attention to morality too much because it played havoc with what we wanted to do. So we either pretended that right and wrong were some sort of subjective concepts ("this is asinine, you must admit," she commented), or tried to plaster over it all with things like responsibility to one's family, to the neighborhood Baptist Church, to one's mate, to security, to a single digit inflation rate and to keeping one's lawn trimmed and green.

But Meg Winters herself knew very well where she was going. And she was also willing to pay the price to get there.

The press conference that George held the next day was a bravura attempt which worked beyond anyone's expectations. A crowd of reporters, some especially flown in from Sydney,

Wellington, and even Hawaii, listened to his firm and conciliatory statement, designed to show our total control of the situation. At the same time he was obviously extending an olive branch to former enemies who had committed no crimes and were willing to acknowledge the changed situation. In his statement he definitely rejected summary trials and executions, making it clear though that those who had tortured and killed in the name of National Unity would be brought to justice.

An Australian reporter asked if Main Island would be liberated within a year. George smiled, coyly suggesting that it may happen much sooner. He could say for sure that the liberation would not take place the next day; but that was the only comfort with which he was ready to provide Lucius Liefenbarger. The comment produced chuckles that lightened up the proceedings.

Someone asked what the official name for the Lower Isle would be, and George's answer was Democratic New Salisbury. He then explained that all nations were regarded as friendly and that they were invited to establish relations with the new regime. And, yes, the Americans have been quite helpful to the Revolutionary Army, but then, weren't the Americans a product of a revolutionary movement themselves? Theirs was, in fact, the only revolution in the history of mankind which resulted in more than 200 years of an uninterrupted democratic system. Democratic New Salisbury would be very much guided by their example.

Only a handful of political prisoners had been liberated on Lower Isle and actually they had been in National Unity Corps prisons only a short time. The rest had already been sent to the Bristol Street Armory in N.S. City for interrogation or they were serving long sentences on the Partrawa Plain. If for no other reason than this, Main Island must be liberated, said George. And soon.

No, the Soviets had not been hostile to the revolutionary movement, he replied to another question. It could be said that perhaps they were a bit more cautious than the Americans. But there were, of course, Marxists in the Revolutionary Army itself and they would certainly be free to exercise their right to contest the coming elections.

He didn't know if his wife would join him or where his residence would be on St. Enoch. He had not had time to pay too much attention to his personal life during these past few months.

For the immediate future Lower Isle would be run by a military government, headed by himself.

The single, most important factor in the success of the Revolutionary Army? He would say it had been the immense support it got from the people. The distaste for the Liefenbarger police regime and the longing for a democratic system had always been there; what was required was an organization which could channel the people's efforts to free themselves. He was proud that the revolutionary movement had been able to provide it.

No, he had not heard that Liefenbarger had cordoned off his father's mausoleum in New Salisbury City, and that he closed it, supposedly for repairs. But he was not particularly surprised. Such places had always been dangerous to any tyrant and this particular tomb was important to those who valued freedom and human rights. It would, however, take much more than the closing of a tomb to stifle the revolutionary spirit on Main Island.

The reporters' questions had not betrayed any particularly extensive knowledge either of the country or of its revolutionary movement. The conference over, we chatted with the reporters, drank coffee and ate cucumber sandwiches which, someone quipped, were really a symbol of parliamentary and other desirable traditions left by the British. Afterwards George privately admitted that he did feel a bit uneasy. Perhaps he should have projected a sterner image, that of a serious statesman rather than that of a zealous revolutionary. On Main Island each of his public appearances from now on would be judged according to the quality of leadership he exhibited, leadership which would have to take the country through these troubled times.

George insisted on being present in front of the barracks as the trucks rolled in around six the following evening. The weary men of the 2nd Battalion of the A-I Regiment filed past him into the mess hall, dazed and numbed by the chill and by the events of the previous forty-eight hours. I spoke to some that I had met before, but George said nothing. He just stood by the entrance to the mess hall, making sure that they saw him on their way in. When they were all inside George went in too. He ate dinner with them, and afterwards approached the microphone which had been set up.

"My name is George Titus," he began, "and I came here because I wanted to personally thank you for what you have done. You have been fired on and we are investigating by whom and why. It certainly was not because we have ordered it. It was a terrible accident in which many of your friends died, and others were badly wounded. It was a senseless slaughter we wanted to do our best to avoid. We are sincerely sorry that we failed.

"You, on the other hand, have been able to contain your wholly justifiable anger. You did not continue to perpetuate the killing. And yet, in spite of our efforts, your commanding officer died last night — a man who had earlier made what must have been the most difficult decision of his exemplary career.

"I come to offer you my hand of friendship. In no way do we consider you a defeated unit, but rather as one that joined us in victory over despotism and terror. For this you have earned the respect and the undying gratitude of all democratically-minded, decent people on our islands."

He was about to step away, considering it no mean achievement that the man whom they had yesterday been sent to annihilate, had today been permitted to address them.

Then the first pair of hands started to clap. It was a hesitant gesture, illustrating the grave doubts with which the men of the battalion must have been beset. Then a chorus of applause broke out, hesitantly at first until all the troops found the proper conviction. The sound became louder, more rhythmical, and then the first few stood up, still applauding, but now adding a long, low cheer that soon reverberated through the space, until there was no one left sitting. The 2nd Battalion had totally and unequivocally transferred its allegiance and was now thunderously greeting its new commander.

George had done his job well. He gazed at the spectacle in front of him, incapable of halting his tears. He waved to them, deeply moved. Sid Capadouca then slowly ushered him out.

Chapter 47

It was now a different sort of Liefenbarger that Copithorne painted. He was a morose, taciturn ruler, who liked to spend increasing amounts of time alone, listening to his favorite Mahler and staring at the ceiling. The Lief had become a prisoner of his efficient organization. Having found even the mini-cabinet arrangement inadequate, he went on to create several committees (usually according to Copithorne's advice), which handled such things as the economy, urban affairs, commerce and communications, security and defense. The Security and Defense Committee was by far the most important now. It included Ormsby (the Lief had completely abandoned the idea of replacing him — there simply was no one else), Mayfield, and the various chiefs of the armed services. Sometimes they met several times a day, at a feverish pace completing a comprehensive plan for the defenses of Main Island. There were other committees dealing with areas as culture and education, but they seldom officially convened; their activity was regulated by memoranda.

The coordinator of this complicated web was, of course, the ubiquitous and seemingly omniscient Frank Copithorne. He ushered the Lief throught the day, juggling schedules, summarizing reports, shielding him from fools and bores, providing for the Lief's transportation, living quarters, even for his meticulously clean uniform and laundry.

And Copithorne noted how important it was to keep the Lief on a tight schedule, to keep him preoccupied to the point of exhaustion. Then, when the Administrator sat alone, listening to the interminable Mahler symphonies, he had little strength left to fully grasp the total dimension of the disaster that had befallen him.

As the Govenor General Pro Tempore, Diebel had initiated some international contacts in an effort to get credits for the rapidly expanding defense expenditures which the Lief was ready to back by the oil from the Thames Delta. One of the few countries mildly interested was South Africa, but serious doubts were expressed as to oil flow; when it was finally established, could it be maintained without interruptions from the rebels on Lower Isle?

Diebel then approached the French with an offer to supply both New Caledonia and Tahiti with New Salisbury oil. There is some evidence that the French toyed with the idea for a while, as they always did with any suggestion that lent an opportunity to slap the beak of the American Eagle, but in the end even they declined.

On occasion the Lief must have been asking himself just how much authority he still possessed. Ormsby and Mayfield paid lip service to an overall defense plan, but each ran his domain quite independently, clashing violently with the other whenever interests overlapped. Internally, both the armed forces and the NUC were now nearly sovereign entities. And Copithorne, as is evident from the increasing number of his signatures on documents from this period, had been delegated an enormous amount of power by the Lief. On occasion he complains in his diaries that his duties kept him from his favorite hobby — flying. He had qualified on a Boeing 727 some months before, and although the Lief kept one always at his disposal, Copithorne seldom had a chance to use it.

Increasingly the Lief wanted to talk with Copithorne about himself. As if to justify all that he had done till now, the Administrator again and again returned to the mammoth leap he had made from the N.S. City Police Force to the N. S. Parliament. Frequently the Lief complained about the unfairness of it all, pointing out it had been far easier for Norman Ruttledge Titus, who was now resting in a revered mausoleum, who never had to bow and scrape for dignity and respect, and who had died stylishly on the parliament's steps to be carried into history with great honors — like some Gothic god — only because he had been born into the proper social strata, while the Lief had always had to bear the stigma of being born out of wedlock.

The Lief vacillated between thoughts of death and reflections on the most intense living he had ever done — those times spent with Ann Schorez. But tormenting suspicions of her betrayal began to drive him to despair.

Chapter 48

Alexandr Voinovich Velikovsky didn't lose much time. He had the embassy arrange for a meeting with the Administrator even before his Japanese Airlines jet touched down in New Salisbury City. As he walked through the airport's glassed corridor, he noted the markedly increased military activity around the place, and a Pan Am jumbo loading up supplies at one of the ramps. Pan American didn't fly to New Salisbury; this was a chartered flight which would take away most of the staff and records from the U.S. embassy. Only three Americans would remain for about a month to close the place down permanently.

Velikovsky had exactly one hour between his arrival and his appointment with Liefenbarger. He used it to cruise around the city, being briefed in the back of the embassy limousine on the latest local developments by the embassy's first secretary. The limousine eventually stopped in front of the Royal Credit Building. In the lobby he was greeted by the servile interpreter.

It couldn't have escaped the Russian's notice how the Lief had changed. The giant's face betrayed an inordinate amount of fatigue and worry. But then, what leader wouldn't be tired and worried with half his country in rebel hands? Just like the airport, Liefenbarger had acquired a frenetic, wartime look. Gone was the dress uniform of the New Salisbury Guards in which he used to strut about. Instead, the Administrator wore an open-collared khaki military shirt with the sleeves rolled halfway up his arms. When the ambassador entered, he was holding a clipboard. A ball-point pen sticking up from his breast pocket reduced even further the former formality of his bearing.

This time Copithorne left the room before he was asked. The ambassador duly answered the Lief's pro forma questions about the trip, then quickly moved on to the main subject. The interpreter sprang into action, the discussion recorded by Copithorne who also observed the meeting on closed circuit TV.

Vel: "It need not be stressed that since we last met the

situation has changed considerably. This, naturally, has been the main subject of my discussion with my government in Moscow. But in spite of the occupation of the Lower Isle of your country, Mr. Administrator, it is in the interest of the Union of Soviet Socialist Republics that your government be provided with as much help as you require in order to withstand the imperialist incursions into your country's sovereignty.

"Under the drastically changed circumstances, however, it is felt by my government that this assistance should be provided within a different framework. It is therefore felt by my government that our original proposal should be altered in the following manner:

"1. Our naval presence in the southern Pacific should be increased, but according to a schedule which is even more accelerated than originally envisaged.

"2. The defense material and low interest credits will be supplied to your government along with military advisers who will be able to suggest the best use of such assistance. I should properly add here that the advisers have already been assembled — some in fraternal Havana in the Republic of Cuba, others in Ho Chi Minh City. Both groups are ready to fly to New Salisbury on a moment's notice. As well, the first shipment of armored personnel vehicles has been assembled at Nakhodka, our port in the Sea of Japan. It is generally quite obvious that speed is essential in this entire undertaking if it is to be proven successful.

"3. It is felt that under the altered circumstances no publicity whatsoever should be given to this new undertaking. Expectedly, the presence of the advisers and supplies from the Union of Soviet Socialist Republics on the Main Island of New Salisbury will not long remain undetected. It is of utmost importance that neither your government nor ours comments in any way on it. The conflict in New Salisbury must not be interpreted as merely another area where the big powers are at loggerheads. What must emerge is the true picture — that of a small island country in the middle of the vast Pacific Ocean which is being threatened by U.S. imperialism. Don't you agree?"

Lucius C. Liefenbarger said nothing. After a few moments he started to slowly pace back and forth across the room. Velikovsky must have been astonished. Under the circumstances he had undoubtedly expected a far more enthusiastic response.

The Russians didn't consider the Lief's survival a safe bet — that much was clear. But it was all still apparently worth the effort; otherwise they wouldn't have offered to send supplies, advisers and the navy. The idea of a Soviet base in New Salisbury was so tempting that they were willing to gamble against overwhelming odds. Evidently the possible loss of a few troop carriers and tanks was not too high a price for them to pay. If necessary, if Liefenbarger was about to be toppled, the advisers would probably be flown out again or taken aboard some Soviet ship in the vicinity without much trouble.

There was one point, however — a crucial one — which Velikovsky didn't bring up this time, but which had figured prominently in the Russians' original plans. The Lief remembered and he was not about to let the ambassador forget.

Lief: "What about the Communists among the rebels, Mr. Velikovsky? Is your government still ready to tell them to go home — that this isn't their fight anymore?"

Vel: "There are no true Marx-Leninists with George Titus anymore."

Lief (to the interpreter): "Did you get that right — is that what he said? That there aren't any Communists on the Lower Isle?"

Vel: "There are Trotskyites and revisionists of all types there, of course, but there are no true Marx-Leninists. Naturally the Soviet Union — the spiritual leader of all true Marxists in this world — has little influence over such types."

Lief: "Naturally."

It could mean several things, the Lief thought. Either the Russians had really lost control of the Communists — and taking into consideration their uncanny ability elsewhere to keep a tight grip on people they have trained, this was highly unlikely — or Titus had cracked down on the Communists. But that was unlikely as well, because for Titus the revolution was far from over. Weakening his movement by eliminating the Communists would not make much sense right now. The Lief must have concluded that there was something else behind the Russians' disowning the Communists on Lower Isle.

Lief: "I understand your proposal, Mr. Ambassador, and I'll take it under consideration."

Vel: "Under consideration? Our intelligence sources suggest that an attack from the south on this island could come any moment."

Lief: "Oh, do they? Then you possess information which you do not wish to share with my government, is that correct?"

Vel: "But all that is common knowledge, Mr. Administrator. *The New York Times* —"

Lief: "I know what *The New York Times* says. What I wasn't aware of until a moment ago was that the Soviet Union took its cue from it. You will be contacted about your proposals, Mr. Ambassador. Meanwhile, I hope you will get some rest. Travel is tiring."

Velikovsky rattled off some stiff farewell noises, then he walked out, followed by the interpreter.

It isn't easy to comprehend why Liefenbarger decided not to crawl aboard the life raft that the Russians were throwing him. In his diaries Copithorne suggests very strongly that the fault lay in the way Velikovsky had presented the whole thing. The Lief had just been humiliated by the rebels and Velikovsky presented the Russian proposal from somewhat the same viewpoint that a vulture eyes a carcass. Appearances have always been most important to the Lief and appearances were now just about the only thing that he had left. This was a point that Velikovsky, the great product of the Party system, was incapable of grasping. The Russians had, in effect, presented the Lief with an ultimatum in such a way that so aroused his disdain it almost equalled that which he harbored for the Americans.

In the final analysis, wrote Copithorne, because Velikovsky had managed throughout the years to completely subdue his ego to the will of the Party, he was incapable of understanding that an ego might have been a major factor in somebody else's decision-making.

I cannot quarrel with Copithorne's reasoning. The trouble is that it doesn't go far enough, because he does mention elsewhere that the Lief was already beginning to develop a death wish, that he had started building for himself a Wagnerian end, a tragedy complete with a funeral pyre and sombre figure. Velikovsky and his gorilla-like Russian advisers swarming all over Main Island, interfering, pushing, and only prolonging the agonizing inevitable end, didn't fit in at all. A tragic hero upholding the real values of this convoluted, degenerated world — that's how the Lief increasingly saw himself. In that role he had to shut his eyes ever more tightly to what Mayfield was doing at Partrawa and at Bristol Street, and he had to stand apart both from the Americans and the Russians. In his mind he saw himself as that small, feeble flame of mankind's hope, eventually destined to be snuffed out by the heavy breathing of the giants.

Chapter 49

On November 15th I raised the Kilmaron question at a Military Council meeting. George countered by suggesting that by bringing it up I was somehow threatening revolutionary unity.

"Who doesn't want to keep us united at all costs?" I yelled at George across the table. "But does that mean that we have to give the Marxists a carte blanche? Because giving them Kilmaron means just that!"

"They've been given neither a carte blanche nor Kilmaron," George replied softly, watching the aroused faces of most of those gathered around the table. Except for the two Justacs, Sid, Meg and myself, they were mostly men and women who had worked in the Resistance in the Lower Isle's cities. This was their first meeting with the Temporary Military Governor — a title George had finally and most reluctantly accepted.

"The commander of Force Delta which administers Kilmaron is one William Hewitt, who likes to call himself a radical socialist. Second in command is D. Smelling, who definitely is. He is one of the beloved Algerian graduates. Other officers include G. Stewart, W. Smithe and W. H. Sherman," I read from my list. "All are left-leaning types who have for years disrupted labor unions and Poly organizations with their rabble rousing. And who, pray tell, is Vic Channing — some sort of a right wing, reactionary type?"

"We can't simply exclude radical socialists. What sort of a democratic revolution would it be?" asked George.

"But why concentrate them in one spot — in one unit?"

"Maurice, practically all units have radicals in them. Even Communists."

"Not to this extent."

"To what extent? Aren't you being just a little bit paranoid?" interjected Meg. "The people we're fighting are on Main Island — remember?"

"Yes, that's right. But they don't constitute a threat to us down here any more."

"Do *these* people?"

"Damn right they do. What was Baracolli doing at Sumawa

when someone tried to wipe out the entire 2nd Battalion of the A-I Regiment?"

"Maurice, for God's sake," George began tiredly, "we have been over that a thousand times. He was with Force Beta which had been ordered there. And yes — he had gone to the service station, but it was because he wanted to see what was going on. There's nothing, absolutely nothing, that would link him with the machine gun over the TV shop. Nothing."

"Pardon me, I don't think I quite understand," said a Polynesian named Ray Rankwete, whose group had been largely responsible for delivering St. Enoch's northern suburbs to the hands of the rebels. "What exactly would have this Baracolli hoped to gain from killing a few government troops that would have likely surrendered in a few hours anyway?"

"Nothing," I allowed after a few moments. "That is, nothing right away. But it would have certainly complicated things and kept the takeover from going smoothly. We have to understand their strategy: the idea is to have the revolution succeed but without George Titus and his democratic ways becoming too powerful. The revolution in Russia in 1917 produced Kerensky whose government wasn't strong enough to keep the Bolsheviks out. Leahy's raid on Fort Wellington was designed to show that the Commies play an important part in the N.S. revolution. It backfired because it also showed that the most important role of all was still played by the A-I Regiment. Fifteen men were killed in Sumawa in front of the petrol station. Probably not as many as the Communists hoped for, but enough to put at least a slight blemish on George Titus's organization of the Day of Descent. And this time — quite unlike Fort Wellington — the Communists have not been publicly associated with the killings."

"I think the whole thing's ridiculous," said the agitated Howell Waynborn, a middle-aged school principal from Kilmaron. "I've met William Hewitt and found him to be a very reasonable and capable man. Since it was Force Beta that had entered Kilmaron first, why shouldn't they be stationed there? I also consider all this talk to be very divisive. I am not a Communist, socialist, or any other kind of radical, but we certainly can't begin excluding them from our midst. I would like to move that we not only express our full confidence in William Hewitt and Force Beta right here and now, but that we also censure Maurice Bech-Landau." He turned to me. "I'm sorry about this, but I consider some of your statements inflammatory, inappropriate and also dangerous."

The murmur that followed increased in volume until George raised his hand to still it. "We're not a parliament and censuring people is not too good a way to battle divisiveness," he said. Then he looked at his watch. "And since in half an hour Kenneth Garbeau will be arriving, I now have to go to the airport."

I went along. In the back of the black Chrysler the discussion resumed, this time between only the two of us.

"Yes, yes Maurice, I've seen the pamphlet and I know exactly what's in it — what it all means."

"Did these workers' committees of Democratic New Salisbury — or whatever the crypto-Commies are called — did they ask you for permission?"

"No, not for this specifically. But they did call to tell me that they'd be organizing a drive among workers and I gave them my blessing. They probably interpreted it as my permission to go ahead and put out the leaflets."

"Everything that's published on this island is supposed to go through the military censor. Do you think this did?"

"Probably not. Maybe it was an oversight. The point I'm trying to make, though, is that I found nothing objectionable in the leaflets. They call for workers to organize themselves and they also call for cooperation with the military authorities."

"And because of that you are convinced that the workers are being organized to help us run the country, right?"

"Of course. I have to assume that. Or we'd all go mad, suspecting everyone everywhere."

"You're right, George, absolutely right if you're talking about the Rosicrucians or about members of the Flat Earth Society. But these are labor organizations — the same groups that have been misused by practically every power-hungry despot in modern history. Their ignorant membership is handed out armbands and they march through the streets, faces tightened up like gorillas and guns slung across their shoulders. It makes them feel so important. And they march and march and call themselves the workers' militia and bring in regimes both on the right and left which first of all step on the workers' necks. And these bright chaps you want tightly organized under Leahy, right?"

"Yes, I *do* want them organized. We have a great opportunity to build on some solid foundations here. When the military government steps down we must have a strong labor organization."

"For what, George? So that the workers' committees can take over, so that Leahy can become another Castro and the rest of us another Cuba?"

"No, no. By that time we will have reorganized our legal system and the police — everything. There's no danger of Castroism. None at all."

I said nothing so George returned to his favorite theme. "Do you know what the single most disruptive aspect of a democratic society is? Labor strife. We solve it by blackmail — either by withdrawing services or by preventing people from working. We act as if our right to blackmail ranked right up there alongside our rights to free speech and habeas corpus."

He leaned closer to me. "Now, suppose that here we have a chance to go back to square one. Not outlawing strikes but making them more compatible with the system within which they operate. Suppose we agreed that any management of a company whose workers go on strike will have to immediately call a stockholders' meeting for a vote of confidence. And suppose that before a union could call a strike, it would have to win by a secret ballot, supervised by a court-appointed administrator — a vote of confidence from its membership. And suppose that the government would be required *by law* to intervene in a labor dispute and if necessary impose a settlement whenever a certain number of the consumers demanded it?"

He became more and more agitated, obviously sensing that he was dealing with an issue with which he could make an international name for himself. "But to do all this," he continued, "we first must have the confidence of labor. We can't refuse them the right to organize because management already *is* organized."

There followed a pause as the Chrysler sped along the airport road, cleared by the escort ahead. There wasn't much one could say against his plans at this stage, so I decided to play my trump. From my pocket I brought out a paper which I handed to George.

"It's an excerpt from Leahy's memoirs which are being published in the East German press," I explained. "And those are the boys you'd like to organize the workers in this country."

George took the paper from me and started reading:

About 7 A.M. we finally reached the George Titus base above Precarious Inlet. We were astonished at the type of guerrilla warfare that they were fighting. In fact, they had not been fighting at all since their debacle at Oriwiki on the Renfrew Peninsula. To put it frankly, they were fat. Fattened by the frequent air drops of supplies to them by the Americans, supplies which included deodorant sticks and cases of expensive French brandy. The empty bottles with which the area was littered and their deep suntans attested to the fact that here was a different kind of a revolution than the one we had been fighting. Several chemical toilets stood in the nearby woods and plastic reclining chairs were scattered around a small pond. These men quite obviously were not here to fight, they were here to officially establish a presence while CIA agents negotiated a change of government in the capital in which no one would be hurt. Liefenbarger would be handsomely paid for gracefully stepping aside, and Titus offered dollars for taking over the reins. So far as the social and economic structure of the country was concerned, absolutely nothing would change: the same bourgeois imperialist elements along with multinational corporations would govern New Salisbury with merely a cosmetic touch-up.

George let the paper slip to his lap. He was staring out the car's windows at the countryside. After a while he spoke.

"All right. Granted that I'm not happy about this; who would be? But I am also aware that the Communists' raison d'etre is the revolution, that they're used to leading all revolutions, that they find it hard to imagine a revolution *without* their leadership. So what is happening here in New Salisbury is not something with which they are equipped to cope. On the other hand, there is their undeniable dynamism, their dedication, their experience and organizational skills — all things that have been and are very useful to our own efforts. This hasn't been written by the Communist Party of New Salisbury but by one of its members. What's more, it has been written by a member who is at present in disrepute."

"They're all in disrepute. It's — "

"Not by their own membership. I mean it looks like Leahy isn't the boss any more."

"How do you know?"

"It comes from the Americans. They aren't sure but it looks like it."

"It may be a trick. They — "

"Maurice, you've got to start thinking differently. This sort of thing will eventually tear you apart."

Our small convoy entered the airport area and wound its way through the back service roads until it came to a stop beneath the control tower, facing the main runway. In the distance a U.S. Air Force 707 was gently touching down against the vivid background of the setting sun.

Chapter 50

Garbeau was tanned and fit, ebullient and effusive in his praise of the revolution, while delivering congratulatory messages from his President and from the Australian Prime Minister. He fitted himself between us in the back of the Chrysler.

"Frankly, they didn't think you could really pull it off. There had been lots of skepticism even around the State Department. They simply didn't like this democratic experiment of yours, they didn't trust it. By the way, how are things here?"

"Fine," said George. "Much quieter than we expected."

"People are wondering how you'll handle the National Unity Corps types you have in your custody."

"Which people?" I asked.

Without batting an eye Garbeau shot back: "People like me."

Both George and I noted that Garbeau was more relaxed, more informal this time. I guess there was less doubt about us to cover up. We existed officially as a physical entity now and that made us all equals. Of sorts, anyway.

"Well, then people like you should rest assured that we'll not have any public beheadings," George noted.

"What about the death sentence?" asked Garbeau.

"What about it?" Titus shot back.

"Well, are you going to abolish it or what?"

"Don't know yet. It's been abolished once already under my father, then put back by Liefenbarger. So the whole thing is fairly entangled and it'll take a while to sort it out."

"What about things like diplomatic recognition? Are you ready to move on that?"

George shook his head. "Not yet. Look, I know it's easy for you Americans — you've been thrown out of N. S. City. But we have to understand the little guy's position too. For them it's much more complicated. Who's really in charge here — Liefenbarger or us? We are in no danger right now and in a few weeks we'll be on Main Island. Then no one will have to start apologizing."

Garbeau then abruptly changed the subject. "There is one thing we would really appreciate: a nice, loud public protest and an explanation to help us with Diana Mulgrave. She's been to Libya, you know. Posed for pretty pictures with Khadafi and with every terrorist they could muster within a thousand-mile radius. Then she announced that in her native country the anti-imperialist struggle goes on — led by Vic Channing."

My interest was aroused. "When was the affair in Libya held?"

"About a month ago."

"So it was decided then, probably decreed from Moscow. Leahy isn't out because of some petty internal squabble here in New Salisbury. That's interesting."

Garbeau looked at me with benign amazement. "You mean you thought that Leahy and Channing and their types decided anything on their own? They'd need a lot more clout for that. Up till now they've cost a lot of money and produced nothing in return. They certainly have to dance to the Russian hit parade."

"I wonder why Leahy was replaced," George mused.

"It usually isn't just one thing. It's rather an accumulation of failures. Like you replace a football coach if he doesn't produce."

"About Diana —" I prompted Garbeau after a while.

"Yeah, about Diana. Well, she's in Paris right now. And in an interview on French television she grudgingly admitted that George and Maurice exist and that you may figure prominently in the revolution here. But that was all. I think she's split right down the middle in her loyalties. Now might be a good time to exert a little pressure from the right direction. She could be a powerful fan of Democratic New Salisbury."

"What do you suggest?" George asked.

"Invite her over here. Show her how things stand. Make her feel like she's being consulted, but for God's sake don't take any of her advice; she once counselled us to make Angela Davis the U.S. ambassador to Moscow. Listen to her as if she has important things to say because they all love that — Fonda, McLaine, Robert Vaughn — they all go in for that in a big way if it's done right."

"I'm supposed to tell her how things stand with whom — the Americans?" asked George innocently.

"With everybody."

George thought it over for a moment. "No," he said conclusively, shaking his head. "I don't think this is the right time for diplomatic or public recognition."

"Why the hell not?" I asked in a manner that was definitely intemperate. "You don't want to offend the Communists?"

"Maurice, I couldn't care less about the Communists' feelings. But to introduce ourselves right now as America's bosom buddies would give the Russians all the ammunition they need. It would also make the Third World really wonder about us. Neither thing would be very good for our future as a sovereign nation. I know that Diana's ramblings are not very pleasant for you Americans to listen to, but basically she's still neutral toward us here. I'd prefer it that way. If she wants to find out how things really are, let her come on her own. I don't think she's the kind of a person that would be impressed by our pleading with her."

We reached the outskirts of the city and the driver slowed down.

"You could be right," allowed Garbeau. "Maybe we're a bit too impatient. I wish we had a little Siberian camp where we could immediately send all actors who decide to go into politics."

Garbeau watched the storefronts as they flashed by, searching for some sign of recent struggle. He found none. A pair of chic women entered a boutique, one of them with a white, fluffy poodle on a leash studded with rhinestones.

"Are you sure you've had a revolution here?" he asked.

"Tomorrow we'll show you Sumawa," I said. "You won't see too many poodles or boutiques there."

Chapter 51

It's hard to pinpoint it exactly, but sometime early in June Victor Channing came to Allan McAlpine's house for an important visit.

No one could have been more surprised at Channing's arrival than the former governor. Preparing the rose bushes for the winter at a cottage that he rented at Cambridge, the southern suburb of St. Enoch, McAlpine brooded over the fact that he had been shunted aside by the military government, that he had not been given a posh office with a flock of assistants and secretaries; that he had been, in effect, let out to pasture.

Part of it was my own doing. After the governor's performance on the Day of Descent, I had managed to thwart all attempts to use McAlpine as a consultant to the military government. There were quite a few of them. He seemed to have contacts everywhere and they all seemed to owe him favors. Finally I called McAlpine personally to say that as the military vice-governor who had to force him to do his duty at gunpoint, I considered him unreliable and therefore of no use to the temporary military regime. I also made it clear, however, that once the democratic system had been restored he would be free to run for any office he chose, adding that I would personally make sure that there were no irregularities in his campaign. Once again, I had done my best not to endear myself in his eyes.

Characteristically, George chose not to involve himself in the affair, totally ignoring several overtures to receive McAlpine and to hear his case. So what remained were those rose bushes to be readied for winter and the cottage at Cambridge, while it must have been increasingly clear to McAlpine that so long as Main Island remained in Liefenbarger's hands there was no hope of Lower Isle having anything but a military government. His return to power must have seemed awfully distant the day Vic Channing walked through his door and offered what appeared to be a fairly logical shortcut.

Actually not *that* logical, when one considers Allan McAlpine's opinion of the Marxists. But Channing, one of the ablest manipulators of people I have ever come across, must have come well prepared for an initially cool reception. I estimate that after he introduced himself and stated his business, he allowed about twenty minutes to half an hour for McAlpine to rant and rave and thereby absolutely spend himself. Channing knew quite a bit about politicians' gut reactions to Communism, but he also knew that in most cases their hatred of it was nowhere near as potent as their love of power.

So Channing listened politely while McAlpine quite likely enumerated for him all the faults of the Marxists. Then it was McAlpine's turn to listen to Channing explain that the Communists didn't want McAlpine to join their party, but to help them prevent New Salisbury from falling into the hands of another dictator. That much must have sounded reasonable to McAlpine. He could distance himself from the unpleasant Marxist totalitarians, but still use their ruthlessness and well-known penchant for outstanding organization to boost himself back into power. Channing, to boot, convincingly explained that he really represented the new, democratic Communists who had been born in Italy and Spain and in other industrialized countries of the West. McAlpine must have seen here further signs of legitimacy that would be helpful to him personally.

What, like so many others before him, he never saw or understood, was that Channing — just as practically every other prominent Communist nowadays — considered Marx-Leninism to be nothing more than a highly maneuverable vehicle. It could be boarded, abandoned, started and stopped, and turned to the left or right. It certainly was not a bible that would have to be followed verbatim. McAlpine counted on Channing to keep his promises because he saw in Channing one of those revolutionary fools, full of ideas about proletarian necessity and scientific inevitability. Channing, of course, was nothing of the sort. He was basically a McAlpine-type opportunist who had chosen a much more potent and dynamic means to get to the top.

From what we know, Channing offered McAlpine the governorship of Lower Isle with substantial administrative freedom. In return, the former governor promised to lend his name to the virulent campaign against George Titus and his military government, with the proviso it would be made amply clear that he — McAlpine — had political convictions which were quite different from the Communists'. And since it was important for the Communists to create the impression that their opposition to Titus was part of a much broader front, McAlpine's separate line was exactly what they wanted.

On June 6th, in the evening, we all met on the top floor of the Hotel Chaucer where George established his headquarters. Aside from George, Garbeau, Meg, the Justacs, Sid Capadouca and several force commanders, there was an American admiral and a U.S. Marines general present. They agreed that the invasion of Main Island was possible, but that it would require the utmost in planning and organization. They and their respective staffs would stay on Lower Isle and help us with the task. Our basic plan was then outlined and at eleven we broke up.

George and Meg drove off toward the waterfront to say goodbye. Meg was going to Main Island aboard a fishing boat — the time had come to coordinate the Resistance activity there.

At the waterfront they walked up and down the dock in the rain, holding hands. Their last kiss was short. She slipped out of his embrace and disappeared aboard a trawler whose engines started a moment later.

Meg came out on deck, just as the trawler started to wind its way to open sea, waving to him until the boat was hidden by the rows of masts and command bridges. George couldn't see it anymore. He could only imagine it setting course out of the bay.

He began to tremble. Worried that he probably wouldn't be able to control the tension much longer, he ran up the dock to the car and huddled in the back seat, feeling cold, tired and anxious despite the blast of hot air the driver was sending to the back.

Under the canopied entrance to the hotel he managed temporarily to regain control of himself. With tight, measured steps he reached the elevator, passing the armed guards at the entrance and the duty officer's desk in the lobby. His driver rode up the elevator with him, walked with him past another desk where an occupant rose and saluted. George was slightly hunched but generally managed to hide his personal crisis; at the door to his suite the driver asked solicitously: "Are you all right, sir? Maybe I could — "

George then straightened up slightly, with his last ounce of strength even managed to conjure up a bit of a smile and said, "Fine. Thanks. We should both get some sleep now."

Inside, George later told me, he hurried across the sitting room to his bath because he was sure he was about to vomit. In the end, though, he only managed to dry-retch among the washbasins and wallpaper full of cherubs. For a while he sat on the lid of the toilet, writhing with the cramps in his stomach. As they slowly subsided he staggered into the bedroom with its ludicrous four-poster bed and he toppled onto the covers. Then he remembered Dr. Webber's pills. Webber had examined him just before the Day of Descent, found him fit, but still handed him five or six pills in a plastic bag: "The real pressures will come once we're down there. Here, put these away until you need them. You're bound to get the shakes once when all this is over."

"All this" was not yet quite over and he already had problems. He swallowed a pill without any water and then, still fully dressed, slipped under the covers. Another wave of nausea came and he felt even colder than he did in the car. The trembling came again and he tried with all his might to regain control. Suddenly, he felt a warm relaxing feeling spread through his entire body. The pill was beginning to take effect. Slowly, cautiously, he stretched his legs from the fetal position, where he had been tightly clutching them. He felt his facial muscles relax; his mouth was no longer twitched and the dull ache at the back of his head was gone. He barely started enjoying his new-found comfort when he felt himself drift off to sleep.

Chapter 52

I shook George awake in the darkness. Half asleep, he asked, "What? What time is it?"

"Four, a little bit after. There is a man here who wants to talk to you."

He sat up and I noticed that he was fully dressed.

"Can't it wait till morning? I really —"

"It can't wait, George. The man came in on the milk run from Wellington. He has to go back in an hour."

The milk run was an Air New Zealand flight that used to fly to New Salisbury City but for the past two weeks had been regularly diverted to St. Enoch. There hadn't been time to conclude a formal agreement about it. The plane usually stayed at St. Enoch only long enough to refuel, then it headed back to Wellington.

"Well, then, hold the plane here a few hours. I'll talk to him later."

I grabbed George and now shook him. "The man's from N.S. City. He was just visiting Wellington. He has a message from Copithorne."

George stared at me in disbelief. "You're kidding."

I shook my head. "The name's John Effington. He's a pet food manufacturer or something, attending some conference in Wellington. But he has to fly back there in an hour if he's not to arouse any suspicion."

Instantly George was awake now. "Wait here. I'll wash my face. And get me some strong coffee, otherwise I'll keep yawning and the man will think he's boring me — which he definitely will not be."

Effington was a short man with small bones, a pencil mustache and dyed hair, who gave the impression that he couldn't possibly be taken seriously. But all that changed as soon as he opened his mouth. In a low baritone and well-metered sentences he recited what Copithorne had told him to say the night before he departed from Main Island.

"The reign of Lucius C. Liefenbarger is over. The idea now is to stop any further bloodshed. Mr. Copithorne is willing to cooperate with you toward that end."

"Why?" George asked. A guard knocked at the door and I accepted a tray of coffee and rolls from him.

"I feel that Mr. Copithorne is able to see the end much more clearly than Mr. Liefenbarger," said Effington.

"What proof do we have that he really means it?" asked George.

"There cannot be any proof yet, sir. Mr. Copithorne is willing to do certain things in return for certain assurances. That is all."

"What assurances?" I asked.

"He would like to have two million dollars deposited in a Swiss account. He also would like a written guarantee that in two years, when passions subside, he will be allowed to come back from exile."

No one said anything right away.

"To me it sounds an awful lot like a Warren Beatty movie," I commented.

But George obviously viewed it differently. "Does Frank Copithorne have a plan for avoiding bloodshed?" he asked.

"Yes, he does. Have you read the report on New Salisbury in the *Guardian*?"

We both nodded.

"It is substantially correct. The only two forces capable of resisting you are the New Salisbury Guards and the National Unity Corps: the Guards is a highly disciplined military unit, and the NUC is composed of the dregs of society who would lose everything if Liefenbarger were defeated. Quite a high number of them are also compromised through killings and torture. But only the New Salisbury Guards are amassed together to form a real military threat; the NUC units are scattered throughout the island. Mr. Copithorne proposes to have the New Salisbury Guards transferred to a place where the invasion would *not* take place."

It was obviously an exposition of intentions that Effington had been practising for quite some time.

"And now you want us to tell you where the invasion will take place, is that right? What exactly do you take us for — complete idiots?" I exploded.

But Effington was not deterred. In his prissy, pedantic way he continued with his exposition. "No, sir. Only one place where the invasion will *not* take place. That is where Mr. Copithorne will make sure that the New Salisbury Guards are amassed."

Finally George responded. "The idea of Frank Copithorne changing sides is so preposterous that it makes us slightly dizzy. Then there is another question that is fairly important: Who are *you*, Mr. Effington, and what is your part in all this?"

Effington seemed to relax a bit more now. "I am a businessman. I have been dissatisfied with Mr. Liefenbarger's regime for quite some time, but until very recently many of us sincerely believed that the rebels in the Cheviot Hills were only Communists."

"Does Copithorne have the same reasons?" George pressed.

Effington smiled enigmatically. Then, for a moment, he gazed at the toes of his shoes.

"I am afraid that Mr. Copithorne is what would be called a realist. He sees an end of an era on the horizon and he is making all the proper arrangements."

"But so far he has taken no risks at all. You have," I said.

Effington looked at his watch. "Yes, and I had better make certain that they remain minimal. My flight leaves at 5:30. There is a National Unity Corps agent with our delegation at Wellington, who keeps track of our whereabouts. He thinks that I am in bed at my hotel."

"How do we keep in touch then? Through you?" asked George.

Effington nodded. "Through my office. Mr. Bech-Landau has my card." He rose. "Well — " Effington extended his hand to George who hesitated a moment, then took it and shook it heartily.

"Tell me, Mr. Effington, do you think it possible to take Main Island with as few lives lost as here?" George asked.

He thought for a moment, then looked for him rather boldly into George's eye. "No. Perhaps if you waited until the Liefenbarger regime decayed a bit more — but no, not even then. Too many people on Main Island will be fighting to their death."

George said nothing, but I knew that he disagreed. It had been done on Lower Isle and it could be done up north too.

"We'll contact you," he finally said just before Effington left.

"What do you think?" George asked as soon as I came back from escorting Effington out.

"I think he is on the level. But I don't think that what he's doing is as selfless as he would like us to believe. I mean, we could give him a few hundred thousand, but then he would be a paid-off mercenary. This way we will keep on owing him. And that will get him a lot more in the long run — a lot more. Copithorne would like to pull that too, but he can't. He sees the Liefenbarger boat sinking and like a good little rat he wants to disengage himself — neatly and profitably."

"So that what you know personally about Copithorne would fit in with what Effington said?"

"Sure. Copithorne has sniffed here, sniffed there, analyzed, and finally come to the conclusion that Liefenbarger and the National Unity Movement have had it. And since morality, loyalty and trustworthiness have about as much meaning to him as they do for a baby rhinoceros, he quickly turned the whole thing into a business proposition. He asks for two million because he knows we'll haggle him down to one. And with that he'll fly off to be among the gnomes of Zurich, taking a long vacation and waiting for things to cool down for Liefenbarger's supporters."

"So you think he expects us to pay?"

"Yes. And it isn't that unreasonable, either. If we don't, he has an alternate plan, I'm sure of that. It probably includes an embezzlement of a considerable sum of money and flight to Easter Island."

"Why Easter Island?"

"Because Switzerland is really cold as hell this time of year and because Easter Island belongs to Chile. It is thereby the nearest landfall around here where he could find some understanding for his particular philosophy of life."

"So you'd be in favor of going along with Effington?"

"I don't think I can really favor anything at 5 A.M. George, I mean besides going back to bed. Let's get another three or four hours of sleep, then talk about it some more."

A few minutes later I drifted off to sleep in my room quite easily. I was relaxed. The news was good: Main Island suddenly seemed much less of an impregnable fortress.

Chapter 53

A few days later, Ann Schorez walked into the main hall of Pitlochry, wearing a striped pantsuit and vest, and a high, stand-up collar. Copithorne watched her in the roomy hall, her black leather purse suspended on a long strap from her shoulder; she in turn watched Lucius Liefenbarger descend the winding staircase. Their eyes met and, to the executive secretary, it was quite clear that she had not come to say goodbye. The last of the American diplomats were leaving on the evening plane.

"I can't go," she said softly. "Don't make me Lucius."

"Being with me probably won't be so pleasant now."

"I know, but it doesn't matter."

It was an insane idea, really, wrote the thoroughly fascinated Copithorne. At this point in his diaries, for the first time he wrote about the end in concrete terms, suggesting that it was likely to be violent, sudden, and chaotic. Copithorne didn't place much faith in the NUC whom, like practically everyone in the upper echelons with the exception of Mayfield, he regarded only as a necessary evil. But he held some hope for the New Salisbury Guards who, according to him, were a crack military unit with far more tradition than the Anti-Insurgency Regiment. The Guards officers may have never respected the Lief personally, but they grudgingly admired his successful rise to power. They also respected his strength and determination and the way that both were concentrated in the office of the Administrator. So long as Liefenbarger held the position of the Administrator, Copithorne was quite confident that the majority of the Guards would defend him to their death.

The question, of course, was if it was enough to ward off the attackers.

The Administrator's executive secretary expressed his doubts in his diaries along these lines, periodically noting that the sight of his leader under seige and the chic American beside him was a highly moving experience. As he watched them step up the stairs with their arms around each other, he came to the conclusion that theirs was a fate quite separate from the rest of

New Salisbury. Whatever would happen to the country within the next few months, and whatever dung history may heap upon the memory of the Administrator, here was a human saga that should be regarded and assessed apart from the political events surrounding it.

When I picked up the telephone a few days later, Rose Kubatan was on the other end, calling from Maui, where she had rented a condominium and was hard at work on a book about us.

"How is the rule of law? Is it as much fun as the revolution?" she asked.

"More. One has to restrain himself more, but I realize that I'm talking a bit above your head. You obviously have no idea what the word means," I cracked right back. "What's up? Coming back soon?"

That had been her stated intention. That's why she had gone no further than Hawaii. As soon as we moved against Main Island she would hurry back.

"Not at the moment. Listen, something came up you should know about. Especially George. A friend of mine called a few moments ago from Honolulu. The AP keeps a lookout for who's coming and going to Hawaii. He says that someone named D. Titus arrived from Vancouver on CP 321 today, then went on to Auckland on an Air New Zealand flight. He should be arriving there now. Anyone we know?"

"Yeah, probably David, George's son. There's a connecting flight from Auckland to St. Enoch he'll be on. Thanks a lot, Rose. I'll check into it. Keep in touch, eh? G'bye."

The more aggressive Australians had already checked. They had even contacted the plane and the young man reluctantly admitted that he was George Titus's son. A horde of reporters waited at the arrival gate in Auckland, but there was also an alert Air New Zealand official who quickly sequestered the young man in the VIP lounge. The flight had had a tailwind and arrived earlier than expected. David Titus had almost two hours before the departure of his flight for St. Enoch, but this time he would travel first class. While reporters fumed outside, he stretched out on the sofa and promptly fell asleep.

When I surmised this through a call to New Zealand, I put down the receiver and the phone promptly rang again. It was Garbeau, who had been told that George was taking a nap and I was second choice for delivering his message. He said that the

Soviets were assembling an unusually large concentration of ships some three hundred miles northeast of Lower Isle. Three supply ships, a tanker, a Kresta class cruiser and three destroyers had been sighted so far, with the aircraft carrier *Kiev* possibly steaming toward the same destination. The Americans would keep on eye on them, but Garbeau thought we should too.

The boy had become a young man. While his father had been in New Salisbury he had acquired the poise and mannerisms of an adult. As David spoke, George gazed at him, admiring the confident smile, his calm way with words, the slow, precise way of expressing his thoughts. David had graduated from high school the previous June, then worked for an automobile parts delivery firm, all the time wondering what exactly he should do with his life. His sister had reluctantly started at the university, but he was not at all sure if that should be his way. He was not a big spender. The money began to accumulate and encounters with his father's pictures on television and in newspapers increased. What had originally been the image of his father as an idealistic, but also naive and somewhat erratic adventurer, gradually began to change into something of a determined, principled man who was willing to sacrifice comfort, safety and perhaps his life for his beliefs. At the point of this realization David's trip to New Salisbury became inevitable.

He asked thousands of questions about the revolution, about the country, about our democratic prospects. George was amazed at how much his son knew about New Salisbury. He had heard about the supply drops at Lake Mawusituki and about the Fort Wellington raid. He had seen pictures of his father in the corduroy cap and with a meerschaum pipe. The excitement of the revolutionary New Salisbury appealed to young David from the very beginning. George introduced him to Lawrence Saunders who, along with several of his friends, had organized a group called Youth for Democracy, an organization whose aim was to counteract the years of totalitarian influence on the islands.

Within days of his arrival David felt at home in New Salisbury. He soon moved out of his father's hotel suite into a bachelor apartment and quickly learned to take his place on those occasions that didn't exactly require his father's presence, but could do with the sound of a Titus name. George was delighted with the way that David had become part of his life — it had filled the void left by Meg's absence, assuaged to a degree the dull pain still associated with the breakup of his marriage, and it effectively reestablished his contacts with the young people, all at the same time.

As normalcy was slowly returning to Lower Isle, David brought a degree of it into his father's personal life. True, much of the relaxed atmosphere was a bit deceptive. In the minds of most people, nothing loomed more darkly than the likely horrors of the coming invasion of Main Island. But they also accepted its inevitability if the idea of a democratic revolution was to retain its meaning. Because of it, the military government on Lower Isle functioned fairly smoothly. Through the introduction of compulsory military training the Revolutionary Army readied itself.

The unwritten rule was that, wherever possible, things should be left the way they had been. The time for momentous changes would come only after the entire country had been liberated. Upholding the rule meant that dollar still bore the likeness of Lucius Liefenbarger, but across his face a red stamp mercilessly informed the bearer that the money was now that of Democratic New Salisbury. Air and surface links with the rest of the world gradually increased. The four smaller jets that had been at St. Enoch on the Day of Descent had been painted and their new designation indicated that they were part of the fleet of the newly established Air Democratic New Salisbury. They were used to connect Lower Isle with New Zealand and Australia which, in spite of frequent protests from the Liefenbarger government, were not likely to return the aircraft to Main Island.

In a series of popular television programs leaders of various political groups — including the new leader of the Communist Party of New Salisbury, Vic Channing — were interviewed and encouraged to publicly discuss pertinent issues.

Although as yet there had been no official recognition of the new country sought or extended — mainly because we were certain it would remain a "new" country for not too long — most Western and some other countries maintained an unofficial representative on Lower Isle whose job was mainly to make sure that their governments would not be overlooked in any future trade agreements. A delegation from Democratic New Salisbury had rented offices near the United Nations in New York. Dr. Karl Webber, formerly the medical officer in the Cheviots — and before that an inmate of the Partrawa camps — was appointed the delegation's head.

Lower Isle prisons were bulging. Former military barracks at Muldoon were now being used as a detention center, mostly for former National Unity Corps members accused of violent crimes. Some with less serious charges against them had been released on bail, usually pending acquisition of more evidence from Main Island. Extreme care was also taken by us that prison conditions did not constitute a type of revenge. To this end we made sure that guards were carefully screened.

Trade and commerce were carried out along basically free enterprise lines except where supplies for the military were concerned. There an especially appointed commission determined fair prices and wages to prevent profiteering. Sizeable loans had been extended to Democratic New Salisbury by the U.S., Australia, and some West European countries, and these were responsible for helping along the initially wobbly economy. The island was slowly recovering from the oppressive centralism of the Liefenbarger regime and from the psychological trauma of the recent upheaval.

Unexpectedly, a man named Krofta visited us who had been second in command at Camp Delta and who now was stationed with the garrison at Marsbury. He explained that he was a democratic socialist but that until now he had hesitated to identify himself as such because of the anti-socialist directions within the movement which had been manufactured, he felt, by one Maurice Bech-Landau. But he had taken part in the organization of the workers and he felt that now was the proper time to translate their organization into the Social Democratic Party of New Salisbury. He wanted permission to do it and promptly got it from George.

There had been a curious twist to his visit. George assured him several times that the organization of a social democratic party of New Salisbury was long overdue and that, if Krofta found it impossible to find the necessary funds for the task, it was not inconceivable that the military government could arrange a loan. The reassured Krofta got up to leave but at the door he turned around once more and after a moment's hesitation asked, "Mr. Titus, I have one more question: When are you going to organize your own party?"

George smiled enigmatically. "Who knows? Maybe I'll even join the socialists."

But Krofta was dead serious. He shook his head. "No, I

don't think you will. To me you seem to be too much of a liberal for that. I have read some of your things. You are not enough of a liberal to fit in among the spineless professional men who are now the backbone of the liberal movement. But you are in the highly enviable position of being able to start your own party — to mold it so it would fit your needs exactly."

"I'm not sure I'd want to do that."

Then Krofta grew even more serious. "That would be a serious mistake, Mr. Titus. I mean if you didn't do it. May I point out something? Even the way you have said that — I am not *quite* sure that I *would* want to do that — indicated a certain amount of vacillation. Without a strong, pace-setting party that would provide the initial momentum there will be a myriad of small fish scrambling for power. You know what that would mean."

Krofta said all that in my presence. He had greeted me when he came in, then accused me of steering the revolution too far to the right, and finally totally ignored me.

After he left, George and I talked about the idea of starting up a new party. It turned out that George hadn't really thought about that too much. As he talked I realized that somewhere underneath his other concerns there lay a deeply buried idea through which he saw himself as something vaguely resembling a middle-aged elder statesman, an adviser to the emerging democratic system. Perhaps as a professor at the University of New Salisbury, perhaps even as its rector. Incredible as it seemed at that time, he had not really considered the idea of entering active politics. But all that shouldn't be misunderstood: it wasn't that he didn't want power, but that he craved a philosopher-king's throne instead of a prime minister's desk.

I strongly suspected that there was quite a bit of his inherent academic snobbism in it, because he certainly hadn't pictured himself without future power or influence. But it would have to be clean power, untainted by election-time maneuverings and general crowd pleasing. In that sense he was still very much the detached academic — although he may have been ready to die for an idea, he was not quite sure if he really wanted to soil his hands by the day-to-day handling of it.

Part Three

THE VICTORY

Chapter 54

Shortly after 2 P.M. on Thursday, January 19th, heads of various departments and force commanders gathered in the conference room on the first floor of Hotel Chaucer to be briefed on the invasion plan. There was no longer much doubt in our minds that we could pull it off — the bulk of our effort was now directed toward minimizing the casualties.

George gave a succinct, reassuring introductory speech, in which he stressed harmony, good organization and capable improvisation as the key to success. Then he dropped a bombshell: he announced that the forty-eight-hour countdown would begin at midnight and that only a wholly unexpected storm over the Wellsbury Strait could cause a postponement of the invasion of Main Island. An aide brought in two boxes of brown envelopes and distributed them among those present.

"Your envelope does not state which of the five possible landing sites has been selected for the invasion. For a good reason. It must be kept secret until the very last possible moment. The paratroopers will be told when in the air, the surface troops when actually aboard ships. The rest — support forces — will know only when the actual landings have begun.

"One more thing," George said at the end of his talk. "Those of you who will be taking part in the invasion itself should never forget that those will be your fellow countrymen that you'll be encountering in battle. It is, of course, expected that you will fight, that you will fire when fired upon and that you will be cautious at all times. But it is important for the future of this country that you will bear in mind that you are *liberators,* not *conquerors.* Unless you conduct yourself as liberators, you'll be making it extremely difficult for any future government to govern justly and democratically."

There was no doubt about it, he had acquired the knack for wooing crowds. It wasn't as much what he said as how he said it. The bit about the liberators was not exactly great oratory, but suddenly the whole room erupted in a standing ovation, expressing the utmost confidence in their commander during a very crucial moment. He now seemed far less surprised by it than he was in the Anti-Insurgency Regiment's barracks. He gave the impression that he considered such dramatic demonstrations of loyalty to be perfectly normal.

Later in the afternoon the two-week sunny, dry spell at St. Enoch ended. It started to rain and the streets became slippery. The muddied cars moved slowly down the wide avenue in front of the hotel, increasing the dismal mood of the scene.

The rest of the day I spent with George, without noting the slightest bit of anxiety in him. Gone were the shivers of near paralyzing doubt at Smithton, but it was hard to figure out what it was exactly that had replaced them. Was it an immense faith in the ability of the Revolutionary Army, his newly developed skill in masking his fears and doubts, or a growing conviction as to his own somewhat mystical infallibility?

The news coming out of Main Island was getting worse. The media there was now in the hands of hard-liners who advocated recalcitrance and determination to fight till the bitter end. It could have all been dismissed as bluff, were it not for the increased slaughter at the NUC headquarters and the atrocities reported from the Partrawa Plain. It was no longer possible to blame it simply on the excesses of Mayfield's men because the wave of terror was no longer sporadic; it was now steadily increasing in its intensity, the responsibility resting on the shoulders of everyone in power on Main Island.

We talked about it over dinner in George's suite to which David and Lawrence Saunders had been invited. Lawrence was in an awkward situation because of the position of his uncle and there was, as a result, a bit of uneasiness around the table at first. Althought Lawrence and I probably disagreed on our handling of his uncle, none of us wanted to talk about it that evening. I tried to joke but my humor was admittedly limp and in the end I became quite thankful to David who began to speak of his support for the revolution — despite the fact I was in total disagreement with what he said.

Basically he expressed his belief in something he vaguely referred to as moral power. It was this power which would eventually emerge victorious on Main Island once the deterioration process there had been completed. It was an argument without cause, without too much logic, precedents, or concrete examples. He had been wordy and confused in his exposition of it, timid in his tone.

"Let me get this straight," I said. "You say that we should fight Liefenbarger with something called the moral force. How?"

"I'm not sure," said David pensively, "but I'm sure there is a way."

"And while we're looking for this damn elusive way, Eddie Mayfield murders his quota each week, right? Don't you think we could be accused of being a bit irresponsible if we did nothing?" I asked.

"Have you ever tried negotiating with Liefenbarger?" asked Lawrence. "I mean the man must realize that —"

"Yes, as a matter of fact, we have," I interrupted. "George here has said publicly over and over again that he would in no way hinder the Lief's departure from Main Island."

"And you think that's enough? You call that negotiating?" asked David.

"Yes, I think that's enough. More than enough. Neither Hitler nor Mussolini had been offered such a way out."

"Do you think they would have accepted it?"

"Christ, I don't know. But that's not the point, is it? What I am saying is that when a beast like Liefenbarger is offered life, he already has far more than is due to him. I don't get it: what is this obsession you have that calls for handling killers with kid gloves? Is that what is meant by moral force and youthful idealism?"

David remained undeterred. He had obviously thought it over before this: "Don't you see, you're only concerned with the killers — with Liefenbarger, Mayfield and Ormsby — the whole pack of them. That's wrong. It's not enough. They don't matter. Or rather they matter very little. Who matters much more is the whole island: all the people. And if you kill right in the middle of them, if you make their home into a slaughterhouse, then you must also expect the worst from them. They'll pick up right where you left off and try to string up every single National Unity man on the nearest tree. Like they would have done here, except that here you have been able to stop it. But I don't think you should kid yourselves — it was stopped here only because the Revolutionary Army most of the time *didn't have to* kill. And that won't be the case up north."

We all assumed that David's words closed the discussion and concentrated on our food for a while. Then, suddenly, George spoke up.

"With all due respect for your youthful idealism and the moral force — whatever that may be — I think that the biggest problem here is the lack of experience. Yours, not mine.

"You have no idea who Liefenbarger really is. Neither do you really know anything about Mayfield and Ormsby. I do. Or rather, *we* do. We have detailed dossiers on all of them, and from those dossiers we have discovered that their psychological makeup is not normal. I don't mean abnormal in the sense of them being raving maniacs, but not so normal that most of us would understand them. And, because I know that I don't understand them, I am also very cautious about applying criteria to them which may only apply to me. I also know there is the real danger that if I start applying such criteria I may be thoroughly misunderstood by them. Example: If I make it known to them, who have used force with such success, that I want to negotiate peacefully, there is a good chance that they will interpret it as my confession of weakness. Why? Because for them the avoidance of bloodshed for any other reason doesn't make sense. In fact, since they remain in power because of bloodshed and violence, they think exactly the opposite. So now I have convinced them that I am weak: I have really invited them to test me. From past experience I'd say that their idea of negotiating would include the taking of several hundred hostages and then threatening to shoot them if we don't accede to their demands. I don't mean that this would be the precise scenario, but it would probably be something close to it. Now do you see why it was impossible to negotiate with Hitler, Amin, and Stalin — to name only the most prominent killers — and why we can't negotiate with Lucius C. Liefenbarger? One can only negotiate on an equal plane. Talking upwards or downwards isn't negotiating. It's either pleading or dictating."

Shortly after dinner we were left alone again. Lawrence and David headed for the Youth for Democracy headquarters. The organization had been incorporated into the invasion plan. Its members now patrolled the capital in pairs, unarmed but with two-way radios.

George tried to return to his reports but he could not concentrate. We then tried to watch an inane television drama, but were interrupted by a message from Garbeau who was now in Hawaii and wanted to wish us good luck. The Russian task force cruised some three hundred miles northeast of N.S. City and the U.S. Navy was keeping a careful watch over it. There was now a liaison U.S. Navy group sitting in mufti at the Operations Center. Eventually I too went to the Operations Center, but I called George a few minutes after ten. There was a message from Meg via the British embassy. She now knew about the invasion plans and the entire Resistance organization on Main Island had been alerted, though only she knew the exact time and place.

George asked if she had said anything else. She didn't; but at least she was alive and well.

That same evening, the bus from N.S. City pulled into Sempal almost an hour late because it had had a flat at its last stop in Lake Haumo. Tires, like all spare automobile parts, being designated as strategic material, were hard to replace. Phone calls had to be made in all directions to get a new one. The two NUC agents in civilian clothes waited patiently in a car around the corner from the bus station, lights out and motor off.

Sempal — the town near which the father of our Herriott classmate Hank Windom used to have what he called a hunting lodge, but what to us looked a lot more like the Versailles Palace. And there we congregated — seven of us from Herriott who were now attending the university, just before Christmas '55 or '56, celebrating something or other, drinking brandy from a cask conveniently placed in the corner of the stone cellar. In a few hours we could hardly stand up. Then someone got the idea to go swimming. With great difficulty we piled into the cars and started toward Wampaha Beach.

George drove. At Sempal, in the middle of the night, he failed to stop or even slow down at an intersection, hitting an old man on his way home from a tavern. We all went along to the police station where George was found to be intoxicated. With equal certainty the police also established that George Titus was the son of *the* Titus. The confusion was phenomenal. Then it was discovered that the injured man was drunk as well and everyone concentrated on that aspect of the affair. The lucky thing for George was that he didn't die right away; he lingered for a week or two and by that time everyone lost interest. The public silence wasn't so much of a cover-up as criminal negligence of the New Salisbury press. By the time the man finally died the whole episode had been virtually forgotten.

I forgot it until I heard that on Thursday, January 19th, Meg Winters, wearing a blond wig and glasses, dressed in a raincoat and carrying a small vinyl suitcase, got off the bus at Sempal. She walked over to a waiting blue Austin and got in.

At that point the NUC agents inside the car near the bus depot alerted others and, within moments, five cars converged on the bus depot, three of them with local police markings.

The Austin desperately tried to wind its way out of the depot, but it scraped against a brick wall, then collided with a parked car. It was now immobile, its front end steaming. Several men with drawn revolvers cautiously approached it from different directions.

One wonders what went on inside the Austin during those last few moments. The only thing we know is that when the lead man walked to within ten meters of the Austin, its right door tore open and the driver, named John Swann, emerged with a gun in his hand. He never had a chance: he was felled by several bullets and died on his way to the hospital.

Meg Winters must have seen the futility of such a maneuver; she used the last few moments to place a cyanide pellet in her mouth and to bite down on it as hard as she could.

Chapter 55

George came down to the Operations Center shortly before the start of the invasion countdown at midnight. He watched the big board on which the progress of various supply, transport and combat activities was being recorded. He sat down silently at a table in his glass-enclosed office, puffing on his pipe and periodically sipping on lemonade brought to him in an enticingly frosted glass from the snack bar.

At 4 A.M., when it was evident that communications were functioning properly, he rose to go up to his suite for a few hours of sleep.

He was up and alert instantly when I woke him up shortly after sunrise. In my face he must have read that it was really serious this time.

"Something came up, George — "

"What? Have we — "

"The Communists are trying to take over."

"Where? How? This isn't one of your — "

"At Kilmaron. The man in charge there isn't Hewitt any more. It's Vic Channing. And Force Delta is now Action Committee One."

George just stared at me, trying hard to digest and sort out what he had just heard.

"But that isn't the worst. Listen to this." I got up off the bed and turned on the radio console in the corner of the bedroom. McAlpine's voice came out loud and clear.

" ... that I have reached this decision after considering the consequences very carefully. We must not replace one dictator with another. The chains which would bind us under a George Titus regime would be not be so different from those we have learned to know so well under Lucius C. Liefenbarger's fascism. Soon you may be asked to send your sons, husbands, brothers — your loved ones — to invade Main Island. We ask that you join with us to make sure that their sacrifice will bear fruit. We ask that you join with us in making sure that the future will really bring democracy back to New Salisbury."

"Have they got the radio station?" George asked.

"Worse. They have the transmitter."

"And McAlpine is there?"

"I doubt it. That's a recording they have been playing over and over again. McAlpine's not known as a hero."

"What else?"

"The workers' committees; they're all action committees now. Some places they've already started shooting it out with the Revolutionary Army."

"What orders did you give so far?"

"For our people to defend themselves. I've also strengthened defenses around this place. But there isn't much happening around St. Enoch. They aren't that crazy."

"Well, how do they hope to — "

But George stopped in mid-sentence because he read in my face that there was more, much more. And that it was awful.

"It's David. They've got David, George. They kidnapped him last night."

He said nothing, now slumping in his pajamas on the edge of his bed. As if someone had pulled the plug and allowed most of life to escape from him.

I took a piece of paper out of my pocket. "Here's the note. They don't want you to say a word publicly about the kidnapping or they say they'll kill him. Here's what they want." I thrust the paper at George. There was no immediate response.

"Read it," he said finally, barely audibly.

"They want fifty per cent of their men in any future government and they want this demand implemented before the invasion of the north. Even if we have to stop the countdown. They want a voice in security, control of workers' committees and of half of the army. Also of education."

George looked up suddenly. "And what about me — where would they like to string me up? From the steeple of the Christchurch Cathedr — "

"They don't want you to resign. Just to give up a few things. They're pretty careful not to box you into a corner."

"How long to comply?"

"Three hours. But I'm sure that could be extended."

George got up and mechanically started to dress. "We'll just have to give in, that's all," he said finally, looking at me pleadingly. "I can't — " He flayed his hands helplessly, then sat down on the edge of his bed again. But in a few moments he disappeared in the bathroom. When he came out again he seemed considerably more composed. Not completely, but at least his eyes seemed clear.

"Do you think they're strong enough to take the Revolutionary Army?" George asked.

"Not yet. They know it, too. What they want right now is a better crack at it. And not only at the army, either."

"What do you think we should do?"

"Get rid of them once and for all. Start by bombing the transmitter into smithereens. We have a mobile one that can cut in. Then move against Kilmaron and against any Commie unit that makes trouble. Disband, disarm and arrest all leaders of the workers' or goddamn action committees. And clamp down McAlpine, this time permanently. We have a good, loyal regiment here at St. Enoch — the Epsilon Force — which can spearhead the drive against Kilmaron. We can lick them, George. In less than a day, I'd say."

But neither of us wanted to open up the other part of the problem. We gazed at each other silently.

"David ... what about David?" George finally asked in almost a whisper.

"There are two hundred people already looking for him. Most likely he's still at St. Enoch. We'll find him."

George nodded. Both of us now realized that the kidnapping was largely designed to make George put David before his ideology. The big question now was if he would.

The news reached Lucius Liefenbarger early in the morning. Copithorne arrived at Pitlochry shortly after eight and went directly to the sunny terrace where the Administrator was having breakfast with Ann Schorez. Copithorne quickly summarized the course of the revolt on Lower Isle for him, concentrating on highlights, never for a moment becoming sidetracked by smaller issues. It was now clear, said Copithorne, that Lower Isle was in the throes of a Communist takeover engineered from Kilmaron.

"So we were wrong after all," mused Liefenbarger between mouthfuls of ham and eggs. "Maybe Titus wasn't a Communist. But it's an understandable mistake to make on our part — thinking that nobody leading a revolution could be that stupid. Evidently it is possible, though."

Ann rose, excused herself and went inside. As he watched

her, Liefenbarger asked, "You think the whole thing could be a hoax? Could it be some sort of an elaborate plan to throw us off guard?"

"No, I don't think so," replied Copithorne. "McAlpine is on the radio explaining things right now, and there are apparently anti-Titus leaflets falling down all over St. Enoch. It would be too risky for everyone concerned. It definitely isn't a hoax."

Liefenbarger finished eating, walked to the railing of the patio and looked at the ocean in the distance. "So George Titus will not be admiring the view from here so soon after all. The Communists are really heartless, aren't they? The question now is whether he realizes what is happening to him."

Suddenly he remembered. He whipped around to face Copithorne again. "The Russian advisers — have they started arriving yet?"

"The first batch is due tonight."

"Get hold of Velikovsky, Frank. Tell him to delay their arrival. We've got to think this whole thing through."

"Do you think it's wise, sir? I mean if the Russians — "

Copithorne wrote that at this point he sensed that he was an entirely different Liefenbarger once more. It wasn't yet the old, confident Liefenbarger but he was more hopeful — as if the good fortune he had been so unfairly denied was finally being delivered to him. He stopped in mid-sentence and altered his tone.

"Yes sir. I'm sure the Soviet ambassador will understand."

"And if he doesn't that's too bad. We are very much in the saddle here and he'd better learn how to start running with us. Sure he won't want to; with the Lower Isle Communists in the driver's seat it would be great to have Main Island full of Russian advisers sniffing around every army base. Sure he'd like that. And in a few months Leahy and his Communists from the south will land here, knowing more about where and what we are than our own generals, eh?"

"Excuse me sir, but it doesn't look as if John Leahy is the leader of the Communists any more. One doesn't hear his name mentioned at all."

"Then who is — McAlpine? He must be the dirtiest chameleon I've ever come across."

"No sir, not McAlpine. He'll probably be discarded as soon as he has served his purpose. He's really just a cover. Much more important seems to be a man named Channing."

"Vic Channing?" asked Liefenbarger, surprised.

"Yes sir, Victor Channing. From Castlereagh, I think."

"That's the one. He was an administrative assistant to Hardwick, when Hardwick sat in parliament. He's a slippery eel, just like Hardwick was. Never allowed anyone to call him a Communist; it wasn't good for his public image. He'd threaten to sue every time. Kept saying that he was a radical socialist, whatever that means."

The telephone rang beside the breakfast table and Copithorne answered it. He listened, thanked the caller and then hung up, turning toward the Lief. "That was Mayfield. They've got Meg Winters. At least they think they do. She has bleached her hair but they're pretty sure that it was her."

"Was?" enquired the surprised Lief. "Is she dead?"

"Yes. She took some poison or something."

The Lief looked out the window, pondering the new information. "This doesn't seem to be a very good day for George Titus, not a very good day at all," he mused.

The Administrator's behavior was suddenly making Frank Copithorne anxious. He was witnessing a major transformation of Lucius C. Liefenbarger before his very eyes. It was as if the Administrator had managed to straighten himself once more and was looking at Copithorne once more from up above — from a position of undisputed authority.

Liefenbarger started talking about a new offensive. He was certain that the Americans would return to his side, that he was ultimately slated to become the champion of a dynamic and independent New Salisbury. According to Copithorne's notes on that morning, Liefenbarger was now certain it would be from Main Island that the invasion would eventually be launched and not vice versa. He instructed Copithorne to call a meeting of armed services chiefs for that afternoon at which the changeover to an offensive strategy would be officially announced and new programs developed which would prepare the army for its role as an anti-Communist liberator.

Several times that morning the Administrator even hinted that he planned to limit the size and power of the National Unity Corps, suggesting that it had become something of a liability. He spoke about enhancing the role of the Corps as a civilian movement once again, about entrusting it with more important informational and promotional tasks, leaving security to the police, and defense to the army.

Copithorne didn't feel particularly comfortable with this change. Expecially not since the reports from Lower Isle had been so spotty and chaotic. True, the radio station seemed firmly in the Communists' hands and the radio was in St. Enoch, but there was little else which would indicate that the Communists were in total control — despite the fact that they themselves repeatedly claimed to be. It didn't seem likely to the wily Copithorne that it could all happen so quickly, that they held positions which would enable them to topple Titus without even a fight. He thought of all the possible explanations for the Lower Isle situation, at the same time trying to keep track of all that Liefenbarger was saying.

In the car he quickly silenced his driver who had heard about the Communist takeover on his radio and who wanted to talk. Frank Copithorne had some extremely important decisions to make in a hurry — decisions on which his life would probably depend. He had to decide if he should start running or wait until the situation cleared up. Of course, by then it could have been too late.

It wasn't exactly easy.

At seven-thirty A.M. there was a phone call from the Reds. I handed the receiver over to George who had by now shaved and was drinking a cup of coffee. He held the receiver in his hands for a few moments before placing it against his ear. I picked up the extension next door when George pointed to it.

"Hello," he finally said into the phone without the slightest bit of intonation.

"Channing here. You've read my note?" The voice was clipped, business-like.

"Yes."

"And?"

But there was only silence. George didn't reply.

"And?" Channing repeated the question once more, this time an octave higher.

"I'm sorry but I'm not used to talking with blackmailers. It takes a considerable getting used to."

"C'mon, c'mon, what do you take me for?" Channing inadvertently lapsed into his native cockney he had been trying to mask. "Get on with it — yes or no?"

"We are willing to discuss your greater participation in the government, but not under these conditions."

"You really take me for an idiot, don't you? Never mind offering counterproposals. You have our proposal which is reasonable enough. We don't want the government — only our rightful share of power."

"How do you know that we will consider ourselves bound by any agreement with you which was part of a kidnapping plot?"

Channing chuckled, obviously satisfied that all the proper arrangements had been made on that score. "Oh well, we know. That one we know for certain — you wouldn't. That's why your boy will stay with us — to make sure that you'll carry out the agreement."

"I see. Is he with you right now?"

Channing hesitated for a moment before answering. "No, but he's O.K. Just fine."

"That's good. Could you have him call me — maybe even record a message from him so I would know that he's all right?"

"Not right away."

"Oh."

"Look, I give you my word that he's all right. Perfectly all right. I'll get a message from him to you."

I was still trying to come to terms with the monstrous anachronism of Channing offering Titus his word, when George responded.

"Good. Then we will hear from you again soon, is that right? Afterwards we will make the necessary arrangements."

"No! We have to know right now. We can't wait. The lad's alive and that's that. Now you come up with your end."

"I have to consult with my people. We will let you know in an hour. Two at the most."

"Fine. You have an hour and a half."

"And during that time you will hold your fire. Everywhere."

"We'll do our best."

I came back to the bedroom. George hung up and wiped the perspiration from his forehead. It hadn't gone exactly the way he wanted it, but it hadn't been an absolute disaster either. We were both certain now that David was still in St. Enoch, otherwise Channing would have put him on the phone.

"Do we go to it then? Our boys are halfway to Kilmaron already, but they can be stopped. And there are twelve jets in the air."

"Any news about David?"

I shook my head. "No George, there isn't."

He sighed, gazed out of the window at the bay. "All right," he said. "We'd better get started."

The fighters launched the attack on the Lower Isle National

Radio transmitter at 8:32 A.M. The first bomb exploded at the base of the main tower, severing two of the stabilizing cables. It then toppled from its concrete pedestal, snapping in several places during the fall.

A few moments later the second wave commenced its attack, concentrating on the low buildings surrounding the towers. The first three bombs exploded between the buildings, toppling the remaining towers and sending the few occupants of the buildings into the open. One by one the buildings then received direct hits.

In less than two minutes it was all over. The transmitter buildings and the towers lay in ruins, a formless, smoking heap.

Chapter 56

"My name is George Titus and I am speaking to you from the Revolutionary Army Headquarters in Hotel Chaucer. Earlier today an attempt had been made by a few individuals to subvert our revolution — to reshape its thoroughly democratic orientation into left wing totalitarianism. It was a desperate attempt, characterized by the suicidal tendencies of those who have taken part in it.

"Led by a man named Victor Channing, these desperate few have attempted to shackle and bring under their control the great democratic majority on this island. People like Allan McAlpine, the former governor of Lower Isle, have lent their names to this deplorable subversion of our democratic cause. Allan McAlpine — whose thoroughly reprehensible background as a henchman of Lucius Liefenbarger has been overlooked because of his readiness to help us reduce the amount of killing during our descent from the mountains — has played a prominent part in this attempt to reinstate totalitarianism on Lower Isle. From it we have learned that such people must not be trusted by us again.

"Isolated pockets of Communists are still fighting their suicidal battles for a totalitarian domination of our democratic revolution. I want to urge those few who are still clinging to their false hope of subverting the freedom-loving spirit of people on this island for their own, nefarious purposes, to cease and desist. The Communist cause on Lower Isle is lost. Any further attempts to install it by force will only result in useless destruction and loss of life.

"Heed the voice of reason. The democratic tradition on both of these islands is deeply entrenched. Our people are not about to renounce it.

"Thank you for listening and God give us help in our struggle."

George got up heavily from his table in the sitting room where the technicians had installed a microphone. He came over to me. "You know what I would like?" he asked. "I'd like to get away somewhere. Somewhere where it's quiet."

"With company or without?" I asked.

"With," George smiled. "Definitely with."

I thought about it for a moment. "All right," I said finally, "I know just the place. Sid Capadouca will man the fort while we're gone. But I'll get a car with a telephone. We should keep in touch. The thing in Kilmaron will start in about an hour."

On the way to Willingdon, the stately Victorian home converted for the aged, I explained. "She's had a stroke George. They thought at first that she would end up as a vegetable, but there is tremendous willpower in her. She can even speak now."

"How did you know where to find her?"

"That wasn't particularly hard. Everyone knows her at Brempton. They all come here to visit her."

I had called ahead. At the door we were met by a welcoming committee and a group of smiling nurses peeking out of the room which adjoined the lobby, watching us sign the visitors' book. Then the director guided us to the room now readied for the distinguished visit with two easy chairs and a vase ablaze with brightly colored carnations on the dresser. Propped up on her high bed sat Gladys Cooper, now in her early seventies, in a plaid housecoat with a shawl across her shoulders despite the relative warmth of the summer morning. Her face was radiant; the visit would obviously make up for the years of misery in the benign prison that Willingdon must have been to her.

There was still a trace of that delightful sparkle in her eyes. Slowly and barely audibly she welcomed us, listening politely to my forced story about my father who once had been a guest in a retirement home but who refused to accept it as such. He proceeded to set up extra telephone lines to his suite and to hire secretaries who darted in and out of the door with messages. And when he expanded his activities into the adjoining room, the management of the home and his family agreed amicably that this was not the proper place for him after all. He died almost a decade later, at his downtown office and with a telephone in his hand.

"Some people just don't know how to retire," I concluded. Mrs. Cooper almost imperceptibly nodded in agreement, then it was obvious that she was meticulously preparing in her mind the right words for what she wanted to say.

"I...couldn't...imagine...myself...either.... Not...easy... There is much...lots of...time to...think.... Lots of time... to think."

She looked at George. "Do you ... have much ... time to ... time to think?"

George shook his head. "Not really as much as I would like — as I'm used to having."

"Your father ... died two days ... after ... after I ... had my stroke.... I have ... often ... thought of you ... George."

But then it became clear that she was too tired to continue; there had been too much excitement and it was time to go. None of us wanted to. In spite of the hospital-like surroundings, there was a bit of a haven here. The tempo of the place was in sharp contrast to the Operations Center and it acted as a cool poultice on our brows. Although Gladys Cooper's eyes betrayed that she knew this would be our last meeting, all of us acted as if we had not understood. I was trying to joke again, George using a few meaningless niceties as his farewells. But there was much more than the words.

Then we were out again, the car quickly pulling away from the reporters who had heard about the visit and wanted George to comment on the situation at Kilmaron.

And I am quite sure that George knew why I had brought him to Willingdon.

I chose a public beach about five kilometers north of St. Enoch. Still early in the morning, there were but a few people sunning themselves on the sand, seemingly oblivious to the crisis further north and the possibility of this beach becoming a battleground. We walked nearer the surf which gently washed the crescent-shaped beach. Near the water we found it all even more relaxing. Through the corner of my eye I noticed a small group of soldiers who eyed us from their jeeps, keeping their respectful distance, making sure that others would keep it as well, but remaining near enough to be instantly at our side when needed.

We took off our shoes and ambled along the moist sand, not saying a word. After a while George spoke first.

"I should call his mother. It's only fair."

"I would wait. A few more hours can't make that much difference and you may be saving her some pretty dreary moments."

"Maybe you're right."

We walked in silence for a while longer, until George stopped dead in his tracks, turned toward me and asked point blank: "Tell me the truth: do you think he's dead?"

"I think no such thing. You're dealing with Moscow-trained Reds, not with some two-bit pack of hoods who will panic and kill at the first sign of trouble. David is their ace in the hole. In the end, when everything else may have failed, he'll be their passport out of here. They aren't about to have it cancelled."

It worked. Not completely, of course, but for a while it diverted his thoughts to other things. Far out over the sea two distant dots moved across the horizon, the faint noise of their engines reaching us. Probably part of the force going to Kilmaron, I thought.

"I wonder if someday they won't say that I fiddled out here on the beach while Kilmaron burned. It *is* a strange place to be, you must admit, when one is fighting on two fronts. A bit like Eisenhower golfing in the middle of the Hungarian revolt."

"He didn't have his son kidnapped."

George just nodded to that one. "Have you talked to Garbeau this morning?" he asked. "The Americans were right about those Russian ships, weren't they?"

This time I nodded.

"You think they're out there, waiting to see how this thing will turn out?"

"I wouldn't be surprised."

George stopped and lit his pipe despite the stiff breeze. "Well, when are you going to start serving me with 'I told you so,' Maurice?"

"I didn't tell you that there would be a mutiny at Kilmaron."

"But everything else came true. You were irritatingly suspicious while I was stupidly trusting, just as I had been with the encyclopaedias. The publishers decided to become progressive and have the Russians write their own sections on history. There were some academics among us who protested — mostly emigré profs at the Slavonics Department and a few right-wing conservatives. Not very important types on any campus. So I joined in with the much larger group that demanded academic freedom, free speech and true objectivity and all sorts of other nonsense. We were, I must say, considerably more articulate than the other group. After a while everyone forgot about it because we were too busy climbing on yet another liberal bandwagon. I forgot about it too — until a year or two later, that is. Then I happened to look into the new edition and I was flabbergasted. Imagine if in 1939 someone had asked the Nazis to write the history of Germany. And you have to remember that the Nazis were far less convincing liars than the Communists: I guess it was because they had so much less time to practice. And do you know what I did about it? Nothing. Absolutely nothing. We used to be so good at justifying moral cowardice!"

I thought about what he said for a moment or two, then I spoke up. "Speaking of academic freedom — remember Podgorsky, the guy we called Parachod?"

"At Herriott? Sure."

"Well, later on — I think you were already in England — he taught Russian at the university. It was the late fifties; everybody hated the Russians. And something happened to old Parachod, the white Russian emigré and the great admirer of the czar. He started defending Khrushchev and the new gang around him. Maybe he was just getting old, but I think that he got very tired of all the knocks Russia was getting and he started reacting in a pretty chauvinistic way. You can imagine how that went over. I was sitting on the university board at the time and we drummed him out so fast he didn't know what hit him. Didn't even give him a chance to finish the semester. He died soon afterwards, developed some sort of cancer. But I am sure that wasn't what killed him."

He said nothing, but from George's face it was obvious he appreciated what I was trying to do.

"You think they expected such violent response from us?"

"No, they wouldn't have tried it if they did. What I think they expected was indecision — hesitancy. And they figured that while we were hesitating they could get hold of many more pressure points."

"Why would they start their coup in the middle of the countdown?"

"Several reasons. One might be that they figured they had no hope whatsoever if they waited until you, in a blaze of glory, liberated N.S. City. They were probably right on that one. The other is that they traditionally like to work in a chaos. That is, chaos everywhere but in their own ranks. And you've got just such a potential situation here: will the Revolutionary Army troops know who their real enemy is? If it's Liefenbarger or Channing or neither? Sure they were taking a chance, but so was Lenin. Sometimes it works, especially if you're faced with democrats."

One of the rebels detached himself from the lead car and started running across the sand toward us. This finally aroused the sunbathers' interest. Some sat up and several recognized us, chattering excitedly and pointing in our direction. The soldier snapped to attention in front of us, sand flying in all directions, and reported: "They've reached Kilmaron, sir. And Channing's on the phone."

"Any news about how it's going there?"

"Not yet, sir."

"We'd better go," said George.

We picked up our shoes and returned to the car. In the back, while still putting them on, George pointed to the phone. "You speak with him. I don't think I'd better anymore."

I hesitantly picked up the receiver just as the car started a wide U-turn.

"Hello?"

"Listen you — " the infuriated Channing shouted into my ear. His tone instantly jolted me out of the relaxed mood of the beach.

"No, no. *You* listen. We already know how little you have on your side. Now here's what *we* have. *We* have destroyed your radio and *we* have taken your babbling McAlpine into custody. *We* have Kilmaron surrounded and total control of all the airspace above it, with planes there ready to bomb all of you into oblivion. *We* have arrested all officials of your damn workers' committees, and put down half-hearted insurrections at Hawar and Devon. All is quiet here at St. Enoch. In other words you have failed and the country is firmly in the hands of the democrats. Now here's what *we* want: we want you to produce David Titus alive and unharmed within half an hour. We want him at the Chaucer Hotel. We want you to put down your guns and start trickling into the Kilmaron Stadium with hands on top of your head. That goes for your men. You and the other leaders will then get a ride to the airport and be flown wherever your red hearts desire — to Moscow, Havana, wherever. But it's a deal only if there isn't another shot fired at Kilmaron. Is that clear, damn it?"

But the line was already vacant. Channing had gone off and ordered an artillery barrage against our tanks which were waiting at Kilmaron airport for orders to enter the city. The hatred then spilled over and the time for negotiating had ended. The methodical levelling of one building after another at the Communist-held airport continued, conducted from the air and from the ground. More artillery arrived from St. Enoch and more fanatical zeal emanated from the defenders until fighting erupted in the streets which were soon littered with bodies and wounded.

By then the defenders and attackers alike had lost all sense of reason. Both were now governed by hatred mixed with the strong instinct for raw survival. The combination proved lethal. The attackers became entranced with their precisely engineered destruction — unbounded, unlimited, totally free to kill, punish, level and liquidate. In the midst of this hell, the local citizens huddled in cellars or tried to flee in long, sad lines along the waterfront, terrified by the explosions, with children whimpering and adults' faces squinting in a daze.

By afternoon the Communists had retreated into the western part of the city, near the barracks that had served as headquarters before their wooden frames had been set on fire to settle down in smoldering, symmetrically spaced heaps. The fire from the Communists then became sporadic, as if only to announce that they were still there. The attacking tanks arranged themselves into neat rows and noisily fanned across the plain where once had stood the barracks, methodically pushing the Communists to the trees by the river, periodically spraying the area ahead of them with machine-gun fire.

Simultaneously a column of trucks was approaching from another direction toward the river until the defenders were left with nothing but the stream behind them. Some tried to surrender but the tanks and trucks were not about to take prisoners, the raised hands and white shirts on the end of rifles served only to make better targets.

In the end there were some twenty men still huddling on the grassy bank as the trucks and tanks relentlessly approached. One by one they threw themselves into the river, either drowning in the swiftly flowing stream or being mercilessly gunned down by the attackers that stood along the bank, their guns ready, as if waiting for small game.

By nightfall there was little left of Kilmaron. The docks remained intact though because the Communists had not attempted to defend them.

But Channing was missing. So were Baracolli and Tolway. Many of their comrades lay in the streets of the razed city. Preliminary counts showed there must have been close to 300.

A few prisoners were taken, however. One of them, whose left arm had just been amputated, claimed that he had seen Diana Mulgrave with Baracolli and Channing, but it could have been just the ravings of a shell-shocked fanatic.

Chapter 57

Most of the detective work had been done in the unusually logical mind of Inspector Chic Dwyer of the St. Enoch Police Department, who sat with his hat still on at the dinette table of David's apartment, drumming his fingers on its vinyl surface. He was pondering the first politically motivated kidnapping with which he had ever been associated, and the decidedly unsettled situation around him which hampered his investigation.

To begin with, he was convinced that David was still alive and in St. Enoch. The bombing of the transmitter and the isolation of Kilmaron had quite likely disrupted communications between the leadership and those who held him. They were all Communists — disciplined, obedient, and thoroughly unaccustomed to thinking as individuals. The orders to the kidnappers must have been that they were to keep David alive until told otherwise. David was somewhere in the city.

Where?

There had been no struggle. No upset chairs or broken crockery. Nothing. That didn't necessarily prove that he had left with his abductors voluntarily — after all, he could have been drugged — but it accounted for the fact that no neighbors had heard anything. It must have happened sometime between midnight, when David came home from a meeting, and 4 A.M., when the kidnappers got hold of Bech-Landau at the Operations Center. Most likely it had happened closer to midnight because time was needed for transferring David to a safer place, and also for Kilmaron to be contacted and orders given to begin with the attempted coup d'etat. A long distance call to Kilmaron Barracks had been made at 2:30 A.M. from a booth at Regent Street to St. Enoch. It must have been the one.

Dwyer's detectives and a Revolutionary Army contingent had already searched the homes of almost fifty known Communist sympathizers in the city, but they found nothing. Even before the search had begun, however, Dwyer thought it unlikely that the boy would be found in the home of any known Communist. It had to be someone else — the Marxists were a lot of things but certainly not fools.

Again he thought about the possible mechanics of the kidnapping itself, trying to imagine the atmosphere of the Meadowgreen Courts, the modernistic and functional concrete and wooden clusters of apartments in a garden setting, at midnight. At night this place must be like a tomb, he thought. After twelve each attempt to start an automobile engine must sound like an artillery barrage. The car would then have to start slowly winding its way out of the complex and chances were that many a curtain would be drawn aside to see who was disturbing the peace.

At that point Dwyer reached for the telephone book to check on all persons who had moved into the complex in the last month.

The first suite they broke into was occupied by a terrified elderly couple watching television. The frail lady with a silver cane beside her chair began to tremble uncontrollably, and was still trembling even after the whole thing had been thoroughly explained to her. In the end she had to be sedated.

The situation was quite different in the ground floor suite No. 6 of Cluster C. As a soldier's boots broke down the front door, two others entered the place via the smashed glass doors. The young woman seated on the couch turned to her gun but failed to reach it before she died, her body having taken several bullets at once.

But the man was closer to his. Before he was hit he fired two bursts through the open door into the bedroom. And there on a bed, gagged and with his hands and feet bound, lay David Titus.

George called his news conference for 10 P.M. The reporters listened to his dramatic summary of the events at Kilmaron, not failing to note in their stories that his usual garb of a nondescript pair of khakis and a short-sleeve shirt had been replaced by Revolutionary Army fatigues. George was also wearing combat boots and there was a revolver attached to his belt for the first time.

A xeroxed copy of his news summary was being distributed which officially announced that Kilmaron had been destroyed and the Communists' attempt at a coup crushed. Although his kidnapped son had not yet been found, George spoke in a calm but firm voice. Maintaining that tone under the circumstances was something of a feat.

"Mr. Titus: Has the invasion of Main Island been postponed?" a Reuters man asked impatiently.

"The invasion of Main Island — if it is found necessary — will take place whenever we feel it most feasible. Both from the standpoint of a quick, military victory and the smallest possible amount of deaths and suffering. Nothing has changed on that score."

That answers nothing, I thought. In the best tradition of all the world's political leadership.

"Mr. Titus," asked a reporter from the newly-formed Democratic New Salisbury News Service, "has the Communist revolt changed any policies of the Revolutionary Army and of your military government?"

George thought about that one for a moment. "Well, yes, there have been some changes. I think that up till now we haven't been quite certain as to what we are primarily — a democratic movement or a Revolutionary Army. That question has now been answered for us by the Communists' treachery. We are first and foremost a Revolutionary Army. So, I would say that there will be a general emphasis on the military organization of the revolution from here on. Such things as military ranks will be used both officially and unofficially from now on. Mr. Bech-Landau and I are now generals, the various commanders of Greek letter forces are colonels, the vice-commanders, lieutenant colonels and so on."

"Does this new emphasis on the military aspects of your movement indicate that your schedule for the transition to a democratic system has been altered?"

"Which schedule?"

"You have stated somewhere, sir — general — that free elections will be held within a year of Lucius Liefenbarger's downfall. Does that still stand?"

"We really don't know yet because we are in the middle of some pretty serious happenings."

"Well, is the schedule being reexamined right now? Is that why you don't know, sir?"

George became visibly irritated. "Kilmaron is still burning, that's why we don't know. We have been attacked and dealt a wound from a side we have least expected. In spite of almost every indication otherwise, we have been led to believe that the Communists would be willing to compete democratically. We do know for certain now that we must not only be strong but vigilant. What that means in terms of democracy's development in our country — or rather in terms of its return here — is impossible to tell so soon."

From the corner of his eye George must have noticed Sid

Capadouca coming in, kneeling down beside my chair and whispering something to me. Just as he finished answering the last question I rose, covering the microphone with my hand.

"They've found David," I whispered.

George swallowed. "Dead?"

"No, but it's serious. There's a car waiting for us."

A ripple passed through the audience. George hurried out through the side door, while I gave a brief announcement concerning David, about whose disappearance the reporters had not been told. George's Chrysler careened through the dark streets. Somewhere along the way we were joined by two motorcycles with their sirens blaring, clearing our way across intersections where lights had turned red against us, past the football stadium, King George High School and the Queen Elizabeth Park, and on into the suburbs to the sprawling Mercy Hospital.

Lawrence Saunders was waiting at the entrance and keeping pace with George's fast tempo up the steps and across a spacious entrance hall to the elevator, all the time briefing him on what had happened. On the third floor, in front of the operating room with its heavily glazed doors, they finally came to a halt. Someone then slipped inside, in a moment reemerging with a man in a wrinkled hospital gown, wearing a cap, and with a surgical mask hanging across his chest.

"I'm Doctor Maldauer," he extended his hand and pointed to a pair of easy chairs nearby. "We're just about ready to operate. One of the bullets hit the spinal cord. I think we can save his life but that may be all."

"You mean a wheelchair."

Maldauer sighed. "I mean a wheelchair."

George reached in his pocket and brought out his pipe. He put it in his mouth without lighting it, quite obviously because it gave him something to do. Maldauer indicated he must hurry.

George took a deep breath and shook his hand. "Good luck, doctor, I'll be waiting right here."

In the corner of the recessed waiting room a short man rose as George entered. Lawrence Saunders introduced him. "This is Inspector Dwyer. He's the one who found him."

George, who had been in deep thought, looked up. His face softened. "Thank you inspector," he said.

Chic Dwyer waved his hands helplessly. "I only wish that — " he started.

"I know. Thank God he's alive though."

"Yes. Thank God for that."

Dwyer wanted to say more but he also sensed that this wasn't the right time. He quietly withdrew.

"We don't know how they got him out of his apartment," Lawrence said, "but whoever had done it must have met him before. It was no problem for them to get inside."

"Who were the people with him?"

"We don't know yet."

George nodded. The long wait was on. He rested his head against the back of the rattan chair and closed his eyes. Lawrence got up to turn out the lights but before he had a chance to, I asked, "We're almost halfway through the countdown. Do we stop?"

George took a deep breath. "That *is* the question, isn't it? What do you think?"

"I think we should go."

George nodded. "Yeah. Liefenbarger would least expect us right now. Are all our units operational?"

"All of them."

"But Kilmaron was an awful blow. What about the commanders — do they want to go?"

"They're split right down the middle. Half of them want to go."

"That's a great help."

George pounded his thigh with his clenched fist a couple of times, steeped in indecision.

"At least Eisenhower had a West Point education to help him. The Oxford one isn't much good here."

"I don't think a West Point degree would make much difference. This really isn't a military decision."

Neither of us said anything. Finally, reluctantly, I spoke. I had changed my mind for some reason. He should know before he made his decision.

"There's something else, George. ... Jesus, I have no idea how to say it."

In spite of my best efforts my voice broke down and tears flooded my eyes. I had known for almost an hour now and had hoped that I could control it by now.

"Is it Meg?"

I nodded.

George paused, terribly afraid to ask the next question. "Is she dead?"

"Yes."

And that had been too much for one day. I fully expected him to keel over, but he didn't. He just sat staring ahead while I haltingly recounted all I knew about what had happened at Sempal — that she had taken the poison she carried with her when they were stopped by the NUC, and that her driver had been killed. There was little else she could have done if the invasion plans were to be kept secret. At that point she knew all there was to know. She also knew about Eddie Mayfield and the Bristol Street Armory and that there was a good chance they would make her talk.

Now there were tears in George's eyes too. I didn't realize it then but I know for sure now that they weren't only those of sorrow and regret but those of the stubborn determination that was growing within him by leaps and bounds. His head remained proudly erect.

After all, it was Meg Winters we were mourning.

I had been terrified that the Sempal factor would hit him so hard that he would collapse. It was the last thing we would have needed at that moment. I decided to try to change the mood, but it was soon made amply clear that my attempt at cheerfulness wasn't needed.

"Is there anything I can do?" I asked. "I mean maybe I could — "

"There is," George replied with a resolution that had so suddenly hardened within him. He got up, and when we followed suit he put his arms around our shoulders, and directed us toward the elevator. "Go back and tell them the countdown is still very much on. Then go up to your room and put on your uniform, General Bech-Landau. I'll join you at the Operations Center as soon as I can."

Lawrence and I stared at him incredulously. In front of us suddenly stood a veritable tower of strength. All the doubt was gone now. The trouble was that neither Lawrence nor I were sure just how it could have been erected so fast, whether it was just a front, or how strong it actually was — if it would be able to weather the storms that were bound to come.

Nor were we quite sure if we liked its designs.

Ninety minutes later Dr. Maldauer emerged from the operating room, took off his mask and revealed for George a big, thoroughly satisfied smile.

Chapter 58

At this point it all becomes a bit complicated, partly because we wanted it that way and partly because for this period there aren't any more Copithorne diaries to fall back on for explanations. Events were moving much too fast and he had no time for making entries.

Early on Friday, January 20th, we got a message off to Copithorne via Effington and via the British embassy, that the New Salisbury Guards should be transferred to Nelson to face the invasion. It meant, of course, that Nelson would definitely not be the invasion site. Word came back to us very soon that Copithorne wasn't at all certain he could accomplish the transfer so quickly; he had hoped to have at least a week during which to work on Liefenbarger.

But it had all been done on such short notice for a purpose. We simply didn't want Copithorne to have the information in his possession for a whole week, so that he would have ample time to figure out or make some other use of it. I suspect that he knew right off the invasion would come on Wampaha Beach. He knew enough to figure out that once Nelson had been singled out as the place where the invasion would *not* take place, it pretty much ruled out *all* parts of the open water — from Partrawa to N.S. City. That left the Wellsbury Strait — Garrick, Wampaha Beach or Wahira. And since Meg had been at Sempal, only fifteen kilometers from Wampaha Beach, Wampaha Beach was the most likely site. Some of my reasoning on all this may be a bit shaky, but I still think that Copithorne knew.

In any case, Copithorne quickly assessed the situation, alerted the airport that the Administrator's Boeing 727 should be readied, then proceeded with his plan.

The plan was in no way simple, because for Copithorne, too, correct timing was all-important. The bulk of the New Salisbury Guards was stationed at Fort Meester, some 250 kilometers east of New Salisbury City and about halfway between the capital and Nelson. So that the Guards could be in full readiness at Nelson by ten on Saturday night, Liefenbarger had to issue the transfer order by noon. Copithorne must have realized he was cutting it all pretty close. The simplest and safest thing for him would have been to cut his losses, get in his car and start toward the airport, leaving the Lief and Titus to fight it out. At this point Copithorne already had well over a million dollars out of the country and that, along with fees for books and magazine articles about the Lief's last days, would have ensured that he did not starve. I suspect, though, that all the money would not have been half as sweet as the feeling that he had once again outfoxed everybody around, and to achieve that he would have to stick around a bit longer.

When Copithorne was very young he had craved power the way some people crave alcohol or heroin. It was an obsession with him to show the world around him which, he felt, had been treating him so harshly, that in the end he would be in the driver's seat, he would be deciding which events were to take place. But then this craving matured, became more sophisticated. As he came closer to power, he realized that power itself attracted too much attention and that it could become a heavy burden, even a liability. He started to understand that a much more enticing prospect was to attach himself to power.

Rose Kubatan quite fittingly once referred to him as the National Lamprey.

It appears that early Saturday morning, after he had made sure that Effington was ensconced at his inaccessible cottage, Copithorne drove to Pitlochry, where the Lief was spending the weekend with Ann Schorez. There he dropped his bombshell. He told the Administrator that the rebels were probably preparing to invade Main Island via Nelson.

The Lief then quite likely asked how Copithorne knew, and Copithorne mentioned Effington's name. The Lief then probably voiced his doubts about the rebels' readiness to launch an invasion so soon after the attempted coup.

That's when Copithorne must have played his trump card, confessing that he may have been all wrong in his assessment of the Kilmaron thing, that indeed the whole Communist revolt may have been a put-up job to throw Main Island off guard.

At that point the Lief must have called either Mayfield or Ormsby — or perhaps both — to see if the preparations at St. Enoch were still going on. Hearing their worrisome answers, he called a meeting of everyone concerned with defence and security at the Parliament Building at 11 A.M. Copithorne had no time to record his observations in his diaries, but he still went through the motions of being an efficient executive secretary and recorded the proceedings on tape.

At eleven the couches and easy chairs scattered around the Administrator's office were filled with uniforms and Copithorne was briefing the military on what he claimed he had heard.

Mayfield: "How come we don't know about all this, Frank?"

Copithorne: "Because I have just heard about it myself only a few hours ago. Together with the news from St. Enoch, I considered it to be important enough to be brought to the Administrator's attention."

May: "Who is this man — your source?"

Cop: "A friend, that's all."

May: "I sort of assumed that."

Cop: "His name is John Effington."

Ormsby: "The pet-food man?"

Cop: "Yes."

Orm: "Can he be trusted?"

May: "We'll soon find out. Let's have a talk with him."

Cop: "The message was confidential. To me. I trust the man and I would also like to keep him as anonymous as possible because he may be of further use to us. Besides, I have already broken my promise to him by mentioning his name."

The gambit was brilliantly designed to appeal to the Lief's warped sense of honor. All eyes must have been on the Administrator who was thinking it over.

Lief: "What did Effington say exactly?"

Cop: "He said that the conference in Wellington was also attended by people from Lower Isle. One night there had been considerable drinking and that from all the talk he got the distinct impression that Nelson would be the place of invasion."

Lief: "When was this conference held — last week?"

Cop: "No. Several weeks ago. Effington didn't think it important until he heard about the preparations at St. Enoch."

May: "Is that all you have? We are to put together our defense strategy here according to some drunken blabber at a New Zealand hotel?"

Lief: "Who were the men with him — did he identify any of the people from Lower Isle?"

Cop: "I don't remember the names, but I can ask him."

He knew, of course, that it was Saturday and almost noon — a gorgeous, sun-basked Saturday and Effington was at his secluded weekend place. He was safe.

Orm: "No, wait a minute. All that can wait. But there are preparations at St. Enoch and we have aerial reports about some strange ship movements. There is no reason why we shouldn't take proper precautions, though not necessarily along the lines Mr. Titus would like us to. I am also highly suspicious of information passed along at drunken parties which somehow makes its way back here. How do we know that it isn't exactly what George Titus would like us to think?"

Cop: "Isn't the way he's letting us know a bit complicated?"

Orm: "Not really, it has to look authentic to us, otherwise it would be worth nothing. Before D Day the Allies dressed up a cadaver as a British pilot and set him afloat off Portugal with false documents about the date and place of the invasion. Then they made sure that the Germans would get wind of him."

Lief: "You don't think that Titus would be invading through Nelson?"

Orm: "No, sir. It doesn't make sense. It's practically the farthest point you can transport an invading force from Lower Isle and the seas are absolutely treacherous around Nelson Bay. Then, beyond the beachhead there is a chain of mountains and a large river to be crossed before they can reach New Salisbury City. They would have to travel something like 400 kilometers. It just doesn't make sense."

Lief: "Where then?"

Orm: "There is only one place: the shortest distance between them and us in the protected Wellsbury Strait."

Copithorne must have felt his heart sinking at this point.

Lief: "Where in Wellsbury Strait?"

Orm: "At Sidwell."

It wasn't as good as Nelson, but it still wasn't Wampaha Beach. Copithorne had registered at least a partial victory.

It was a bit like the bad and good news joke. The good news was that while the Revolutionary Army was wading up on the Wampaha Beach, the elite New Salisbury Guard regiment would be getting ready to valiantly defend Sidwell. The bad news was that the two forces were eventually bound to meet head on in between the two places.

In the process they would level Wahira to the ground.

Chapter 59

The new officer in charge of the National Unity Corps detachment guarding Pitlochry was a captain named Hawkes who possessed a boyish face with an almost constant smirk on it. As soon as the Administrator and Ann Schorez arrived, Hawkes reported to him.

Ann went up to her room but the Administrator halfheartedly listened to the captain's recounting of all the security arrangements he had made. Finally Liefenbarger stopped the officer to ask him from whom he was being so vigorously protected. At first Hawkes was somewhat taken aback. Then, strengthening his smirk, he replied, "From anybody sir. Anybody at all. After all, you *do* have enemies, you know."

Exchanging the New Salisbury Guards detachment for a NUC one had been a move advocated by Mayfield for weeks, but with the transfer of the Guards to the south shore it had been decided upon and carried out within hours. The Lief must have known very well that the move would further increase Eddie Mayfield's prestige and power; at the same time he was probably too tired by all the intrigues to do anything about it. In two places on the beach Hawkes soon had his maroon-shirted men build a wall of sandbags and place machine guns. It would shatter the serene, bucolic setting of the place even more.

According to Hawkes's later testimony Ann, dressed in close fitting slacks that made the men turn their heads and with a sweater thrown over her shoulder, came out to sit with the Lief on the terrace after dinner. They watched the sun sink into the ocean, sipping on their cups of espresso. And Hawkes, who claims he made it a point to be always close by, says that the Lief without a doubt already knew that all was lost, that he told Ann Schorez so, and that he had begged her to leave several times.

Of course Ann refused. She told him that if the situation was as hopeless as he believed it to be then they should both fly off, leaving the islands to be fought over by Titus and the Communists. But by now the Lief was absolutely certain of his own destiny, of his *Götterdämmerung* type of end which somehow, at least in his own eyes, would assure him a place in history among the tragic greats. To make the whole thing even more entangled, it was precisely this insistence of his on an heroic end that must have especially appealed to Ann Schorez. There was a hint of it already in her Virginian upbringing, where the memory of the tragic figure of General Lee in his grey tunic offering his sword to the crass Grant and the defenders of the Alamo had not dimmed. Except that it existed only as a distant ideal while it was being progressively overshadowed by the Americans' penchant for the pragmatic and at times decidedly unheroic behavior.

Certainly the ways of the U.S. foreign service had lately been guided more and more by that which had worked, not necessarily by that which was right. Robert E. Lee and Davy Crockett had never been much of an ideal there. Here, at the stately Pitlochry, the mood must have resembled that of some noble legend. With the sun-tanned and khaki-clad Lucius C. Liefenbarger at her side, it was relatively easy to forget all about Mayfield's torture chambers and so many other, less appealing characteristics of his regime. Glorious self-sacrifice must have seemed marvelously appropriate over the espresso sipped on the patio out of Rosenthal cups. It was all coming to a magnificent conclusion that seemed straight out of Sir Walter Scott and she was proud to be part of it.

Of course, helping along with her decision to stay was the fact that at this point she was doubtlessly deeply in love with Lucius C. Liefenbarger.

Sometime after 1 A.M. Sunday morning, George Titus pushed against the back of his recliner at the Operations Center and closed his eyes. When he opened them again he had been asleep close to two hours. The activity of the place was of a different pitch now. The general atmosphere seemed subdued; there were fewer people around. It wouldn't be for long — we were only about an hour away from the invasion.

The giant board in front informed him that the weather was still holding, that there had been no change in the forecast. The atmospheric pressure on Main Island was high and there was practically no wind. Three troop-laden ships were on station. They were cruising some eight kilometers off shore and should have no trouble launching their lifeboats to begin ferrying their men to the beach. The two supply ships, Main One and Main Two, were also cruising on station, waiting for the first signs of daylight to come alongside the Casino Dock at Wampaha Beach to start unloading the vehicles they carried. Earlier, Main One had radioed that the sleeping resort town was already in the hands of 200 rebel paratroopers who had landed shortly after midnight on the road to Sempal.

As George watched, a young man ascended the steps toward the board. Then, standing on his tiptoes, alongside Squadron 345 he wrote the words "in the air." The 345 was a reconnaissance group. It would soon be followed up by two fighter squadrons.

George rubbed his eyes. I was watching him inside his glass cage as a soldier approached my desk, snapped to attention and handed me a piece of paper torn off the teletype machine. Instantly I lost all interest in the board in front of me. For a moment or two I stared at George, then at the paper in my hands. It was from the Theta Force commander, a man named Brownlee who wore a waxed mustache and had once been a regimental sergeant major. Force Theta was the new garrison at what had once been Kilmaron.

> Channing, Baracolli and Tolway
> apprehended while trying to leave
> area. Also actress Diana Mulgrave.
> Holding in custody. Advise further
> disposition.
>
> Brownlee

What I did next was undoubtedly a mistake. But it was past three in the morning, and we had all been under a great strain. Although the message was good news, I didn't consider it to be important to what our real worries were at Wampaha at that moment. I handed the message back to the soldier and directed him to the glass door, to George's office. Then I bent back over my map again, for the umpteenth time studying all the possible inland approaches to Wampaha Beach.

When I looked up again, George was holding the piece of paper up against the wall, and with a flat pencil that tradesmen use was writing something across it. He then folded it, handed the paper back to the soldier and turned away. Outside the office I intercepted the man and took the paper away from him. It read:

Establish identity beyond any doubt,
then execute all four detainees.

Titus

In two steps I was at the door to the glass office. "You can't be serious," I said, quickly closing the door behind me. "It's no good. We can't do it this way. Besides — Diana Mulgrave! What did she have to do with it?"

George spun around to face me. "We? *I* am doing it that way, Maurice. And *I* am doing it that way because we have finally stopped kidding ourselves and become a revolution. The genuine blood-and-guts, maiming and dismembering article that we should have been from the very start. Then Kilmaron would still stand today and David wouldn't have a bullet through his spine."

"How do you know? How do you know that anyone would have followed you if you were offering exactly the same thing that they had under Liefenbarger?"

"But they would have followed Channing, wouldn't they? The result: Partrawa reopened along the Gulag lines and the National Unity people would have gotten a red star on their caps. Does *that* make sense?"

"The Communists had no chance. Kilmaron was a desperate attempt that had no chance at all. It had been engineered by fanatics — by the true believers."

"It had, eh? Well, then this is insurance that there won't be anymore of them." George pointed to the paper. "That's the end of true believers on these islands."

"For God's sake George, that's exactly the opposite. It's giving them a good start. You are creating a veritable triumverate of martyrs. In two, maybe three years, the Kilmaron affair will be known as a brutal suppression of all progressive people's rights. No matter what the university profs will be writing in their monographs. David's kidnapping and crippling will be neatly detached from it and your summary execution of the three Communist leaders will overshadow everything else. You'll spend your time not running the country but running around the country looking for new ways to excuse yourself."

"That's funny, really funny, your saying that. You were the one who advised me to pounce on the workers' committees, remember?"

"I'd still advise it. There is a world of difference between murdering your opponents and denying them a foundation on which to build."

"You don't think they'd kill me if they had the chance?"

"Yes. And they wouldn't bat an eye while doing it."

"Well then?"

"We're past the eye-for-an-eye stage. We have to be. All children have to grow up eventually. Tit for tat stays behind with all other childishness. We can't move ahead on that basis, George. Not in New Salisbury, not where life is supposed to be decent."

"So I should sit here and turn the other cheek?"

"No. That's in the Bible. Something else comes into play when you start giving unto Caesar."

"There is no universal meaning here, Maurice. None. There is only the urgent need for the survival of this revolution. People have already died in droves and in a few minutes there will be fresh corpses. It all has to lead somewhere. We *must* protect their sacrifice."

"What about McAlpine? He was part of it. If there's anyone that — "

"He hasn't ordered any killings."

"Why can't Channing and the others be tried? We could —"

"Because that would be giving them a forum. The time for discussions is gone. We aren't talking anymore — not after Kilmaron."

Spent, I fell into a chair in the corner of his office. "I'm too beat to dredge up more arguments," I said. "I don't even know if there are any others. It's more of a gut feeling and it tells me that this is a hell of a mistake, that it will only cover us all with blood and mire and it will rid Leahy of his three main enemies in one fell swoop. At least postpone the decision, George! Wait until we have a hold on Main Island."

He thought about it, but only for a moment. "No," he said finally. "It would only be worse then. This is the right time. The *only* time."

"Think of all the Mrs. Coopers we'll be brutalizing. We're stripping all the thin covers off people until there is nothing left but the thick, black hide of a beast. Until there is nothing that sets us apart from *them*. I don't particularly relish a picture of Gladys Cooper as a beast — do you?"

George stared into the darkness and spoke up without looking at me. "I understand what you are doing and I respect it. But we can continue to function properly only if we dare to tear out the roots of this whole Kilmaron thing. There is no other way."

I got up, opened the door, then turned around once more to face him. "War is the great simplifier, isn't it?" I said.

Sitting down heavily at my desk I realized I had been wrong. I didn't even glance at the board because what was happening on it wasn't anywhere as important as what had just happened inside us. Somebody offered me a cigarette from across the desk, I accepted it, lit it and started smoking as if I had never managed to get rid of the habit. I also walked across to the snack bar and got myself a cup of the bitter, greenish coffee. It was better than sitting at my desk and doing nothing but see Diana face a firing squad, in confusion and disbelief, because war and revolution and violence had always been to her only a bunch of technicians on a Hollywood backlot who pulled wires that set off firecrackers among which zigzagged Errol Flynn in a meticulously pressed lieutenant's uniform.

And hatred? Hatred was to her what Jane Fonda reserved for the right-wing senators and nuclear reactors. Now Diana's first lesson in revolutionary definitions would also be her last one.

To be perfectly honest with myself, it wasn't Channing and his friends or even Diana Mulgrave personally who were my main concern. I had used all the arguments I could think of and they still weren't enough. And it was I who was mainly responsible. It was I who had created this monster who was now devouring us all.

I must have dozed off for a few moments in spite of my agitation. Someone had laid down another message on my desk. I stared at it, rubbed my eyes, then stared again.

"Sid — you saw this?" I called to Sid Capadouca a few desks away.

"I put it there."

"There is no doubt about it?"

Sid shook his head.

I grabbed the paper and a second later tore through the glass door. "Copithorne double-crossed us. The Guards haven't been diverted to Nelson. They've gone south."

George got up from his seat. "Where to — south?"

"Wampaha — where else? We've got to call the whole thing off."

"But we don't know for sure that they've gone to Wampaha, do we? They might have been sent somewhere else."

"We've got to call the whole thing off!" I kept raising my voice.

"We can't."

"Why? For God's sake why?" Now I almost screamed. "Anybody trying to come ashore at Wampaha will be wiped out now."

George glanced up at the clock. "There are two hundred paratroopers there already. Think of the slaughter if we abandon them."

I stared at him helplessly. "Jesus, I forgot."

George flicked on the ceiling light, then walked over to a large wall map hanging on the far side of his office. I stared at him in amazement. The man was a picture of calmness.

"The same road from Fort Meester leads to Wampaha, Wahira and Sidwell. It leads even to Garrick until it branches off here at Lake Haumo. It doesn't look like the Guards moved to Wampaha Beach because we would have heard about it already from the paratroopers. They are somewhere else, at Wahira or Sidwell. As soon as it's light the planes will spot them. In the meantime let's start landing the troops."

The paratroopers encountered little opposition at Wampaha. The sleepy National Unity Corps lieutenant in charge who reached for his gun as they entered his office received a bloody and painful wrist for his trouble, while the rest of his colleagues accepted it as fair warning. As instructed, they tore all the insignia from their maroon chests, then obediently crowded into the cages in the back of the office which had been originally intended for their enemies. Regular town police were then summoned to the station, disarmed, and immediately recruited again as advisers to the Revolutionary Army's military police.

Having posted patrols on the road to Sempal, Wahira and Garrick, the paratroopers concentrated on the two freighters bristling with heavy guns and vehicles which were to tie up along the recreational Casino Dock jutting from the beach. The water level had been tested earlier and found to be deep enough at high tide, but no one had ever docked a ship of that size there.

The paratroopers' commander, Dragan Justac, stood on the dock as the howsers from Main Two were being tied. Simultaneously with the docking operation and the emergence of the first rays of the sun, our fighters circled the area then neatly divided into two groups. One of them headed west toward Wahira, the other east to Garrick.

The dock soon became a beehive of activity as the booms began lowering the vehicles and guns on it. Justac and his men then retreated out of the way, back onto the beach. The first hurdle had been overcome.

But was it the first hurdle? The landing of 200 paratroopers in the dead of the night and their quick reorganization on the dunes had in itself constituted a hurdle we had managed to get across. So had been the taking of Wampaha Beach by firing only one shot through the wrist of a local NUC man.

The row of ships could be seen quite clearly on the horizon now. Those with good eyes could even recognize the first launches approaching the beach. It had all gone so incredibly smoothly.

There was still no hint of sunrise when Frank Copithorne loaded up his Lancia in front of the apartment overlooking Victory Gardens, and started toward the airport. The weather couldn't have been better. It was still cool, but there wasn't a cloud in the sky and the air was absolutely still. The sports car passed through the three cordons of guards at the airport, then came to a stop underneath the Boeing.

It didn't take long to load up his baggage while Copithorne preflighted the aircraft, then called for the starter truck. According to the airport's records, the plane took off at 4:03 A. M. with Copithorne alone at the controls.

The Boeing 727 has a range of about 4,500 kilometers, more than enough for it to reach Rarotonga, Copithorne's destination. But Copithorne took off with a plane whose fuel gauges registered full when, in fact, they were half empty. That little sleight of hand had been engineered by James Moriarty, chief of the maintenance crew. Moriarty, who had been active in the Resistance for several years, sensed that when his crew had been ordered to ready the plane for a possible night takeoff, it would be to enable Lucius Liefenbarger to make a quick getaway. He had weighed the various possibilities and came to the conclusion that of greatest benefit to the people of New Salisbury would be the quiet disappearance of the Administrator in the waters of the blue Pacific.

So Frank Copithorne took off at the controls, seated in the nose of the doomed aircraft. It would be the rear end of the fuselage with luggage and several volumes of his diaries that would be found floating peacefully about three hundred kilometers southwest of Rarotonga.

Chapter 60

At 7 A. M. Lucius C. Liefenbarger finished shaving, put on a freshly ironed uniform of the New Salisbury Grenadier Guards and started down the long winding steps for breakfast. It had been an enchanting night, with the sound of the surf coming in through the open window, with a thoroughly theatrical moon and soft breeze from the sea which periodically ruffled the chiffon curtains. Alternately they had made love and slept. At one point he had opened a bottle of champagne and they sipped their glasses, speaking about whatever came to their heads but carefully avoiding any reference to the rapidly nearing conflict or to the wall of sandbags outside their window.

Liefenbarger reached the bottom step and had turned to the terrace when the telephone rang in the reception room. An NUC sergeant appeared from nowhere, picked up the receiver and a moment later nodded to the Administrator.

"It's for you sir. General Ormsby."

Liefenbarger must have known instinctively that it was over, that the hours allotted to them had run out, that the sunshine and promise of the bright morning were nothing but a sham. Without a word he took the receiver from the sergeant's hand. He identified himself, then listened.

"They've landed. At Wampaha Beach. Thousands of them. They have control of the skies and are unloading tanks and guns at the Wampaha dock."

"And the Guards?"

"They are at Sidwell."

So you have been wrong the second time, the Lief must have thought. You have missed them when they came down from the hills and now you've missed them again. Maybe Sandhurst was not as useful as you thought, but it doesn't matter any more.

"Are you moving the Guards over?"

"Yes sir. They're on their way."

Liefenbarger paused before asking the next question. "Through or around Wahira?"

"It hasn't been decided yet. I wanted to consult with you."

"About what?"

"About Wahira. The port is strategically highly important now."

"Go through, Ormsby. You have to go through. And get ready for a hell of a fight." He hung up, noticing Captain Hawkes standing in the shadow of the staircase.

"Get me Copithorne on the phone, will you captain?" he asked him, once more turning in the direction of the terrace. The phone would be reconnected there.

"Excuse me, sir, but Mr. Copithorne left last night. I thought you knew — "

"Left? He wasn't even here last night."

"No, I mean that he flew off, sir. In the jet."

"Where to?"

"His flight plan was made out to Rarotonga, sir. We thought you knew. The order had been signed by you and it had your stamp."

Liefenbarger stood thunderstruck for a moment. Mayfield must have known that Copithorne was flying off to join his Swiss accounts, but he let him go. Why shouldn't he? Copithorne with his influence on the Lief constituted an undesirable complication. With him and the Boeing gone Liefenbarger would be completely dependent on the NUC.

"That's right, Rarotonga," the Lief said, as if remembering. "He has to meet with — but I forgot it was already this week." It was all, of course, for Hawkes's benefit.

"Excuse me, sir, but shouldn't I get General Mayfield on the phone? He left instructions that he wanted to speak with you when you got up."

"Mayfield? No, not right now. After breakfast."

He turned around and for the third time started in the direction of the terrace. He had been right about Copithorne; the man knew how to take care of himself. But did he really think it through — biding his time in some dreary Swiss or Chilean exile? Halfway down the corridor leading to the terrace Lucius C. Liefenbarger saw Ann Schorez in the act of raising a tea cup to her lips with the sun on her hair and the dazzling blue sea in the background.

Was Copithorne the winner?

Through the doorway he caught sight of the two silver dots, then realized that they were moving, that they were airplanes and probably were not friendly. Maroon uniforms were scampering toward the sandbags, two soldiers manning the anti-aircraft gun. The planes swept in low, their Democratic New Salisbury markings clearly visible, their cannons firing bullets which kicked up the sand, then tore the sandbags and the rose garden beyond. The noise intensified each moment.

Liefenbarger started running because he clearly saw that the line of fire was advancing toward Ann who was frozen in fear at the breakfast table. And then he saw it would be too late no matter how fast he ran. There was one more small anteroom to be crossed, where guests used to put their umbrellas and gum boots but, when he was two steps away from the gothic doorframe, the snow-white breakfast table on the terrace crumbled as if crunched by a giant hand, the roar now deafening, the tranquil scene replaced by havoc, scattered debris, and a silver sugar bowl rolling down the terrace toward the beach.

When Lucius Liefenbarger finally reached her, he knew that she had already left him. She was gone, not in the romantic scene of a sleek candle being snuffed out, but brutally, painfully and crudely: the way a snow-white chiffon dressing gown becomes spattered by blood mixed in with skull fragments; the way a leg becomes grotesquely bent underneath the torso when the torso is lifelessly hurled to the ground; the way pieces of crockery and bits of food cover a body whose eyes are still opened in astonishment and terror, even though there is nothing more to be seen.

He knelt over her, knowing that there weren't any more hours, minutes or seconds, that it had all reached its dreadful finality. He stayed beside her in spite of Hawkes's faint warning that the planes would be back, that they were merely turning around for another pass. And then he heard the whine of their dive again, but this time they were firing at the other side of the mansion, at the entrance. Hawkes was shouting frantic orders which were effectively drowned out by the din of the engines and guns.

Chapter 61

The three trucks in the convoy pulled out of the back door to the armory complex, following Mayfield's drab-colored Ford and four men on motorcycles. They skirted the armory's back wall toward King Edward Avenue with its verdant median, then continued along it toward Queen's Park. Although it was noon, when the park was usually packed full by lunching secretaries from nearby offices, it was almost deserted. There had been no fighting yet in the capital itself, but there seemed to be indications all around that it was bound to come. The convoy passed the gently rolling west side of the park and headed toward the fortress-like military headquarters, built by the British at the time of the worst excesses of Victorian presumptuousness. The convoy stopped in front of the main entrance and two guards beside their striped guardhouse saluted mechanically as General Mayfield, Commander in Chief, National Unity Corps, entered the building. He was followed by a group of some fifty men, all armed with automatic weapons and extra magazines fastened to their belts.

Mayfield entered the conference room first, his revolver drawn. Behind him his men fanned out through the room. Some of the officers attempted to stand up in outrage, but they were gruffly pushed back into their seats, then disarmed. One or two initially tried to resist, then thought better of it. Mayfield waited indifferently by the door until all the small arms taken from the officers had been piled up on the floor in the corner, and watched Orsmby defiantly take out his weapon, hold the revolver by its barrel, then slide it across the highly polished table.

"I am, as of this moment, assuming command of all of New Salisbury's armed forces. On land, in the air and at sea. I am charging you, commanders of the various services, with treason. You will be taken into custody and tried as soon as the present emergency conditions are over."

"May I ask why?" Orsmby asked haughtily.

"Defeatism, general. That's what's wrong with all professional soldiers. You've decided to give up. You forget that we're not at some military college maneuvers but in the middle of a battle against the Communists. You don't see the power of the spirit of our people — that this spirit is strong enough to face and defeat a bunch of gangsters."

"I've never said we cannot defeat Titus's forces."

"But you've ordered the Guards to move out of Wahira, haven't you?"

"Wahira cannot be held. If we try to hold unto it we will destroy not only the city but the New Salisbury Guards as a fighting unit."

"And surrender will not destroy them?"

"According to our plans, the unit will withdraw at night in the direction of Partrawa. There it will regroup with units of the Queen's Regiment from Nelson."

"Nobody will withdraw and regroup, general. That's the kind of bullshit that gets cooked up in comfy conference rooms like this. It doesn't take into account what happens to the morale of a regiment that has had to pull back from the most important part of the southern coast."

Ormsby said nothing. Mayfield was not giving him a chance to anyway. The senior officers were being handcuffed and taken away, the junior ones dismissed and ordered to leave the headquarters immediately.

Mayfield then sat down in the chair moments before occupied by Ormsby. He began to study the operational map of southern coast of Main Island that was spread on the table in front of him.

Late Sunday afternoon, Branko Justac already knew that there was absolutely nothing that he could do, that in spite of his general's uniform, in spite of his title of a Commander of the Invasion Forces, in spite of his driver waiting respectfully for him next to the jeep and a group of aides hovering nearby — that in spite of them all he was alone. He had been, in effect, appointed the executioner. He looked down the empty runway from which moments ago three C-130s lifted another 200 paratroopers and their equipment to their destination near the capital, under the command of his son Dragan.

He worried just like any father would worry, but not as much as he worried about the fate of Wahira, spread in front of him. Most of all, though, he worried about his role in the destruction.

The invasion had been completed without a single casualty.

The timetable had been followed closely with two ships unloaded and away from the Casino Dock well before the tide started to recede. Almost two thousand men had been landed on the undefended beach, leaving their launches to jump into the knee-high, warm, calm and sunny sea. The rebel units which had quickly regrouped on the beach now stood poised to the north and south of Wahira, ready to march into the city. It was a maneuver designed to provide them with a magnificent port and a base from which to fan out, not only north and west toward the capital but also east toward Partrawa, toward the camps in one of which, Branko hoped, his son would still be alive.

But it would be costly. When the New Salisbury Guards Regiment heard about the landing, it simply broke camp and started marching towards Wahira. Maybe as much as a battalion was already inside the city — it had been left there as a detachment while the rest was on its way to Sidwell. Now the Guards were moving back into Wahira, despite the fact they had been first showered by leaflets exhorting them not to shoot at their countrymen, and to begin negotiating and to stop all hostilities (the word "surrender" being meticulously avoided). An aerial bombing came later when there had been no response, followed by machine-gun showers with which the rebels greeted them. Despite all the exhausting efforts to keep them from entering Wahira, the New Salisbury Grenadier Guards still advanced, unit after unit being swallowed inside the old port city with its narrow streets. There they were invulnerable to attack from the rebel tanks.

The determination of the Guards was something on which none of us had counted. The Guards were not a newly-formed unit like the Anti-Insurgency Regiment. They had fought at Ypres, at the Mareth Line and Inchon Reservoirs. To assume that their loyalty could now be instantly altered by a piece of paper had really been absurd. They served not Lucius Liefenbarger or the National Unity Movement, but New Salisbury City. Whatever commands emanated from there were the proper ones, no matter who was behind them. Legitimacy was of utmost importance. The cheap leaflets we showered on the Guards most likely even strengthened their determination to resist.

So most of the Guards Regiment was now inside Wahira, the first, historical capital of the colony. The town's imposing white colonnade overlooked the bay and harbor and docks below. It included the nineteenth-century office of the British Overseas Trading Company (now a museum), with the governor's mansion a bit to the side, and built on such an angle that a glimpse of the distant Central Mountains could be caught from the ballroom windows.

Branko had first seen Wahira right after the war, at the offices of the British Mission in Italy, where a young employee suggested that he make his future home in New Salisbury. Branko had already left Yugoslavia forever. At that point he was ready to go anywhere in the world and nothing he had seen so far had matched the tranquility and loveliness of the Wahira scene on a postcard in front of him. The hatred and the raw wounds didn't seem to be healing around him in Yugoslavia, and that violence was only countered by greater violence. From all he had heard, violence seemed quite foreign to a place like Wahira.

In the end the reality wasn't that different from the picture. He had landed at Wahira with his young wife aboard an Australian ship in 1946 and for a while he was determined to make his home there. But Wahira steadily lost its economic importance. The port facilities at competing Nelson and New Salisbury City had been built up during the war at the expense of the quaint Wahira and its future seemed uncertain. It was certain, however, that it had already become the domain of the rich, especially of the war profiteers. Land prices around the old town atop the cliff skyrocketed as those who could afford them started building their summer homes there in mock-colonial style. Swimming pools and golf courses proliferated where once had contentedly grazed the cattle of the early settlers. A landing strip for easier commuting from the capital had been built that Branko was now standing on.

Thirty years ago he had sensed that Wahira, for all its charm and beauty, would not be the rugged, unspoiled New Salisbury for which he had come. Within days he had left for Precarious Inlet.

But in his mind Wahira had never been replaced as a symbol of that New Salisbury for which he had travelled halfway across the world.

A few minutes before departure of the C-130s he had been handed a dispatch from St. Enoch which had effectively brushed aside all his arguments for bypassing Wahira on the rebels' way to the capital. It directed him to start an attack on Wahira as soon as his forces were in a position for it. Time was of the essence. Air raids had already started in and around

New Salisbury City; now the paratroopers were about to land south of it. It was important that all of Main Island be kept in constant turmoil. Any successful attempt by the Lief's forces to regroup, to coordinate their defenses, would be costly.

In the spring of 1944 they had stopped somewhere along the tributary to the Morava and he, along with ten others, had gone ahead to see what was between them and the main road along which the Germans were planning to pull back their Panzers. First there was the stream, churned up by melting snow, which they forded by submerging themselves up to their waists in the icy water, holding their weapons and ammunition above their heads. Exhausted, on the other side every inch of their stiff bodies begged for a rest. But time had been important there too, and Branko got his group back on its feet, climbing up the soggy side of the valley toward a village which seemed even more picturesque than most he had seen painted on gingerbread hearts at the fair in Novi Pazar, where his grandmother used to take him before the war. A little further there was a path which could support the small artillery pieces and supply wagons that his unit dragged along. But first the village — and for the life of him Branko could never remember its name afterwards — had to be taken. A single German in one of the straw roof cottages at the top of the hill would have a perfect target for anything passing below.

The village was quiet enough. Unnaturally quiet. That much Branko and his men sensed as they approached the first house. Yet it wasn't deserted — deserted homes smelled and felt differently. So they stayed in the bushes at a distance until, at the entrance to the third house, they were greeted by a figure of a husky peasant who ran out to them, his back bent almost to the ground, catching his breath and at the same time explaining that there were five or six Germans, some sort of a rear guard or something, scattered throughout the village one in each house, and that along with each German was a whole family — kids, grandma, cats and dogs.

They had no more than an hour. The main part of his unit would be arriving and there was no way of slowing it down now. Seconds were ticking away mercilessly, relentlessly, making Branko's brain skip and skid as he kept up the pressure on it to come up with a solution. But the only way out was already obvious to everyone. Anything else would endanger the unit and let the Panzers pass unhindered north toward Skopje and Pristina. So they went into the man's house, made torches from his firewood and dipped them into a sticky pitch until they burned with black pungent smoke that hurt one's eyes. Then they took the torches to a spot which was the village center. The one among them who spoke the language shouted to the Germans that those who would come out with their hands up would be allowed to live. But everyone — the Germans, partisans and the villagers alike — knew that this was a war where both sides had stopped taking prisoners a long time ago. Still, the warning had been shouted like some sort of a pagan ritual whose meaning had long ago been forgotten. The unguarded families then came running out of their houses, but that was a mistake. The Germans fired at them through the windows, killing a woman and the baby she was carrying with one bullet, a teen-aged girl with another.

The fury was then unleashed. They threw their burning torches at the straw roofs of the houses, putting a red rooster up there, as the villagers used to say. Some came running out and there was even one German, whom Branko's men grabbed by the feet and dragged into the adjoining woods, still screaming and pleading for mercy. The flames spread until half of the village was gone and with it the idyllic scene which only a few moments before had been like the Yugoslavia he had known before the war, near his native Luznik. Now neither Luznik, where his mother died as his family's house had been levelled by German guns, nor this place, existed anymore. In their place was a land afflicted with ugly, frenzied hatred.

Astonished, they all watched a door to a stone-walled, barn-like building slowly opening. Through it, at first hesitantly, and looking around cautiously, a girl emerged. She couldn't have been more than six, in a short-sleeved cotton dress which was far too inadequate for the early spring weather. She advanced slowly through the bellowing clouds of smoke, sometimes coughing, at times quickly getting out of the way of a fiery tongue that reached for her, but never losing sight of her destination — of the group of men with guns slung across their shoulders huddling on the edge of the woods. She carried something in an earthen jug which she protected with her hand from all sorts of perils, relentlessly advancing toward the group until she was close enough for it to be clear it was one particular man she was coming to — the unshaven, wet and muddy Justac, who was now trembling because of the cold and because death had just passed by. He stared at the child, trying to keep himself warm by shuffling his feet and placing his hands under his armpits.

The girl finally stopped right in front of him, her terrified mind probably recalling help she had once somewhere on some occasion asked for and received, perhaps from some obscure relative who vaguely resembled Branko. She raised her head, revealing two eyes so blue and so frightened that he had never forgotten them. And along with that look she remembered what once had worked, what probably had once brought warmth and security.

"Would you like some wine, uncle?" she asked, offering him the jug.

Branko then lost control. For the first time in that gruellingly long, grey, monstrous war his face began to twitch and he felt the warm stream of tears descend down his cheeks. He still had the strength to turn on the heel of his boot, to practically crawl into the underbrush behind him. His body was trembling with emotions that had now reached the top and spilled over. And he was no longer big enough to contain them.

"General, they just called. They're ready — the force is ready to start."

Branko looked at the young rebel officer in a short-sleeved shirt standing alongside him on the landing strip, his weapon slung carelessly across his shoulder. In his eyes Justac saw the eagerness — the thirst for excitement the man doubtlessly felt was rightfully his. Branko felt tired — tired the way a man feels at the end of a long day's work whose worth is in doubt. Through the corner of his eye he saw part of the old church with the Kahikatea trees around it and he took a deep breath. Earlier in the day he had sent a message to St. Enoch, asking that the assault be delayed until morning, but he also knew that it couldn't be because there was the timetable with the paratroopers already on their way north. A pause would give the Guards time to shore up their defenses, maybe even to build barricades.

He started toward his jeep. "Come on, I'll give you a lift," he called to the young officer.

The other men boarded their vehicles too and started down the runway toward the city. From the top of the hill Branko Justac watched the long rows of tanks, artillery pieces in place behind them, as well as the trucks being loaded with men further on.

It was starting up again, and he had the horrifying feeling that it was all completely out of his hands now.

Chapter 62

The door to my suite opened and a young corporal ushered in Rose Kubatan. Long hours aboard a plane had wrinkled her clothes and dishevelled her hair. Obviously she had come straight from the airport. I looked up from my papers.

"Hello Rose. Had a nice flight? It sure doesn't look like it."

But Rose was not in the mood for jokes and she showed it in no uncertain terms. She ignored the tone of the greeting, addressing me in her raspy voice. "What the hell's happening, Maurice?" she asked, advancing toward me menacingly. "I just heard that Channing and Baracolli have been shot."

"Yeah — well, you see, we're in the middle of this revolution here."

Rose gave me time. She said nothing, just standing there with a questioning expression on her face.

"Why don't you sit down? Anywhere. On that couch or chair — anywhere."

But she remained motionless in the same spot, silent. I knew it meant that I had failed to deflect her attack. Now I would either have to get rid of her or defend myself.

"So what do you want to hear — that it was a mistake? It was. A terrible one. And it wasn't only Channing and Baracolli but Tolway and...and Diana Mulgrave."

Rose's eyes widened. She selected a cushion on the couch and sat down. "That puts you right alongside the Bacongos and Castro."

"Now wait a minute —"

"I mean it Maurice. We can sit here and argue the degree of comparison till the cows come home, but that's not what the TV commentators will be talking about or what the papers will come up with. The question of degree is one of the first casualties in any fight with the Communists. Stalin — that bloody beast — made such a hullaballoo about Julius and Ethel Rosenberg that the whole world forgot about his Katyns and Gulags and forced collectivizations. You know why? Because he knew that the democrats have to justify each and every death. Can you?"

"I don't have to justify anything. I didn't make the decision."

"George?"

I nodded.

"So we're back to the original question: What the hell is going on here, Maurice?"

"Meg Winters is dead."

"Oh God."

"They caught up with her on Main Island and she only had time to swallow the pill."

"God."

"George was in love with her. Head over heels. So Meg is gone and David is barely alive and unable to walk. George feels guilty about letting her go up north, he feels guilty about his own life, about allowing the Reds to stay bunched together like that, and about allowing the workers' committees. He feels guilty about everything and everybody. Mixed in with it all is his anger and thirst for revenge."

"So he will undo everything he has — you have — put together here. The whole goddamn glorious thing will go up in smoke."

"Not if he snaps out of it in time."

Rose nodded in silence. I think that at this point she understood my dilemma and regretted having come on so strong.

"What's happening to the rest of the world?" I asked after a while.

"Same old shit. This was the only place without the same old shit. I'm halfway finished with the book. Best thing I've ever done — optimistic, bright, dynamic rah rah rah type of thing. You can't imagine what it's done for me personally. I mean there I was in a condominium at Maui and I actually put on a bathing suit again and went frolicking into the surf. Bulges and everything. For the first time I was able to convince myself that the bulges didn't matter, that what I was doing did. That's why the news we got on arrival at St. Enoch was such a cold shower. Not just a cold shower. Like being bludgeoned to death by ice cubes.... Is this thing at Kilmaron finished?"

I nodded. "That isn't the worst of it. The New Salisbury Guards are holed up at Wahira. They're surrounded and we're hitting them hard but they won't give up. When it's finished I guarantee you there'll be nothing left of the place."

"Oh God, Wahira of all places."

"Yeah."

We sat in the half-darkened suite, staring at each other.

"Rose," I finally asked, "does it still look like we have a chance from where you're standing? Everything that shouldn't have happened is happening. At times it feels like what I'm doing or trying to do has absolutely no bearing on anything anymore."

"You're still winning, aren't you?"

"I don't know. We're beating Liefenbarger, but I don't know about winning—"

"Stop it, Maurice, or I'll never go out in my bathing suit again. What about the government?"

"What about it?"

"Is it still democracy you're in it for? Do you still know what you're fighting for?"

"*I* know."

Rose sighed. "What's happening up north? If Liefenbarger sends Ormsby over with his sword, will you accept it?"

"*I* won't have to make that decision."

"George doesn't consult anymore, is that it?"

I shook my head.

"A bit of a Frankenstein situation, eh?"

That brought me back. I had two people to convince, so I was properly vehement. "No, that's not it at all. We've just had it so incredibly easy till now. So there's stress. We're not used to it but we try and cope. Maybe we haven't got the hang of it yet, but it's coming. In the long run though it changes nothing. Absolutely nothing."

Rose got up to come closer to the desk behind which I sat. She leaned over it toward me. "You know what you are Maurice? You're scared. Scared of your friend turning into a relatively mild-mannered Hitler and your precious revolution into anything but mild-mannered. That you're going to the dogs and that you've also unleashed them against anybody who isn't fanatically behind you...and that's exactly the way it looks to me. You've got a military dictator who is blasting detractors to kingdom come. Uncomfortable? Let me tell you something buddy, it's gonna get a lot more uncomfortable once you don't have a Liefenbarger to kick around. Once you run out of excuses."

I said nothing.

"What do you plan to do? You *do* have a plan, don't you?"

"I'll stay with him."

Rose smiled for the first time since she came in. "Sounds a

lot like a proper marriage vow. And that's good because temptations are going to increase for both you and George from now on. This is where the going gets really rough."

"I know."

Rose Kubatan was on her way out but I didn't want her to go. I also so much wanted to be back in the mountains with her, along with the smell of pine in the fireplace, the cleansing snow and the rarefield atmosphere.

"You want to come down to the Center for a cup of coffee?" I asked, getting up.

"What Center?"

"The Operations Center."

"Am I allowed in there?"

"I think I can get you in," I said.

Chapter 63

The suburbs had been relatively easy to take. The wider streets were readily accessible to the tanks which rolled past manicured lawns and newly planted, sweet-smelling Rewarewas. When they reached the old section, they were helplessly stopped. The streets narrowed and cobblestones replaced the smooth pavement. That's where the first machine-gun fire was heard, where the streets had been walled up by barricades, and where it seemed as if every window had a marksman in it.

The sun set and the sound of gunfire increased because the rebels became more frustrated, realizing that their armor was now useless, that they could not move forward any more and that the defenders could not be gouged out of their lairs except by destroying the lairs. Hand grenades then came into play and artillery shells began to level the rows of old townhouses with the snipers inside. Fires broke out and ran together like rivers until the entire center of town was in flames, but by then no one seemed to care any more. They had tasted blood and killing and destruction and they no longer knew how to stop — they didn't want to know. In the heat and in the eerie light reality, reason and logic vanished along with thousands of the painful civilizing years. Men had shed their historic encumbrances. They became mammals again, hairy mammals, part of the primeval order of things on this earth, staking out their territory, wordlessly, savagely and effectively eliminating all that stood in their way. They fitted themselves back into the biology books, into the environmentalist's natural cycle. Just like the jackals, stampeded herds and other killers, they became simple, universal and predictable.

Few noticed that dawn had come. The smell and heat of the burning city along with the sound of the angry guns had provided for an atmosphere which was no longer dependent on the sun's rise and descent. Men killed and were killed; they destroyed and maimed quite apart from the distant laws of the universe, but quite in tune with the custom on this savage planet. Those among the rubble of the city were now thoroughly oblivious to where they were. But they felt strongly again as to *who* they were. They became primates again.

Progressively the number of the defenders grew smaller. At what had earlier been a small park with three Rimu trees, a group of them gathered, huddling under a smouldering facade. They weren't talking; they just stood because their bodies dictated a rest. But then, suddenly, the building above them crumbled, breaking into hundreds of fiery pieces, burying half of them and sending the rest with insane screams back into the streets. The jungle had more lives — killing, being killed, killing along with the fiery cacophony.

Then it was light again and most of the fires had died out, leaving behind rubble that had been the city. What once had been the pride of the country was now a charred, still smouldering black outline of a formerly warm, vibrant place with children, tourists and sidewalk cafes. By then very few were still fighting. What remained were the dead and dying and the utterly exhausted. The occasional shot which still rang out was more like an involuntary death twitch, emphasizing the end rather than denying it.

Quietly and unobtrusively the ambulances, trucks and stretcher-bearers entered the citadel, attendants piling black, hideous bodies one atop another until the trucks were full. The drivers then started down the hastily cleared road toward the suburbs again, and beyond, to the plain where the bulldozers had already started digging a gigantic grave, where men under the watchful eye of their officers searched through pockets and documents, trying to identify as many as possible — a grim, ghoulish task to which no one was and no one wanted to become accustomed.

A small group of people who had hidden in the cellars now started to form; it grew and became alive with chatter and animation until the embarrassed officer in charge tried to disperse them. But they reformed at other places around the common grave, their fears now changed into curiosity. As the children became tired of the scene they grew restless and started to play. Soon the plain resounded with laughter and joyful sounds which matched the activity there the way day matches the night.

There was no more Wahira. The few now grotesquely combed and manicured suburbs which remained intact had lost their raison d'etre. The citadel with its old church, the British Overseas Trading Company, the governor's mansion and the patrician townhouses beyond were no more. Neither was there a proud regiment called the New Salisbury Guards that had fought at Ypres, Mareth Line and Inchon. Instead, a few dazed, bloodied men staggered out of the ruins of the city and were taken to a resort hotel at Wampaha Beach that had been made into a prisoner-of-war center.

At the airport the rebel forces were reassembling. The exact situation at the capital was still unclear. The paratroopers had encountered some resistance but it was sporadic and not at all coordinated. A rebel committee was in control of Garrick. Sempal and Lake Haumo were also now in the hands of rebel sympathizers and there were no more government troops between Wahira and Partrawa. The road to the capital was clear.

Branko Justac listened to situation reports at the airport terminal building outside Wahira, once more watching the cargo planes being loaded with men and supplies, hearing the fighters circling above, at the same time being aware of the citadel's smoking ruins in the other direction which his eyes carefully avoided. All air facilities on Main Island were now reported to be in the hands of rebel pilots.

Although there was still some fighting around the fleet headquarters at Nelson, it was sporadic and the local rebel commander reported that there couldn't be more than a handful of the diehard National Unity Corps men still alive. In most other places the revolution was over.

We had won.

Chapter 64

On Monday Lucius Liefenbarger half woke up as the sun's first rays penetrated the tall windows of his bedroom. He lay, his foggy mind trying to reconstruct just why he was there, and who had put him in his own bed. Slowly he turned his head to look at the clock radio beside him, finding it hard to focus, at the same time feeling a sharp pain in the back of his skull. His eyes eventually focused enough for him to discern that it was close to ten o'clock.

He was dizzy. As he felt slightly more certain on his feet, he shuffled off toward the closet. There he put on his robe and inadvertently caught sight of his reflection in the mirror. He was appalled. The dishevelled, matted hair, the great dark rings under his eyes, the stubble across his face and his deathly pallor presented a visage which was so depressing that he had to hold on to his chair while trying to accept it as his own.

Gradually he started recalling things: the airplanes, Ann Schorez, her bloodied torso in his arms. But he remembered nothing further. He shuffled out of his room and onto the landing outside, approaching the banister with his arm outstretched, then grabbing hold of it. Below him, at his table in the reception hall, napped Hawkes. Liefenbarger failed to muster enough strength to call him. Instead he made only a raspy sound.

"Captain —"

Hawkes swung his leg from the table, looked up, then started up the steps. "You shouldn't be out of bed. It's been too much of a shock. The doctor says you must rest."

Liefenbarger didn't resist as he was led by his arm back inside the bedroom, to his bed. It must have been an enormous strain for him to get up and walk. He wanted to rest. But he also wanted to know.

"Ann — what have you done with her?"

"She's dead, sir. She died at — " but Hawkes stopped, realizing that the Administrator remembered it all.

"We gave you a sedative, sir. We had to. It was such a shock."

"What have you done with her?"

This time Hawkes understood what he meant. "We buried her, sir."

"Where?" Liefenbarger persisted, closing his eyes with exhaustion.

"In the rose garden."

"What's happening? Have the rebels — "

"The Communists have launched an assault on Wahira but they have been twice repulsed. The New Salisbury Guards are now preparing to counterattack and throw the Communists back into the sea," the captain recited as if from some manual.

"Ormsby — have him call," the Lief muttered with increasing difficulty.

"That can't be done," Hawkes said arrogantly. "General Orsmby is under arrest."

"Why?" the Administrator whispered.

"Because of his defeatism. He was about to order the New Salisbury Guards out of Wahira."

Liefenbarger wanted to say more, but he didn't have the strength. He drifted off to sleep.

The first thing that struck me about the place was the eerie silence. As we walked in about noon on Monday the freed men stood about, sometimes in groups, but these seemed to be more accidental than the product of conscious demography. Their sunken eyes stared at us silently. They didn't speak to each other; they didn't address us — the liberators. They merely stood in their places like monuments to suffering and pain, in their ragged sweat-stained clothing, with skulls shaved and bones pushing against a thin layer of grey skin.

The place itself added more despair: there was no grass and practically no trees. The ground seemed made of baked clay, in some places hardened into rock, and was covered with a layer of dust that whirled about with even the slightest breeze, covering men's faces and parching their lips. Behind them in symmetrical rows stretched the barracks, made of warped planks and topped by corrugated roofs that must have been stifling, baking ovens in summer, and tormenting ice boxes in wintertime. Earlier we had driven past the potash mine which was unique in that there wasn't the slightest bit of machinery in or around it. Men with shovels and picks had scraped the ground until they collapsed and died. Then new ones took their places. The whole Partrawa Plain with its three vast camps became something of a repository of humans — a press where the prisoners were squeezed until they had no more to give, then thrown away as pulp.

In one place there suddenly appeared a patch of green, like a grotesque piece of scenery left from last night's performance that had nothing to do with today's production. As Rose Kubatan and I stared dumbly at the incongruity, Branko Justac, who was accompanying us, stepped closer to explain.

"A common grave. Something of a garbage dump to the camp authorities."

I suddenly remembered. Turning to Branko abruptly, I asked, "Your son. Is he — "

But even before Justac started shaking his head sadly, the sorrow was already visible in his eyes. The sorrow of the thousands of dead and wounded at Wahira along with the deep wound of his own, personal loss.

"They shot him the day we came down from the mountains. Him and fifteen others. On personal orders from Mayfield."

For a moment I thought I saw tears in his eyes.

"I'm sorry," I said with a helpless gesture.

We moved on through the silent Camp 1, among the clusters of men who had forgotten all about being created in the Lord's image, about families and children and music and poetry. Men who concentrated all their remaining meagre strength on getting food, shelter, and a bit of warmth. Near the gate one of the emaciated prisoners made a few unusually quick steps toward me, then grabbed hold of my hand and kissed it. But he was an exception; he must have arrived at the place only recently because as yet he didn't resemble the walking dead. And he still remembered enough to distinguish one uniform from another.

The five maroon-shirted guards who had been captured huddled together inside a compound separated from the rest of the camp by a double row of barbed-wire fence. There were gaping holes on their uniforms where once had been ostentatious decorations, one or two even in grey riding pants denoting senior officers. But most of these had left hours before, reportedly setting out toward the coast, where they crowded aboard fishing boats, frantically trying to avoid the clutches of New Salisbury's advancing retribution. Some had been seen retreating toward the Central Mountains. There, in a perversion of the idealism of the Revolutionary Army, they announced that they would continue resisting.

The National Unity Corps Guards retreated into the far

corner of the compound as our group entered it and only then did we begin to realize that Camp 1 had been designed not only as a place of slow, lingering death in the main, but also as a place for a much faster one, where pain increased with speed. The Delinquency Block — inside the only stone structure in the vast camps — contained minute cells without windows, with bare lightbulbs which either burned day and night or were switched off permanently so that the prisoner lived in perpetual darkness, sometimes chained to an iron ring in the wall, with a dented slop bucket in the corner as the only piece of furniture. There were gallows in the center courtyard among the buildings, along which each prisoner was led into the Delinquency Block and on which several hundred of them had ended their lives. There were white-tiled rooms with curved, perforated tables where beatings were administered and whose blood-spattered walls could be easily hosed down. Leather straps were used for tying a prisoner into a ball and leaving him forgotten in some corner for hours.

There were instruments of torture that would have been accepted as standard fare only in mediaeval castles or in some late night horror movie; pathetic scratches on the wall where the condemned were trying to keep track of time, and escape insanity. Outside, in the courtyard, was a wall with three layers of wood panelling to absorb bullets — near which young Justac must have died.

This no longer is a grainy black-and-white documentary on the rise and fall of Nazism; this is my country, I thought. We will never be able to point the finger again.

The curious thing about the women's compound in Camp 3 was that it was so hard to distinguish from the rest. The woe that was women here was just as skeletal and ragged, just as shaven and silent as the men. They had been working inside a tall structure in the middle of the camp, assembling machinery of all kinds, mostly reconditioned pieces, in two twelve-hour shifts, seven days a week. Here too most of the guards had been men — sadistic dregs of society who had been given authority and who clearly understood that only their unequivocal support of the Liefenbarger regime could maintain them in their positions. A rebel officer who accompanied Branko, Rose and me, rattled off fearful statistics on death, suffering and neglect, but it really didn't matter anymore. The thousands killed here paled before a mental picture of even one such silent, emaciated woman, slowly dying while chained naked to a stone wall of the detention barracks, gloated over by a maroon shirt staring at her through the door slot.

Watching the walking dead men and women on the liberated Partrawa Plain, the gallows and the torture instruments, Rose was already beginning to write her dispatch in her head — the one that made the point so clearly that all atrocities are ultimately connected:

How naive it is to single out General Pinochet and his pathetic, bemedalled, strutting generals in Chile without placing blame on the lawless arrogance of the late Allende and his road that could have ended nowhere else but in totalitarianism. Because here, as in Chile, the maroon-shirted sadists had been brought in on the fears of anarchy produced by the wide-eyed, irresponsible radicals. The Bolsheviks had been brought in on the wings of a bloody Russian civil war and fears produced by the First World War; Hitler then could build on the Germans' fear of Communism, as demonstrated by Stalin, who was committing his mass murders not too far to the east of them. It's all tied together in a dreadful chain of radical excesses. Whenever the law is circumvented and bent all out of shape, and whenever in its place is substituted the fear of a red star, or of a maroon or any other colored shirt, there will emerge the terrible danger of yet another Partrawa Plain.

The modernistic outline of the picturesque town of Partrawa, once the center of New Salisbury's artists, appeared before us. The car started its slow descent toward it and the airport. A Lear Jet was waiting there to take Rose and me to New Salisbury City.

We were quiet at first, thoroughly overwhelmed by what we had just seen. It was a horrifying revelation of Liefenbarger's ways, of New Salisbury's ways, of ourselves.

"Do you think that now, with a heritage like this, we can ever function normally again? I don't think any of us imagined anything like it," I said.

"Look at Germany."

"But that was at least in time of war. And fear. The worst concentration camps and gas chambers didn't spring up until about seven or eight years after the Nazis came to power. There was no war here and what did we have to fear? Not hunger, poverty and misery. Not at all. What we feared was the lowering of our grand living standard. We worried that our houses wouldn't rise in value quickly enough, that we wouldn't be able to afford a new dishwasher or a second car. That's why we called on the Messiah and were instantly ready to abandon a quarter of a century of freedom, justice and decency. It's a scathing condemnation of ourselves. Of democracy."

"Oh, I don't know. I don't believe in precedents among nations any more than I do in precedents among people. That's why therapists change their styles every few years — from Freud to Jung and Fromm and on to Skinner and the Primal Scream. We don't know and they don't know, but we go on anyway because that's the way we are programmed. And not even that is exactly right because the tapes inside us seemed to be changed with greater frequency nowadays."

"But there *are* certain things we can predict. I'm terrified of what will happen when the Partrawa pictures start appearing in the newspapers and on T.V."

"What exactly *can* you predict? The Germans looked at pictures from Auschwitz and Mauthausen, paid off billions to the survivors, and nowadays movingly commemorate Kristalnacht. The Russians have had a chance to read about Ivan Denisovich and they heard Khrushchev expose Stalin's crimes. But they still believe their glorious Party when it says that Dubcek was in cahoots with the neo-Nazis and that the Hungarians and the Czechs respectfully requested to be invaded. *Which* people are you talking about?"

We drove along silently until I spoke: "I guess it wasn't the people I was actually so much worried about. It was George. What will happen to us and to our future when he stands on the threshold of the Delinquency Block, Rose?"

And here she had no idea about how to reassure me. We both became pensive again.

Captain Hawkes watched the armed figures approaching along the beach and made an instant decision: it was time to get out. There simply wasn't any thing left to fight over. The Administrator was an empty hulk who meant nothing now.

Hawkes had already heard about Wahira. He knew that no viable fighting unit capable of stopping or even slowing down the advance of the rebels existed anywhere on Main Island any more. He knew that General Edward Mayfield had assumed command and while he favored that, he was also aware that there was nothing to assume command of any more. Hawkes's Pitlochry detachment, on the other hand, was still intact.

There had been no casualties among his men during the aerial attack.

He watched the rebels advancing slowly and cautiously toward the mansion. It gave him ample time to withdraw his men from the sandbagged machine-gun nest, and then from the rest of the area. At first he toyed with some token resistance followed by a quick withdrawal, but then he quickly discarded the idea. There would be more time to get away if the invaders didn't know how long ago they had left.

In the bedroom upstairs Lucius Liefenbarger reawakened for the second time that day, this time to the sound of running feet and muffled commands. He was still slow getting out of bed, but felt steadier on his feet. When he finally opened the door, the mansion was already deserted. He was about to go downstairs, but then for some reason changed his mind. Instead, he came back inside the bedroom, walked toward the window and drew the chiffon curtain slightly to the side.

And then he saw them. In their green American fatigues they were easily identifiable. As if hypnotized by the sight, he watched them fan out across the beach, then across the rose garden, finally approaching the mansion itself across the stone patio in front of it.

At that moment Lucius Liefenbarger, more in the manner of a reflex than conscious thought, walked back to the clothes closet and opened its door. He took a holster belt from a hook in the side of it, pulled out his pistol and inserted a magazine in it. He could hear them clearly now in the entrance hall. Opening the door onto the landing, he took the two steps toward the banister.

The sight of him standing there stopped all sound and movement along the green uniforms below. They stared upwards — confused, incredulous, and astonished. Liefenbarger had finally met the enemy he had been hearing, reading about, and at times doubted existed. To play the role to its proper end, he lifted his hand with the gun in it over the banister, then fired twice into the crowd below.

He only heard the first part of the burst that hurled bullets against him. There was a searing hot feeling on the left side of his head, followed by a general slowing down of not only his own motions but everyone else's. He let go of the banister and slid down to the floor, at the same time hearing the sound of several feet running up the curved staircase, his mind using all its resources in order to force the body to do something about it, to provide at least a flicker of proud defiance that should have properly been part of the whole thing. But there was no response.

He lay there on the carpet; from the left side of his face seeped a pool of blood, his eyes dull and unseeing. No one will ever know just how satisfied he was with the performance, but the general consensus of those who were witnesses was that he had done it well. Exceptionally well.

Chapter 65

I had nothing to do with George's triumphant return to Main Island. That had been orchestrated by Vilamko and Cameron, the two young P.R. men who had attached themselves to him when George descended to St. Enoch, although I don't remember ever seeing them with him in public. It must have been because there was a vast sartorial difference between them. They were of the grey-suited type and when without a tie, it was with an angorra sweater and a foulard. Vilamko had once taken some courses under George at the University of British Columbia. He later joined a New York advertising firm and became the anonymous author of "the end justifies the jeans" slogan for Rodeo King Jeans. That brought him up through the ranks of young executives, but it hadn't brought him any closer to the political power he had always craved. In that he was positively Copithornian. A transfer to George's staff in New Salisbury finally did the trick. Cameron was simply attached to Vilamko.

And so on Tuesday morning George Titus's plane, filled to the brim with reporters and camera crews, took off from St. Enoch with Kilmaron its first stop. There a sombre-faced Titus rose on a makeshift platform and spoke about "an alien, deleterious doctrine" that "preyed on proudly independent, peace-coveting democracies." He vowed "vigilance and determination" in dealing with Communism, then boarded his plane again for Partrawa.

His two-hour walk through the camp was meticulously recorded by TV cameras and news photographers. Here he said nothing, but made sure that his shocked face was eloquent enough. His guide explained the use of the torture instruments, pointed out the gallows and opened a solitary cell with traces of blood still on its walls. The cameras zoomed in. Outside in the courtyard George asked to be alone and was recorded as he paced in a remote corner of the camp, deep in thought. Then he rejoined the group. When asked for a comment, in a voice fighting surges of emotion, he said softly, "We must never, never allow another Partrawa."

At Wahira George eyed the still-smouldering heaps that had

once been the old city, and promised ample sums for reconstruction so that "this sad memorial to a nation divided can be justly swept into the dustbin of the past."

Two days later a documentary on George's return to Main Island was shown over New Salisbury television. It ended with him emerging from a plane at N.S. City Airport, smiling and waving to the crowds, then stepping in front of the microphones again to plead that "we let this mark a new beginning for our peoples, a beginning of mutual trust and hope for a just, democratic future."

But then this slick Vilamko-Cameron scenario became somewhat marred by the affair at the Towers. The two neo-gothic structures had been standing on each side of the military headquarters since the winter of 1863, when a small British garrison held out here against repeated onslaughts of the fierce Polynesians. When in October relief finally came, exactly fifteen men remained alive inside the fort — one-tenth of the original contingent. And that's where Mayfield, Ormsby and practically every ranking officer on the island were now holed up.

George listened while being briefed on the situation by Dragan Justac. We were on the way to the Oceanic Hotel, where his headquarters were being hastily set up, the same Oceanic where once we used to grace the terraces in our white dinner jackets, waltzing and mamboing until dawn.

"Have you spoken with them?" asked George.

"No, I haven't. I don't think that I am the right person for that."

"I'm sorry. I have heard about your brother." Dragan's jaw momentarily tightened.

"They want a safe passage out of the country," I filled in the awkward gap.

"Absolutely not. Not now. They could have left before."

"That's what they have been told," Dragan reported.

"But why Ormsby?" George asked. "And why all the other generals? Have they all gone crazy?"

I shook my head. "We hear that they are prisoners. Mayfield simply marched into the Towers and took over."

George thought for a few moments. "Well, how can we get at them?" he asked finally.

"Maybe we should show you," I said, directing the driver to Queen's Park. A few minutes later we stood at the edge of the exuberantly green Queen's Park, George gazing at the Towers beyond it through a pair of binoculars.

"There are two ways, sir," the commanding major beside us explained. "One involves fewer casualties for us but also the total destruction of the Towers. We would smash down the sides of it with artillery, then move in with tear gas and gas masks. It would all be too quick for any organized resistance."

"There is no other way?" George asked.

"There is," broke in Dragan. "The way they used to do it in the Middle Ages. Starve them out. It would take a couple of months. You could cut off their water but they probably have plenty stored."

"But then you'd have a fort under seige in the middle of the capital," I broke in. "The people inside would become something like martyrs. This is the last time that the city will be deserted like this. By tomorrow curiosity will win out."

George turned to the major. "What about the area around here?"

"We have evacuated everyone as soon as we got here, sir."

George's brow furled and I spoke up again.

"There are at least ten officers in there who are Mayfield's prisoners. Let's not forget them."

George spun around. "Like they remembered all the civilians at Wahira, eh? When did Ormsby last bother finding out who was and who wasn't an innocent bystander?"

The major looked at his watch. "Whatever we do, sir, it should be decided on as soon as possible. Before it gets dark."

"You've got your artillery in place?"

The major nodded.

"Then call them once more. Give them five minutes to get out and then blast them...to kingdom come," ordered George, and he then climbed back into the car.

I spoke to him through its window and not particularly eloquently. I still haven't gotten used to the new man, to the new situation; I found it all much too unexpected for an effective protest — if there was such a thing under the circumstances.

"You can't, George. We can't just like this..."

"The hell I can't," he said, "and the hell *we* can't. Here is a ready-made way to dispose of those beasts. Without lengthy and complicated trials that would tear the country apart. The hell we can't."

"But we must have justice. And we must have trials — that's what all this killing has been all about."

"No, no, that's not what it has been all about. It was to get rid of some cancer and that's exactly what we're doing — radical surgery."

The worst thing about it was that for a moment I saw a smirk on his face. He was laughing at all of us. I grabbed the door of the car until my knuckles became white.

"Listen, goddamn it. This isn't just your country. There are others who have something to —"

But I could only get as far as this. The major gently moved me aside and I was left standing there as the car sped away. And when I tried to interfere with the major's orders, he put me under escort and had me taken to the Oceanic. I heard the first explosions and saw the whole wall of the Towers collapse just as we were rounding the corner.

So much had been won and right away lost again.

Chapter 66

The rest constitutes a bit of an anticlimax. I went out with the proverbial whimper. Late in the afternoon came the phone call from Brownlee, who had just been appointed George's executive officer, thereby replacing me as vice-commander. He officially informed me that I was being temporarily relieved of my duties in the Revolutionary Army and that I was *requested* not to wear my uniform. I was told to vacate the suite at the Oceanic as soon as convenient and to move into the Hotel Angel where a room had been reserved for me.

The move to the Angel was significant. I was, in effect, being told to stay out of the limelight, that my case had not yet been decided. My conduct from now on would play a major part in the decision making.

I was thankful for such small favors. George Titus could have had me exiled that same night and then of course I could have never researched this book. Instead, I donned blue jeans with a denim jacket, a pair of sunglasses (sometimes even a fake mustache) and proceeded to gather material. George, who must have known what I was doing, didn't seem to mind. I was allowed access to Copithorne's diaries. I spoke to countless people of the Liefenbarger era, visited Captain Hawkes at a prisoner compound near Hamilton and also the sulking but occasionally helpful Governor Allan McAlpine in the N.S. City prison. (The Bristol Street Armory was no longer used; it was being readied to reopen as a national museum.)

I interviewed Lawrence Saunders and young David Titus in his wheelchair several times. Initially they responded in a lively, highly informational way. But then our relations became progressively cooler until it became clear they were influenced by George. Eventually we agreed to terminate the whole thing.

The most bizarre meeting of all was with the Maoist-anarchist-Trotskyite, wild man Guernsey, who was in the same prison as McAlpine. He had been apprehended while organizing a plot to assassinate George and, somewhat in the manner of McAlpine, now viewed me as a poor sucker who had carried

George Titus to victory, then received a swift kick in the behind
for his trouble. Except that McAlpine never said so, he merely
suggested it. But Guernsey never stopped repeating his view;
embellished in Marxist jargon with colorful obscenities
thrown in for good measure, he was still shouting at me as he
was being led away.

Mostly I kept to myself, writing notes, making xerox copies
of documents which I then managed to get out of the country. I
guess that shows I must have known from the start that I
couldn't carry off my new role, that I was bound to fail the
Titus loyalty-through-sycophancy test.

I was written about. Newspapers and magazines abroad
asked what had happened, requesting — sometimes even demanding — interviews and viewed me with utmost suspicion
when I refused. The most difficult "no" to give was the one to
Rose Kubatan. We met, walked along the Quay and I tried to
explain that as a would-be chronicler of the revolution I had to
remain silent until I had all the material in my possession. I felt
that she was gradually beginning to understand my position
but then, the following day, on February 15th, Branko Justac
was summarily dismissed from his post as Chief of the Revolutionary Army. He was replaced by Carey Hunt, a former
Force Commander from the mountains, who now was best
known for instituting such neat things as nightly curfews and
tightened regulations which closely resembled the imposition
of martial law. Among the N.S. University students he
promptly acquired the nickname Madman Hunt. Branko and
his son Dragan quietly returned to Precarious to resume their
fishing.

Rose came to the Angel and suggested that I make a public
statement on behalf of the Justacs. Again I refused. She then
put together a series called *The Entrails of a Revolution* in
which Branko Justac and Meg Winters were practically deified
and I played the part of a court jester. I was hurt but I think that
even then I understood her anger, her disappointment. I guess
we were all destined to stop wearing our swimming suits
eventually. I felt then (as I still feel today) that my ability to
freely gather material for *The Statement* was much more
important than a futile public statement on behalf of the
Justacs, which would not have helped them and would have
quite likely resulted in my immediate expulsion from the
country.

Anyway, I travelled to Precarious to explain to Branko and

Dragan and they seemed to have both understood. Without much bitterness Dragan expressed concern about George's fondness for holding giant rallies instead of getting down to the giant task of reorganizing the country and defusing some of its most volatile elements.

As expected, after the series appeared Rose was ordered out of New Salisbury within forty-eight hours. The thoroughly alarmed Kenneth Garbeau flew in and attempted to make George into at least a token democrat. Before he left he came to see me, trying to clarify the new situation in his own mind, but what with my noncommittal silence and George's increasingly obvious authoritarianism, I don't imagine that his anxieties were much relieved.

New people started rising to the top — unknown, genuflecting "yes men" who had spent the previous year not in the mountains but in warm offices with generous salaries. They said nothing that had not been approved by the prime minister; they were properly vague when it came to the date for the elections; and properly bombastic when it came to lavishing praise on George Titus at rallies and from reviewing stands at military parades.

Although I had no idea what I could possibly say to him, I still asked for an audience with George. When the negative answer came along with an explanation of how busy he was, I knew it was all over. That my choice had been narrowed down between living in New Salisbury in total obscurity or not living there at all.

On Monday, March 13th, my Air New Zealand jet took off from N.S. City for Auckland. I was one of the last ones from the original gang to leave; for those from our mountain group who chose to dally, the N.S. City prison was a much more likely destination. But I had gone voluntarily.

The revolution was being swept clean, then streamlined.

Chapter 67

Hawaii again. Honolulu with its throngs in cotton shirts, outrageous mumus and badly-fitting Bermudas. I have an apartment near the Ala Wai Canal, but there is no newsletter; there is no Resistance group. Instead, there is a fairly generous pension which arrives every month from the Department of Veterans Affairs in New Salisbury City. The space reserved for rank and type of service on the accompanying slip is always left empty.

There are damn few people for whom I still seem to exist. During the year that I have already spent here Rose Kubatan came to visit twice, the first time expecting an outburst from me. But the *Entrails of a Revolution* are largely forgotten now and we are good friends again, except that her work now takes her mostly to the Middle East, and I am out of the way.

There have been numerous accusations hurled at George Titus although I refused to participate in them. They came in articles and programs bristling with quotations from his own books and public pronouncements that identified him as a devout democrat. Then it was all contrasted with what was actually happening on the islands.

When Titus's version of the Diana Mulgrave execution had been released shortly after my arrival in Honolulu, I was sorely tempted to release my own. George claimed three Communists had been killed in a skirmish resulting from an attempt by other Communists to rescue them. At the last moment, the wider implications of the whole thing emerged for me. If I spoke up against George from my palm-fringed paradise, I would be fully supporting the Communist version of the events. In the end it could be argued that I really knew nothing about it, that I had not been there, that all I had seen was the message received at the Operations Center. That I had never been anywhere near the scene of the killings.

Besides, the trials that came during the first year of the Titus rule were a model of propriety. George wisely started with those who had the most to answer for — the NUC officers, Partrawa Guards and guards from the Bristol Street Armory. When the evidence of their bloody deeds was presented, there were few who objected to their death sentences. Mixed in with them were people like Diebel and Metcalf, who had been found guilty but received no prison terms. It was all, of course, orchestrated by Vilamko and Cameron for the benefit of the press and public opinion, with George appearing at one press conference after another, patiently explaining, movingly admitting the normal amount of human fallibility that is certainly present in emotional affairs such as revolutions. In spite of the generally hostile international press, George basically held his own as a statesman in the eyes of the world; at home he strengthened his already steel grip in many ingenious and varied ways.

He quickly, for example, saw the advantages of taking on a title of the prime minister. But there was no elected parliament, no cabinet representing its majority, no governor general, and as yet, no hint of a constitution which would provide the basis of a new democracy. The regime was quick to reach for pre-Liefenbarger laws to shore up its actions but, of course, it also feels equally justified in ignoring them whenever it is convenient.

Murky personalities are emerging from their depths and are beginning to play important roles. Brownlee, the commander of Theta Force who had Channing executed, is now in charge of security. Lawrence Saunders seems to have instantly outgrown his youthful idealism when he was offered an adviser's post by George. He crisscrosses the country, sometimes accompanied by David Titus in a wheelchair for greater emphasis, preaching devotion to his master. There are even rumors that McAlpine is out of prison, and has become a discreet consultant to George, being groomed for an important position on Lower Isle.

Vilamko and Cameron, of course, reign supreme. Alongside them John Effington is occasionally heard from, and Sid Capadouca is still something like the head of George's household. More like a valet though — certainly not like an executive secretary à la Copithorne.

But there is no real totalitarianism. Not yet, anyway. What exists on the islands to day could best be described as benign authoritarianism. There is no organized opposition because there is still a great amount of fatigue. The general idea, I guess, is to get on with the rider they have, that he may not be wearing the shining armor everyone had expected, but at least he is firmly in the saddle. And as long as he keeps his visor open, he even shows a disarming smile.

And as we get older, our thirst for battle diminishes. A month ago I officially petitioned the prime minister for permission to return to New Salisbury. Although I have never been officially exiled, I still feel it is the courteous thing to do — to prepare George for my return, I mean.

But, of course, he has no intention whatsoever of allowing me to return. He would be a fool. And I want to end on a Biblical note, taking a cue from Rose Kubatan, who definitely thinks that the Word of God is back in. It comes from the Second Epistle to the Corinthians, where Paul says:

> Did Titus make a gain of you?
> walked we not in the same spirit?
> walked we not in the same steps?